Praise for the early novels of George R. R. Martin

THE ARMAGEDDON RAG

"The best novel concerning the American pop music culture of the '60s I've ever read."

—Stephen King

"George R. R. Martin takes us on a wild, melodramatic, mystical hallucinatory voyage through the last two decades. Beautifully written. I couldn't put it down."

—Timothy Leary

"Moving...comic...eerie...really and truly a walk down memory lane."

—*The Washington Post*

"A knowing, wistful appraisal of...a crucial American generation...poetic, nostalgic, daring."

—*Chicago Sun-Times*

"The wilder aspects of the '60s—the frenzied idealism, the cultism, the orgiastic rock music—roar back to life in this hallucinatory story by a master of chilling suspense."

—*Publishers Weekly*

"Vivid, perceptive, and passionate, *The Armageddon Rag* is George R. R. Martin's best book so far....A must for anyone who mourns the '60s—or who loved good, old-fashioned rock 'n' roll."

—Stephen R. Donaldson

"What a story, full of nostalgia and endless excitement for everyone! It's taut, tense, moves like lightning and it proves George Martin is...a master."

—Tony Hillerman

"Martin builds a never-been time in musical history in all its glory; the only thing the book lacks, to my mind, is a soundtrack album."

—SFSite.com

"Like a 'road movie' blended with amateur detective mixed with heavy rock and is one of the best goddamn books that I've ever read. Although originally released in 1983, it is a master class in how to write characters and develop them, set mood, etc. It even tells a story. . . . This book has a hearty recommendation for anyone with a liking for rock, old lyrics and a stonking good story."

—SF Crowsnest.com

WINDHAVEN
with Lisa Tuttle

"The pace never slackens, shifting easily from moments of almost unbearable tension to others of sheer poetry and exhilaration. Martin and Tuttle make wonderful professional music together."

—*Fort Worth Star-Telegram*

"Twenty years after the first publication of this novel, it still stands the test of time."

—*Talebones*

"A book for adults and children who have dreamed of flying with their own wings, and for story listeners of all ages for whom dreams are as potent as realities. A truly wonderful book."

—Jane Yolen

"I didn't mean to stay up all night to finish *Windhaven* but I had to!"

—Anne McCaffrey

"It's romance. It's science fantasy. It's beautiful."

—A. E. van Vogt

FEVRE DREAM

"Reads more like a strongly themed historical novel than gothic horror . . . far more engaging and meaningful than the usual flip-page violence that passes for horror fiction nowadays."

—*The Washington Post Book World*

"Grace, suspense, and just good old-fashioned knockout story-telling make it the kind of chiller one reads with unabated enthusiasm . . . and rereads with the rare commitment accorded only to the best tale-spinners."
— Los Angeles Herald Examiner

"A chilling vampire novel that will have those little hairs on the back of your neck standing at constant attention. A five star beauty [and one of] the best two books of the season."
— Boston News Digest

"[Here] solid characters, vivid descriptions of an opulent world, a plausible explanation of vampirism and some genuinely chilling scenes create one of the best. . . . The most satisfying and frightening novel of its kind since Stephen King's *Salem's Lot*."
— Roanoke Times & World Herald

"Spectacular, simply one of the best frighteners to appear in years . . . inventive, lucid, and genuinely scary — I'd recommend this to anyone who scoffs at genre writing."
— Time Out

"Skillfully balances historical realism and flights into fantasy and obsession. Its characters linger in the mind, along with the beauty of the great boats and the greater river."
— Locus

"A skillful blend of adventure, supernatural horror, and accurate historical settings . . . Exceptionally good, this deserves superlatives in almost every respect."
— Science Fiction Chronicle

"Will delight fans of both Stephen King and Mark Twain . . . Darkly romantic, chilling and rousing by turns, moody and memorable, Martin's novel is a thundering success."
— Roger Zelazny

DYING OF THE LIGHT

"I read *Dying of the Light* for the first time when I was fourteen, and it blew the doors off of my idea of what fiction could be and could do, what a work of unbridled imagination could make a reader feel and believe. Almost thirty years later I find that it reminds me of all that with as much power as ever, and that its heartbroken universe feels even more like home."

—Michael Chabon

"The Wild West in outer space, complete with a chase that will keep you awake. Slick science fiction."

—*Los Angeles Times*

"The kind of imagination that makes science fiction worth reading ... An effective, affecting story."

—*Galaxy* magazine

"George R. R. Martin has the voice of a poet and a mind like a steel trap."

—Algis Budrys

"Each of George R. R. Martin's stories is a gem, cut with verve and polished with abundant skill, reflecting the face of humanity in its many facets—its mood colored, highlighted by a master of misplay ... by a lover of his tools and trade."

—Roger Zelazny

DREAMSONGS

"Science fiction, fantasy and horror fans alike will be blown away by the diversity and quality of stories as well as by Martin's extensive and frank commentary about his life and experiences in the publishing and television industries.... Both physically and thematically immense, this extraordinary collection is one to cherish."

—*Publishers Weekly* (starred review)

"A collection that achieves its aim in highlighting the true challenge creative writing presents and the magic that can appear if we attempt it.... From 'The Fortress' forwards, the reader will find nothing that could be described as less than excellent, whilst occasionally encountering a piece that is truly breathtaking.... George R. R. Martin's *Dreamsongs* will fill the world with their sound for some time to come and what better to follow a song than a Dance?"

—SF Crowsnest.com

Praise for

A SONG OF ICE AND FIRE

A DANCE WITH DRAGONS

and betrayal, success and failure are blurred and morally ambiguous. . . . At the end, I felt shaken and exhausted. I can't recall the last time a work of science fiction or fantasy had that kind of effect on me. I'm almost glad that it will be years before I have to do this all over again. Because it will take me years to recover."

—Salon

"By turns thrilling, funny, scary, emotionally devastating, oddly inspirational, and just plain grand...This is top-notch kitchen-sink storytelling—part straightforward pulp, part high fantasy—that will leave you thirsty for more. Luckily, Martin has two more books on the way. But let's not rush the man, people: When the writing is this good, it's worth the wait."

—*Entertainment Weekly* (Grade: A)

A FEAST FOR CROWS

"Of those who work in the grand epic-fantasy tradition, Martin is by far the best. In fact . . . this is as good a time as any to proclaim him the American Tolkien. . . . *A Feast for Crows* isn't pretty elves against gnarly orcs. It's men and women slugging it out in the muck, for money and power and lust and love."

—*Time*

"A Song of Ice and Fire is firmly at the top of the bestseller lists, probably because it's the best fantasy series out there."

—*Detroit Free Press*

"George R. R. Martin has created the unlikely gene of the realpolitik fantasy novel. Complete with warring kings, noble heroes and backroom dealings, it's addictive reading and reflects our current world a lot better than *The Lord of the Rings*."

—*Rolling Stone*

A STORM OF SWORDS

"George R. R. Martin continues to take epic fantasy to new levels of insight and sophistication, resonant with the turmoils and stress of the world we call our own."

—*Locus*

"Like a cross between a complicated game of chess, a quirky Stephen King tale and *Braveheart*, Martin's epic advances his series with gritty characterizations, bold plot moves and plenty of action."

—*St. Louis Post-Dispatch*

"If you are a fantasy fan and you're not reading Martin, you're cheating yourself of some of the best the field has to offer."

—*San Francisco Chronicle*

A CLASH OF KINGS

"Martin amply fulfills the first volume's promise and continues what seems destined to be one of the best fantasy series ever written."

—*The Denver Post*

"High fantasy with a vengeance."

—*The San Diego Union-Tribune*

"So complex, fascinating and well-rendered, readers will almost certainly be hooked by the whole series."

—*Dallas Morning News*

A GAME OF THRONES

"Reminiscent of T. H. White's *The Once and Future King*, this novel is an absorbing combination of the mythic, the sweepingly historical, and the intensely personal."

—*Chicago Sun-Times*

"I always expect the best from George R. R. Martin, and he always delivers. *A Game of Thrones* grabs hold and won't let go. It's brilliant."

—Robert Jordan

By George R. R. Martin

A Song of Ice and Fire
Book One: A Game of Thrones
Book Two: A Clash of Kings Book
Three: A Storm of Swords
Book Four: A Feast for Crows
Book Five: A Dance with Dragons

The Lands of Ice & Fire
The World of Ice & Fire: The Untold
  History of Westeros and
  the Game of Thrones
A Knight of the Seven Kingdoms
Fire & Blood

Dying of the Light
Windhaven (with Lisa Tuttle)
Fevre Dream
The Armageddon Rag
Dead Man's Hand (with John J. Miller)

Graphic Novels
A Game of Thrones, Volumes 1–4
A Clash of Kings, Volume 1
The Mystery Knight
Windhaven
Starport

Short Story Collections
Dreamsongs: Volume I
Dreamsongs: Volume II
A Song for Lya and Other Stories
Songs of Stars and Shadows
Sandkings
Songs the Dead Men Sing
Nightflyers
Tuf Voyaging
Portraits of His Children
Quartet

Edited by George R. R. Martin
New Voices in Science Fiction,
  Volumes 1–4
The Science Fiction Weight-Loss Book
  (with Isaac Asimov and
  Martin Harry Greenberg)
The John W. Campbell Awards,
  Volume 5
Night Visions 3
Wild Cards I–XXII

Co-edited with Gardner Dozois
Warriors I–III
Songs of the Dying Earth
Down These Strange Streets
Old Mars
Dangerous Women
Rogues
Old Venus

THE
ARMAGEDDON
RAG

GEORGE R. R. MARTIN

BANTAM BOOKS TRADE PAPERBACKS
NEW YORK

2012 Bantam Books Trade Paperback Edition

Copyright © 1983 by George R. R. Martin

Published in the United States of America by Bantam Books, an imprint of the Random House Publishing Group, a division of Random House, Inc., New York.

Bantam Books and the rooster colophon, and the spectra colophon are registered trademarks of Random House, Inc.

Originally published in hardcover by Poseidon Press in 1983 and in paperback by Pocket Books in 1985. Later republished in trade paperback by Bantam Spectra in February 2007.

Library of Congress Cataloging-in-Publication Data
Martin, George R. R.
The Armageddon Rage / George R. R. Martin.
p. cm
ISBN 978-0-553-38307-2
eBook 978-0-553-90123-8
1. Science Fiction.   I. Title.
PS3563.A7239 A7   1983
813'.54—dc22   83013597

www.bantamdell.com

Book design by Lynn Newmark

ACKNOWLEDGMENTS

Quotations from "The Second Coming" by W. B. Yeats appear throughout. Reprinted with the permission of Scribner, an imprint of Simon & Schuster Adult Publishing Group, from THE COLLECTED WORKS OF W. B. YEATS, VOLUME I: THE POEMS, REVISED, edited by Richard J. Finneran. Copyright 1924 by The Macmillan Company; copyright renewed © 1952 by Bertha Georgie Yeats.

"Those Were the Daze" (Stephen W. Terrell), copyright © 1981 Stephen W. Terrell, Sidhe Gorm Music, BMI. Used by permission.

CHAPTER ONE
    "Those Were the Days" (words and music by Gene Raskin), TRO— Copyright © 1962 (Renewed) 1968 (Renewed) by Essex Music, Inc., New York, NY. Used by permission.
CHAPTER TWO
    "Bad Moon Rising" (John Fogerty), copyright © 1969 by Jondora Music. Used by permission.
CHAPTER THREE
    "Did You Ever Have to Make Up Your Mind?" (words and music by John Sebastian), copyright © 1965 by Alley Music Corp. and Trio Music Company. Copyright renewed. International copyright secured. All rights reserved. Used by permission of Alley Music Corporation and Trio Music Company.
    "Daydream" (words and music by John Sebastian), copyright © 1966 by Alley Music Corp. and Trio Music Company. Copyright renewed. International copyright secured. All rights reserved. Used by permission of Alley Music Corporation and Trio Music Company.

THANKS

The Nazgûl would never have played at all were it not for Gardner R. Dozois, who asked me to write a story for an anthology he hoped to do, and thereby set some wheels to turning. And they would never have sounded as good had it not been for my trio of rock consultants, Lew Shiner of the Dinosaurs, Stephen W. Terrell of the Potato Salad Band, and Parris. To all of them, my thanks.

George R. R. Martin
October 1982

To the Beatles,
    to the Airplane and the Spoonful and the Dead,
    to Simon and Garfunkel, Joplin and Hendrix,
    to Buffalo Springfield and the Rolling Stones,
    to the Doors and the Byrds, the Mamas and the Papas,
    to Melanie, to Donovan, to Peter, Paul, and Mary,
    to the Who, and the Moody Blues, and Moby Grape,
    to Country Joe and the Fish, Paul Revere and the Raiders,
    to Bob Dylan and Phil Ochs and Joan Baez and Joni Mitchell
    to the Mothers of Invention and the Smothers Brothers,
    to the Hollies and the Association and the Beach Boys
       and even Herman and the Hermits,
    to Creedence Clearwater Revival,
    to lost innocence and bright, shining dreams,

and, especially, to Parris:
    looking at you, I hear the music.

THOSE WERE THE DAZE

(with apologies to Norman Lear)

Oh, the way that Hendrix played
Everyone was getting laid
Dope was of the highest grade
Those were the days

Always knew who you could trust
Cruising in your micro-bus
They were them and we were us
Those were the days

All the things we're into then
Tarot cards, I Ching, and Zen
Mister, we could use a man like
      Timothy Leary again!

Hardly needed any cash
Everybody shared their stash
Always had a place to crash
Those were the days!

THE
ARMAGEDDON
RAG

ONE

Those were the days, my friend/
We thought they'd never end

It was not one of Sandy Blair's all-time great days. His agent had picked up the lunch tab, to be sure, but that only partially made up for the way he'd gotten on Sandy's case about the novel deadline. The subway was full of yahoos and it seemed to take forever to get him back to Brooklyn. The three-block walk to the brownstone he called home seemed longer and colder than usual. He felt in dire need of a beer by the time he got there. He pulled one from the fridge, opened it, and ascended wearily to his third-floor office to face the stack of blank paper he was supposedly turning into a book. Once again, the elves had failed to knock off any chapters in his absence; page thirty-seven was still in his typewriter. You just couldn't get good elves anymore, Sandy thought morosely. He stared at the words with distaste, took a swig from the bottle in his hand, and looked around for a distraction.

That was when he noticed the red light on his message machine, and found that Jared Patterson had phoned.

Actually it had been Jared's secretary who made the call, which Sandy found amusing; even after seven years, and everything that had happened, Patterson was still a bit nervous about him. "Jared Patterson would like Mister Blair to contact him as soon as possible, in connection with an assignment," said the pleasant professional voice. Sandy listened to her twice before erasing the tape. "Jared Patterson," he said to himself, bemused. The name evoked a hell of a lot of memories.

Sandy knew that he really ought to ignore Patterson's message. The sonofabitch deserved no more. That was hopeless, though; he was already too curious. He picked up the phone and dialed, mildly astonished to discover that he still remembered the number, after seven years. A secretary picked up. "*Hedgehog,*" she said. "Mister Patterson's office."

"This is Sander Blair," Sandy said. "Jared phoned me. Tell the poltroon that I'm returning his call."

"Yes, Mister Blair. Mister Patterson left instructions to put you through at once. Please hold."

A moment later, Patterson's familiar mock-hearty voice was ringing in Sandy's ear. "*Sandy!* It's great to hear ya, really it is. Long time, old man. How's it hanging?"

"Cut the shit, Jared," Sandy said sharply. "You're no happier to hear from me than I was to hear from you. What the hell you want? And keep it short, I'm a busy man."

Patterson chuckled. "Is that any way to talk to an old friend? Still no social graces, I see. All right, then, however you want it. I wantcha to do a story for *Hedgehog,* how's that for straight?"

"Go suck a lemon," Sandy said. "Why the hell should I write for you? You fired me, you asshole."

"Bitter, bitter," Jared chided. "That was seven years ago, Sandy. I hardly remember it now."

"That's funny. I remember it real well. I'd lost it, you said. I was out of touch with what was happening, you said. I was too old to edit for the youth audience, you said. I was taking the *Hog* down the tubes, you said. Like shit. I was the one who *made* that paper, and you damn well know it."

"Never denied it," Jared Patterson said breezily. "But times changed, and you didn't. If I'd kept you on, we'd have gone down with the *Freep* and the *Barb* and all the rest. All that counterculture stuff had to go. I mean, who needed it? All that politics, reviewers who hated the hot new trends in music, the drug stories . . . it just didn't cut it, y'know?" He sighed. "Look, I didn't call to hash over ancient history. I was hoping you'd have more perspective by now. Hell, Sandy, firing you hurt me more than it did you."

"Oh, sure," Sandy said. "You sold out to a chain and got a nice cushy salaried job as publisher while you were firing three-quarters of your staff. You must be in *such* pain." He snorted. "Jared, you're still an asshole. We built that paper together, as a communal sort of thing. It wasn't yours to sell."

"Hey, communes were all well and good back when we were young, but you seem to forget that it was my money kept the whole show afloat."

"Your money and our talent."

"God, you haven't changed a bit, have you?" Jared said. "Well, think what you like, but our circulation is three times what it was when you were editor, and our ad revenues are out of sight. *Hedgehog* has class now. We get nominated for real journalism awards. Have you seen us lately?"

"Sure," said Sandy. "Great stuff. Restaurant reviews. Profiles of movie stars. Suzanne Somers on the cover, for God's sake. Consumer reports on video games. A dating service for lonely singles. What is it you call yourself now? The Newspaper of Alternative Lifestyles?"

"We changed that, dropped the 'alternative' part. It's just *Lifestyles* now. Between the two H's in the logo."

"Jesus," Sandy said. "Your music editor has *green hair*!"

"He's got a real deep understanding of pop music," Jared said defensively. "And stop shouting at me. You're always shouting at me. I'm starting to regret calling you, y'know. Do you want to talk about this assignment or not?"

"Frankly, my dear, I don't give a damn. Why do you think I need your assignment?"

"No one said you did. I'm not out of it, I know you've been doing well. How many novels have you published? Four?"

"Three," Sandy corrected.

"*Hedgehog*'s run reviews on every one of them too. You oughtta be grateful. Firing you was the best thing I could have done for you. You were always a better writer than you were an editor."

"Oh, thank you, massa, thank you. I's ever so thankful. I owes it all to you."

"You could at least be civil," Jared said. "Look, you don't need us and we don't need you, but I thought it would be nice to work together again, just for old time's sake. Admit it, it'd be a kick to have your byline in the old *Hog* again, wouldn't it? And we pay better than we used to."

"I'm not hurting for money."

"Who said you were? I know all about you. Three novels and a brownstone and a sports car. What is it, a Porsche or something?"

"A Mazda RX-7," Sandy said curtly.

"Yeah, and you live with a *Realtor*, so don't lecture me about selling out, Sandy old boy."

"What do you want, Jared?" Sandy said, stung. "I'm getting tired of sparring."

"We've got a story that would be perfect for you. We want to play it up big, too, and I thought maybe you'd be interested. It's a murder."

"What are you doing now, trying to turn the *Hog* into *True Detective*? Forget it, Jared, I don't do crime shit."

"Jamie Lynch was the guy that got himself murdered."

The name of the victim brought Sandy up short, and a wisecrack died in his mouth. "The promoter?"

"None other."

Sandy sat back, took a swig of beer, and mulled on that. Lynch had been out of the news for years, a has-been even before Sandy was fired from the *Hog*, but in his day he had been an important man in the rock subculture. It could be an interesting story. Lynch had always been surrounded by controversy. He'd worn two hats: promoter and manager. As a promoter, he'd organized some of the biggest tours and concerts of his day. He'd ensured their success by booking in the bands he controlled as manager, and by denying those bands to rival concerts. With hot talent like American Taco, the Fevre River Packet Company, and the Nazgûl under his thumb, he'd been a man to reckon with. At least up until 1971, when the disaster at West Mesa, the breakup of the Nazgûl, and a couple of drug busts started him on the long slide down. "What happened to him?" Sandy asked.

"It's pretty kinky," Jared said. "Somebody busted into his place up in Maine, dragged him into his office, and offed him there. They tied him to his desk, and, like, *sacrificed* him. Cut his heart out. He had one after all. Remember the old jokes? Ah, never mind. Anyhow, the whole scene was kind of grotesque. Mansonesque, y'know? Well, that made me think of the series you did back around the time that Sharon Tate got offed, you know, that investigation of . . . what did you call it?"

"The dark side of the counterculture," Sandy said dryly. "We won awards for that series, Jared."

"Yeah, right. I remembered it was good. So I thought of you. This is right up your alley. Real Sixties, y'know? What we're thinking of is a long meaty piece, like those in-depth things you used to go for. We'll use the murder as a news peg, see, and you could investigate it a bit, see maybe if you could kick up something the police miss, y'know, but mostly use it as a springboard for a sort of retrospective on Jamie Lynch and his promotions, all his groups and his concerts and his times and like that. Maybe you could look up some of the guys from his old groups, the Fevre River gang and the Nazgûl and all, interview 'em and work in some where-are-they-now kind of stuff. It would be sort of a nostalgia piece, I figure."

"Your readership thinks the Beatles were the band Paul McCartney was with before he got Wings," Sandy said. "They won't even know who Jamie Lynch *was*, for Chrissakes."

"That's where you're wrong. We still have lots of our old readers. The kind of feature I see on this Lynch business will be real popular. Now, can you write it or not?"

"Of course I can write it. The question is, why should I?"

"We'll pay expenses, and our top rate. That ain't nothing to sneeze at, either. You won't have to sell the paper on street-corners afterward. We're beyond that."

"Terrific," Sandy said. He wanted to tell Jared to go get stuffed, but much as he hated to admit it, the assignment had a certain perverse attractiveness. It *would* be nice to be in the *Hog* again. The paper was his baby, after all; it had turned into a pretty wayward and superficial kid, but it was his, nonetheless, and still had a lingering hold on his loyalties. Besides, if he did this Lynch piece, it would help restore some of the old *Hog* quality, if only for an instant. If he passed, someone else would write the article, and it would be more trash. "I tell you what," Sandy said. "You guarantee me that I'll get cover billing with this, and you put it in writing that the piece will be printed just the way I write it, not one word changed, no cuts, nothing, and maybe I'll consider it."

"Sandy, you want it, you got it. I wouldn't think of messing around with your stuff. Can you have the piece in by Tuesday?"

Sandy laughed raucously. "Shit, no. In-depth, you said. I want as much time as I need on this. Maybe I'll have it in within a month. Maybe not."

"The news peg will go stale," Jared whined.

"So what? A short piece in your news section will do for now. If I'm going to do this, I'm going to do it right. Those are the conditions, take 'em or leave 'em."

"Anybody but you, I'd tell 'em to get shoved," Patterson replied. "But hell, why not? We go way back. You got it, Sandy."

"My agent will call and get everything in writing."

"Hey!" Jared said. "After all we been through, you want things in writing? How many times did I bail you out of jail? How many times did we share a joint?"

"Lots," Sandy said. "Only they were always *my* joints, as I recall. Jared, seven years ago, you gave me three hours' notice and bus fare in lieu of severance pay. So this time we'll get a written contract. My agent will call." He hung up before Patterson had a chance to argue, turned on the answering machine to catch any attempted call-backs, and leaned back in his chair with his hands behind his head and a faintly bemused smile on his face. He wondered just what the hell he was getting himself into this time.

Sharon wasn't going to like this, he thought. His agent wasn't going to like it, either. But *he* liked it, somehow. No doubt running off to Maine to muck around in a murder was a silly thing to do; the more rational side of Sandy Blair knew that, knew that his deadlines and mortgage obligations ought to come first, that he could hardly afford the time he'd have to expend on this for the relative pittance that *Hedgehog* would pay. Still, he'd been restless and moody lately, and he had to get away from that damned page thirty-seven for a while, and it had been entirely too long since he had done anything silly, anything spontaneous or new or even a tad adventurous. In the old days, he'd been just wild enough to drive Jared crazy. Sandy missed the old days. He remembered the time that he and Maggie had driven to Philly at two in the morning because he wanted a cheese steak. And the time Lark and Bambi and he had gone to Cuba to harvest sugarcane. And his attempt to join the French Foreign Legion, and Froggy's search for the ultimate pizza, and the week they'd spent exploring the sewers. The marches, the rallies, the concerts, the rock stars and underground heroes and dopesters he knew, all the off-the-wall stories that had fattened his clipbook and broadened his horizons. He missed all that. He'd had good days and bad days, but it was all a lot more exciting than sitting in his office and rereading page thirty-seven over and over again.

Sandy began to rummage through the lower drawers of his desk. Way in the back he kept souvenirs, things he had no earthly use for but couldn't bear to throw away—handbills he'd written, snapshots he'd never gotten around to sticking in a photo album, his collection of old campaign buttons. Underneath it all, he found the box with his old business cards. He snapped off the rubber band and extracted a few.

There were two different kinds. One, printed in deep black ink on crisp white cardboard, identified him as Sander Blair, accredited correspondent of the National Metropolitan News Network, Inc. It was legit too; that was the real name of the corporation that published *Hedgehog*, or at least it had been until Jared sold out to the chain. Sandy had come up with the corporate name himself, reasoning—quite accurately, as hindsight demonstrated—that there would be occasions when a reporter for the National Metropolitan News Network, Inc., would have a much easier time getting press credentials than a reporter for something called *Hedgehog*.

The second card was oversized, with metallic silver ink on pale purple paper, depicting the paper's namesake symbol picking his teeth and diapered in an American flag. In the upper left it said, "Sandy," and down under the cartoon, in slightly larger print, "I writes for da *Hog*." That one had its uses too. It could open doors and loosen tongues in situations where the straight card would be worse than useless.

Sandy slid a dozen of each into his billfold. Then he picked up his beer bottle and strolled downstairs.

When she got home at six, Sharon found him seated cross-legged on the living-room carpet, surrounded by road maps, old clipbooks of stories from the *Hog*'s heyday, and empty bottles of Michelob. She stood in the doorway in her beige business suit, with her briefcase in hand and her ash-blond hair rumpled by the wind, staring at him in astonishment from behind tinted glasses. "What's all this?" she asked.

"A long story," Sandy replied. "Get yourself a beer and I'll tell you."

Sharon looked at him dubiously, excused herself, went upstairs and changed into a pair of designer jeans and a loose cotton blouse, and returned with a glass of red wine in hand. She seated herself in one of the big armchairs. "Go ahead."

"Lunch was a bummer," Sandy said, "and the fucking elves didn't write a word for me, but the ghost of hedgehogs past raised his corpulent head on my return." He told her the whole story. She listened with the same pleasant professional smile she wore when selling brownstones and condos, at least at the start. By the end, though, she was frowning. "You're not kidding, are you?" she said.

"No," Sandy said. He'd been afraid of this.

"I can't believe this," Sharon said. "You've got a deadline, don't you? Whatever Patterson is paying won't make up for the novel. This is stupid, Sandy. You've been late on the last two books. Can you afford to be late again? And since when have you turned into a crime reporter? What's the use of messing around in things you don't understand? Do you know *any-thing* about murders?"

"I've read half the Travis McGee series," Sandy said.

Sharon made a disgusted noise. "*Sandy!* Be serious."

"All right," he said. "So I'm not a crime writer. So what? I know a lot about Jamie Lynch, and I know a lot about cults. This has all the earmarks of a Manson kind of thing. Maybe I can get a book out of it, a whole different *kind* of book, something like *In Cold Blood*. Consider it a growth experience. You're real big on growth experiences."

"You're not talking growth," Sharon snapped, "you're talking regression. *Hedgehog* is giving you a license to be irresponsible, and you're crazy for it. You want to drive up there and play Sam Spade and talk to has-been rock stars and old yippies and relive the Sixties for a month or so, at Patterson's expense. You'll probably try to prove that Richard Nixon did it."

"LBJ was my guess," Sandy said.

"He's got an alibi. He's dead."

"Aw, shit," Sandy said, with his most engaging grin.

"Stop trying to be so damned cute," Sharon snapped. "It isn't going to get you anywhere. Grow up, Sandy. This isn't a game. This is your life."

"Then where's Ralph Edwards?" he asked. He closed his clipbook and put it aside. "You're really upset about this, aren't you?" he asked.

"Yes," Sharon said curtly. "It's not a joke, no matter what you think."

She had finally worn him down; annoyance was contagious. But he decided to give it one last chance. "I won't be gone too long," he said. "And Maine can be lovely this time of year, with autumn just beginning. Come with me. Make it a vacation. We need to spend more time together, and if you came along, maybe you'd understand my side of it a little better."

"Sure," she said, her voice acid with sarcasm. "I'll just phone up Don at the agency and tell him I'm taking off for, oh, who knows how long, and he should cover for me. Fat chance. I have a career to think about, Sandy. Maybe you don't care, but I do."

"I care," he said, wounded.

"Besides," Sharon added sweetly, "it would be a bit awkward having me along if you decided to screw around, wouldn't it?"

"Damn it, who said I wanted to . . ."

"You don't have to say it. I know you. Go ahead, it doesn't bother me. We're not married, we've got an open relationship. Just don't bring anything home with you."

Sandy stood up, fuming. "You know, Sharon, I love you, but I swear, sometimes you piss the hell out of me. This is a story. An assignment. I'm a writer and I'm going to write about the murder of Jamie Lynch. That's all. Don't get bent all out of shape."

"You use such quaint nostalgic expressions," Sharon said. "I haven't gotten bent out of shape since college, dear." She rose. "And I've enjoyed about as much of this as I can stand. I'm going to my study to work."

"I'm leaving first thing tomorrow morning," Sandy said. "I *was* thinking maybe we'd go out for dinner."

"I've got work," Sharon said, walking to the stairs.

"But I don't know how long this will take. I might be gone . . ."

She turned and looked at him. "It had better not be too long, or I might forget all about you and change the locks."

Sandy watched her back as she climbed, frustration building within him with every click of heel against wood. When he heard her enter her study, he stalked into the kitchen, grabbed another beer, and tried to return to the preparations for the trip, but it took only a moment to realize he was too mad to concentrate. What he needed was music, he thought. He took a sip of beer, and smiled. Some *rock*.

Their record collection filled two tall cabinets on either side of the speakers, huge old JVC 100s that had given Sandy years of faithful service. Sharon's cabinet was packed with blues, Broadway show tunes, and even disco, to Sandy's never-ending dismay. "I like to dance," Sharon would say whenever he got on her about it. Sandy's records were all folk and vintage rock. He couldn't abide what had happened to music in the past ten years, and the only albums he bought these days were reissues he needed to re-place old favorites worn out by play.

Sandy wasted no time selecting music to suit his mood. There was only one possible choice.

There were five albums, filed between the Mothers of Invention and the New Riders of the Purple Sage. He pulled them out and sorted through them. The jackets were as familiar as the features of an old friend, and so too were the titles. The first, *Hot Wind out of Mordor*, had a kind of Tolkienesque cover, hobbits cringing in the pastel underbrush while volca-noes belched red fire in the distance and the dark riders wheeled above on their scaly winged steeds. *Nazgûl* offered a surreal landscape of red sun and scarlet mist, twisted mountains, and shapes half-living and half-machine, all vivid, fevered, hot. The big double album was shiny black, front, back, and within, without lettering, empty but for four tiny sets of hot red eyes peering from the lower left-hand corner. There was no title. It had been called the Black Album, in deliberate parody of the Beatles' White Album. *Napalm*, which followed, showed children in some jungle, crouching, burning, screaming, while oddly distorted jets streaked overhead and vom-ited fire down on them. It wasn't until you looked closely that you realized the scene was a restatement of the cover for *Hot Wind out of Mordor*, even as the songs within were answers to the group's earlier, more innocent com-positions... though they had never been entirely innocent.

Sandy looked at each album in turn, and replaced them in the cabinet, until he held only the fifth album, the last one, cut only weeks before West Mesa.

The jacket was dark and threatening, done in dim shades of black and gray and violet. It was a concert photograph, retouched to remove the audi-ence, the hall, the props, everything. Only the band remained, the four of them standing on some endless empty plain, darkness hulking before them and below them and pressing in, the shadows slimy and acrawl with suggestive, nightmarish shapes. Behind them a vast, glowering purple sun etched their figures in relief and threw long shadows black as sin and sharp as the cutting edge of a knife.

They stood as they'd always stood when playing. In the back, among the drums done up in swirling patterns of black and red, Gopher John sat scowling. He was a big man, moon-faced, his features all but lost in his thick black beard. In his huge hands the sticks looked like toothpicks, yet he seemed to crouch, for all his size, to hunker down among those drums like some great fierce beast surprised in its lair. In front of Gopher John's dark nest stood Maggio and Faxon, flanking the drums on either side. Maggio hugged his guitar to his bare, scrawny chest. He was sneering, and his long dark hair and droopy mustache were moving in some unseen wind, and his nipples looked vivid and red. Faxon wore a white fringe jacket and a thin smile as he plucked at his electric bass. He was clean-shaven, with long blond braids and green eyes, but you would never guess his brilliance by looking at him.

And up in front stood Hobbins, legs spread, head thrown back so his waist-long white hair cascaded down behind him, eyes blazing scarlet, one hand clutching a microphone and the other clawing the air. He wore a black denim suit with buttons made of bone, and on his crotch was sewn an American flag with the Eye of Mordor where the stars ought to have been. He looked like something supernatural, slight and small yet possessed of a vitality that shrieked at the darkness and held it at bay.

Against the great purple sun was a single word, in spiky black lettering, that looked like a lightning bolt mated to a snake. *Nazgûl*, it said. And down below, very faint, gray against the blackness, it whispered *Music to Wake the Dead*.

Sandy slid the album out of the jacket cover and placed it carefully on his turntable, set it in motion, and turned up the amp all the way. Tonight he wanted it loud, the way it had been when he first heard it, back in '71, the way the Nazgûl meant it to be played. If that bothered Sharon, upstairs shuffling her papers, that was her tough luck.

For a moment there was only silence, then a faint noise growing louder, something that sounded like a teakettle whistling, or maybe a missile coming down. It rose until it was a shrill scream that went knifing through your brain, and then came the heavy sound of drums as Gopher John laid down the backbeat, and then the guitars cut in, and finally there was Hobbins, laying full-force into "Blood on the Sheets." The opening lyric gave Sandy a strange small shudder. *Baby, you cut my heart out,* the Nazgûl sang, *Baby, you made me bleeeeed!*

He closed his eyes and listened, and it was almost as if a decade had gone away, as if West Mesa had never happened, as if Nixon was still in the White House and Vietnam still raged and the Movement still lived. But somehow, even in that tattered past, one thing remained the same, and in the darkness, lit by the songs of the Nazgûl, it was etched clearer than ever.

Jamie Lynch was dead. They had, indeed, cut his heart out.

TWO

I see a bad moon a-rising/
I see trouble on the way

Sheriff Edwin Theodore was called "Notch" by all and sundry in his jurisdiction, for reasons that were not readily apparent to Sandy Blair. Notch was a small, gaunt man with terrific posture, a narrow pinched face, rimless glasses, and iron-gray hair that he combed straight back. He looked as if he ought to have been holding a pitchfork and staring out of a painting. Sandy took one look at Notch and decided to call him Sheriff Theodore.

The sheriff fingered Sandy's crisp, white, officious business card while looking dubiously at Sandy himself. For a moment, beneath Theodore's pale watery scrutiny, Sandy felt like it was 1969 again and he had hair down to his ass and a stainless-steel peace medallion on a leather thong around his neck. It was an effort to remember that, scruffy as he was, he didn't look much worse than any other reporter. Maybe he was wearing jeans, but at least they were *expensive* jeans, and his brown cord jacket ought to be acceptable enough, even if it was a bit on the old side. He ran a self-conscious hand through his mop of thick black hair and felt briefly thankful that he had long since given up wearing his beard.

Theodore handed back his card. "Never heard of no National Metropolitan News Network," he said brusquely. "What channel is that?"

"Not television," Sandy said, deciding that he'd better play it straight.

"We publish a national music and entertainment tabloid out of New York. With Lynch's rock connections, the story is a natural for us."

Sheriff Theodore replied with a small, parsimonious grunt. "Press conference was two days ago," he said. "You missed it. Most of the other newspaper boys come and gone by now. Ain't nothing new."

Sandy shrugged. "I'll be working a feature slant," he said. "I'd like to interview you about the case, talk over whatever theories you're working on, and maybe go out and take a look at Lynch's house, where it happened. Do you have any leads?"

Theodore ignored the question. "Did my talking at the press conference. Got nothing else to say. Ain't got time to be repeating myself for every fool reporter comes up here late." He looked around the office with a disgruntled expression on his face and beckoned to one of his deputies. "I'll have one of my men run you out to Lynch's place and answer your questions, but I can't spare him more than an hour, so you get what you want quickly, Mister Blair, or the National Metropolitan News Network is going to be shit out of luck. You understand that?"

"Uh, sure," Sandy said, but Theodore hadn't waited for an answer. A bare few minutes later, he was packed into one of the sheriff's cars, heading out of town in the company of a gangling, horsefaced deputy named David ("Call me Davie") Parker. Parker was about Sandy's age, though his receding brown hair made him look older. He had an amiable smile and a clumsy way of moving.

"How long will it take us to get to the house?" Sandy asked as they pulled out from the curb.

"Depends on how fast we go," Parker replied. "It isn't far as the crow flies, but it's all back roads. Takes a while."

"I'm only supposed to have you for an hour."

Parker laughed. "Oh, that. Don't worry about it. I'm coming off shift and I got nothing better to do, so I might as well run you out to Lynch's. Notch is just out of sorts with reporters. Two of them spelled his name wrong after the press conference."

"It *is* Theodore?" Sandy said, checking his notes.

"Yeah. But it's Edwin, not Edward."

Sandy was double-checking that when the deputy said, "Speaking of names, you're Sandy Blair, right? The writer?"

"Uh, yeah."

"I've read your books. Two of them, anyway."

"Which two?" Sandy said, astonished.

"*Open Wounds* and *Copping Out*," Parker said. "You sound surprised."

"I am."

Parker gave him a shrewd sidelong glance. "Cops *do* read, you know. Well, some cops. And this isn't the wilderness you New Yorkers think it is. We get movies up here, books, newspapers, even rock and roll."

"I didn't..." Sandy began, then thought better of it. "What did you think of the novels?" he asked.

"*Open Wounds* was too depressing for my taste," Parker said. "You write pretty well, I'll give you that. Didn't like the ending of *Copping Out*."

"Why not?" Sandy said, a bit bemused at the idea of chewing over the merits of his first novel with a deputy in the Maine woods en route to a murder site.

"Because your hero is an asshole. What's the point? He's finally gotten a decent job, he's making some money, being responsible for the first time in his life, and he chucks it all. For what? Even he doesn't know. If I remember right, it ends with him walking down a street, wondering where it leads. It doesn't even bother him that he's out of work, that he's let down everybody who was counting on him."

"But that's the point," Sandy said. "It *doesn't* bother him. It's a happy ending. He's free. Finally. He's stopped selling out."

"Wonder how long that lasted," Parker said.

"What does that mean?"

"When did you write that book?"

"I started it back around '69 or so, but I didn't get around to finishing it until I left the *Hog* seven years ago."

"Well," said Parker, "all this bopping around being free was fine back then, but I'd be curious to know how it's lasted. How's your guy like poverty after a decade of it? Where does he crash these days? Bet you he don't get laid as often now as he did in your book. I'd like to see this jerk in the Eighties, friend. I'd lay odds he's selling out again."

"*Touché,*" Sandy said glumly. "All right, the novel's a bit naïve. What can I say? It was a reflection of its time and social context. You had to be there."

Parker glanced at him. "I'm about your age."

"Maybe it depended on which side of the barricades you were on."

"I wasn't on either side. I was over in 'Nam, getting shot at while you and your characters were getting stoned and getting laid." The deputy was still smiling, but there was a faint bitter edge to his voice that Sandy found unnerving.

"You weren't there on account of me, friend," Sandy said. The subject made him uncomfortable; he changed it. "Let's talk about this Lynch business. Who did it?"

Parker had a warm laugh. "You come right to the point. Hell, we don't know who did it."

They had turned off the main road some time back and were winding their way through a thick stand of woods, all orange and rust in the late afternoon light, on a narrow dirt track. The car was riding roughly, but Sandy spread his notebook on his knee and stared down at some of his questions. "You think the killer was local?" he asked.

Parker spun the car deftly around a sharp turn. "It's doubtful. Lynch kept to himself pretty much. This damned road ought to tell you that much. He liked his privacy, I guess. Oh, I suppose there was some friction between Lynch and those who had dealings with him. I mean, he didn't exactly blend in. But nobody had any reason to go *kill* him, much less do it . . . well, the way it was done."

"Cut his heart out, you mean?" Sandy said, making a note. The motion of the car turned his handwriting into a scrawl.

Parker nodded. "This is Maine. That's a New York kind of thing to do. Or maybe California," he added thoughtfully.

"Did they find it?"

"The murder weapon?"

"The heart."

"No. Neither one."

"All right," Sandy said. "So it wasn't local. Any suspects, then? You must be investigating someone."

"Well, we're playing with a couple of theories. Nothing really seems to fit, though. We thought maybe robbery at first. Lynch might have been washed up in the music business, but he was still rich as hell. Except there's no evidence that anything was taken."

"You're forgetting the heart," Sandy said.

"Yeah," said Parker, noncommittally. "The other thing we're thinking is that maybe drugs were involved somehow. Lynch had a couple of convictions, you know."

Sandy nodded. "He supplied hash and coke to his groups. That's well known. Does it tie in?"

"Oh, maybe. Rumors were that Lynch had lots of wild parties. Rumors were he kept drugs on hand. We didn't find any. Maybe somebody killed him for his stash."

Sandy wrote that down. "OK," he said. "What else?"

The deputy shrugged. "There's some other funny things about this murder."

"Tell me."

"I'll do better than that. I'll show you. We're there." They swung around another curve and over the crest of a hill, and suddenly there was Jamie Lynch's house ahead of them. Parker pulled the car to a halt on the gravel of the circular driveway, and Sandy climbed out.

Surrounded by woods on all sides, the house sprawled comfortably amid the riot of autumn foliage. It was a modern, tasteful place, built of red-gray stone and natural wood, with a red flagstone patio to one side and a large outdoor deck above it. A dozen steps of unfinished wood led from the base of the drive to the front door. All the windows were tightly shuttered. A large tree was growing through the roof.

"There's a little creek runs through the living room too," Parker volunteered. "This place is even more impressive at night. Lights up all around here."

"Can we go inside?"

Parker extracted a set of keys from his jacket. "That's why we're here."

They went in the front door. The interior was wood-paneled and deeply carpeted. Each room was on a slightly different level, so they went up and down small three-step staircases constantly and it was hard for Sandy to decide how many floors he was dealing with. Parker gave Sandy a quick tour. There were skylights, stained-glass windows, and—as advertised—a creek running through the living room, around the trunk of the old tree. The kitchen was modern and clean. The four bedrooms had water beds, mirrored ceilings, and fireplaces. And the sound system was incredible.

Lynch had an entire wall of records, and speakers mounted in every room. It could all be operated from the living room, the master bedroom, or Lynch's office, Parker said. He showed Sandy the nerve center, hidden behind a sliding wooden panel in the vast living room. It looked like the bridge of the starship *Enterprise*. The main speakers were taller than Parker and wafer-thin. "You could have played at Woodstock with an amp like this," Sandy said in astonishment. "This is concert-level stuff."

"It's loud," Parker agreed. "That's a factor in the case."

Sandy rounded on him. "How so?"

"I'll get to that," the deputy said. "First, let me go through this with you. C'mon." They went back to the entryway. Parker opened another sliding wall panel to reveal more lights and switches. "Security system," he said. "Lynch had alarms on alarms. Paranoid fellow. You'd think somebody was out to kill him. The alarms were never tripped. No one broke in. Death came walking right up to the front door."

"Meaning he knew the killer?"

"So we think. Either that or it was the Fuller Brush man."

"Go on."

"Well, we construct it this way. The killer or killers drove up open as you please, got out, came up the front steps. Lynch met them and let them in. The lock wasn't forced or anything. They went into the living room. That's where the argument began. We found evidence of a struggle, and we think Lynch was overcome quickly and dragged back to his office, unconscious or unresisting, maybe dead. But we don't think so. The living-room carpet shows drag marks. You haven't seen the office yet. Come with me."

Sandy followed him dutifully back through the living room. This time Parker pointed out the marks in the carpet before he took out the keys again and unlocked the office door.

Jamie Lynch's workspace was an interior room, three times as long as it was wide, with a slanting skylight overhead but no windows. The only furniture was a big horseshoe-shaped mahogany desk, a chair, and twenty black filing cabinets that looked very stark against the deep milk-white carpeting. One long wall was covered floor to ceiling with mirror tiles, inlaid with decorative swirls, to make the office seem larger than it was. All the other wall space was taken up by posters and photographs; glossies of Lynch clients famous and infamous, pictures of Jamie and various celebrities, concert posters, political handbills, album cover blow-ups, commercial posters. Sandy looked them over with a faint pang of nostalgia. There was Che and there was Joplin, cheek-to-jowl. Nixon was selling used cars next to the infamous pornographic American Taco poster that had gotten a concert canceled and almost caused a riot. The far north wall, behind the desk, was taken up entirely with old Fillmore posters. "Quite a collection," Sandy commented.

Parker sat on the edge of the desk. "This is where they killed him."

Sandy turned away from the posters. "On the desk?"

The deputy nodded. "They had rope. They bound him to the desk top, spread-eagle, one loop around each limb." He pointed. "See the bloodstains on the carpet."

There was a large ragged stain by one of the legs and a couple of smaller ones around it. Against the white carpet they were painfully obvious, now that Parker had pointed them out. "Not much blood," Sandy said.

"Ah," said Parker, smiling. "Interesting point. There was a lot of blood, actually, but our killer was fastidious. He pulled down one of the posters and spread it across the desk under the victim, so the wood wasn't ruined. You can see where it's missing." He nodded.

Sandy turned and looked, and finally noticed the blank spot among the posters, high on the east wall, about ten feet from where they stood. He frowned, bothered, yet unable for the moment to say why. "Weird," he said, turning back to Parker. "How was Lynch found?"

"The music was too loud."

Sandy took out his notebook. "Music?"

Parker nodded. "Maybe Lynch was playing a record when death arrived. Maybe whoever did this put one on to cover up the sound of Lynch screaming. Either way, there was this album playing. Over and over, endlessly. And it was playing loud. You said it yourself, this isn't exactly your run-of-the-mill home hi-fi. It was three in the morning and we got a noise complaint from Lynch's nearest neighbor, a half-mile down the road."

"That loud?" Sandy said, impressed.

"That loud. It was stupid, too. Our man probably only missed the killer by a minute or two on that dirt road. It doesn't add up. Whoever did this, they were real careful otherwise. No prints, no murder weapon, no heart, very little physical evidence, no witnesses. We got a tire track, but it's too common, useless. So why crank up the stereo like that? If they wanted to hide Lynch's screaming, why not turn it off after he was dead?"

Sandy shrugged. "You tell me."

"I can't," the deputy admitted. "But I've got an idea. I think it was some kind of hippie cult thing."

Sandy stared at him and laughed uncertainly. "Hippie cults?"

Parker was looking at him shrewdly. "Blair, you don't think every reporter who comes nosing around gets this kind of grand tour, do you? I'm giving you all this because I figure maybe you can give me something in return. You know things that I don't. I know that. So talk."

Sandy was flabbergasted. "I've got nothing to say."

Parker chewed on his lower lip. "I want to give you something off the record. Can you keep this out of your story?"

"I don't know," Sandy said. "I'm not sure I want to take any off-the-record information. Why is this so secret?"

"Since the news of Lynch's death appeared in the papers, we've already had three clowns call up to confess. We'll have more. We know the confessions are fake because none of them can answer a few key questions we ask them. I want to give you one of those questions, and the answer."

"All right," Sandy said, curious.

"We ask them what was playing on the stereo. The answer—"

"My God," Sandy said, interrupting. "The Nazgûl, right?" He blurted it out without thinking. Suddenly, somehow, he knew that it had to be.

Deputy Davie Parker was staring at him, a very strange look on his long horseface. His eyes seemed to harden just the smallest bit. "That's real interesting," he said. "Suppose you tell me how you happened to know that, Blair."

"I just...I just knew it, the minute you started to say it. It *had* to be. Lynch was their manager. The album...I'll bet anything it was *Music to Wake the Dead*, right?"

Parker nodded.

"Listen to the first track on that. There's a lyric about cutting someone's heart out. It seemed so...I dunno, so..."

"Appropriate," Parker said. He wore a small, suspicious frown. "I listened to the record, and I noticed that lyric too. It got me thinking. Manson and his bunch, they were involved with some album too, weren't they?"

"The Beatles' White Album. Manson thought the music was talking to him, telling him what to do."

"Yeah. I knew a bit about that. Went and got a few books down at the local library. But you know a lot more, Blair. That's why I thought maybe you could be of help. What about it? Could this be another Manson thing?"

Sandy shrugged. "Manson's in prison. Some of the family are still out there, but mostly in California. Why come to Maine to off Jamie Lynch?"

"What about other nut cults? Like Manson, only different?"

"I don't know," Sandy admitted. "I've been out of touch with that lunatic fringe for a long time, so I can't really say what might be going down. But the Nazgûl...it would have to be someone our age, I'd guess, to get their obsessions from the Nazgûl. They're a Sixties group, broken up for more'n a decade now. *Music to Wake the Dead* was their last album. They haven't played or cut a track since West Mesa."

Parker's eyes narrowed. "That's another real interesting thing you just said, friend. Keep going. What's West Mesa?"

"You're kidding," Sandy said. Parker shook his head. "Hell," said Sandy, "West Mesa is famous. Or infamous. You never saw the TV coverage? They even made a documentary."

"The reception was real bad in the DMZ," Parker said.

"You ain't no rock fan, I know that much. West Mesa was a rock concert, one of three everybody's heard of. Woodstock was dawn and Altamont was dusk and West Mesa was pure, black, nightmarish midnight. Sixty thousand people outside of Albuquerque, September 1971. Small as these things go. The Nazgûl were the headliners. In the middle of their set, somebody with a high-powered rifle blew the skull off their lead singer, Patrick Henry Hobbins. Eight more people died in the panic that followed, but there was no more shooting, just that one bullet. They never caught the killer. He vanished in the night. And the Nazgûl never played again. *Music to Wake the Dead* was already recorded, and they released the album about three weeks after West Mesa. Needless to say, it made a whole shitpot of money. Lynch and the record company put a lot of pressure on the three surviving Nazgûl to follow up with a memorial album for Hobbins, or replace him and keep the group together, but it never happened. Without Hobbins, there was no Nazgûl. West Mesa ended them, and it was the beginning of the end for Jamie Lynch, too. He'd promoted that concert, after all."

"Interesting," Parker said. "So we have two unsolved murders."

"What, thirteen years apart?" Sandy objected. "It can't be connected."

"No? Let me tell you about the poster, Blair."

Sandy stared blankly.

"Our fastidious killer pulled a poster from the wall, remember, and used it to cover the desk. Lynch was killed on top of it. It was pretty messed up, but after we cleaned it some we could make out what it was. It was kind of a moody lithograph of a desert landscape at sunset. Above the sun were four dark figures riding some kind of flying lizard things, like dragons or something, only uglier. At the bottom it said—"

"I know what it said," Sandy interrupted. "Jesus H. Christ. It said *Nazgûl* and *West Mesa*, right? The concert poster. But you can't . . . it has to be a coincidence . . ." But as he said it, Sandy turned, and realized what had been bothering him before, when Parker had pointed out the blank space on the office wall. He whirled back. "It's not a coincidence," he blurted. "Whoever killed Lynch could have used any of the dozen posters that were right behind the desk, in arm's reach. Instead they walked all the way down there and climbed up on something to pull down the West Mesa poster."

"For an old hippie, you're not so dumb," Parker observed.

"But *why?* What does it mean?"

The deputy got up from the edge of the desk and sighed. "I was sort of hoping you'd tell me that, Blair. I had this fond idea that when I told you about the poster and the album you'd suddenly light up and clue me in on some secret cult that worships these guys and goes around murdering people in time to their music. It would have made my life one hell of a lot simpler, believe me. No such thing, huh?"

"Not that I know of," Sandy said.

"Well, I guess we go to the horse's mouth, then. We'll bring in these three musicians and have them questioned."

"No," Sandy said. "I've got a better idea. Let me do it."

Parker frowned.

"I'm serious," Sandy said. "It's part of my story, anyway. I have to interview people who knew Lynch, work up a sort of retrospective on him and his times. It would be logical to start with the Nazgûl. If any kind of cult has sprung up around them or their music, they ought to know about it, right? I could let you know."

"Are you trained in techniques of interrogation?" Parker said.

"Interrogation my ass," Sandy said. "I'm me and you're you, and I'll get more out of the Nazgûl than you could. We used to have a saying in the old days. Da *Hog* knows things the pigs don't."

The deputy grinned. "You may have a point there. I don't know. I'll have to talk to Notch about it. Maybe. This Nazgûl connection is kind of a long shot anyway, and we've got a hell of a lot of other leads to follow up, people to question. We're going through all his correspondence and files. A lot of people didn't like him much. Notch will probably go along if I say he should. Can I trust you to keep in touch?"

Sandy raised his hand, palm open. "Scout's honor."

"Somehow you don't look much like a scout," Parker observed.

Smiling, Sandy kept his hand up but lowered three fingers and split the two remaining into the familiar V. "Peace, then?"

Parker nodded. "I'll see what I can do. You sure you can take care of yourself? I have a bad feeling about this. One of your musicians could very well be the killer. Or all three of them. Lynch had five inches and forty pounds on you, and they cut his heart out with a knife."

"I'm not going to do anything dumb," Sandy said. "Besides, I've interviewed these guys before. Once in 1969, again in 1971. They aren't killers. If anything, they seem to be the victims in this little scene, don't they? First Hobbins, now Lynch."

"Maybe somebody doesn't like their music."

Sandy gave a derisive snort. "Their music was just fine, deputy. You ought to listen to that album for something besides clues. It's powerful stuff. Listen to Maggio's guitar riffs in 'Ash Man,' and to Gopher John's drumming. And the *lyrics*. Hell. The second side especially; it's all one long piece, and it's a classic, even if it is too damned long for most radio stations to play intact. There was nobody quite like the Nazgûl, before or after. They were so good they scared people. Sometimes I think that was the motive behind West Mesa, that it was Hoover or the fucking CIA or someone like that, scared shitless because Hobbins' singing and his goddamned charisma were turning people on to the message in the music. More than a band died when that shot was fired. It killed an idea, crippled a movement."

"Myself, I like Johnny Cash," Parker said laconically. "Come on, I'll take you back to town, and we'll talk to Notch before I have second thoughts about letting you loose on this thing."

Sandy smiled. "You realize, Davie, that your second thoughts don't matter much? We do have a first amendment still, and I can go ask questions of the Nazgûl whether Notch likes it or not."

"Don't tell Notch," Parker replied.

They turned out the lights behind them as they went back to the car. Sandy paused for a moment in the darkened living room. Night had fallen, and he could see the dim circle of the moon through the skylights, its pale light cut into a half-dozen different colors by the stained glass. Seeing the room in that strange light, Sandy felt a pang of nervous fear. For a brief second the slow liquid gurgle of the creek sounded like blood might sound gurgling from a dying man's mouth, and the sound of leaves scratching across the skylight became the sound of fingernails scrabbling at a wooden desktop in agony. But it lasted only an instant; then the noises were mere noises again, the ordinary night sounds of leaf and stream, and Sandy told himself he was being foolish.

Outside, Parker had started the car, and the headlights glared at him as he stumbled down the stairs. If he tried, it would be all too easy to hear the sound of music coming faintly from the dark, empty house behind him; to hear the distant thunder of drums, and the forlorn wail of guitars and voice, and snatches of song from the lips of a man long dead.

Sandy did not try.

THREE

It's not often easy, and not often kind/
Did you ever have to make up your mind?

Sandy found a room for the night in a motel on the outskirts of Bangor. It was cheaper and dingier than he would have liked—with Jared Patterson footing the bills, he was determined to go first class—but the conversation with Notch had been longer and more acrimonious than anticipated, once he'd made it clear that the help he was offering did not include betraying any journalistic ethics or violating any confidences. When he got to Bangor he was tired, and glad for a bed, any bed, so he pulled his Mazda over at the first VACANCY sign.

Luckily, Jared Patterson hadn't changed his unlisted phone number in the past four years. Sandy took a faint satisfaction in waking his erstwhile employer out of a sound sleep. "You're in trouble, Patterson," he said cheerily. "That's my daughter there in bed beside you, and I'll have you know she's only fifteen. We're going to send you to jail and throw away the key."

"Who the hell is this?" Patterson demanded in a confused, wary voice. Sandy could picture him sitting bolt upright in his jockey shorts, trying to rub the sleep out of his eyes.

"Tsk. I'm wounded. This is Clark Kent up in Maine, chief. Your star reporter. Don't you recognize the voice?"

"Oh, Jesus," Patterson muttered. "Seven years, and I'd almost forgotten your asshole stunts, Blair. What the hell do you want? Do you know what time it is?"

"Three-seventeen," Sandy said. "Exactly. I have a digital watch now, you know. I got mugged three years ago and the bastard took Spiro, would you believe it? I need some information from the *Hog* morgue. Here, write down this number."

There was a brief muffled conversation on the other end as Jared said something and someone else answered. It did sound like a fifteen-year-old girl, Sandy thought. "All right," Patterson said. "I've got a pencil. Give it to me."

Sandy gave it to him. "What I need are the present whereabouts of the three surviving Nazgûl. In case the disco queens you've got working for you now don't know who the hell they are, the names are Peter Faxon, Rick Maggio, and John Slozewski. If you clowns have kept the files up to date, the information ought to be there. Get back to me as soon as you can to-morrow. I've done everything I can up here, and I want to get rolling."

"Sure, sure," Patterson said. "Hey, as long as we're at it, you want to look up some of the guys in Lynch's other groups too?"

"No," Sandy said curtly.

"Todd Oliver used to be with American Taco, didn't he? He's lead singer for Glisten now. You ought to interview him, at least, so we'll have one current name in with all these has-beens."

"Fuck Todd Oliver," Sandy said. "Man's got no pride. If he'd play for Glisten, he'd do anything. I refuse to interview any man who wears a silver lamé jumpsuit on stage. Just the Nazgûl, please. The reasons need not con-cern you, but let me tell you, this story is going to be more interesting than we thought. Give your friend a kiss for me. Bye." He hung up, smiling.

The smile faded quickly in the dinginess and silence of the motel room, however. Bone-weary as he was, somehow Sandy did not think sleep would come easily, and he was strangely reluctant to turn out the lights. Briefly, he considered phoning Sharon back in Brooklyn, but he discarded the idea with-out even reaching for the phone. She'd be furious with him if he called at this hour, especially since he really had nothing to tell her. Sandy sighed. For the first time in a good number of years, he found himself wishing for a joint. It would relax him nicely, but it was a futile thought. He had smoked so little in recent years that all of his connections had long ago dried up and blown away.

Thinking of connections led to other thoughts, however. He took out his notebook and glanced through the names and numbers he'd jotted down at home. Old friends, old contacts, old sources. Most of the numbers probably weren't even good these days. People move around a lot. Still, if he needed them—and you could never tell on a story like this—the num-bers would give him a place to start tracking them down.

He lingered over one number, considering. Finally he smiled. Maggie wouldn't mind, he thought. Not unless she had changed beyond recognition. Sandy reached for the phone and dialed.

The number, as he'd expected, was disconnected, but Cleveland information still had a listing for a Margaret Sloane. Sandy wrote down the number and hoped it was the same Margaret Sloane. He placed the call anyway, and listened to it ring.

On the tenth ring, someone picked it up and a familiar sleepy voice groused, "Yeah?" into the receiver.

"Hi, Maggie," he said quietly. "It's Sandy."

"My God," she said. "Sandy? Sandy *Blair*!" With every word she seemed to be coming a bit more awake, and Sandy was pleased as hell by the sheer delight in her voice. "My God, is it really you? Are you in town? Tell me you're in town!"

"Afraid not. I'm in Maine, of all places. Believe it or not, I'm working for Jared again."

"That cretin."

"Yeah, well, it's only a one-time thing. Jamie Lynch got himself killed and I'm doing the story on it. Everyone on the *Hog* staff these days sprang full blown from Jared's forehead in 1976, so I'm the only one that's qualified. I'm about to go interview the Nazgûl, wherever they may be, and I thought maybe I might pass through Cleveland."

"And you damn well better stop and see me, you hear? What has it been, three years? I've read your books. Sarah was me, wasn't she? In *Kasey's Quest*?"

"Hell, no," Sandy said. "All my characters are fictional, and any similarity to real persons living or dead is strictly coincidental. It says so right under the copyright."

"You asshole," Maggie said affectionately. "At least you said she was good in bed."

"She was."

"But you *killed* her!" Maggie wailed.

"Don't you think it was more poignant that way?"

"I'll give you *poignant*. Are you really coming out?"

"Maybe," Sandy cautioned. "Don't count on it. I have no idea where the Nazgûl have gotten themselves to. If they all live on Guam now, I'll have to fly out and take a pass. But if it's humanly possible, I'd like to drive, and stop and see you on the way."

"Driving, huh? You coming in the Hogmobile?"

Sandy laughed. The Hogmobile had been a green 1966 Mustang,

covered with leftover flower decals from the '68 McCarthy campaign. He'd put nearly 180,000 miles on her before she finally gave up the ghost and went to wherever dead Mustangs go to pasture. "She passed away some time ago," he told Maggie. "I've got a new car now."

"Sigh," said Maggie. "I liked the old lady. Ah, well. What do you call the new one?"

"Call?" Sandy said. "I . . . well, I guess it doesn't have a name." It seemed a strange admission even as he said it. He'd bought the Mazda almost two years ago. When had he stopped naming his cars? he wondered. He'd *always* named his cars, ever since the very first one, a rusted-out black VW Beetle he'd gotten when he was seventeen and immediately christened Roach.

"Nothing's wrong, is there?" Maggie asked. "You sound odd all of a sudden."

"No," Sandy said, a bit ruefully. "Nothing wrong. I was just sitting here talking and all of a sudden I realized that I was maybe getting older than I like to admit. But never mind about that. What are you up to these days?"

Maggie told him, and they talked about mutual friends who'd gone this way or that, and then about the old days, and somehow it got to be five in the morning with Sandy hardly noticing. "This is going to cost a not-so-small fortune," he said finally, as they were hanging up. "Good thing Jared is paying for it. I'll be seeing you as soon as I can."

"You damn well better," Maggie replied, and when he put the phone back into its cradle, Sandy felt quite good indeed, and very tired, and he had no trouble whatsoever falling at once into a deep, dreamless sleep.

The phone woke him just before noon. "I want to order a pepperoni pizza, and hold the anchovies," the voice said.

"You're too fat for pizza, Jared," Sandy said wearily. He pulled over his notepad. "You got the addresses?"

"Yeah," Patterson replied. He sounded grumpy. "You have a lot of ground to cover. John Slozewski lives in Camden, New Jersey, of all the goddamned places. Maggio is in Chicago. And Peter Faxon owns a big house out in Santa Fe, New Mexico. You want us to make airline reservations for you?"

"No," said Sandy. "I'll drive."

"Drive? It'll take you *forever*."

"I have as much time as I need, remember? Don't complain. I'm saving you money. Now, give me those addresses. Phone numbers too, if you've got them." He copied them down carefully, promised Jared that he'd never phone at that ridiculous hour of the morning again, no sir, and said goodbye.

Down the road a bit, he found an International House of Pancakes, where he put away an order of bacon and eggs and a couple of gallons of coffee. It left him feeling vaguely human, even if he did slosh a little as he drove back to the motel. He packed quickly, then sat down on the edge of the bed and phoned Sharon at work.

"I'm kind of busy right now," she said. "Can't it wait?"

"No, it can't," Sandy said. "I'm about to check out of this place and drive down to New Jersey, and I don't know when I'll be free to call you again." Briefly, he gave her his itinerary, but when he started telling her about Lynch she cut him off.

"Look, Sandy," she said, "it's not as though I'm not interested. I am. But this is a bad time. I've got a client with me, and I'm already late for a show-ing. Call me tonight. Oh, and by the way, Alan phoned." Alan was his liter-ary agent. "He's not thrilled about your new career as a private eye either. You're supposed to call."

"Great," Sandy said.

"Which one of your idols was it who kept saying, 'You knew the job was dangerous when you took it'?" Sharon asked.

"Superchicken," Sandy muttered.

"Ah. I figured it was either him or Gene McCarthy."

"All right, I'll call Alan. Lay off. Thanks for the message."

Alan Vanderbeck was on another line when Sandy phoned. Alan Vanderbeck was almost always on another line. Sandy held patiently, soothed by the knowledge that it was Jared Patterson's money he was burn-ing up. Finally Alan came on. "So," he said. "The prodigal idiot. Sander, just what in the name of creation are you thinking about?"

"Good to talk to you too, Alan. Did you get all of Patterson's promises in writing? I left a message on your machine."

"Sure, I got them. You're going to get the cover, and no cuts, and as much time as you like, and *Hedgehog*'s top rate. You care to know what that is? Five hundred bucks, Sander. That's fifty for me. I've got better things to do with my time. And so do you, for that matter. I'm not thrilled by the way you leave me a message and duck out of town. I'm not thrilled by this whole thing. I told Sharon."

"Yeah, she told me. You're not thrilled and she's not thrilled. I'm the only one that's thrilled. Good for me."

Alan sighed a very put-upon sigh. "How long is this going to take?"

"I don't know. It's mutating in some interesting ways. Maybe a month, maybe two."

"Perhaps you recall having lunch with me just a few days ago? Perhaps you also recall that I reminded you that the deadline on the new novel is barely three months off? You cannot afford to use two of those three months for some quixotic four-hundred-fifty-dollar gesture to your lost youth, Sander. Haven't I stressed that?"

"Damn it, Alan, don't tell me what to do!" Sandy said, feeling a bit peevish. "I'm tired of people telling me what to do. Look, things weren't going too well on the novel. Taking off and doing this story ought to be good for me. Maybe it will get me past my block. So I miss the deadline. Big deal. I haven't noticed the world holding its breath. I was two months late delivering *Kasey's Quest*, and nearly a year late on *Open Wounds*, wasn't I? You can't create to a fucking schedule, damn it!"

"No, Sander," Alan said. "It won't wash. The circumstances are different this time. You got a lot of money up front on this book, mainly because *Copping Out* did well, but the publishers are regretting it now. You seem to have forgotten that *Open Wounds* still hasn't found a paperback publisher."

"It got good reviews," Sandy protested.

"That's not enough. It's selling shitty. I've warned you, if you're late on delivering the new one, they're going to cancel the contract right out from under you and demand their money back. We can't give them the opportunity."

"You're too damn pessimistic," Sandy said. "It won't be that bad. I'm going to do this one story for Jared, that's all, and then I'll be back to work on the novel. Hell, maybe I'll even make that deadline. If not, you'll find some way to placate them."

"I'm an agent, not a magician," Alan said. "You overestimate my powers of persuasion. Look, let me make myself perfectly clear—"

"Jesus," said Sandy. "You sound like Nixon."

"Be that as it may," Alan persisted, "I'm going to warn you right now that I'm not in business to make five-hundred-dollar deals with *Hedgehog*. If you don't deliver this novel, and the contract gets canceled, you had better start looking around for other representation."

"Maybe I should start looking around anyway," Sandy said.

"Maybe you should," Alan agreed. He sighed. "I don't want to do this, Sander. I like you, and I like your work. But this is for your own good. Forget this story, come back to New York and get to work. You have professional responsibilities."

"Screw professional responsibilities," Sandy snapped, "and get off my case, Alan. Don't you have a call on another line?"

"As a matter of fact, I do. I just thought perhaps I might talk some sense into you. I can see that was a misplaced hope. Think about it, Sander. It's your decision."

"Glad you remember that," Sandy said. "Goodbye, Alan. I'll keep in touch." With a conscious effort, he refrained from slamming the receiver down into its cradle and dropped it very softly into place.

He was in a sour, surly mood as he checked out and lugged his suitcase to the car. Most of the day was shot already, and the talks with Alan and Sharon had left him feeling hassled and depressed. Maybe they were right, Sandy thought to himself. Maybe it was stupid to be working on this Nazgûl thing instead of the novel. Maybe he was being immature and irresponsible. But damn it, he had a right to be a little immature at times, didn't he? It wasn't as if he'd run off to join the circus. He was doing a story, and it might turn out to be a damn *good* story too, a big one, an important one. Maybe he'd even win some kind of goddamned *award*. He tightened the straps that held his suitcase in place, stepped back, and slammed down the rear hatch of the Mazda harder than was really necessary. For a moment he stood in the motel parking lot, seething, wanting something on which to vent his frustration, finding nothing. He felt like kicking the car. He'd stubbed many a toe on the tires of Roach, Jezebel, the Battleship Missouri, and the Hogmobile through the years, letting off steam.

The Mazda, though, the Mazda wasn't kickable. It sat there in the parking lot, sleek and gorgeous, all low and bronze-colored and shining, with its sunroof and its power antenna and its rakish black rear-window louvres, looking fast as hell and twice as sexy even standing still. Sandy had always dreamed of owning a sports car. He loved his Mazda. Yet somehow it wasn't an old friend the way the other cars had been, wasn't the kind of partner in adventure and adversity who might understand and forgive an occasional pissed-off kick that hurt toe more than tire. No. It was a lovely driving machine. It was a status symbol, something to take pride in, to buff-wax. It held its value really well...but that was it. Roach had been a buddy. The Mazda was a fucking *investment*, he thought. He glared at it and walked around to open the door.

Then he stopped. "The hell with it!" he said loudly. He slammed the door shut again, kicked the front tire as hard as he could, and hopped around the parking lot on one foot, grimacing and grinning in alternation.

He was still grinning ten minutes later, out on the road, whipping down the highway at seventy as the little rotary engine made a smooth purring noise. He glanced down at his tapes, picked up an old Lovin' Spoonful cassette, and shoved it into the tape deck, turning up the volume so the music filled the interior. *What a day for a daydream,* John Sebastian was singing, *custom made for a day-dreamin' boy.*

"Daydream," Sandy said. He liked the sound of it. It was frivolous, fun, something you weren't supposed to do but did anyhow. "Daydream," he said to the Mazda, "get a move on. We got us a date with a gopher in New Jersey." He pressed down on the accelerator, and the speed began to climb.

FOUR

Look at the sky turning hellfire red/
Somebody's house is burning down, down, down

Sandy hated the New Jersey Turnpike with a hatred that passed all understanding. It was a bitch of a road, always lousy with traffic, and it cut through some of the most ghastly country this side of Cleveland, a stinking no man's land of sanitary landfills, oil refineries, auto graveyards, and hazardous waste dumps. The road was shrouded in a perpetual grayish haze with its own distinctive odor, a miasma of carbon monoxide, diesel exhaust, and malignant chemicals, and a whiff of it was enough to evoke old fears in Sandy.

In the old days, he'd gotten busted on the turnpike more than once, cited for fictitious traffic violations, and searched for drugs. The turnpike cops had been as bitterly anti-freak as any in the country, and they used to lie in wait for hippies and longhairs and go after them with an almost crazed zeal. If your car had the wrong sort of bumper stickers, you were in trouble on the Jersey Turnpike, and driving that road in the Hogmobile, with its spray of McCarthy daisies, had been like declaring open season on yourself.

Now all that was long past. Daydream was respectably expensive and entirely flowerless, and the old hostilities had waned, yet something about the road still unnerved Sandy. The very smell of it made him think of flashing lights in his rearview mirror, of tear gas, of narcs and bloody nightsticks and Richard Milhous Nixon.

Even the turnpike food gave him indigestion. It was a relief to turn off for Camden.

The Gopher Hole sat on a major feeder road, less than a mile from the turnpike entrance ramp. From the outside, it was an ugly place, all cinderblocks and green aluminum siding, neon tubing on the roof spelling out its name, a cardboard sign filling up the only large window. The sign said LIVE MUSIC. Though the building was big enough, it looked small, surrounded by the vast empty expanse of its asphalt parking lot. Sandy pulled Daydream into a slot near the door, between a black Stingray of ancient vintage and a trim little Toyota. They were the only cars in attendance. He climbed out, stretched, slung his jacket over a shoulder, and went on in.

The day outside had been cloudy-bright, and it took his eyes a minute or two to adjust to the cavernous darkness within. He lingered in the entry foyer by the coat-check room until he could see where he was going. By the door to the main hall was a sign on a wooden tripod advertising the nightly performance of a band called the Steel Angels, who smiled out at him from a glossy. They had very white teeth, Sandy thought. Beyond the sign was the large empty club. He could make out a stage, still littered with instruments and sound equipment, a dance floor, a large number of tables and chairs, and at least three bars, a long one by the west wall and two smaller circular ones out in the middle of the floor, ringed by barstools. The paneled walls were covered with old rock posters, which reminded him uncomfortably of Jamie Lynch's office.

Behind one of the round bars, a youth was setting up and talking to a big fellow in a pin-striped suit who was leaning against the rail, looking something like a Mafia hit-man. Sandy glanced around and saw no sign of anyone else, so he walked toward them. They both watched him approach. "We're closed," the barman finally called out.

"I know," Sandy said. "I'm looking for Gopher John. When do you expect him?"

The man in the pin-striped suit cleared his throat. "I'm John Slozewski," he said. He held out a hand. "You're Sandy Blair, right? I remember you."

Sandy shook the hand and tried not to do a double take. Gopher John Slozewski had been a huge, glowering bear of a man who liked to dress in ragged jeans and loose tie-dyed smocks. With his vast black beard, his moon face, ruddy cheeks, and paunch, he had sometimes reminded Sandy of a sort of dark analogue to Santa Claus. The man shaking his hand was a stranger he would have passed in the street with scarcely a second glance. Slozewski had lost weight; his face was no longer round and cherubic, and he was trim under that vest. The beard was gone, and the black hair, just starting to recede now, was fashionably combed and styled. Only the size hadn't changed. The hand that enveloped Sandy's was huge, the same powerful red fist that had hammered out the righteous, relentless beat of the Nazgûl in full flight. "I never would have known you," Sandy said.

"Times change," Slozewski replied. "I got my place to run here. Mister John Slozewski can run it a lot smoother than any hairy-ass hippie called Gopher John. Would you believe it, I'm a member of the Chamber of Commerce now. What are you drinking?"

"A beer," Sandy said.

"Draw one, Eddie," Slozewski said. The barman filled the glass and pushed it over to Sandy. Slozewski nodded at him. "Go set up the main bar so we can talk, OK?" The barman left. "So you're still with the Hog, huh?"

"Yes and no," Sandy said. He sipped his beer and eased himself back onto a bar stool. "This is a freelance assignment. Mostly I write novels these days."

"Good for you," Slozewski said flatly. Neither his voice nor his face betrayed any hint of warmth, but Sandy knew that was misleading. Gopher John Slozewski had been famous for his perpetual scowl, and his short, curt manner with the press and the public. That, and his wild drumming, had gotten him the reputation of being a little bit mean, a little bit crazy, and more than a little bit stupid. None of it was true, as Sandy had found out the first time he interviewed the Nazgûl. If anything, Slozewski was one of the gentlest and friendliest men in the world of rock, but his charms were well hidden by his innate shyness and reserve. It seemed he hadn't changed much in that respect. After making his comment, he sat quietly, waiting for Sandy to continue.

Sandy took out his notebook. "You've probably figured what I came to talk about," he said.

Slozewski looked at the notepad and smiled thinly and fleetingly. "Look at that," he said. "Been ages since I've seen a reporter write down stuff. The new ones all use little tape recorders." He sighed. "You probably want to ask me about Lynch, right? And the Nazgûl?"

Sandy nodded.

"It figures," Slozewski said. "I was kind of hoping that maybe the Hog wanted to do a little write-up on my place here, you know. We could use the publicity. But I didn't think it was likely." He scowled. "They ought to do a piece on the Gopher Hole. You tell Patterson that for me, OK?"

"Will do," Sandy said. "It's a nice place," he lied.

"Hell," said Slozewski, "you're just saying that. It's just another goddamned bar to you. I know how tacky the place looks outside. Cinder blocks and all. I'm not dumb. But you don't know the half of it. This is an important place."

"Important?" Sandy said.

"The Gopher Hole is kind of a dream come true for me," Slozewski said. "I put everything I had into this place, and I'm losing money on it, but I don't give a fuck. I'm paying back some dues, the way I see it." He scowled. "Music's a tough game. I remember how hard it was, breaking in. I always remembered that, even after we got big."

"The Nazgûl?"

Slozewski nodded. "You saw the end of it, those years we were on top. You never saw the beginning. Mean times. We had a new sound, raw and angry like the times, and we did all our own material, Faxon's stuff. No one wanted to hear it. No one wanted to hear us. When we did get a gig, we'd get these bozos in the crowd requesting all kinds of dumb shit. Standards, you know? And we'd get managers leaning on us to do that crapola. And the pay was... hell, there ain't no word for it. We all had second jobs on the side. I was a cook at Denny's, on the graveyard shift." He shrugged his massive shoulders. "Well, when we made it, I made up my mind that I was going to make things easier for kids breaking in. That's what the Gopher Hole is all about. You ought to come back in a couple of hours and hear the Steel Angels. They're damn good. New Wave kind of sound, you know? Not commercial, but good. That's the only kind I book. To play here, they have to be doing their own stuff, original. No disco crap, either. I give them a start, a regular gig if they need it. And I pay them decent money, too. I'd pay them better if I could, but we haven't been doing as well as I'd like." He shrugged again. "But what the hell, I can afford it. The music is what's important, not the money. But you don't want to hear all this, do you? You want to hear about Jamie Lynch."

"And the Nazgûl," Sandy said. "Sorry. Maybe I can get Jared to do a little item on your place."

"I'll believe that when I see it," Slozewski growled. His voice was as rumbly and deep as it had been in his performing days. "Look, I don't mind talking to you, but I'll tell you right up front that I think you're wasting your time. I don't know diddly-shit about who killed Jamie, and I care less. And I'm sick of talking about the Nazgûl."

"Why?" Sandy asked.

"Why was Lennon sick of being asked about the Beatles breaking up?" It was a rhetorical question. Slozewski walked around the edge of the bar and continued as he methodically began to fix himself a drink. "Next month I'll be thirty-seven years old. Forty isn't so far off. A lot of life. I've got a place I'm real involved in, trying to do something good for music. I was a good drummer for a long time. After West Mesa, I had a three-year gig with Nasty Weather, and then with Morden & Slozewski & Leach, and for a little bit with the Smokehouse Riot Act. The Riot Act could have been one hell of a band too, if only Morden and Jencks hadn't been such flaming assholes. We did some good tracks. If we'd stayed together, we might have made people forget all about the Nazgûl. Do I ever get asked about that, though? Nah." He scowled and shook his head. "All they want to know about is the Nazgûl. I'd be the last guy to put down the Nazgûl, mind you. We were *good*. We were a world-class rock band. I'm proud of that part of my life. West Mesa ended it, though. Some crazy out there in the dark squeezed a trigger, and it was over, and we had to move on. Only they won't let me. You hear what I'm saying? I'm John Slozewski, and I want to be treated like John Slozewski, not just like I'm one-fourth of the Nazgûl. Fuck that shit."

Slozewski's deep voice had taken on a faintly petulant tone. Sandy listened to him with a certain amount of astonishment, hoping it didn't show on his face. Gopher John's post-Nazgûl career had been less than distinguished. Nasty Weather, which had formed around Slozewski and Maggio in the aftermath of West Mesa, had been a derivative band at best. The Smokehouse Riot Act had shown a lot more promise and a lot more originality, but internal dissension had torn them apart after only one album. And the less said about Morden & Slozewski & Leach the better. You would have thought that Gopher John would just as soon have all those groups forgotten.

Still, Sandy managed a thin, sympathetic smile. "I know where you're coming from," he said. "My first book, *Copping Out*, sold twice as well as the later ones. I still get these reviews that say it's been all downhill ever since. Sets your teeth on edge, doesn't it?"

Slozewski nodded. "Damn straight."

What Sandy didn't add was that he agreed with the conventional wisdom in Gopher John's case. Jim Morden, Randy Andy Jencks, Denny Leach, and Slozewski's other, later partners had all been competent professional musicians, but not a one of them had been fit to set up Hobbins' microphone or string Peter Faxon's bass. Tact prohibited his pointing that out, however. Instead he said, "Still, I can understand why you're sick of questions about the Nazgûl, but I'm sure you see why Lynch's murder has to kick up a lot of interest, right?"

Slozewski scowled. "Yeah, OK. Don't mean *I've* got to be interested, though."

"Have you had a lot of media people coming round to ask questions since the news got out?"

"Not a lot," Slozewski admitted. "A guy from a wire service phoned for a quote, and one of the Philadelphia TV stations sent out a crew. I talked to them, but they didn't use any of it. I didn't have much to tell 'em. Nothing interesting." He sipped at his drink. "Got nothing interesting for you either, but if you want to ask questions, go ahead. I got a couple hours till we open."

"You have no idea who might have killed Jamie Lynch, then?"

"Nah."

"Or who might have wanted him dead?"

Slozewski's laugh was a nasty little chortle. "Half the fucking *world* wanted Lynch dead." He shrugged. "At least that was so ten years back. Lynch hadn't done anything nasty to anybody *recently*, I got to admit. He wasn't in a position to. But back when he had clout, he was a ruthless sonofabitch. I guess whoever killed him was someone who held a grudge."

"Some grudge," Sandy said. "You sound like you didn't get on well with Lynch yourself."

"No comment," said Slozewski.

"That seems a little ungrateful," Sandy said. "I thought Jamie Lynch was responsible for discovering the Nazgûl. He gave you your break, made you one of the biggest things in rock."

"Yeah, sure. He made us big. He made us rich. And he made himself richer, too. I pay my dues, Blair, that's why I run this place like I do. I know how to be loyal. But Jamie used up whatever loyalty he had coming a long, long time back. He knew how good we were when he found us. He knew how hungry we were, too. You ought to have seen the contract he signed us to. What the fuck did we know? We were four kids who wanted to make music, get on the cover of *Hedgehog*."

Sandy wrote it all down. "You saying Lynch took advantage of you?"

"He *used* us. And he fucked us over royally." Slozewski's voice had a bitter edge to it all of a sudden. "You ever wonder why the Nazgûl didn't play at Woodstock? We were big enough. We wanted to be there. Still pisses me off that we weren't. Lynch kept us away. Said he'd get us on breach of contract if we went against him, sue us for millions. That fucking contract gave him sole discretion over when and where the Nazgûl played, you see, and he didn't think Woodstock would be good for us. *Good for us! Jesus!*" Gopher John's big knuckles were white where he held his glass. "And then there were the drugs," he added.

"Lynch provided drugs for all his groups," Sandy said. "He had connections, everyone knew it. So?"

"So. Yeah. So. You don't get it. Drugs were just like another way of *controlling* us, you see. Oh, hell, I was real fond of hash, still am, and a little recreational trip every now and again never hurt nobody. That's cool. I could handle it. And Peter never touched the stuff. Not even grass. He was like that. Hobbins and Maggio, though, they had problems. By the time of West Mesa, Hobbit couldn't even go on without a mess of pills and a slug of whiskey, and Rick was shooting up regular. It hurt his music, too. You don't know how many times we had to redo some of those tracks on *Napalm* and *Wake the Dead* to get Maggio's guitar sounding right."

"And you blame Jamie Lynch for this?"

"Hell, Jamie gave old Rick his first needle. As a Christmas present, would you believe it? All wrapped up with a white ribbon. It drove Peter right up the goddamned wall, let me tell you. Lynch didn't care. Giving us free drugs gave him more control. He was a real moderate user himself. Jamie Lynch was a power junkie."

"Sounds nasty," Sandy said.

"Yeah, it was nasty all right. That wasn't the only thing, either. Rick liked the groupies too, especially when he was wired on one thing or another, or after a set. We wouldn't be backstage for ten minutes before he'd have his pants down and some girl sucking him off. Well, there was this one night, after a concert in Pittsburgh, and Maggio was getting it on with these twins, and all of a sudden Jamie comes barging in with a Polaroid and starts snapping away. Faxon was gone, Hobbit and I were wasted, so nobody did nothing. We all thought it was a big laugh. Maggio giggled and mugged for the camera." John Slozewski's scowl was so deep it looked like it was carved into his face. "Turns out those twins were under age. They were *fourteen*! They didn't look it, I tell you that, but they were, and Jamie knew it. Well, we never saw those pictures, but Jamie joked about them all the time. Just kidding around, you know, about how we better do like he said or he'd sell them somewhere, heh-heh-heh, and we all laughed. Maggio laughed harder than anybody. Only I could look at his face, and he was sweating every fucking time, no matter how hard he laughed. *He* knew Jamie wasn't joking. The fucker meant it."

"Why all the sweat?" Sandy asked. "He wouldn't have been the first rock star to get caught in bed with jailbait. Half the groupies on the circuit were under age."

"Yeah, maybe. You don't know Rick, though. He was just a skinny

Catholic kid from the Southside of Philly. An *ugly* skinny Catholic kid. He never could handle it. He'd try any drug Jamie got him, and fuck anything with two legs that was willing to spread 'em, but all the time he was sort of *nervous* about it. Like any minute some *nun* was going to come along and hit him with a fucking ruler. Those pictures bothered him plenty. Peter took care of it, though."

"Faxon?"

Slozewski nodded. "One night he got Jamie drinking, and managed to convince him that he wanted to ogle the pictures a little, you know, and somehow he got Jamie to take 'em out and pass 'em around. And then Peter just took 'em away and ripped 'em into little pieces, right in front of Lynch. It didn't make much difference. Lynch had lots of handles on us." Slozewski finished his drink and set it aside. "Hey," he said, "you aren't going to *print* this, are you?"

"Don't you want the world to know the truth about Jamie Lynch?"

"Oh, come *on!*" Slozewski protested. "Can't we keep this off the record? I don't give a flying fuck what the world knows about Lynch, but Maggio's got enough problems. I don't care much for him, maybe, but that don't mean I want to mess him up more than he's messed up already."

Sandy gave a sympathetic shrug. "I don't know," he said. "I've got to interview Maggio. He might hang himself with his own words. If he doesn't, though, I'll see what I can do to soften the stuff about him. Maybe." He held up a hand hastily. "No promises, but it's Lynch I'm interested in, mostly. I knew his rep, but I never really knew the details. I can see why you aren't wearing black."

That drew a rueful, hangdog grin out of Gopher John. "Yeah, well, I told you."

"What about recently? Since West Mesa?"

"I didn't have much contact with Jamie Lynch after West Mesa," Slozewski said. "By choice. His contract was with the Nazgûl, you see. With the four of us. He *owned* the Nazgûl. Did you know that? You know what Hobbins used to call him?"

"Mister Lynch Sir?"

Slozewski laughed. "No. But you can figure it out. You know where the name came from, don't you? The Nazgûl?"

"Patrick Henry Hobbins," Sandy said. He'd included the anecdote in both of his earlier interviews with the group; it was a well-known piece of their history. "Hobbins was quite short, only five-two, and he had all that white hair, including some on his feet, and he smoked a pipe. Filled it with grass, but it was a pipe anyway. So when *Lord of the Rings* came out, it was

natural that he got nicknamed Hobbit. That got him into the whole
Tolkien bag, and he was the one who named the group the Nazgûl, after
the flying baddies in the books."

"Yeah," said Slozewski. "So guess what he named Lynch?"

It had been a long time since Sandy had read the Tolkien trilogy. He
had to think for a minute. "Sauron," he said finally. "Sauron owned the
Nazgûl."

"Give the man a beer," Slozewski said. He drew one and shoved it
across the bar. "Jamie loved it, actually. After *Hot Wind out of Mordor*
climbed to the top of the album charts, he gave us four matching rings to
commemorate the success."

"Cute," Sandy said. He took a sip of the beer. "I'm not sure I understand, though. What do you mean, Lynch owned the Nazgûl?"

"He owned the name," Slozewski explained, "and he owned the right to
manage any band that included at least three of us, so we couldn't just
break up and re-form under a different name to get ourselves out from under. He had us just where he wanted us until West Mesa. But when Hobbit
was killed, it changed everything. Lynch wanted us to get a new lead singer
and go on. Peter was having none of it, though. He freaked out after West
Mesa, just gave up, and Rick and me formed Nasty Weather, which Lynch
got no part of. There wasn't one fucking thing he could do about it, either.
I used to hear from him every year or so, always full of schemes for getting
the Nazgûl back together. He'd try to sell me on the idea, and I'd tell him to
fuck off."

Sandy tapped his pen thoughtfully against his notepad. "Let me get this
straight," he said. "Jamie Lynch *still* managed the Nazgûl?"

"If you can manage a band that ain't existed since 1971, yeah, he managed us. Fat lot of good it did him, with us all going our own ways. Jamie
was such a bastard, though, he wouldn't let go of that contract, not for anything."

"Did the question ever come up?"

"Oh, yeah, a couple times. When I opened this place three years back, I
thought I could get a lot of publicity by having the Nazgûl do a set on opening night. Just a gimmick, you know, a few old songs, not a real revival. But
it would have packed the joint, and Peter was willing to do it as a favor, and
Rick was *eager*. Things haven't been so good for Rick, and I guess he saw it
as a shot. Well, Jamie stomped on the idea. Demanded some absurd fee
that I couldn't afford and threatened to sic a high-priced lawyer on me. It
wasn't worth the hassle, so I dropped the whole idea." He snapped his fingers and pointed one at Sandy. "The other time was just like a month ago.

I got this letter from a promoter, weird guy by the name of Morse, who had this scheme for a big Nazgûl comeback tour. He'd already sold the idea to Maggio, who called me and pleaded with me to go along. Well, hell, I wasn't really the least bit interested. I didn't need the money that much, and the Gopher Hole means more to me now than the Nazgûl. But I could tell how much Maggio wanted it, and there was no sense in getting into a nasty argument with him over a dead issue. So I said sure, I'd go along, but they had to get Jamie's approval. See, I knew there was no way in hell that Jamie Lynch was going to turn over the Nazgûl to any other promoter. Sure enough, that was the last I ever heard of it. Jamie killed it dead one way or the other, him and that contract of his, that wonderful iron-clad unbreakable lifetime contract."

Sandy glanced up at Gopher John, and then off toward the vacant stage, with its clutter of instruments and sound equipment. He chewed on the end of his Flair thoughtfully. "Lifetime," he said. "Interesting word, that."

Slozewski frowned. "Hey," he said. "That's right."

"With Jamie Lynch dead, you may be hearing from that other promoter again. What's his name?"

"Morse," Slozewski said. "Edan Morse. Shit. I hadn't thought of that. I'm going to have to have it out with Rick, then. No way I'm going to just chuck everything I'm trying to do with the Hole here and go back on the road. Besides, it wouldn't work anyway. I can't imagine having the Nazgûl without Hobbins."

"A new singer?"

Slozewski grunted derisively. "Yeah. You might as well set up a Beatles reunion and hire Peter Frampton to fill in for John. Fuck no. It would never work. Besides, Peter would never do it."

Sandy grinned. "Frampton or Faxon?"

"Either one," said Slozewski. "You want another beer? You're dry."

"Well..." Sandy said. "I don't know. I could use something to eat, though."

"Got no kitchen here," Slozewski said. "I could get you a bag of potato chips, maybe." He looked at his watch. It was a digital watch, Sandy noted. Somehow he found that vaguely surreal, the very idea of Gopher John of the Nazgûl wearing a digital watch. It was like the idea of Richard Nixon having sex; you knew it happened, but somehow it was too utterly strange to contemplate. "Look," Slozewski said, "the rest of my people will be getting here soon, and the band will be coming in to set up and rehearse. You won't be able to hear a thing. You want to go get dinner? There's a pretty good steakhouse about a mile down the road."

Sandy got up and stretched. "That sounds like a perfectly wonderful idea," he said. He picked up his coat. "Let's go."

Out in the parking lot, Sandy hesitated between Daydream and the black Stingray parked beside it. "You want to take your car or mine?" he asked Slozewski.

Gopher John laughed. "The 'Vette belongs to Eddie," he said. "That one's mine." He pointed to the tiny Toyota on the other side of Daydream.

"We'll take mine," Sandy said. He unlocked the doors, and Gopher John wedged himself in on the passenger's side.

The steakhouse was only a bit farther than Slozewski had said, and nearly empty. "Jared Patterson is paying for dinner," Sandy said after they'd been handed the menus. They both ordered rare prime rib, along with a bottle of the most expensive wine in the house. The restaurant was a quiet place, with red tablecloths, candles burning in little teardrops of colored glass, and thick dark carpeting. Sandy sat staring out the window at sunset while they waited for cocktails to arrive and Gopher John chatted with the owner, a fellow member of the Chamber of Commerce. Beyond the window cars sped by, and one by one their headlights began to come on as the gloom outside thickened. Sandy wondered how to ask Slozewski the questions that remained, and how much to tell him of what had gone on up in Maine. By the time the drinks and Gopher John came back to the table, he had made up his mind.

"A few more questions," he said, taking out his notepad once more.

Slozewski rolled his eyes up to the ceiling. "I hate you fucking journalists," he said in an even conversational tone. "Go on."

"I want to know about your fans," Sandy said.

"I got a cat that's real excited about me."

Sandy smiled. "The Nazgûl must have had a few weirdos hanging around in the old days. Fringe types. Was there ever any one particular person? Or a group of people, maybe? People who were real into your music?"

"Lots of people were into our music. Hundreds of fucking thousands. Millions. We were the Nazgûl. Shit, you know that."

Sandy waved impatiently. "Yes, but I don't mean ordinary fans. I mean nut cases, people who maybe thought you were speaking right to them, who tried to live by your music, who identified with you."

"We had a big fan club. They called themselves Orcs."

"No, no. I mean *dangerous* people. Manson types. Mark David Chapman types. You know."

"Nah," said Slozewski. "Nothing like that. Brown-nosers and groupies and Orcs, that's what we got." He tasted his drink.

Sandy frowned and took a slug from his own Scotch-and-soda. This wasn't working, he thought. Either there was no Nazgûl cult or Slozewski didn't know about it, or he was holding back, but Sandy didn't know how to find out which one it was. "One last thing," he said. He set down his drink. Moisture had formed on the outside of the glass. He stared at it and absently drew a peace symbol with a finger. "Where were you on the night of September 20th?"

Slozewski laughed. "This one or the one back in 1971?" he asked.

Sandy stared up at him. "*Jesus,*" he blurted. He couldn't believe he'd been so stupid. "I'm a fucking *moron,*" he said loudly. "It's the same fucking night, isn't it? September *20th!*"

Comprehension dawned in Slozewski's dark eyes. "Oh," he said. "You mean Jamie got himself killed on the same night." He scowled. "That's weird."

Sandy pounded the table. "It's more than weird," he said angrily. He had decided not to tell Slozewski all that he'd learned from Davie Parker, but now he abruptly changed his mind. Gopher John *had* to know. "This is kinky in the extreme. Jesus, why didn't I *realize!* Sharon was right, I'll never be the hippie Sherlock Holmes. Listen, it wasn't any coincidence that Lynch got killed on the anniversary of West Mesa. There's more to it than that." He told Slozewski about the album, playing over and over, and about the poster that had been taken down and spread out under Lynch's body. Halfway through his account, their salads arrived. Slozewski took up his fork and began to eat with methodical slowness, chewing each bite thoroughly, his eyes never leaving Sandy's face.

"I see," he said when Sandy was done.

"That's why I asked about a Nazgûl cult," Sandy said. "We thought maybe someone like that was responsible. Someone unhinged by your old music."

"Nah. I don't know of anybody like that."

Sandy ate a forkful of salad, hardly tasting it, and put down the fork again. "Where *were* you that night?"

"At the Gopher Hole," Slozewski said. "Same place I am *every* night. Unless it was a Sunday. It wasn't a Sunday, was it?"

"No," said Sandy. "Well, you're clear then."

Slozewski shoved away his empty salad bowl. "Clear?"

"You've got an alibi."

"Do I need one?"

"The killer offed Lynch on top of one of your posters, while playing one of your records, on the anniversary of your last concert, in a manner described in one of your lyrics. What do you think? You admit there was no love lost between you. If you don't have a cult of crazed fans, then suspicion is naturally going to fall on you and Maggio and Faxon."

"Well, I was here," Slozewski said, frowning. "It ain't Rick or Peter neither. No way, you hear?"

The waitress cleared away the salad bowls. Sandy had hardly touched his. "There's another thing," he said, as she served the prime rib.

Slozewski stared at him. "Yeah?"

"You might be next."

"*What?*"

"Think about it," Sandy said. He cut into his meat deftly, put on a bit of horseradish, swallowed hastily. "Hobbins, now Lynch."

"Oh, fuck," Slozewski said derisively. "You can't be real, man. Even if you are, I'm safe till September 20th rolls around again, ain't I?"

"Maybe," Sandy said, "but I'd watch out if I were you."

"I always watch out," Slozewski said. Then he fell to his dinner, eating in a grim methodical silence. Sandy watched his hard, scowling face for a minute before returning his attention to his own prime rib. They dined in an uneasy quiet.

It wasn't until dessert and coffee that conversation resumed. "I don't like this," Slozewski said, as he stirred three heaping spoons of sugar into his cup and tried to whip it into dissolution. "Not one fucking bit. I don't know what the hell is going on, but I ain't got nothin' to do with it." He grimaced. "You're going to talk to Rick and Peter?"

Sandy nodded.

"Watch out for Maggio," Slozewski said. "He's had some bad times. He's a little crazy sometimes. I hope he isn't involved. Don't like Rick much, but I never thought he'd do nothin' like this."

"He played a wicked guitar," Sandy said.

"The best. At least at the start, before the drugs. The drugs ruined him. He could have been world class, but after West Mesa he just got worse and worse. If anyone had a good reason to hate Jamie Lynch, it was Rick." He paused for a moment, and then started talking about Maggio and the Nazgûl, about the way they had gotten together. "I wasn't the first drummer, you know," he said. "I just liked their sound, though, so I hung around, made myself useful. That's why they started calling me Gopher John. Finally Peter gave me my chance, and I showed him what I could do. The next night Regetti was out of it and I was drummer."

"This guy Regetti," Sandy said. "Was he bitter? Maybe he's the killer."

"Nah. He died in a motorcycle accident before we even cut our first album. He was OK, you know, but I was a better drummer." He went on, and talked for a long, long time.

Sandy listened respectfully. "You miss it," he said, when Gopher John fell silent.

"Yeah, a little," admitted the big man in the pin-striped suit, and for a moment, across the table, Sandy could glimpse the ghost of a wild-haired, scowling young man in a tie-dyed poncho and jeans, a magical madman surrounded by black-and-red drums, his cheeks flushed, his hands a blur, hammering out the thunder. "I miss performing," he said. "There's nothing like it, not a goddamned fucking thing in this goddamned fucking world, Blair. You see them out there, thousands of them, *hundreds* of thousands, and they move, they move and sway and dance and clap their hands, and all because of you, your sound. Your music fills them, does things to 'em, and somehow you get something back, you know? You can feel it. Energy, like. It comes pouring off the audience and into you, and it makes you crazy, it makes you *better*. You're like some kind of fucking *god* up there." He looked pensive. "And the music," he added. "I miss that most of all. The bands that play the Gopher Hole, hell, I *try* to like them. I mean, I know music can't stand still, and the new sounds are ... well, you know, if we put them down, then how are we any different from the assholes who put down our sound? So I give them a place to play, the ones who deserve it. Only, down deep, I know something. I *know* it." He leaned forward conspiratorially. "They're not as *good* as we were," he said softly.

Sandy laughed and felt warm. "Most of them, in fact, are shit."

Gopher John Slozewski leaned back and grinned. He glanced at his watch briefly.

"Should we be getting back?" Sandy asked.

Gopher John shrugged. "Yeah, I guess. The place is open now. The Steel Angels will be starting their first set. Only, you know, I don't really feel like it. To tell the truth, the place runs damn good without me. Want another cup of coffee?"

"Sure," Sandy said.

Slozewski raised a finger and summoned the waitress. They lingered over coffee for a long time, sitting in the quiet of the steakhouse while Gopher John talked about the old days, and the Nazgûl, about the concerts and the rallies and the songs. He rambled and reminisced and recounted old anecdotes in a voice grown faintly wistful, no doubt because of the wine. Wine had a way of making you wistful, Sandy thought. From time to time, Sandy would break in with a laugh, or with a story of his own about some acquaintance they'd shared in the rock world or the Movement. Mostly he just listened, though, staring out the window absently as Gopher John rolled on, and the coffee cups were refilled and then refilled again. The check came and Sandy covered it with his Visa, while cars plunged through the Jersey night, headlights stabbing blindly ahead. Sandy watched them and wondered why they were all in such a hurry to reach that darkness on the road ahead, that darkness that swallowed them whole. Once he saw the lights of a jetliner pass overhead.

Later, much later, he heard sirens and glanced out just in time to see a blur of passing light, flashing frenetically. "Some hippie must have gotten on the turnpike," he said, interrupting Gopher John.

"What?" Slozewski said.

"Cops," Sandy replied, gesturing. "Didn't you see them? You can still hear the sirens."

Slozewski frowned, and listened. "Nah," he said. "That's a fire truck." And so it was; the noise grew instead of diminishing, and two long red trucks passed by in an almighty hurry. A minute later came an ambulance, and an even bigger fire truck, and finally two cop cars, whose sirens did indeed have a completely different sound. "What the hell is going on?" Slozewski muttered. He got up suddenly. "Come on."

Sandy grabbed his jacket and his Visa receipt and followed Slozewski out into the parking lot. Gopher John was standing next to Daydream, staring off down the road. He said nothing.

Down where he was looking, the whole eastern sky was suffused with reddish light.

Another police car rushed by. Gopher John sniffed. "I can smell the smoke," he said.

"Industrial fire?" Sandy said. "A lot of plants out that way, right?"

Slozewski turned his head and stared at him. "Yeah," he said. "And my place is out that way, too. Let's go."

"I hope it's not..." Sandy started.

"Let's GO!" Slozewski roared, his voice suddenly ugly and afraid.

Sandy glanced briefly at the spreading red wound on the night sky, then hurriedly unlocked the doors of Daydream. A minute later, they were on the highway, speeding toward the conflagration. Gopher John had his arms crossed tightly against his chest. He was scowling and silent. Sandy drove with a sick feeling in the pit of his stomach.

Long before they got there, they knew. The road took a small curve past a Midas Muffler shop and a Burger King, and then they could see it clearly, the flames licking at the night, the thick clouds of greasy smoke rolling up and away, the ring of fire engines laying siege. Gopher John said nothing at all. Sandy pulled into the parking lot and slammed on the brakes without bothering to find a parking place. The lot was full; full of police cars and fire trucks, and cops and firemen rushing everywhere shouting orders, and wild-eyed crowds of civilians staring at the fire and calling one another's names and sobbing. And cars. The lot was full of cars. The place had been packed, Sandy thought as he stared at all the cars.

He felt the heat on his face as soon as he opened the door and climbed out. It was a chilly October night, but he had no need of his jacket. Slozewski had gotten out faster and was already plunging through the crowd. Sandy put his car keys in his pocket and followed. Some of the people, he noted, had torn clothes and faces smudged by smoke. There was a lot of smoke. He passed a young girl, who was screaming hysterically and pounding her fists on the asphalt of the lot while a friend tried to restrain her. Sandy looked at her helplessly, then back at the fire. Water was pouring from the encircling hoses, but it seemed to have no effect on the blaze. As he watched, a huge gout of bright orange flame went roaring up, and the crowd shuddered like a single frightened animal and edged backward, away from the fresh wash of heat and the acrid scent of smoke.

He found Gopher John up by the police line, arguing with an overweight cop. "You *got* to let me go in. I own the place. It's *mine*."

"Nobody goes in," the cop said. "Can't you understand? You want to get yourself burned up, Mister?"

"But I'm the *owner!*" Slozewski insisted.

Sandy put a hand on his shoulder, but Slozewski glared at him and shook it off. His face was red with reflected light, and fires danced in his eyes. "There's nothing you can do," Sandy told him.

Slozewski ignored him. "Let me *by!*" he said to the cop.

The policeman just shook his head curtly and called out to one of his fellows. Two other cops came over. "He says he owns the place," the fat one remarked.

"Would you come with us?" one of the other policemen said, taking Slozewski by the arm.

Gopher John stared at him. He shook his head and let himself be led off through the crowd. Sandy started to follow, but the fat cop grabbed him by the sleeve. "Hey, where you think you're going?"

"I'm press," Sandy said, trying to shake off the grip.

"So?" the cop said. "You wait here."

Sandy waited. The fire burned on and on. No one came out of the building, and no one went in. Sandy went back to his car and got his notepad, then moved around asking questions. The crowd was full of dazed, crazy, smoke-smudged kids. They all looked so *young*, he thought. A girl in a torn dress and heavy green eyeshadow babbled at him, but seemed to know nothing. A fat boy with a crew cut shrugged and said, "I just seen it burning and come to watch." Several people told him the fire had just come, "out of nowhere." Sandy saw one man sobbing convulsively, but when he tried to question him, another man pushed him away hard, saying, "He can't find his girlfriend, you hear? Get the hell out of here, fucker. Leave him alone, hear? Asshole. Motherfucker." And then a torrent of abuse that got louder and louder. Sandy backed away from him uneasily, glanced around for the police, and shouldered through the press of people.

Finally he found someone who claimed to have seen it all, a thin youngish man with dirty blond hair cut short, a gold loop through one ear, a green leather jacket, and a bleeding lip. "They pushed me down," he said, wiping away the blood with the back of his hand. But he was pleased to be interviewed. "Jim," he said, when he told Sandy his name. "Don't say James in the paper, OK? I'm Jim. I was there, yeah. It was real ugly. The Angels were playing, and everybody was dancing, and then all of a sudden I thought I heard someone yelling, but I wasn't sure, 'cause the music was so loud. So I went on dancing. And then these guys come pushing through the dance crowd, crazy, screaming something. They just pushed into people. That's how I got this." He used his hand to wipe away more blood. "Then I smelled smoke, though, so I got up real quick, and people were yelling fire, but I couldn't see nothing except a little smoke coming through this door, over the top, you know? Through the crack. It didn't look like much. And the band stopped all of a sudden, and one of these bartenders went running up to the door—"

"What door?" Sandy demanded.

"Some *door*, I don't know. In the back. It said employees only on it, I remember that. Anyway, this guy runs over to it, and the smoke is coming out the top, and he grabs the knob and pulls it open, and then all this *fire* comes out. All at once, you know. With this big *whoooosh*!" He spread his arms along with the sound effect. "The guy who opened it just got *crisped*, you know." Jim had a sickly smile on his face, and his eyes glittered with reflected flames. "And other people caught fire too, I saw them running around, burning up, you know, rolling on the floor. So then I figured I'd better get out of there fast. I was right by an emergency exit, so I jumped for it, but the fucker wouldn't open, so I pushed my way back to the main door and got out. Everybody else was pushing, too. I saw people getting stepped on. You should of seen the place go up! The firemen couldn't get inside for shit, neither. A bunch of them run in and came running out again real fast."

"OK," Sandy said. "Thanks." He moved away.

"Jim," the man called after him. "Not James!"

"Fuck," Sandy muttered. He moved around until he found one of the firemen in charge, talking to another reporter. "You know how it started?" Sandy asked him.

"Not yet," the fireman said. "We're investigating."

"How about fatalities?" the other newsman asked.

"At least five dead. Two died of smoke inhalation, and three were trampled to death in the panic. It appears that the fire blocked off two emergency exits in the back, and two others were locked, leaving only the main entrance. We suspect the final death toll will be higher. *Much* higher. A lot of people never made it out of there."

"Can you give me a number?" the reporter asked. "I'm on deadline."

"Fifty at least. Maybe as much as a hundred. Don't use my name, that's just a wild stab."

"But *why* were the fire exits locked?" Sandy asked.

"Go ask the owner!" the fireman snapped, moving off.

Sandy pocketed his notepad and drifted back to the police barrier to watch the flames shrink. He stood quietly, hands shoved deep into his pockets. Finally the last orange snakes twisted and died, long after the roof had collapsed in a huge gout of smoke. The red death-glow that had drenched the darkness was gone, but the fire trucks continued to pour water onto the smoking ruins. The bystanders and survivors got into their cars and left until only a handful remained. Sandy was one of them. When the wind blew, the air was heavy with ashes.

He found Gopher John Slozewski standing alone by a deserted police barrier, his face as gray and ashen as his building. Sandy put a hand on the big man's shoulder, and Slozewski turned toward him. At first the dark eyes held no recognition. Then, finally, he nodded. "Oh," was all he said. He looked back at the remains of the Gopher Hole.

"I'm sorry," Sandy said.

"All those dead," Slozewski said to no one in particular. He did not look at Sandy. "They ain't even sure how many. More than West Mesa, though. A lot more. They say the fire doors were locked." At last he turned. "Blair, you got to believe me, it couldn't be. Red told me to lock those doors. He was the assistant manager, you know, and he said kids were sneaking in and not paying the cover charge and that we ought to lock the doors and stop 'em. But I told him no way. I swear it!"

"Maybe he locked them anyway," Sandy said.

Slozewski looked once more at the ruins, staring as if the weight of his gaze could somehow make the twisted, blackened beams rise and knit themselves anew. His face was blank of expression, unlined and innocent as a child's. In despair, he had lost his scowl.

"Do they know how it started yet?" Sandy asked.

Gopher John Slozewski laughed bitterly. "They think," he said. Then, very quietly: "Arson."

FIVE

Yesterday, all my troubles seemed so far away/
Now I need a place to hide away/
Oh, I believe in yesterday

She opened the door to him and said nothing at all, but her smile was all the greeting he needed. It was the same whacko lopsided gee-whiz smile he remembered, beneath the same crooked nose, and it had been too damn long since he'd seen it. He found himself smiling back, and when he did Maggie stepped forward and they hugged fiercely for a long long time. When at last they broke the embrace, she held his hands in her own and said, "Jesus, it's good to see you. Really."

"Yeah," said Sandy. His voice sounded vaguely goofy, but he went on anyway. "Yeah," he repeated. "For me, too." Maggie was like a breath of fresh air from the past. For three frustrating days he had been fighting the obstinancy of Jersey cops, trying to tie up the fire story that Jared had demanded for *Hedgehog*, and having acrimonious talks with Sharon courtesy of Ma Bell. He found he needed Maggie's smile.

"Come on in," she said, moving aside. "We eat soon. Still like lasagne?"

"My fourth favorite thing in the world," Sandy assured her. "Comes right after books, sex, and pizza." He followed her inside. The place was smaller than the one she'd had five years ago, the last time he'd visited, but then she no longer had roommates to contend with. A beat-up old sofa, a large floor-to-ceiling bookcase, and an antique buffet dominated the cramped living room. In a corner by a narrow window looking out on an alley there was a comfortable-looking recliner with two cats on it, a huge fat Siamese and a smaller orange short-hair.

"Ho Chi Minh?" Sandy said, surprised. The Siamese opened one eye and peered at him suspiciously.

"None other," Maggie said. "He's old and crotchety as hell, but he hangs in there. The new guy is Orange Julius. Chase 'em off and sit yourself down while I get us some wine. We got a lot of catching up to do."

The cats protested loudly as Sandy evicted them from the recliner and settled in. Maggie went out to the kitchen and came back shortly with a bottle of Chianti and two glasses. He held while she poured. Then she sat on the floor, crossed her legs, sipped the wine, and smiled up at him. "So," she said, "how's your love life?"

Sandy laughed. "You come right to the point, don't you?"

Maggie shrugged. "Why the hell not?" She had hardly changed at all, Sandy thought. She was wearing faded jeans and a loose white peasant blouse, beneath which her breasts moved freely. She'd never worn a bra as long as Sandy had known her. That had been one of the first things he'd noticed when they met, way back in 1967. It had turned him on enormously. Maggie had never been a classical beauty. Her mouth was a bit oversized and somehow a little lopsided, especially when she smiled, and her nose was large and still crooked where it had been broken by a cop's nightstick during the '68 Democratic convention. But she had nice green eyes, and a generous mass of reddish-blond hair that always seemed windblown, even inside, and more animation to her than any woman Sandy had ever known. Maggie had been the first great love of his life, as well as the first lay, and sitting there in her living room looking down at her, he realized suddenly that he had missed her enormously.

"My love life," he mused. "Well, I'm living with someone. I think I wrote you about her."

"Maybe," she said. "You know me and letters." Maggie was a notoriously lousy correspondent, bad enough to defeat all of Sandy's efforts to keep in touch. Not only did she never answer letters, she *lost* them, and couldn't recall whether or not she'd ever gotten them. "Was this the dancer?"

"No. That was Donna. We broke up a couple of years ago. This is the realtor. Sharon."

"Right," Maggie said. "You did write me about her. Hell, the letter's around here someplace, I guess. So you moved in together, huh?"

"We *bought* a house, believe it or not," he replied. "I had some money from a book, and Sharon convinced me I'd do better buying real estate than sticking it in a bank. It seemed like a good idea at the time." He sipped his wine. "Now I'm not so sure, though. It's going to be messy if we break up."

"Hmmm," Maggie said. "That doesn't sound optimistic. You been having troubles?"

"Some," Sandy said, vaguely. He felt a bit awkward. Maggie had always been his best friend as well as his lover, and even after they'd gone their separate ways he had always found it easy to confide in her, but it *had* been a long time since he'd seen her, and it felt a bit like betrayal to tell her too much about his fights with Sharon. "Maybe we can work things out," he said after a hesitation. "I hope so. I mean, she's a good person and all. Very bright, very competent. Very much into her career. Only lately, well, we haven't been communicating all that well." He made a face. "A lot of it is my fault. The writing hasn't been coming well lately, and I've been kind of...I don't know, restless, I guess. Moody. Until this story came along, anyway, and Sharon hates the idea of this whole *Hedgehog* gig."

Maggie finished her wine and climbed to her feet, then extended a hand to pull Sandy out of the recliner. "You're going to have to tell me all about it, you know. I'm dying to know how Jared got you in bed with him again, after what he did. But let's talk about it over your fourth favorite thing in the world."

They ate at the kitchen table, but it was covered with a real honest-to-goodness tablecloth and the dinner service actually matched, prompting a comment from Sandy about how things changed, and a sly smile from Maggie. One thing hadn't changed at all; she still made a mean lasagne, very spicy, heavy on the cheese and tomato sauce. Sandy had lunched on a plastic cheeseburger somewhere along the Pennsylvania Turnpike, and he attacked the food with a vengeance. Maggie kept the wine glasses full of Chianti from the wicker-covered bottle in the center of the table. In between bites, Sandy regaled her with the whole Nazgûl story, from Jared's phone call right on through. He found that he was eager to lay it all out to someone, and Maggie had always been a great listener.

The story and the lasagne were finished about the same time. Sandy pushed his plate away and gave a theatrical groan. "God," he said, "I'll never eat again."

Maggie smiled. "So go on. Are they holding Gopher John for the arson, or what?"

Sandy shook his head. "He's cleared on that. It turns out the place was badly underinsured, and it doesn't make sense to burn down your own money-losing business unless you've got it covered. But it *was* arson. They turned up traces of kerosene and plastic explosive. Only Slozewski wasn't responsible. Hell, I could have told them that much. If you're going to torch your own property, you hire a pro, and he does it in the wee hours, so nobody gets hurt. Not when you're open and packed. The final death toll was seventy-nine, and twice that number injured. Slozewski is clear of the arson charge, but he's still in deep shit. They might bring him up on criminal charges on account of those fire doors' being locked, and the families of the kids that died are suing him for millions. I feel sorry for the guy. I'm convinced it wasn't his fault. I saw how much that place meant to him."

"You really think it was some nut out to get the Nazgûl?"

"Sure looks like it, don't it? Hobbins at West Mesa, Lynch murdered two weeks ago, and now this? Damned if those cops in Jersey would listen, though. Parker was more reasonable. I think I've got him half-convinced. He said he'd get in touch with cops in Santa Fe and Chicago, try to keep an eye out for Faxon and Maggio, for whatever good it'll do." He got up from the table. "Want help with the dishes?"

Maggie dismissed them with a wave. "Dump them in the sink and let 'em soak. They'll keep. You won't."

They took what was left of the wine back to the living room, and Maggie lit a couple of candles instead of turning on the lights. This time they both sat on the couch. Ho Chi Minh came over and hopped into Maggie's lap, where he settled himself with a proprietary disdain. She stroked his cream-covered fur as they talked, but he was too proud to purr.

"I'm going on to Chicago from here," Sandy said. "Maggio lives down in Old Town and plays weekends for some sleazo bar band. Maybe he can tell me something." He hesitated, then plunged ahead. "And I've got another idea too, one I wanted to ask you about. When was the last time you heard from Bambi Lassiter?"

Maggie gave him a sharp look and a smile. "Oh," she said, "maybe a year or so back. I got the letter around here somewhere." She gave a vague wave toward the bookcase, which was stacked full of ratty paperbacks, and Sandy peered at it and noticed for the first time that she had letters and envelopes and various other random papers stuck in among the books, some lying on the shelves, others doing duty as placemarks. "What do you want with Bambi?" she asked.

"I tried phoning her, but my number is six years old and useless, and I've got no leads to track her down," Sandy said. "Bambi always had contacts with the real underground, and I'm hoping she can put me in touch. I've got a hunch."

"There's hardly any underground left," Maggie pointed out. "Why would they be involved?"

Sandy shrugged. "Don't know. But they found plastic explosive in the Gopher Hole, remember? That's enough to make me suspicious. It can't hurt to check it out."

"I suppose not," Maggie said. "I'll hunt around for that letter before you leave." She carefully evicted Ho Chi Minh from her lap, kicked off her slippers, and stretched out, laying her feet in Sandy's lap. It was done without a word being exchanged, an old and familiar and comfortable sort of motion that took Sandy right back. He put his hand on her foot. She had never been much of one for wearing shoes. There was a thick ridge of callus on the outside of her big toe, and a pad of it, hard and leathery and starting to crack, all along the underside of the foot itself. He traced it with a finger, took her foot firmly in hand and began to massage it. His fingers remembered. Maggie sighed. "Jesus, I love that," she said. "You were the best damn foot-rubber I ever had, Sandy."

He smiled at her and kept up his ministrations. "We all have our talents," he said. Then they fell quiet. Ho Chi Minh came back and hopped up on the couch and settled in again on Maggie's stomach. Finally he began to purr as she stroked him. Maggie sipped wine from time to time and stared off at the candle flames with a small crooked smile on her face. And Sandy rubbed her foot and fell to thinking.

"You're looking pensive," Maggie observed at last.

"Remembering," Sandy said. He shifted his attentions to her other foot.

"Remembering what?"

He smiled. "Oh, other days, other apartments, other foot-rubs." He paused and reached for his wine glass and held it up briefly in front of the flame before he took a sip. "I remember when wine parties at your place meant drinking Boone's Farm out of Flintstone jelly glasses," he said. "And sitting on the floor, too. You didn't have any furniture except that black bean-bag chair that Ho Chi Minh used to spray on all the time."

"I had cushions," Maggie said. "Made them myself."

"Cushions," Sandy said. "Yeah, right. I was never any damn good at sitting cross-legged. My feet always went to sleep. I was worse at eating off a plate balanced in my lap. Got food all over me."

"It didn't stop you coming," she pointed out.

"No," Sandy said fondly. "No. It didn't." He pointed. "No bookcase then. Just old boards and those cinder blocks that Froggy and me swiped from that construction site for you. And maybe half as many paperbacks. And that big cable spool you kept saying you were going to strip and stain and turn into a table. And all your posters."

"You didn't mention my mattress in the back room," Maggie said. "Haven't forgotten that, have you? We balled on it often enough."

Sandy grinned. "Mattress?" he said. "What mattress?"

She gave a snort of disdain. "I remember how you used to read us whatever you were working on, and afterward we'd talk about it."

"The criticism was unduly influenced by Boone's Farm," Sandy said. "I won't forget those arguments with Lark, though. I was never radical enough for him. Whatever I read, he'd just smile and say it was competent bourgeois entertainment, but he couldn't see how it would help the revolution any."

Maggie gave a sudden whoop of delight. "Shit, I'd forgotten that. You're right. Good old Lark. You know what Lark is doing these days?"

"Haven't a clue," Sandy admitted.

Maggie's grin was so big it threatened to crack her face clean in half. "Look him up when you're in Chicago to see Maggio," she urged. "He's in the book. Look under L. Stephen Ellyn."

Sandy felt his mouth drop open. "L. Stephen Ellyn?" he said dumbly. Lark Ellyn had always been perversely proud of his first name, no matter how much gender-confusion and kidding it caused. Sandy had ragged him about it when they first met, and Lark had told him coolly that his namesake was a creature of song and beauty, gifted with the ultimate freedom of flight, and that therefore Lark was an appropriate name for a man committed to love and freedom, whereas *Sander* meant "defender of mankind" or some such bullshit, with all the militarism and sexism that implied. Lark was real big on the symbology of names. "*L. Stephen Ellyn?*" Sandy repeated. "No, c'mon."

"Really," Maggie said. She held up a hand as if to swear. "L. Steve is a real comer in the ad world, too. Account executive."

Sandy stared at her. Then he giggled. Helpless, he giggled again, then burst into laughter. "No, no," he muttered, "it can't be, c'mon, it can't," but Maggie just kept insisting, and Sandy kept on laughing. "L. Stephen Ellyn, oh, no, Jesus H. Christ on a crutch, you can't tell me...*no!*"

That was the start of the real silliness. After that, they made jokes about L. Stephen Ellyn for ten minutes or so, and drank some more wine, and started singing old songs in horribly off-key voices, and drank some more wine, and somehow got onto old TV theme songs, and worked through *Superchicken* and *George of the Jungle* and most of the Warner Brothers westerns and *Car 54, Where Are You?* before getting sidetracked by too much wine and *Tombstone Territory.*

"*Whistle me up a memory,*" Maggie was singing uncertainly, though loudly. "*Whistle me back where I want to be. Dum dum, something something Tombstone Territory!*" she finished with a flourish.

Sandy felt a bit dizzy from the wine, and what she was singing seemed very profound and terribly, urgently important. "And where *do* you want to be?" he demanded suddenly.

Maggie stopped singing, refilled her glass, grinned at him. "Huh?" she said amiably.

"Where do you want to be?" Sandy said again. "Do you know? What kind of memories are we whistling up? Where they going to take us?" He ran his fingers through his hair, confused by the sound of his own voice. "I'm drunk," he said, "but it doesn't matter. I just . . . I dunno, it's confusing. What happened, Maggie?"

"Huh?" she said. "Happened? To what? *Tombstone Territory?*" She giggled. "It got canceled, Sandy."

"No," he snapped. "To *us*! What happened to *us*!"

"You and me, honey?"

"You and me," he repeated, "and Bambi Lassiter, and Jared Patterson, and Gopher John Slozewski, and Jamie Lynch, and Froggy, and Slum, and Jerry Rubin, and Angela Davis, and Dylan and Lennon and Jagger and the Weathermen and the Chicago Seven and William Kunstler and Gene McCarthy and the SDS and . . . and *L. Stephen Ellyn,* for Chrissakes! *What happened to us all?* To *everybody?*" He waved his arms wildly, in a great all-encompassing motion that took in the hopes and dreams and demonstrations, that took in riots and assassinations and candlelight parades, that took in Bobby Kennedy and Donovan and Martin Luther King, that embraced Melanie and the Smothers Brothers and the hippies and the yippies and the Vietnam War, that swept across the memories of a turbulent decade and the destinies of a whole generation of American youth, and that nearly knocked his glass of Chianti off the arm of the sofa. He recovered and caught it just in time.

Maggie moved over and put an arm around him. "Time happened," she said. "Change happened, love."

"*Change,*" Sandy said bitterly. "Maggie, we wanted change, that was what it was all about. We were going to change the fucking world, weren't we? Shit. Instead the fucking world changed *us*. It changed Lark into somebody named L. Stephen Ellyn, and it changed Jared into a rich asshole, and it changed Jamie Lynch into a coffin and Gopher John into a pinstriped suit, and I ain't even sure what it's changing me into, but I don't like it. *I don't like it!*"

Maggie hugged him. "You're shaking, honey," she said softly.

"The wine," Sandy muttered, but he knew it wasn't so. "Fucking wine has me sick but they say there's truth in wine, you know. Truth. Remember truth? It was real big in the Sixties, along with peace and love and freedom. What did we do with all that stuff, Maggie? It's like we all forgot, forgot everything we were, everything we stood for." He sighed. "I know, I know, it's all past now. We're grown up, we're getting old. But I tell you, Maggie, we were *better* then."

"We were *younger* then," she said with a smile.

"Yeah," Sandy said. "Maybe that's all. Maybe I'm just going through a mid-life crisis, right? Mourning my lost youth. Sharon thinks so." He looked at Maggie stubbornly. "I don't buy it, though. It's more than that. I remember . . . I remember, hell, I know things were shitty then, we had the war, and racism, and Nixon and old Spiro, but you know, we also had . . . I dunno . . . like, a kind of *optimism*. We knew the future was going to get better. We *knew* it. We were going to *make* it so. We were going to change things around, and we had the youth, right, so time was on our side. We knew what was right and what was wrong, and we knew who the bad guys were, and there was a sense of *belonging*." His voice got quieter as he spoke, winding down of its own accord. "It was the dawning of the goddamned fucking Age of Aquarius, remember? When peace will guide the planets, and love will steer the stars. Only peace and love sort of went out with bell-bottoms and long hair and miniskirts, and I sure as hell can't tell who the bad guys are anymore." He grimaced. "I think some of them are us."

"Hey," Maggie said, shaking him gently. "Lighten up. It isn't so bad, honey. So it's not the tomorrow we dreamed about. Things never turn out the way you think they will. We *did* change it, Sandy. We stopped the war. We changed the colleges and we changed the government, and we changed all the rules about men and women and love and sex. We even got rid of Tricky Dick, finally. So it's not the Age of Aquarius. It's still different than it would have been without us. And better." She leaned over and kissed him quickly on the end of the nose. "Think of it like this: if it hadn't been for the Sixties, the Fifties would have gone on and on forever."

Sandy shuddered and smiled at her.

"And you've done well personally, love," Maggie went on. "You've written *books*. That's something. You've made a mark on the world."

Sandy's tentative smile withered, and he looked away from her, thinking, yeah, in wine there is truth. "I'm a real big success," he mumbled, with more than a tinge of bitterness in his tone. "Every book I write sells less than the one before, my agent is about to fire me, the *Times* says I have as much literary relevance as *Steal This Book* or *The Greening of America*, and I've got this *terrific* case of novelist's constipation, which is a real good metaphor now that I stop to think about it, because if I ever do get this god-damned novel written I have a hunch it's gonna be a turd. In eight months I'm going to run out of money for my half of the mortgage payments, which ought to confirm all of Sharon's ideas about how irresponsible I am. Sharon and I have this great relationship. We've got a contract, you know, sort of like a marriage contract except we're not married, spells out every-thing in writing, *everything*, like all the housework, and the financial shit, and what happens if we decide to split. Every goddamned thing, except what we do in bed. That we play by ear, so'z we can keep things sponta-neous. It's wonderful, our relationship. We share equal responsibility, and we give each other space, and it's all open so we can both fool around. The only thing wrong is that I don't think Sharon *likes* me very much." Sandy felt very drunk, and very sorry for himself. He picked up his glass and found it empty. "Need more wine," he said.

"All gone," Maggie replied.

Sandy stood up. "Then I will get some!" he announced. "You have to come with me. Otherwise I'll get lost. Point me to a 7–11, crazy lady. Besides, you got to meet Daydream."

Maggie pulled herself up and took his hand. "Daydream?"

"My car!" Sandy said. "I named her. It's your fault. You shamed me into it. Come *on*." He pulled on her arm and dragged her out the front door and down the block. At some point they started running, hand-in-hand, with Maggie laughing as she ran. Sandy wasn't sure what she was laughing about. For that matter, he wasn't sure why they were running.

By the time they stumbled up to his Mazda, they were both out of breath. "There she is," he proclaimed with a sweep of his hand. The street was dark and deserted. There was only the two of them, in their shirt-sleeves, Maggie barefoot. It was cold out, Sandy realized suddenly. But Daydream waited silently under the yellow halo of the streetlamps, sur-rounded by other parked cars. Sandy made a trumpeting noise. "I want ooohs and aahs, woman. This is no ordinary vehicle. This is a Mazda RX-7, with powers and abilities far beyond those of ordinary Fords. This is Daydream."

"Oooh," Maggie said, giggling. "Aaaah." She moved into the shelter of his arms, looked up at him, kissed him on the nose.

"Don't you want to go for a ride?" Sandy asked.

"Oh, no," she said, smiling slyly. She moved closer, put her arms around him.

"Wine," he muttered. "What about wine?"

"Had enough wine," Maggie said. She was looking at him. Her eyes were big and green and playful.

"Had enough wine," Sandy said. "Good, because I can't find my keys. In my jacket, I think. Back at your place. We have to go back."

"Oooh," Maggie said. "Aaaaaah." She started to unbutton his shirt. One button. Two. Three.

Sandy didn't resist. "You're as drunk as I am," he said accusingly.

Four. Five. She tugged, and the shirt tails came free of his jeans. One button left. Six. Then she was yanking it off.

"Here?" he said. "*Here?* Daydream is watching. She's only two years old. Can't see filth like this. We'll give her a trauma." He blinked.

Maggie dropped his shirt on the concrete, pulled up his undershirt. It got stuck as she tried to get it up over his head. She left him that way, pressed against the car. He reached up and tried to untangle his tee shirt, and felt Maggie kiss his bare chest. It was cold out there. He pulled the tee shirt free, dropped it, and she ran a tongue around one nipple, making him shiver. Her hands were undoing his belt buckle. "I had a hard-on like this once in 1959, when I saw my cousin Sally taking a bath," he announced. "It was so hard it hurt."

Maggie pulled down his jeans. "This isn't fair," Sandy said. "I'm freezing to death, and you're completely dressed."

She stood up, grinning, and undid her own blouse. "Fair enough," she said. Her breasts were pale in the dim light of the Cleveland street. No bra, Sandy thought. Still. Some things never change. Never any bra. But she was lovely. He reached out, very tentatively, and touched her left breast. "The left was always my favorite," he said solemnly.

Maggie stepped free of her jeans. "Hi," she said, grinning wickedly. "You're not naked."

Hurriedly, awkwardly, Sandy stripped off his briefs. "I'm going to die of the cold," he said. "Come here."

Maggie shook her head. "Oh, no," she said. She bent quickly, snatched up the pile of clothing, and took off.

Sandy watched her run down the block, flabbergasted. It took him a long time to figure out what was going on. Then he realized that he was standing stark naked on a street in Cleveland at some ungodly hour of the morning, alone. "Hey," he yelled, and he began to spring after her.

His legs were longer, but he wasn't used to running barefoot, and stones underneath hurt like hell, and anyway he was in rotten condition. Maggie increased her lead. He saw her wheel around a corner, put his head down and rushed after her, and bowled right into a big black dude in a pimp suit who had materialized out of nowhere. The guy glared at him, and backed off. Strange naked white guys running through the night were clearly outside his realm of everyday experience. "Sorry," Sandy muttered. "Just training for the Olympics." Then he was off again, thinking that the guy probably didn't even realize that the original Olympics had been conducted in the buff. "Missed the whole fucking point," he muttered, and he ran.

Maggie was waiting in the door of her apartment. Sandy came panting and staggering up to her. "You evil bitch," he said, trying to catch his breath. His heart was thumping in his chest. All the running seemed to have dissolved the miasma of the wine. Only the lust was left.

"Hi," Maggie said softly. She took his hand, pulled him inside, and shut the door. It was warm, but Sandy was still shivering. Maggie put her arms around him and kissed him.

When she broke away, they were both smiling. "Sure you want to go through with this?" Maggie asked.

Sandy groaned. "Oh, Jesus," he muttered. Her breasts were brushing against his chest, ever so lightly, the merest touch. He wanted her so badly he ached.

They kissed again. "I've got a bed now," Maggie said. "A real one. Think you can handle it?" Her hand went down between his legs, touched him lightly, and then closed firmly around him. "Come on," she said, and she led him into the bedroom.

"Oooh," she said as his hands roamed across her warm, smooth skin. "Aaah," she said, when he began to kiss her. But then the playfulness stopped and things got more fevered, more urgent. They were hungry, both of them. Sandy remembered her body, remembered the things she liked. He did them, and she responded, and one thing led to another, and the darkness seemed lit by their heat. When Maggie came, her arms grew tight around his chest, squeezing with a terrible desperation, and her mouth opened soundlessly. Sandy came a few strokes later, but he did not pull free of her afterward. It was warm inside of her, warm and safe and comfortable, and he liked the feel of her arms around him, and so they held each other and savored the fading moments of the after time, and Sandy felt her tears on her face but said nothing. There was nothing to say.

Finally, as if by unspoken agreement, they broke apart. Sandy could see Maggie smiling in the darkness, inches from his face. She kissed him lightly on the end of the nose. "Bastard," she said affectionately. "You haven't changed. You still leave me with the wet spot."

"Oh, Maggie," Sandy said. He felt himself tremble, though it was warm in the bedroom, in the afterglow of their lovemaking. "I've *missed* you. I've missed this. You're crazy. I love it. I love you. I never did know what you were going to do next. You turn me into a horny thirteen-year-old."

He could feel Maggie's smile as much as see it. "And Sharon?" she murmured. "Doesn't she make you crazy, love?"

Sharon's name sobered him a little. The mention was enough to change things, somehow. Sandy could sense himself drawing back, though he did not move an inch. "Sharon," he repeated reluctantly. "It's different. Not bad. We're good together, at least in bed. At least in the sack we both want the same things. Sharon's very sexy. Uninhibited. Giving. Only, I dunno, it's different." He sat up, wrapped his arms around his knees. "She's *not* crazy. Maybe that's it. She's not even the least little bit crazy. I need crazy."

Maggie's fingers traced the curve of his spine, gently, idly. "You need sanity too, love," she said. "Remember? That was why we broke up. I was too crazy for you. You wanted more stability. You wanted sane."

"I wish I knew what the hell I wanted," Sandy said. "I don't think I want to go to where Sharon is headed, but at least she's headed someplace. Me, I just kind of wander from day to day." He turned around to face Maggie, caught her hand lightly, kissed it. "And what about you?" he asked. "I've been so wrapped up telling you about my life, I haven't even asked you about yours."

Maggie shrugged lazily. "I tend my garden," she said. "I work in an office, bullshit typing stuff. I read. I go out now and again and get laid. Some days I'm lonely. Mostly it's okay."

"Men?"

"Sure. A few special ones since you. Lived with a guy named Bob for two years. He taught high school. Finally I was too crazy for him. I'm active in the women's movement. I'm trying to save money to go back to college. Never should have dropped out."

"I *told* you that," Sandy said.

"I know. At the time, the revolution seemed more important. Courses were such bullshit. Who needed a piece of paper. Huh?"

Sandy smiled ruefully. "I remember the cant," he said.

"I'll be all right," Maggie said. "I missed you. I've made my mistakes. I get the regrets every so often. Who doesn't? But I'll be all right, Sandy." There was a hint of resignation in her voice as she said it that somehow made Sandy feel very sad.

He lay down next to her again, gathered her into his arms, and kissed her. Now that the sex was over with, the wine was coming back into his head and reclaiming the domain lust had driven it from. He muttered things softly to Maggie, and she muttered back, and at some point in the course of the muttering they crossed the line that they had crossed so often together in years past. "I'm not asleep," Sandy heard himself declare stoutly, but the declaration itself woke him, and he realized sheepishly that Maggie's accusation had come hours earlier, that it was almost dawn now, and Maggie was snoring softly in his arms. Her face was very close to his. In sleep, much of the animation had drained out of it. Sandy could see the lines under her eyes, the heaviness beneath her chin. Her nose was too big and crooked where it had been broken, and her half-open lips were wet with saliva. He found himself thinking of Sharon, no doubt asleep in their Brooklyn brownstone, in the big brass bed, her ash-blond hair spread out on the pillow, her trim body sleek in a silk camisole. Beautiful, as Maggie would never be beautiful. And she loved him, in her own way. She had been good to him. Yet right then, Sandy was glad he was here, and not there. He kissed Maggie softly, so as not to wake her, snuggled closer, and gave himself back up to sleep.

SIX

Show me the way to the next little girl/
Oh don't ask why, oh don't ask why

Sandy had known Old Town pretty well during his undergraduate days at Northwestern. Even then it had been touristy, overpriced, and crime-ridden, but you could hear some good music there. More likely folk than rock, but good stuff anyway, so Sandy wasn't averse to returning.

Unfortunately, Rick Maggio *lived* in Old Town, but that didn't mean he *played* in Old Town. Sandy found himself doubling back on his own tracks and taking Daydream down the Dan Ryan south of Chicago to find the one particular sleaze-pit where Maggio's band had its nightly gig.

Cleveland, and Maggie, had left him feeling pretty good, but his first sight of the tavern where Maggio played was enough to sour whatever remained of Sandy's good mood. The Come On Inn was a dismal little place sandwiched between two gaudier and larger bars on a frontage road near the Indiana border. The big C in the electric sign was defective, kept going off and then struggling fitfully to come back on again. A neon Budweiser sign occupied one window. The other displayed a cardboard placard that said LIVE MUSIC — NO COVER. All around the country, Sandy thought, bands called Live Music were playing badly tonight in bars called Come On Inn on highways known only as Frontage Road. It was a species of generic entertainment; they ought to make the musicians wear white jumpsuits with BAND on their backs in plain black lettering and the UPC symbol on their pockets. He sighed and went on in.

Inside, the Come On Inn was a narrow place with a beery smell, mirrored to make it look larger. The band was laboring away on a crowded stage behind the bar. They weren't playing very well, but it didn't matter much, since no one was listening. Sandy went to the back and found himself a table against one mirrored wall. He glanced around while he waited for the waitress to notice him. Only one other table was full, occupied by a glum graying couple who were more interested in staring at their drinks than in talking to each other. Three more customers at the bar: a solitary woman drinking alone and watching the act, and two men in workshirts arguing about the Bears. They were loud enough so that Sandy caught snatches of their conversation above the raucous, uncertain music. The lack of trade didn't surprise him. The bars next door had been topless joints, while the Come On Inn offered only LIVE MUSIC.

When the waitress finally showed, she proved to be a hard-faced, buxom girl—barely out of high school by the look of her—with too much eyeshadow and an air of being old and cynical beyond her years. Sandy ordered a draft and resolved to nurse it well. Maggie's Chianti had left him with a godawful wine hangover that morning, and he wasn't up for a reprise. "Who's playing?" he asked the waitress.

She looked at him dully. "Playing what?"

"The music," Sandy said, raising his voice just a tad so she could hear him above the band's rendition of "Help Me Make It Through the Night."

The waitress threw a disdainful glance at the stage. "Oh, *them*," she said. "Those are the Rolling Stones. Doncha recognize Mick Jagger?" She tossed her short dark hair and walked away.

Sandy leaned back to wait for his beer. He didn't recognize Mick Jagger. In fact, it took him a disoriented minute to pick out Rick Maggio. Four of them were responsible for the racket up there. They had a skinny little girl on keyboard, a drummer who looked like he'd just gotten out of Treblinka, a red-headed kid on bass, and a big, grossly fat man playing lead guitar. Maggio wasn't the sort to dye his hair or go in for a sex change, which meant he had to be the lead guitarist, but it was hard to accept. It wasn't until the singer turned and faced him directly that Sandy could discern a hint of Maggio in the puffy face under those lights. When recognition came, it depressed him.

He remembered older, better days. He remembered a scrawny kid who could make a guitar scream and wail and thrum and beg for mercy. He remembered a singer so energetic that his shirt would always be dripping sweat halfway through the first set. So he'd take it off, ball it up, and flick it out into the audience, playing on bare-chested, his ribs etched clearly under his skin. Girls would scream and fight over those sweaty shirts, usually tearing them to sweaty ribbons. "I love it, man," Maggio had told Sandy in an interview once. "Makes 'em cream in their jeans."

If he took off his shirt now, Maggio might provoke screams, but more from disgust than sexual frenzy. He'd gained all the weight that Gopher John had lost, but on him it looked worse. Where Slozewski had been big and broad, Maggio was just sloppy fat. His face was puffy, the once-sensual sneering lips gone blubbery. His long Fu Manchu mustache had been cut and trimmed and now had a beard to keep it company, but the beard was scraggly and looked like a mess of used Brillo pads glued to his face. Sandy suspected that it hid a double chin. Maggio wore jeans, a gold lamé vest, and a green tee shirt with big dark patches under the arms where sweat had soaked through. The tee shirt was too small. It bound around the stomach, and when Maggio twisted too quickly it rode up on him, giving a glimpse of pale white skin.

The waitress put his beer on the table, on top of a cocktail napkin decorated with mother-in-law jokes. "Two dollars," she said.

"For a *draft?*"

She shrugged. "It's one dollar when the Stones ain't playing."

Sandy pulled out his wallet and extracted three dollar bills and one of his purple-and-silver business cards with the hedgehog cartoon. "Two for the beer, and one for you if you give this card to Mick Jagger when the band takes its break. Tell him I want to talk to him."

She looked at the card uncertainly, and then back at Sandy. "You a real reporter? For true?"

"Sure. Doncha recognize Dan Rather?"

She snorted and moved off.

The beer had too much head on it. Sandy sipped it and leaned back again to listen to the music. The band was truly ghastly, he decided after listening to them butcher "Michelle" and derail "The City of New Orleans." The red-headed bass player was faking most of the lyrics. The drummer was off in a world of his own and liked to jump in with drum solos at totally inappropriate times. The girl on keyboard sometimes seemed to be playing different songs than the rest of them. As decayed as he might be, Maggio was still clearly the only thing that gave the group any professionalism whatsoever. He played listlessly, as might be expected, but every so often you could hear a flash of his old style, and his voice still had the same raw raspy edge to it that had worked so well as a counterpoint to Hobbins' singing in the days when the Nazgûl were flying high. It was a nasty voice, full of poison and pain and possibilities. It made Sandy sick to hear it singing "Tie a Yellow Ribbon Round the Old Oak Tree."

Mercifully, the break arrived right after the first Barry Manilow song. The waitress handed Maggio the card as he was climbing down from the stage. He glanced at it, baffled, and then across the bar to Sandy. The bafflement gave way to a wary, faintly hostile look as he rounded the bar and came across the room. "What's the joke, man?" he demanded in a hard unfriendly voice when he arrived. He dropped the card on Sandy's table, in a puddle of beer.

"No joke," Sandy said, sitting up a bit. He gestured to the other chair. "Sit down. I'll buy you a drink."

Maggio looked angry. He made no move to sit. "I get my drinks free, man," he snapped. "Don't do me no fucking favors. What kind of shit you trying to pull? You ain't from no *Hedgehog*, so don't gimme any of that crapola."

Sandy was a bit taken aback by the vehemence in Maggio's voice. "Hey," he said. "Back off. I *am* from *Hedgehog*. Sandy Blair. Hell, don't you recognize me? I interviewed you twice before."

"Yeah? When?"

"In '69, in Boston, right after the release of the Black Album. And in '71, two weeks before West Mesa. You were with this weird-looking black girl with a shaved head, but you asked me not to mention her in the story. I didn't."

That seemed to put a dent in Maggio's hostility. He even smiled briefly and took the chair opposite Sandy. "Hey, yeah, I remember that," he said. "She was a sweet piece of tail. Maybe you're straight. What was that name again? Blair?"

Sandy nodded.

"Well, sure," Maggio said, "I think I'm remembering now. We got interviewed a fucking million times, man, it's hard to keep all you clowns straight. Press guys were like groupies, a whole 'nother bunch in every fucking city, trying to suck you off for whatever they could get." Maggio must have suddenly realized how offputting that all was, because he paused abruptly, stared hard at Sandy's face, and then broke into one of the most fatuous fake smiles that Sandy had ever seen. "Hey, man, yeah," he said, "I remember you now. Hell yes. You were different, not like them other guys. You wrote some good stuff, sure. Heeeeey! Sandy old man, it's been a long time!"

It was all about as sincere as Richard Nixon's Checkers speech, but

Sandy decided not to press it. "I had a big beard back then," he said to give Maggio a graceful out. "That's probably why you didn't know me."

"Oh, yeah. Sure, man. That's it." Maggio turned and beckoned the waitress over. "Still good for that drink, man?"

"Sure," Sandy said.

Maggio ordered Chivas on the rocks. When it arrived, he sipped at it tentatively. "So what can I do ya for, man?" he asked. "You on a story, or what?"

Sandy nodded.

A hint of wariness returned to Rick Maggio's puffy, restless eyes. "Hey, look, you ain't going to do one of them hatchet jobs on me, are ya? You know, how far he's fallen and all that crapola?" He waved his hand vaguely, indicating the squalor of the Come On Inn, his band, all of it. "I mean, that ain't *fair*, Sandy. This isn't me, you know. I'm just playing with these assholes as kind of a favor to a friend, you know how it is. I'm balling that little girl on keyboard, and she wanted to get a group together, so I'm helping out. It's only a temporary gig."

"I understand," Sandy said. "That's not what I'm interested in. I want to ask you about Jamie Lynch."

Rick Maggio relaxed visibly. "Oh, *Jamie*," he said. "Sure. I read about it. What kind of animals would do something like that?"

"You tell me."

Maggio's expression got uncertain. "Tell you? What, man? I don't know nothing about it. It's just sad, man."

"Is it?"

"An indictment of our times," Maggio said. "You can quote me."

Sandy made a pretense of noting the quote. "It's funny," he said, "but I wouldn't have thought you'd have cared much about Jamie Lynch getting killed."

The singer's eyes narrowed just a little. "What are you saying, man?"

"Just that you had no reason to love Lynch."

Maggio responded with forced, raucous laughter. "Who told you that, Sandy?"

"Gopher John Slozewski, for one."

"Oh," Maggio said. "Well, hell, we used to have this joke about John. What do you get when you cross a gopher and a Polack?"

Sandy shrugged.

"Our drummer," Maggio said, guffawing. "I mean, the Gopher was never the brightest guy around. He misunderstood stuff. Like me and Lynch, I guess. Jamie *made* us. Hell, we had our hassles. What group doesn't hassle with its manager? But that was a long time ago, and we go back a long long way, man. Why did the Gopher think I might have something against Jamie?"

"Oh, a couple reasons," Sandy said. "The drugs, for one."

"The drugs," Maggio repeated. "See what I mean? Dumb shit Polack thinks I'd get upset with a dude who gives me free drugs. Shit, man, I wish I had somebody giving me free drugs *now*."

"How about the pictures of you and the Pittsburgh twins?"

Just for a brief moment, Sandy thought he saw Rick Maggio flush. It vanished in an uneasy grin. "Fuck, I'd almost forgotten about that. They were something, I tell you. Wish I had their names now. Real prime. And by now they'd be legal, too. Let's see, what'd they be? Something like twenty-six, twenty-seven. You oughta go interview *them*, Sandy boy. But hey, look, the Gopher just didn't get it. Jamie took a few pictures, sure, but it was just a joke. A real yock. Those little numbers didn't mind one bit, they just wiggled and stuck out their behinds and smiled for the camera. And it never bothered me none. So Jamie liked to kid around a little. Big deal. I was cool, I could take it." He hesitated. "Hey man," he said, "you ain't gonna put nothing about this in your story, are ya? I mean, it don't bother me or nothing, but my old lady might get weird about it."

"I don't think I'll need it," Sandy said carefully, giving no promises. "Slozewski also said that you wanted to get the Nazgûl back together, you and some promoter you'd hooked up with. True?"

Maggio smiled. "So the Gopher got one right. We're *going* to get back together. Wait and see. Edan will fix it all. It'll be a sensation, man. Biggest fucking comeback in rock history. You tell Jared Patterson to put that on his fucking cover instead of fucking Farrah Fawcett. You tell him Rick Maggio and the Nazgûl are coming back, better than ever."

Sandy thought the fantasy was a little pathetic. He squelched a wise-crack about how Maggio seemed to have changed the name of the band. "This all set?" he asked.

Maggio finished his drink and shook his head. His long dark hair hung down around his bloated cheeks in ropy strands and swayed with his denial. "Nah, but Edan's working on it."

"Edan," Sandy echoed. He flipped back a few pages to the notes on his interview with Gopher John. "Edan Morse, right?"

Maggio nodded. "You know Edan?"

"Slozewski mentioned the name. Slozewski also said that Jamie Lynch wanted no part of it. What about that?"

"OK, OK," Maggio said in a hassled tone. "So Jamie Lynch was being a pain in the ass. Sure, man. So what?"

Sandy shrugged. "So if the cops wanted to get suspicious, they might say you had a motive for killing him."

Maggio turned awkwardly in his seat, put two fingers in his mouth, and whistled. "*Francie!*" he yelled. "Get your ass over here!"

All conversation in the Come On Inn ceased at the shrill sound of Maggio's whistle. It resumed tentatively as the keyboard player detached herself from the table where the band was sitting and made her way across the room. As she neared, Sandy saw that he had not been mistaken about her age. Rick Maggio still liked them young. Francie looked maybe seventeen; a child playing at being a woman. The word that came to mind was waif. She reminded Sandy of some of the runaways he had known in the Sixties, flower children wilting too early in the winter of the world, sustained by nothing but fading memories of their summer of love. Francie was very short. Pretty in a vaguely innocent way. Long, stringy blown hair, big brown eyes, hollow cheeks, lots of rings on her fingers. She was wearing a dirty white tee shirt with a transfer that said PLEASE DON'T SQUEEZE THE CHARMIN over pictures of two rolls of toilet paper, end on, placed in what should have been strategic spots. Only Francie's thin, boyish figure offered no Charmin to be squeezed, so the effect was more pathetic than erotic. Her smile was a wispy, uncertain thing that flickered on and off like the big C in the electric sign outside.

When she reached their table, Maggio grabbed her arm, pulled her to him, and sat her on his knee. "This is Francie, my old lady," he told Sandy. "Francie, tell this fucker where the hell I was the night Jamie Lynch got his heart cut out."

"He was with me," she said in a small voice. "We didn't have a gig that night, so we stayed home and watched TV and balled. Honest."

"All right," Sandy said, though he thought that Francie had been ready with a reply all too quickly. Almost as if Maggio had rehearsed her.

"See?" Maggio said, grinning. One of his hands went around her and up under her shirt, searching for Charmin. To wipe away the bullshit, no doubt, Sandy thought.

Francie ignored him and let the hand wander and squeeze. "You really from *Hedgehog?*" she asked.

Sandy nodded.

"You going to do a write-up on us? How do you like us?"

"Well, it's not really my kind of music," Sandy said politely. "I like harder rock."

She gave a tiny little nod, not at all surprised. "I didn't think you were here for us. Just for Rick, right? Rick's too good for us, really. He's a genius. He was with a lot of big groups, you know? With Nasty Weather, and Catfight, and the Nazgûl." Maggio was grinning behind her, his hand still working at her breasts. She acted like she didn't notice it.

"I know," Sandy told her. "I covered the Nazgûl once. I was a big fan." He looked at Maggio. "You really think you can get the band together again?" he asked.

"Hey, man, I wouldn't josh ya. I said so, didn't I?"

Sandy shrugged. "Sure. But I've got my doubts."

"Well, you just doubt away, it's gonna happen. Just wait."

"You got some obvious problems," Sandy said. "F'rinstance, I seem to recall that Hobbins is dead."

Maggio's smile was broad and almost complacent. "Edan's got that figured. Wait'll you see. It'll blow your fucking mind."

"Oh? How's he plan to replace a dead man?"

"No comment," said Maggio. "Just wait and see, man. Or ask Edan."

"Maybe I'll do that," Sandy said. "How do I get in touch with him?"

Maggio was wary. "Edan don't like people giving out his number," he said. "Maybe I'll ask him about you. If he wants to talk, he'll look you up."

"Interesting," Sandy said. "Why's he so secretive?"

Maggio pulled his hand out from under Francie's shirt and looked uncomfortable. "I told you, I'll ask him about you. Edan don't like being talked about."

"I see. All right, let's get back to this Nazgûl comeback. You say this Edan Morse has some scheme for replacing Hobbins. Fine, I'll give you that much. What makes you think Faxon and Slozewski will go along?"

"They'll go along."

"Why? They have lives of their own now. They don't need the Nazgûl anymore."

Maggio flushed, and his face took on a strange, angry, bitter look. "Like I do, right? That's what you're thinking. They don't need the fucking Nazgûl, but Maggio sure as hell does, that washed-up old creep, can't even hack it no more, playing in dumps like this, living with teenaged sluts like her." He gave Francie a rough push on her shoulder, and she moved off his knee, wordlessly, blank-faced. She stood awkwardly, not knowing whether to leave or stay.

"I didn't say that," Sandy protested.

"Fuck, man, you don't have to *say* it. You're thinking it, though, ain't ya?

Well so fucking what? You think I need the Nazgûl?" His voice dripped with sarcasm. "Not me, man. Fuck, why should I want to get together with those assholes again? Why should I want to cut more albums, and make millions of fucking dollars, and have hot little twats tearing off my pants every fucking time I turn around? What a fucking *bore* that would be. Me, I like playing Cal City and Gary and East St. Louis, seeing all them swell Ramada Inns, listening to Moe and Larry and Curly Joe trying to stay in key behind me while the douchebags in the audience shoot off their mouths and swill beer. I like sweating like a pig and getting shit for it. Why the *hell* should I ever want to play with real musicians again?" He slammed his empty glass down on the table so hard that Sandy thought for a moment it might shatter.

"You haven't answered my question," Sandy said quietly. "So you want the group back together. What about Faxon and Slozewski?"

"Fuck Faxon and Slozewski," Maggio said angrily. "A prig and a dumb Polack, who needs 'em. Gopher John wasn't even *in* the fucking Nazgûl at the start. He just hung around and ran errands. Go fer this, go fer that, you get it? There's other drummers out there. I don't need him, man, you hear me?"

"You can't be a Nazgûl reunion all by yourself," Sandy pointed out.

"Shit, man, I *told* you, they'll go along. I guaran-fucking-*tee* it, you hear me? Stick that in the *Hedgehog*! They *owe* me, both of those fuckers. They ripped me off good. Gopher John got himself a fancy nightclub, Faxon lives like a fucking king, and what do I have? Nothing. Shit. Nada. That's what I have. The Nazgûl would have been nothing without me. You think those assholes would be grateful, but no, no, it was always stick it to old Rick. After Nasty Weather smashed up, I asked that dumbass Polack to form a new group with me, but no, he goes off with Morden and Leach and leaves me out in the cold. And Faxon just sits there in Santa Fe on his fucking mountain, getting fat on his publishing rights. He got *plenty* and I got *nothing*. And he could care less. They owe me, both of them. You know why they screwed me? I'll tell you why. Because of the chicks. The chicks always got the hots for me. Faxon never touched any of them but you knew he wanted to. He was so horny the come ran out of his fucking *ears*, but he'd never do nothing about it. And the Gopher, what he got was my sloppy seconds. I was the one they all wanted, they only fucked the Polack 'cause I told them to. See what you get trying to be nice? The chicks dug me better, so now they both got it in for me." He looked at Francie with a face so flushed and ugly and angry that Sandy thought for a second he might hit her. "I got all the prime cut in those days, not third-rate little cunts like her," he said. "And I shared, damn them. So they are gonna come around, you hear? *They owe me.*" He stood up abruptly, angrily, so fast the chair fell over behind him with a loud clatter. "I don't think I got no more to say to you, man," he said. Then, to Francie, "Come on, we got to play for these assholes."

But as Maggio stormed away from the table, she lingered behind. She looked downcast, but Sandy saw no hint of tears in her eyes. She must be used to it, he thought.

When Maggio noticed that she hadn't come with him, he swung around and stared. "Hey!" he yelled. "Come on!"

"I just wanted to . . ." Francie began.

He laughed a very mean laugh. "You *wanted* to," he said mockingly. "I'll *bet* you wanted to. Well, just go ahead. Fuck him, see if I care. Maybe you'll get your name in *Hedgehog.* I don't need you, cunt. I don't need anybody." He winked at Sandy. "Try her out, old boy," he said. "She ain't prime, but she's not bad for what she is." Then he swung around again and stomped back to the stage. Everyone in the bar was watching him. Maggio had finally gotten the audience's attention.

Francie stood a small hesitant step closer to Sandy. "He gets like this sometimes," she said. "He don't mean nothing by it, really. He says mean stuff, but he never hits me or nothing. He's not a bad guy, Mister, not down inside. It's only that he's been having bad luck, and it gets him mad. He used to be a star. Please don't write nothing mean about him in *Hedgehog,* OK? It would hurt him real bad if you did."

Sandy rose from the table, frowned, and put his notepad back in his pocket. "You're a lot more than he deserves, Francie," he said to her, smiling. He reached down and took her shoulder and gave it a small squeeze.

"I'm not, really," she said, averting her eyes. "Rick deserves the best. I can hardly play at all."

"There are more important things than music," Sandy told her. He reached under her chin and raised her head to look him in the eyes. "The truth now," he said. "Were you really with him that night?"

"Honest," Francie said.

Before Sandy could frame another question, a stabbing blare of music came from the stage, as Maggio drew an angry chord from his electric guitar. "All right, you assholes," he said loudly into the mike. This time everyone was looking at him. The red-headed bass player and the drummer sat behind him with wary looks on their faces. "We got a jerko reporter here who don't think Rick Maggio can hack it anymore. He's going to learn.

Right now. So you people can stick your requests up your little bitty assholes, and tie your yellow ribbons round your little bitty cocks, because
now we're going to *rock and roll!*" He roared the final words and jumped
and landed heavily, shaking the stage, and then the whole dingy little joint
shook to the challenge of his guitar. The opening chords were awfully familiar, and Maggio's raw, evil voice grabbed hold of the lyrics the way a
man in pain grabs hold of a scream.

> *Ain't gonna take it easy*
> *Won't go along no more*
> *Tired of gettin' stepped on*
> *When I'm down here on the floor*

He glared at Sandy as he sang, with an old familiar sneer on his face. As
he bulled into the chorus, Sandy had a strange, brief flicker of double vision, as if the puffiness and the beard and the layers of flab were all part of
some grotesque illusion, false and somehow insubstantial, and only now
was he seeing through them, to where the real Rick Maggio lay trapped.

"*Cause I'm ragin'!*" Maggio sang.

"*RAGIN'!*" his back-up men echoed.

They knew enough of the old Nazgûl hit to make a pretense of playing
with him. The bass guitar was uncertain and the drums weren't half as
fevered and angry as they ought to be. But at least they knew their lyric,
their single one-word lyric, and they put a little rage into singing it. Maggio
grinned and drew pain from his guitar.

"*Yes, I'm ragin'!*" he sang.

"*RAGIN'!*" they screamed.

The amps had been wrenched up all the way, so talk was impossible and
the Come On Inn throbbed to the sound. Some of the audience looked
scared. Sandy couldn't blame them; Maggio looked scary. "Ragin'!" had always been his song, the only cut on *Music to Wake the Dead* where he'd
sung the lead instead of Hobbins, and he was pouring all of his hurt and
venom and twisted passion into it now.

"*How I'm ragin'!*" he cried.

"*RAGIN'!*" roared back.

Sandy remembered West Mesa. The lights had gone scarlet and surreal
and Maggio had stepped forward, skinny, sneering, to perform the song, his
big track off their new, unreleased album. And by the third line of the chorus, the audience had gotten the idea, so when Maggio snarled "*Ragin'!*"
sixty thousand people shouted it back at him. Red light and bloodlust and

naked rage at all the cruelty of the world; sixty thousand voices come to-gether. Almost sexual.

> *Ain't gonna tote no rifle*
> *Ain't gonna sweep no floor*
> *Screw them liars in their suits*
> *I ain't takin' anymore!*

It was flawed, it was amateurish, yes. But still it had power. Raw, nasty power. Sandy felt it. He could sense the blood that Maggio was giving his guitar, the pain in the voice, the building anger.

> *Cause I'm ragin'!*
>
> > *RAGIN'!*
>
> *Yes, I'm ragin'!*
>
> > *RAGIN'!*
>
> *How I'm ...*

And then, suddenly, sickeningly, it ended. The music died with a shud-dering whine like nails on a vast blackboard, the back-up musicians froze and goggled at one another.

Down under the stage, the bartender had pulled the plug.

Rick Maggio floundered like a man who has been interrupted while making love, who has been yanked forcibly and roughly out of his partner in the instant just before orgasm. He looked dazed and sick. Then, when he finally realized what had happened, he went white with anger. "*What the fuck do you think you're doing?*" he screamed down at the bartender. "*Get your fucking hands off my equipment. I'll kill you, you cocksucker!*"

The bartender was wiry, fiftyish, with a jutting chin, wrinkles, and flint chips for eyes. "You got it wrong, Mister," he said. "You not killing nobody. You punks just pack up and get out of here real quiet now. I don't want no trouble. And you can forget the money, too."

"You *hired* us!" Maggio said. "We made a deal."

"I hire you to come in and play some music. Nice music, what my cus-tomers like to hear. I didn't hire you to hear you foul mouth talking filth, or to have you scare away my trade, or make people deaf with that garbage you were singing. Get out, punk, before I call the cops."

Maggio yanked off his guitar savagely and jumped down from the stage. He looked real ugly. "We did two fucking sets, man," he said. "You owe us money."

The bartender took a small step backward, reached under the bar, and came out with a Louisville slugger. "Get out," he repeated. "You touch me, punk, and I break all you fingers." Looking at him, Sandy could believe it, too.

Maggio clenched his fist, raised it, lowered it, and turned away with an effort, shaking. The rest of the band had already started to pack up. Maggio looked like a man about to crack. Sandy didn't want to see that. The idea left him feeling nauseated. It was time to go. He touched Francie lightly on the arm. "He was good," he told her. "Tell him that. Tell him I said he was good."

She nodded, understanding. Then she went to Maggio and wrapped her thin arms around him and held him while he trembled. Beaten, white, impotent.

Ragin', thought Sandy as the door closed behind him.

SEVEN

**Hello darkness, my old friend/
I've come to talk with you again**

Driving back up the Dan Ryan into the heart of Chicago, Sandy was glum, too dispirited even to push a cassette into his tape deck. He wasn't sure where he was headed. No more than Rick Maggio was, he thought, or Gopher John or Maggie or poor dead Jamie Lynch, no more than any of them. But it was late and growing later and he was too weary for the road, so he found himself pulling off and cruising through the empty streets of the Loop, pulled by a lassitude that was almost a compulsion.

He took a room for the night in the Conrad Hilton. "The fifteenth floor," he told the desk clerk when he checked in. The man looked at him, gave an uncaring shrug, and handed over a key.

When the bellman left, Sandy's watch read a little past midnight. An hour later back in New York, he thought. Just the time to call Jared. He decided he'd pose as a late-night DJ doing a trivia quiz and ask Jared to sing the theme song from *Superchicken*.

When Patterson's sleepy, befuddled voice finally came over the receiver, however, Sandy found he had neither the energy nor the inclination for the ruse. "It's me, Jared," he said wearily. "I've got something I want you to check for me."

"Can't you call at a civilized hour, goddamnit?" Patterson complained. "You *promised* not to bother me at home. What the hell am I going to do with you, Blair?"

"You're going to find out about Edan Morse for me," Sandy said.
"Who?"

"Morse, as in code," Sandy said. "First name Edan." He spelled it.

"Who is this guy?" Jared asked.

"That's what you're supposed to tell me," Sandy said. "I don't know, it's probably nothing, but the name has come up with both Maggio and Slozewski. He's a promoter or something, wants to do a Nazgûl reunion."

"Hey!" said Jared. "That'd be something, right? Really put the icing on this story of yours."

"It won't happen," Sandy said. "This guy Morse is deluding himself. Still, I want to know who he represents, what kind of groups he's worked with, what kind of ties he has in the music business. Have one of your green-haired teenyboppers dig through the morgue and send me a full backgrounder. I'm at the Conrad Hilton in Chicago. Express mail it there. I think I'll be here a while."

"Why?" Patterson asked. "Didn't you see what's-his-name yet?"

"Oh, yeah," said Sandy. "But I've got to run down you-know-who." He hung up, leaving Patterson thoroughly confused, he hoped.

In truth, Sandy didn't know how long he would be staying in Chicago, or why he wanted to. A lot of his memories were here in this city, and on the Northwestern campus up in Evanston, and those old memories had been restless lately, stumbling around in his head like so many newly risen zombies. Maybe that was it. Maybe Chicago would help put them to rest. And he felt somehow that he ought to look up Lark Ellyn, for reasons he did not understand. Lark and he had never been close, even in the old days, though circumstances had pushed them together a lot. In the past decade they had drifted apart totally, vanishing from each other's world. Yet in some obscure way, Sandy knew that Lark Ellyn was a part of his story, just as Maggie had been. The thought came almost as a revelation, but when it came he knew it was right. All his reporter's instincts told him that this was larger than the Nazgûl, and infinitely larger than the slaying of Jamie Lynch. He nodded to himself, sleepily, and promised to try to figure out just why that was so on the morrow, and to set up a dinner date with old L. Stephen Ellyn as well.

He never undressed or turned out the light; sleep took him fully clothed, sprawled on the narrow single bed in the old hotel.

His dreams were confused and chaotic. The Nazgûl were up on a stage, playing in some great dark hall. People were dancing feverishly. Sandy saw that some of them were on fire. Maggie whirled by, laughing. Blood was running from her nose, and her partner was a charred, blackened skeleton, bits of smoking flesh falling from him as he moved to the music. He saw other faces he knew; Lark, Slum, Bambi. Jamie Lynch was there, frenetic, wired, despite the gaping bloody hole in his chest. Around the perimeter of the dance floor, vague shapeless demons were gathering. Sandy could see them in the darkness, and he cried out, trying to warn people, but the others were blind, they paid no attention to him. They danced on and on. The Nazgûl were playing the "Armageddon/Resurrection Rag" from *Music to Wake the Dead*. It was a long, long song, it filled the entire second side of the album, and the dancers were lost in it, oblivious. While the music played, they could not hear Sandy's shouts of warning, they could not see the enemy. Yet the demons were gathering, gathering and taking shape; he saw an army forming around them, in blue uniforms and khaki, with rifles and bludgeons and dark helmets that hid the inhuman, demonic faces. Up on the stage, Hobbins whirled and writhed and sang of death and rebirth. Up on the stage, Gopher John scowled and played his drums in a terrible driven frenzy. Up on the stage, Maggio sweated blood until it soaked through his shirt. He took it off and tossed it away; underneath his flesh was swollen and green and decomposing. Women with flowers painted on their cheeks fought over the bloody shirt. Sandy caught a whiff of tear gas and screamed at them, and they looked up, they all looked up, but it was too late, it was too late, the demons were coming . . . and the song went on forever.

He woke, jerking up out of the bed and crying out, trembling for a moment until the nightmare released its hold on him and he looked around and saw the bare, drab hotel room. Running his fingers through his tousled black hair, Sandy took a deep breath, then pulled himself to his feet and went to the bathroom and drank a glass of water from a glass that had been sanitized for his protection. And then a second.

As he drained the second glass, he realized why he had come to the Conrad Hilton, and why he had asked for the fifteenth floor.

He would not sleep here, *could* not sleep here. He looked in the mirror. His clothes were rumpled by sleep, his eyes just the smallest bit bloodshot, his hair an unkempt mess. He splashed some water on his face, pulled out his suitcase, changed into a fresh pair of jeans and a blue cashmere sweater, combed his hair. Then he took his coat from the chair on which he'd tossed it, and went silently out into the hall.

The hall was dim and quiet. Sandy couldn't remember whether it had changed or not. Probably, he thought. Probably they had changed the paint, or the carpets, or something. He couldn't remember. It looked the same. The same as it had been.

Everything was empty, still. All the doors were closed and locked for the night. But it didn't matter. Locked doors were no protection. Far, far away, he heard the elevator open, and then he heard footsteps, running footsteps, shouts and screams. And he knew it was happening again. Dazed, still half-asleep, Sandy moved down the hall, watching the room numbers. He turned a corner and froze. It was all there. They swarmed from the elevators, swirled down the halls, asking no questions, answering none, swinging, kicking, hurting. Dark blue figures and others in khaki, with clubs raised and bloody and of course the guns, undrawn yet still there, moving at their sides. Faceless, badgeless, pouring from the elevators, and in their eyes you could see that you were the enemy, nothing human at all, the enemy, the enemy, and they came at you, and they *hit* you, and nothing you said or did would hold back those clubs. There was chaos in the hall. They were pounding on doors, kicking in others, yanking out the kids inside, slapping them, pushing them, screaming at them to get out, get out, *get out.* They heard no appeals. He heard the nightsticks crack against arms, teeth, skulls. It was not a sound to forget, not ever a sound to forget. He heard the grunts, the moans of pain, the epithets that went both ways. He saw one slim black kid trying to stand up to them, and they just bowled into him, clubs swinging, surrounded him, hitting and hitting and hitting. Blood on the nightsticks. Then one of them looked up and they saw him. The mouth opened silently, the cold eyes narrowed, and the blue-clad arm pointed, and they moved toward him. Sandy backed up, backed away, and then he was running, screaming a warning, plunging down the halls as fast as he could, around the corners, all the time hearing the footsteps behind him. Ahead was operations. Ahead was the suite. Safety, safety, the ones in charge, they wouldn't club the ones in charge. The doors to the suite were open. He rushed on in. They all looked up at him, startled. Four of them were playing bridge. Others were scattered around the room, talking softly, shuffling papers, drinking the bitter wine of defeat, licking their wounds. Sandy started to shout at them, lock the doors, close the doors, but it was too late, too late, the enemy was among them. They rushed in, clubs swinging. He saw one bridge player raise a hand to ward off a blow, heard the sickening crunch of contact, saw the nightstick splinter. Someone was demanding a warrant, shouting something about a warrant, and they were hitting him, and then he did not shout anything anymore. "*Stop!*" Sandy yelled. "*Stop it! What's going on here!?*" He shied away from a blow, an arm across his face.

He opened his eyes then, dizzily, and the hall was empty. Dead and empty. He was panting. No, he told himself. Nothing here, nothing here.

No shouts, no screams, no sounds of blows. How could there be? It was not 1968. Those passions were long dead. He did not believe in ghosts. All those closed doors hid only empty rooms and a scattering of conventioners and airline personnel and tired travelers. The only sound was the whir of the elevators, off in the distance around the corner.

He shoved his hands deep in his jacket pockets and headed toward the sound, punched the button, waited. Finally the elevator arrived. When the doors opened, some old memory, some instinct made him shy away. But there was nothing inside. He entered and rode down to the lobby.

"I want a different room," he told the desk clerk. He handed over his key. "Here," he said. "Have the bellman move my stuff. I'm going out for a walk. I'll get the new key when I come back."

The clerk nodded, politely, noncommittally. "Yes, sir. Was your room unsatisfactory?"

"I don't want to be on the fifteenth floor," Sandy said. "I want to be on a different floor."

"You requested that floor," the clerk pointed out. He was an older man, slender and prim, his thinning hair combed carefully back. He had dark, disapproving eyes.

"I was there before," Sandy muttered, looking away, running his fingers through his hair. "Oh, God, yes, I was there before."

"Yes, sir. When was that, sir?"

Sandy looked at him, wondered if he'd worked at the Hilton then, if he'd been on duty that night. "You know," he said. "You know damn well. That was where operations was. Headquarters was up on the twenty-third floor, I remember that, up where Gene was, but the fifteenth was ours too, the fifteenth was operations, and that was where they came for us."

"You were throwing things," the clerk said, and it looked odd, the way he spoke without moving his lips. "You were throwing ashtrays, and bags of urine, and human excrement. You were throwing things from your windows. You deserved it."

"No," Sandy said. "Lies, all lies. I was there, dear God, yes. No one threw anything, not us. It was a goddamned fucking *lie*, you hear?" But the man was staring at him, smirking at him, mocking him behind that polite smile. Sandy felt sick. He spun, lurched across the lobby, toward the doors, feeling haunted and hunted. The lobby was full of faceless blue shadows, and masked Guardsmen, and they glared at him as he passed. He passed through them, running, staggering, desperate for air.

Michigan Avenue was deserted as far as the eye could see. Sandy glanced at his watch, leaning back against the side of the building. It was half past four. Across the street was the dark, threatening emptiness of Grant Park, a great darkling plain of brown grass and concrete under the glittering cliffs of the parkside buildings. He moved toward Michigan and Balbo, driven by something he could not articulate.

The ghosts were there, too. Sandy stopped, shivering in the cold October air and the wind off the lake, remembering another night, a hotter night, warm and muggy, when the slightest breeze was a welcome relief. All around him phantoms stirred and took on shimmering, insubstantial shapes. The armies of the night, he thought. And there they were. On one side of the street was a ragtag, brightly colored, taunting mass of children, armed with ribbons and banners and flowers and slogans. They are all so *young*, Sandy thought, and remembered how different it had seemed back then, how very different. There were no faces, never any faces, only blurs, images, and emblems. Young blond hair, clean, shimmering, flowing past innumerable trim waists. Faded, worn jeans with flower patches. Headbands. Daisies. Granny glasses, halter tops, paisley shirts, bell-bottoms, armbands, headbands. Yippies and hippies and Mobe people and Clean for Gene. Holding hands. Singing. Chanting. Lips moving silently. The front rank was all young women, pretty young women, girls really, and dimly he saw the marshals moving through the crowd, heard them saying, "Chicks up front, get the chicks up front. Keep it calm. Keep it calm." The whole in constant motion, people shoving this way and that, turmoil, stirring, everything blending together, a great melting of shadow forms. Banners waving above it all, red flags and black flags, slogans painted on sheets, the peace symbol and the Viet Cong flag, everywhere banners shifting and swaying and snapping when the wind came sighing off the lake. Everyone swaying, girls and guys and banners all together, hands joined, arms linked, swaying, lips moving.

And there, against them, the others; a line, a rank, stiff and straight and martial. Against that stirring, moving, living mass, no motion at all. Blue uniforms. Helmets. Dark faces, faceless faces, legs braced, badges, dark oily guns snug in black leather holsters riding beefy hips. Faces like masks. Waiting. Clubs and violence and hatred barely held in check.

Peace and love and law and order, ghosts, phantoms, dead now, gone, yet now they stirred again, somehow, somehow. Sandy could see them, could see the tension building, could see everything but the faces, the faces were somehow twisted, blurred.

He moved between them, stumbling almost, into the middle of the street, turning around and around, remembering the way it had been. *He* was in that ragtag army, he knew, wearing a marshal's armband, trying to keep order. And Maggie was in there too, up front somewhere, shouting things, chanting, her nose still straight, unbroken. And the others, all the others.

Sandy moved toward the still army, the blue army, the army that waited silently, its rage held in check. Faceless shadows in dark uniforms, eyeless, mouthless, the sticks and the guns somehow more vivid than anything else about them. He stood in front of them. "No," he said, and the whole rank turned their heads slightly to stare at him, and he felt the weight of all those eyeless blank inhuman stares. "No," he said again. "Don't do it, you can't do it. Don't you understand? This is where it changed. Peace, that's all they want, that's all. McCarthy. They're kids, that's all. Working within the system. They want the convention to listen. That's why they are here. They still believe, really they do, don't mind the flags, the Cong flags, all that shit, that's not where it's at. Listen to me, I'm in there, I remember, I know how it was. We worked so hard, and we won, the peace candidates, Gene and Bobby, they won all the primaries, every damn fucking one, and they still don't listen. Don't you see? When you charge them, when you start hitting, it changes, it all changes. You harden them. They stop believing. It all gets worse and worse. This is the last chance, the last moment before it all changes. Let them pass! Dear God, *let them pass!*" But the shadows had looked away from him now, the shadows no longer listened. Sandy found that he was crying. He held up his hands in front of him, as if he could somehow restrain the charge to come, repress the violence that he could feel building and gathering all around him. "They're *not* your fucking enemy!" he screamed, at the top of his lungs. "We're your *children*, you assholes, we're only your goddamned children!"

But it was too late, too late, suddenly he heard the whistles and the sound of running feet, and a flying wedge of blue shadows came racing down Balbo and smashed into the stirring, chanting army of the young, and it shattered and broke, and then the other lines were moving forward, and way behind, flanking, the masked faceless shadows of the Guard spread in a great enveloping pincer, pinching them in, gathering them together, pressing, and it all disintegrated into chaos, knots of phantoms struggling together, running, faint screams adrift on the wind from the past. Briefly came a moment of calm, the forces pulling back, and Sandy heard the marshals again, shouting, talking to their squawk boxes. "People are getting hurt," they were yelling, and yelling too about the medical center, and kids in white medical armbands were kneeling over the victims, all bloody and battered. Some of the banners had fallen, and lots of faces were red now, red with blood, red with fury, red with a rage that would build for years. "Keep it cool," the marshals were saying, and Sandy saw himself, so god-damned achingly young, wearing a jacket even, all Clean for Gene, dark hair messed now but once carefully combed, so bewildered, it wasn't sup-posed to be like this, the belief was already going, the faith that elections meant something, the anger was coming instead. "Keep it cool," he called, such a young voice, like all the other marshals'. "Lots of people are hurt, keep it cool," and more, but then the words were drowned out, swallowed up. He heard the chant again, echoing down all the years. Ghost voices, hundreds and thousands of ghost voices, joined together in a great cry. "The Whole World Is Watching, the Whole World Is Watching, the Whole World Is Watching, the Whole World Is Watching, the Whole World Is Watching." Over and over and over and over, louder and louder and louder and louder.

And then the small truce shattered and splintered, like a mirror hit by a bullet, the mirror that captured the face of a generation, so when it splintered that face became distorted, fractured, never whole again. The blue shadows came racing forward, and in the wind of their wild charge the candle of sanity was blown out for years. The clubs were lifted and came cracking down, and battle was joined. They hit everyone, anyone, those who were chanting and those who were silent, those who taunted and those who begged, those who hit back and those who ran and those who cringed away. They clubbed the kids and the old ladies and the oper-atives in business suits, the marshals and the medical staff, the injured in the streets and the crazies spitting, the ones with press passes held up as futile shields, the ones behind the cameras, the cameras themselves, the men and the women and the boys and the girls, if it moved they hit it, and the world disintegrated into screams and rushing feet and fists and the crack of nightsticks and the crunch of shattering bones. In the center of the intersection, Sandy stood with his hands at his sides, watching it hap-pen again, his hands curling into helpless fists. The ghosts rushed all around him, and one plunged right through him, and he had the awful sick feeling that it was he who was the phantom. He saw his younger self shouting into a walkie-talkie, saw it knocked from his hands, saw the nightstick descend, saw himself run, ducking, weaving. Maggie staggered past, pale blood trickling from her broken nose, her blouse ripped, grin-ning and holding aloft a nightstick that she'd snatched somehow. They surrounded her and took it away, and Sandy watched the clubs swing, and she vanished. The whole world was watching, he thought. He looked up, and in the lighted windows above the street he thought he could see faces, rank on rank of faces, looked down on the carnage swirling and shrieking through the streets of that toddling town below. And above the buildings were the stars, a million million stars. Sandy stared at them, and as he did each star became an eye. The sky was full of slitted yellow eyes, cold and malevolent eyes, eyes drinking in the riot in the night. More than the whole world was watching.

"No!" Sandy screamed. He cringed away, covered himself with his arms, shaking.

How long he stood like that he could not say. But finally the fear passed. He lowered his arms reluctantly. The stars were only stars. He could see Orion. The night was cold, the wind was blowing, and the streets of Chicago were empty.

Of course they were empty, he thought. They had been empty all along. Years had passed, and all the things he had seen were gone, dead, scattered, half-forgotten.

Wearily, he walked back to the Hilton, alone, hands deep in his pockets.

He took the room key from the desk clerk. They had moved him to the seventeenth floor. The room was virtually identical to the one he had fled, yet somehow it did not feel the same. Sandy found he could not sleep. He pulled up the shade on his window and sat looking out over the lake, until dawn first started to lighten the eastern sky. Then, suddenly, he was very tired. He undressed and went to bed.

He had forgotten to leave a wake-up call. When he finally awoke, it was almost three in the afternoon, and the events of the night before seemed like a bad dream. Sandy was sure it had been nothing but one long nightmare until he yanked open the room door and stared at the room numbers. He was on the seventeenth floor. He closed the door again and leaned back against it, frowning. He had been pushing himself much too hard, he decided; too little sleep, too many miles.

An ice-cold shower washed away the blurred memories of the night before, and Sandy emerged determined to put his personal ghosts behind him and get on with the business at hand. He slipped into a clean pair of jeans and a thick sweater, and looked up the address of Lark Ellyn's agency in the yellow pages. It was a quarter to four when he left the Conrad Hilton. The agency was up on Michigan Avenue. Rather than worry about parking, Sandy took a cab.

Ellyn's office was on the top floor. The reception area had thick carpeting, comfortable chairs, and a pretty dark-haired woman behind a big walnut desk.

She looked as though she'd been born for an environment like this; Sandy couldn't imagine her in any other setting. "Mr. Ellyn, please," he said to her.

"Do you have an appointment?"

"Nope," Sandy replied. "He'll see me, though. I'm an old friend." That was maybe stretching it a bit, but still . . . "Tell him it's Sandy Blair."

"If you'll kindly have a seat."

Lark Ellyn emerged from the agency's inner labyrinth a few minutes later. He was very different, and very much the same. Instead of jeans, tee shirt, and vest, he wore a three-piece brown suit and a striped tie. The head-band was gone, the mustache was gone, and the hair he'd once tried to wear in a white boy's imitation Afro was now razor-cut and blow-dried. Yet the man inside the new uniform was unchanged. Short, trim, with an an-gular face, a pinched nose, healthy chestnut hair and thin eyebrows. His walk was the same too, and from the instant he entered the room he pro-jected a self-conscious intensity that Sandy remembered very well.

When he spied Sandy, he put his hands on his hips and smiled. Lark Ellyn's smile had a faintly mocking edge to it. It was a sharp, superior sort of smile, and he'd always used it just before he said something critical or cut-ting. Sometimes he just smiled and said nothing at all, but the effect was the same. The smile was supposed to let you know that the criticism was all in fun, that Lark didn't really mean it. Well, he did and he didn't; Sandy had figured that out a long time ago. Facing that smile now, Sandy remem-bered how and why it was that he and Ellyn had never gotten along.

"Blair," Ellyn said. "This must be my lucky day." He looked Sandy up and down. "Putting on a little weight, I see. You look like hell."

"It's good to see you too," Sandy said, rising.

Ellyn crossed his arms against his chest. "Can I do something for you?"

"Not particularly," Sandy said. "I was in town working on a story, and I thought I'd look you up. Maggie suggested it."

"Maggie Sloane?"

"No, Maggie Thatcher," Sandy snapped. "Of course Maggie Sloane. Hell, Lark—"

"Steve," Ellyn corrected quickly. "Look, I'm almost done for the day. Why don't you have a seat and wait a few minutes while I wrap things up, and then we can go out for a drink."

"Fine," Sandy agreed. He settled back into his seat and picked up a magazine.

By the time Lark Ellyn reemerged, Sandy had read all the interesting ar-ticles and several that weren't. "Sorry to keep you," Ellyn said when he reemerged, leather briefcase in hand. "Something came up that couldn't wait. I'm on a big account at the moment. Billing a cool million and a half. Have to keep the clients happy." He led Sandy toward the elevators. "So you're working on a story, you say? Still a yellow journalist, then?"

"Actually, I'm a yellow novelist now," Sandy said as Ellyn punched the button. "I've published three books."

The elevator doors opened. "Hey, real good," Ellyn said as they entered. "I'm afraid I haven't seen them. They keep me pretty busy around here, and I don't have time to keep up with pop literature. You know how it is."

"Hell yes," Sandy said. "It's a thankless task anyway, keeping up with pop literature. You're lucky you're out of it."

Ellyn raised a thin dark eyebrow and smiled. "Same old Sandy."

Sandy grinned right back at him. "Same old Lark."

That put a damper on the Ellyn smile. "All right, Sander, cut it out with the Lark stuff. It's Steve now, unless you'd prefer Mr. Ellyn."

"Not me, boss," Sandy said.

"I took enough ribbing about my name when I was a kid. I don't want any more. I have a position to maintain around here. Everyone thinks my first name is Lawrence. My friends call me Steve. You understand, Blair?"

"No Lark?"

The smile returned. "You got it." They arrived at the lobby. "Now that we've got that unpleasantness out of the way, what say we go on over to Rush Street and get ourselves a drink. There's a place called Archibald's that gives you two-for-one during happy hour."

"You want to go to a Rush Street bar?" Sandy said in a bemused tone. "Everyone knows the Rush Street bars are full of stewardesses, secretaries, and middle-aged account executives in three-piece suits."

"Too classy for you, Blair?" Ellyn said.

"Lead on," Sandy said.

The bar was sandwiched in between two other bars, all of them crowded. It was a narrow place, full of ferns and people who seemed to know one another. Ellyn called the bartender by name and waved to three women at a table in the back. He and Sandy found stools up by the window that looked out on the street. Sandy ordered a beer; L. Stephen Ellyn ordered a gin and tonic. They each got two. "This round is on me," Ellyn said.

"If you want a fight, you're looking at the wrong guy," Sandy said. He took a sip of beer from his stein.

Ellyn removed his tie and stuffed it in his pocket, then undid the collar button on his shirt. His eyes had the same intensity that Sandy remembered from a long time ago. "It has been a long time, Blair."

"About a decade."

Ellyn nodded, smiling. "Can't say I've missed you much."

Sandy grinned.

"Now," said Ellyn, "this is the part where I'm supposed to tell you all about my life, and you're supposed to tell me all about yours. Then after we are both suitably bored, we order a few more rounds of drinks and get into the part about the good old days and all the crazy things we did. I tell you the news about the people I've kept in touch with that you barely remember, and you return the favor. We get thoroughly sloshed and walk home arm in arm, and as we part we promise each other fervently that this time we will keep in touch. We don't, of course. Maybe I send you a Christmas card. You, being a hippie, don't believe in Christmas cards, so you don't reciprocate. You get crossed off my list and we never see each other again. One of us reads an obit for the other in the alumni newspaper a few years down the line." He smiled. "That's the script, right?"

"Doesn't sound like you like your part much," Sandy observed.

Ellyn smiled his mocking smile and took a healthy swallow from his gin and tonic. "Sentiment bores me. So call me a cynic."

"You're a cynic," Sandy said agreeably.

"I see your wit's just as sharp as it was when we were both sophomores at Northwestern," Ellyn said. "I hope you'll spare me the accompanying wisdom."

"Wisdom?"

Ellyn made a sharp, impatient gesture with his left hand. "You know, Blair. The friendly concern over what has become of me. The patronizing put-downs of my lifestyle. The glib little digs about selling out. The jokes about gray flannel suits. The appeals to my youthful idealism. All delivered with an air of condescending wonderment about the way I've changed and punctuated by repeated fervent assertions that you can't *believe* I work in an ad agency, that you can't *believe* I live in Wilmette, that you can't *believe* I own stock and real estate and wear a suit and drink in Rush Street singles bars, you just can't *believe* it, not me, not Lark, not Mister Radical of 1968." He raised one sardonic eyebrow. "You see, Blair, I know it all already, so let's both save some time and not go through it again."

"Do I detect a faint note of defensiveness in the air?"

"Wrong," Ellyn snapped. "I'm not the least defensive about the choices I've made. I'm just bored by all this, Blair. I've gone through the whole waltz with your friend Maggie, and she wasn't the first. It's an old tired song. Golden oldies were never my style. So skip it, even though it pains you. I know that was why you came."

"So *that's* why I came," Sandy said. "I was wondering."

"Only because you didn't think things through. You never did. You saw Maggie, right? And she talked about me. So all of a sudden you show up on my doorstep, looking like some refugee from a peace demonstration. For the first time in ten years, you want to see me. Why else? Because you wanted to smirk, Blair. Because you wanted to feel superior, in your own juvenile bubbleheaded way. We were never that close. It wasn't friendship that sent you my way, pal. Not only are you an airhead, you're a transparent airhead." He sat back and swirled his gin and tonic lazily, smiling at his big finish. "Well?"

Sandy finished his first stein, picked up his second, and lifted it to Ellyn in salute. "You're good," he said.

"What?" said Ellyn. "No heartfelt denials?"

"Nah," Sandy said, considering it carefully. "There's a little bit of truth in what you say. Hadn't even realized it myself, but you're right. I always knew you were a jackass, but you used to disguise yourself well. I was sort of looking forward to seeing you in full jackass regalia."

Ellyn grinned in victory.

"I guess I thought you'd be abashed," Sandy continued. "By all rights, you ought to be. You're a walking cliché, La—Steve. The purebred counterculture sellout. An ad agency! Really, how trite can you get? You know, I half expected that you'd try to cop a plea that you'd gone underground to help the revolution."

"I do help the revolution, I *do*," Ellyn said with his sly smile. "Just last year I handled a revolutionary new underarm deodorant."

"You're even stealing my lines," Sandy said with rueful admiration. "You've got it all down pat, don't you? Blast 'em out of the water before they even get the tarps off their guns."

"You sound a little shaky, Blair. Want another drink?"

"No," Sandy said. He slumped back in his seat, and regarded Ellyn dourly while he signaled for another round. Sandy suddenly felt very tired. "Put away the knives, Lark. I'm not up to it today. I had a rough night. Just enlighten me, OK? What happened? How did Lark become L. Stephen? I'm curious."

The drinks arrived. Ellyn lifted his third gin and tonic, sipped, smiled, sipped, set it down. "A simple process, Blair. The same process that changes Billies into Williams and Bobbies into Roberts. I grew up. It's called maturity."

"Maturity," Sandy echoed tonelessly. It was one of Sharon's favorite words when things got nasty in their brownstone. He hated that word.

"I was the original peace-and-freedom kid," Ellyn said, "but that lifestyle got old awful fast after college. Face it, Blair, living hand-to-mouth may be fine and romantic at twenty, but it's boring at twenty-five, depressing at thirty, and downright grotesque at forty. You get hungry for all those middle-class comforts you put down when you were a stupid kid. The Sixties were a joke. We were wrong all along. We were spoiled children mouthing off, and we didn't know a damn thing about the world or how it worked. The *revolution*! Come *on*! What a frigging *laugh*! There was never going to be no revolution."

"I can't argue with that," Sandy said. "You were the revolutionary, Lark. I was the one who went Clean for Gene, who worked for peace candidates. Within the system, remember? Not you, though. You said that was a waste of time. In fact, you said it helped perpetuate bourgeois oppression, because it created the illusion that the system worked. The whole thing had to come down, you said, and the faster the better. Elect fascists, that's what you suggested."

"So I was an immature asshole," Ellyn said.

"And now you're a mature asshole," Sandy snapped.

"At least I've changed."

"You know," Sandy said, "that's the funny thing. You *haven't* changed. Not really. *I've* changed, whether you realize it or not. Maggie has changed. I think I'm going to look up Bambi and Slum and Froggy, and when I do, I bet they'll have changed. But not you."

"Something wrong with your eyes, Blair," Ellyn said. He smiled and tugged on the lapel of his expensive suit.

"That's surface and you know it. Inside, you haven't changed a bit. When it was chic to be radical, you were more radical than anybody else. Though, come to think of it, you never really put yourself on the line, did you? No arrests on old L. Stephen's record, huh? Now, of course, it's chic to be successful, and you're more successful than anybody else. Me especially, right?"

"You said it, Blair. I didn't. It's a competitive world out there. I'm a winner. You're a loser."

That was the final straw; now Sandy was definitely pissed. "It was always a competition with you, Lark. Even when we were all firmly against competitiveness, you made certain you were *more* against it than the rest of us. You're a fraud, Lark, but there's no change there, so don't give me this bull about maturity. You were *always* a fraud."

"I'm a fraud who pulls down a nice six-figure salary, lives in an expensive house, and drives a big car," said Ellyn.

"I have a Mazda RX-7. Want to drag, bozo?"

Ellyn laughed. "Oh, that's perfect," he said. "Talk about juvenile competitiveness!"

"It's the same song you been singing all along," Sandy said. "I'm just not trying to be all wry and sophisticated and subtle about it."

"Sandy, you know that buying a sports car is a terribly trite way of reasserting your masculinity in the face of your waning sexuality. What color is this overpowered phallus of yours?"

"Fuck off," Sandy said. "Your little act isn't even consistent. That crack was pure Lark. L. Stephen ought to have a sports car of his own. A Maserati at the least. You know, in the old days I never quite understood the chip on your shoulder, why you were always putting me down. But I'm mature enough to see through you real easily now."

"Go on. This is fascinating."

"Envy," Sandy said.

"Me?" Ellyn laughed. "Envious of *you*?"

"Envy and insecurity," Sandy said. "I beat your time with Maggie, was that it? Or was there something else? Or was it just that you felt so small inside that you had to cut everybody else down to size? And your name was part of it, right? All those years growing up, and every kid you met made fun of you when you introduced yourself, so you learned to attack first, so you wouldn't have to defend. Keep them all off balance, right?"

"You're beautiful when you're angry," Ellyn said dryly. "Don't stop. I love parlor psychoanalysis. You've got quite an imagination. You ought to try your hand at writing."

Sandy knocked off the last inch of beer in the bottom of his stein and stood up. "I have," he said. "In fact, I wrote you into *Kasey's Quest*. I had the police beat you to death."

Ellyn looked confused. "Huh? The girl was the only one got..." He realized what he was saying and stopped.

"Sarah was the character's name," Sandy said. "Why, I thought you didn't have the time to keep up with pop literature?"

The famous Ellyn smile curdled faster than milk left out in the desert sun, and a dark flush crept up his neck. Sitting there in his three-piece suit, drink in hand, he suddenly looked pathetic. "You have no right to judge me, Blair," he said coldly.

"No need to," said Sandy. "You're too busy judging yourself. Only you better realize that swapping Mao's little red book for *Dress for Success* won't make you a better person." It was a good exit line. Sandy exited.

Rush Street was crowded with happy-hour drunks. All the smart young women and the sharp young men, aging rapidly. Sandy shoved his hands into his pockets and walked back to his hotel, feeling tired and drained. The ghosts he'd seen in the streets last night were not the only ones doomed to fighting ancient battles over and over and over.

EIGHT

Who'll take the promise that you don't have to keep?/
Don't look now, it ain't you or me

Sandy found a pink telephone message slip waiting for him back at the hotel. He looked at it numbly. Jared Patterson had phoned. The report on Edan Morse, no doubt. Maybe something big had turned up if Jared called instead of using Express Mail. But Sandy wasn't up to it right then. He crumpled the slip in his hand and dropped it into one of the lobby ashtrays.

Up in his room, he kicked off his shoes, turned on the TV set, and phoned down to room service for dinner. It was overpriced, but Jared was paying. He tipped the bellhop handsomely and settled in to watch a rerun of *Happy Days* while wolfing down chicken cordon bleu. Richie and Potsie were having lots of problems, but the Fonz had resolved everything neatly by the end of the half-hour. Sandy found himself wishing he knew the Fonz. Of course, he had known kids like the Fonz back in the Fifties, but most of them would rather beat the crap out of you than solve your problems.

He was drinking coffee when the news came on. Sandy sat up and took notice. "In our lead story tonight, Maine sheriff's police announced an arrest in the bizarre murder of former rock promoter Jamie Lynch," the blond, vapid anchorwoman said. Sandy stared at the picture behind her well-tailored shoulder. A big, dark-haired man in a red-and-green plaid jacket was being propelled toward the camera, and a waiting police car, by

two deputies. One of them was unmistakably David ("Call me Davie")
Parker. Then the scene shifted, and Sheriff Notch Theodore was hustling
the same big guy into jail, surrounded by the usual gaggle of press people.
The anchorwoman droned on for a minute, and then blithely switched to a
story about a pregnant panda, leaving Sandy ignorant and royally annoyed
at TV news. He switched off the set, found Parker's home number in a corner of his wallet, and called.

It rang six times before Parker picked it up. "Yeah?" he said.

"Just saw this weird show on the tube," Sandy said. "At first I thought it
was a *McCloud* rerun. Then I said, no, that's Davie Parker. What the hell is
this shit? Who was that guy?"

"Figured you'd be calling, Blair," the deputy said amiably. "That guy, as
you put it, is one Paul Lebeque. We just arrested him for the Lynch murder. He's a Canuck migrant worker. French-Canadian, you know. Seasonal
farm laborer. We get 'em up here, too. Snowbacks."

"I don't care how he makes his living. How's he connect with Jamie?"

"Lynch connected with Lebeque's sister rather than the man himself, if
you get my meaning."

Sandy frowned. "A girlfriend?"

"More like a one-night stand. An old story. She was a cute kid, eighteen
or so. Lynch met her somehow, got her to one of his parties, gave her some
nice coke, took her to bed, and forgot about her. She had to have an abor-
tion. Her brother found out. For the past few weeks he's been mouthing off
in bars on both sides of the border about what he did to that heartless bastard who screwed and abandoned his kid sister. Get it—*heartless* bastard."

"I get it," Sandy said. "I don't believe it, but I get it. A fucking *migrant*
worker? Defending his sister's rep? Come *on*, Parker. Do you buy that?"

"Notch is the one who bought it. He's sheriff, remember? I'm only a
deputy."

"What about those trick questions of yours? The album on the stereo,
the poster? Did this Lebeque guy know the answers?"

"Lebeque said the record was already playing when he arrived. He
didn't even notice what it was. He just turned it up loud so that nobody
would hear Jamie screaming. As for the poster, he says that he didn't take it
down at all. Lynch had removed it, for some reason. It was already there on
top of the desk."

"So why the ropes?" Sandy demanded. "Why the whole ritual sacrifice
thing?"

"Lebeque says he wanted Lynch to know what was happening to him, to
feel good and helpless and scared before he died."

"No," Sandy said. "No, no, *no*! It's a crock and you know it, Parker. What about the date? The fact that it was the anniversary of the West Mesa killing?"

"Coincidence," Parker said.

"What about the fire at Gopher John's place in Jersey?"

"No relation to our case," Parker said.

"I don't believe it," Sandy insisted. "This is ridiculous. You know damn well that the Lynch killing ties in with the Nazgûl somehow."

"We checked that angle. All three of your musicians had alibis. Notch decided it didn't connect."

"Of all the stupid, moronic . . ."

"Ranting and raving won't help, Blair," Parker said. He paused briefly. "Look, if you quote me on this I'll deny it, but the truth is, I think you're right. Lebeque's a hard case, but he's a little nutso, too. I don't think he did it, but he's only too glad to take credit for it. The way Notch threw the questions at him, anybody could have come up with plausible answers on the record and the poster. Notch doesn't want to be sheriff all his life. He'd like to run for statewide office. Solving this case so quickly is going to get him a lot of attention."

"But this guy is *innocent*!"

"You don't know that," Parker said reasonably. "You suspect. So do I. But there's nothing we can do about it. Notch is satisfied, we've got Lebeque in jail, and we're shutting down the investigation."

"Son of a bitch," Sandy said furiously. "Well, you clowns can do whatever you like, but I'm going ahead as planned. And when I shake loose the real killer, you're going to have egg all over your face."

"You have something?" Parker asked.

"Well," said Sandy, "not really. Not much, anyway. But I've got a hunch. All my instincts . . ."

"Notch isn't much impressed by instincts."

"I have a name," Sandy said.

"Go on."

"Why should I? What's the point? You've got Lebeque behind bars, you've got a motive, you've got a confession. Why should you care?"

"I shouldn't," said Parker, "but I do. Notch ain't going to like it, but I'm still willing to work with you on this."

Sandy hesitated. If Parker was straight, he might be useful. He decided to go ahead. "All right," he said, "it isn't much, but it is worth checking out. Edan Morse."

Parker repeated the name. "Who is it?" he asked.

"A promoter, or would-be promoter," Sandy said. "He wanted to get the Nazgûl back together. Lynch stood in the way. More than that I can't tell you. Maggio was real reluctant to talk about him."

"Hmmm," said Parker. "Interesting. The name sounds vaguely familiar. He's probably one of the half-million guys with letters in Lynch's files. I'll check it out and get back to you."

"You do that," Sandy said. He hung up, still feeling stung. No getting around it; he was going to have to talk to Jared, too. Might as well get it over with. He dialed.

Jared sounded almost jovial. "I guess you heard the news?"

"Yeah. So where's that report on Morse I asked for?"

"Oh, that. Never mind that. I had a couple of girls on that this morning, but they drew a blank. Nothing in the morgue, and our music editor has never heard of the dude."

"I don't suppose it occurred to you to have your reporters call around, huh?"

"Call? Who were we supposed to call?"

"Oh, promoters, agents, rock singers, record company execs, say. For a start."

"Hey, *Hedgehog* is the Bible of rock music, Sandy. If we ain't heard of him, nobody has. Besides, I told them to drop it when I heard about the arrest. What's the point?"

"The point is, those morons have got the wrong guy. Lebeque didn't do it."

Jared perked up a bit at that. "No? Hey, that's great! If you can prove that, the *Hog*'ll really have something."

"I can't prove it. Yet."

"Well, what d'ya have then?"

"Suspicions," said Sandy. "Instincts. Trust me."

"*Trust* you?" Jared was aghast. "Hey, look, we can't go out on that kind of limb just on your hunch."

"The *Hog* became famous by going out on limbs."

"That was in the old days. We're respectable now. We call 'em *police* instead of *pigs*. We listen to 'em. They say they got the guy killed Jamie Lynch, and I'm inclined to believe 'em. Sandy, I know how hard you worked on this, and it breaks my heart how it turned out, but you got to face facts. Your Nazgûl angle is deader'n Elvis. Give it up. The way I see it, if you hustle your ass back to Maine, maybe you can get an interview or something, and we can still salvage a story. I'd like it by Tuesday, for next week's edition, but I'm even willing to give you an extra week if you need it. How's that for nice?"

"Blow it out your ear, Jared. I'm not going to Maine. I'm going to New Mexico to talk to Peter Faxon. And I'm going to do this story the way we agreed."

"No, Sandy," Jared said. A hint of coldness had crept into his voice. "We have a reputation to protect."

"Jared, this is the kind of story that *made* us! So the cops have arrested the wrong guy! It makes it even better for us. A migrant worker at that. Minority oppression, right? We do an exposé, it rips the lid off everything. We've done it before."

"If you had anything concrete, sure, sounds good. But you don't. Hey, I'm all for big, juicy stories, but all you can say is 'Trust me.' I'm not going to lay out all the money you want for some nostalgia piece on an old rock band. Without the Lynch connection, it's garbage. So if you want to collect a check, you better hightail it back to Maine."

"I'm doing this the way I intended," Sandy said, "the way we discussed."

"Hey, great," said Jared. "Good luck selling it somewhere."

"I sold it to *Hedgehog*."

Jared laughed. "Better think again."

"We have a contract," Sandy said stiffly.

"I'm breaching it," Jared snapped. "So sue me. You'll get your five hundred bucks eventually. It'll only cost you ten times that much in legal fees." He laughed again, a braying, snorting sort of laughter that drove Sandy right up the wall. Then he hung up.

Sandy sat listening to the dial tone. "I don't believe it," he said to himself loudly. "I don't fucking *believe* it!" He slammed the receiver back into its cradle angrily and sat on the edge of the bed, helpless, his fists clenched. He thought of calling Sharon. Then he thought better of it. Sharon would just tell him to come home and get back to work on his novel. What the hell was the use? Maybe he ought to go home. The cops claimed to have Lynch's killer in hand, and his assignment had been yanked out from under him. Maybe it was time to toss in the towel. This whole thing had been a mistake from the start. Sharon was mad at him, Alan was mad at him, and nothing good had come out of his poking around, except maybe for his bittersweet reunion with Maggie. What was he trying to prove?

He had a life waiting for him back in Brooklyn. Maybe it was time he settled down and lived it. He had to finish page thirty-seven and then go on to page thirty-eight. That was the rational, sensible, mature thing to do.

Thinking of it made Sandy want to puke. The novel was going to be a disaster and he knew it; that was why it had become too difficult to face. He had no stomach for maturity. He'd seen too much of it this trip. Maggie, worn down and trapped in dead-end jobs, lonely, starting to get desperate. Lark, pumping down the gin and tonics, working hard to convince himself that he was wonderfully happy. Gopher John, ashen as he looked at the fire, radiant when he talked about the old days, about what it had been like to play with the Nazgûl. Rick Maggio, ragin'. The ravages of time. That was his story; that was more important than his novel. Jared didn't want to buy it, and Alan didn't want to sell it, and Sharon didn't want to hear about it, but Sandy knew it was the story he had to tell. It was *his* story too, in a way.

Sandy knew it was crazy. He didn't even have a paper behind him now. He'd be working entirely on spec. Still, that might be for the best. Maybe he'd be able to sell it elsewhere. There were better markets than the *Hog*. He could try for *Playboy* or *Penthouse*. He could even show the piece to *Rolling Stone*. That would *really* get Jared's back up. Maybe they wouldn't take it, though. Maybe he'd have to give it away to some low-rent rag somewhere. But it didn't matter. He had to finish it anyway. The story had begun as something interesting, something that might be fun. It hadn't been fun, not at all. It would probably be even less fun as it went along. But he knew he had to see it through. Lynch might have been a first-class shit, but he was owed that much. Not to mention the people who died in the Gopher Hole fire, and even this Paul Lebeque. The clown was set up to take a fall for a murder he didn't commit, and nobody cared. Not the cops, not the *Hog*, not even the guy himself. So it was up to him, then.

He could almost hear Sharon's derision. "How Sixties," she'd say. "The valiant underdog fighting alone for justice," she'd say. "You read too many issues of *Spider-Man* as a kid," she'd say. "I don't suppose it's ever occurred to you that maybe you're *wrong*," she'd say. "Hell, no. Not Sandy Blair, boy crusader, on the side of the angels. You're *never* wrong. Your hat is as white as driven snow, right?" He'd heard it all before. He couldn't argue with her. But he didn't care.

Sandy took out his notebook. After the notes on Slozewski and Maggio, he'd written "Faxon" on a blank page, and underlined it. Now, beneath it, he added "Edan Morse," with a question mark after the name. He chewed on the end of his Flair for a second, then, impulsively, added three more names. He'd seen Maggie and Lark, after all. He might as well hunt up Slum and Bambi and Froggy, make a clean sweep of it. They were all a piece of this, too. Maggie had provided him with an address for Bambi Lassiter; the alumni office could lead him to the others.

Satisfied, he tucked the notebook away, got up, and methodically started to pack. All of a sudden his weariness had evaporated. All of a sudden he was restless, and anxious to hit the road again. Tank up with coffee and drive all night, he thought, tossing clothes into his suitcase.

Before he left, he glanced in the mirror. He needed a shave. Badly. He rubbed the stubble under his chin. And grinned. What the hell, he thought. It would be interesting to see how he looked in a beard again, after all these years.

NINE

It was twenty years ago today/
Sgt. Pepper taught the band to play

The phone was only inches from his pillow. When it rang, it screamed, a merciless trilling loudness. Sandy shuddered out of sleep and lurched for it, and succeeded only in knocking the receiver to the floor. He pulled it up by the cord. "Yeah?" he said.

"Four-thirty, sir. Your wake-up call."

Sandy muttered something unintelligible and hung up. He sat up unsteadily, cradling his head in his hands. Four-thirty, he thought. Faxon was insane. The motel room was black and chilly. Sandy wanted nothing so much as to curl up under those warm blankets once again. Instead he pushed himself to his feet and headed for the shower.

It was a short shower; he couldn't get any hot water. The cold helped a little. When he'd dried himself and emerged, he was almost half awake. The coffee shop wouldn't open for hours, but fortunately the Albuquerque motel had a few amenities, even if hot water was not among them. He made himself a cup of instant coffee on the plug-in unit above the sink and stirred in the powdered creamer that had so thoughtfully been provided. He sipped the coffee slowly. By the time he'd finished, it was ice cold. Even hot, it was a strong candidate for the worst coffee he'd ever had in his life. But the caffeine restored him to some semblance of humanity.

The knock came as he was buckling on his jeans. "One sec," Sandy called out. He yanked a shirt over his head quickly and tucked in the ends while opening the door. Peter Faxon was leaning casually against the door frame. "Be with you in a minute," Sandy told him. "I just have to get some shoes and socks on. I'm not usually functioning at this hour. Normally I rise at the crack of noon."

"No rush," Faxon said. He stepped into the room to wait. The years scarcely seemed to have touched him. His hair was still long, though the blond braids had given way to a kind of Prince Valiant shag that framed his long cool face. Sun-bleached and golden and straight, Faxon's hair seemed even finer and paler than Sandy remembered. His bangs came to just above his startling green eyes. He had tiny lines around the corners of those eyes now, from squinting into the sun too much, and the deep, dark, layered tan of a man who has spent a lot of time outdoors. He looked trim and fit in a blue chambray work shirt, old patched jeans, and crooked denim cap. A big turquoise-and-silver buckle adorned his intricate, handmade belt. With his blond, All-American good looks, Faxon seemed like the sort who'd be more at home singing surf rock or cowboy ballads than the hard-driving rock of the Nazgûl. He fooled people that way. Faxon had never quite seemed to belong with the others, but the truth of it was that he had been the group's creative brains: a consummate musician and a brilliant songwriter.

Sandy pulled on his boots, rose, and offered his hand. "Thanks for seeing me, anyway," he said. "I didn't expect you to come down to Albuquerque for me. Just hope I'm coherent enough to ask some decent questions. Like, for starts, where are we going, and why?"

Faxon smiled. "We're going up on the West Mesa," he said. "Come on, we're running late."

The parking lot was eerily still in the vague predawn light. A faint chill was in the air, and the barest breath of wind. Faxon walked around to the driver's side of a big red-and-white Blazer. Sandy climbed in next to him, uneasily. "The West Mesa?" he said, as Faxon flicked on the headlights and backed out.

"Don't worry," Faxon replied, "the guy with the gun is long gone."

The streets of Albuquerque were almost deserted at this time of the morning. There was a battered Ford pick-up about a block behind them that Sandy noticed when he turned to see dawn starting to break over the Sandias to the north and east, and once they glimpsed another car at an intersection, but that was it. Everything was empty, hushed, yet somehow very alive as well. As dawn broke, the street lamps and headlights seemed to fade. It was a strange, intoxicating hour.

They were headed west, out of the city. After a while, they began to climb; houses became few and far between. The street lamps went out. Faxon turned and turned again, on to roads that became progressively smaller. Sandy looked back and saw the same pick-up behind them. As he watched, its headlights went out. "You're being followed," he said.

"I know," Faxon said, smiling. "My family."

Sandy was confused, though a bit relieved. "What's going on?"

"You'll see."

They were up on the West Mesa itself now. The land was flat and dry and dusty. Dirt roads ran through wide, desolate fields, shorn and empty, and between barbed-wire fences. Vegetation was scarce; some pinyon, a few juniper, stubby little cacti. Dry brown tumbleweeds blew across the road. Faxon ran them over nonchalantly. The Blazer kicked up a cloud of dust as it went, obscuring the pick-up behind them. Sandy looked out the window, remembering. This was where it had happened. Somewhere in this desolation, a sniper had lined up Patrick Henry Hobbins in his crosshairs, and it had all come to an end. Here: this was where the music had died, where the dream had turned into nightmare. But none of it looked familiar. The landmarks had been the trailers and the stage, set amid a sea of sixty thousand people. All gone. All that remained was untouched high desert emptiness, with no way to tell where anything had been.

Faxon made a sharp right where two dirt roads met, and ahead of them Sandy saw that the shoulder was lined by about a dozen cars and trucks. In the field to their left, something big was stirring, rising. For a brief, surreal moment, it looked as though the ground itself was heaving up in some vast wave, about to spit forth the mother of all gophers. Then it became clear. It was a balloon. A big blue-and-white balloon with a checkerboard pattern, lying on its side on the ground, filling and fluttering as he watched.

Faxon pulled off the road and parked behind another four-wheel drive. The Ford pick-up slid in behind him. Sandy was watching the balloon. Its gas burner was roaring, and a cluster of people were gathered around it, holding the bag. They didn't hold it long. All at once the bag, nearly full now, lurched up and righted itself, shaking most of them off. Two men climbed into the basket, and the others let go. Slowly, with infinite languorous grace, the balloon ascended into the morning sky, drifting off until it was only a small blue dot in the distance. It was gorgeous.

Faxon brought his family over and introduced them. His wife, Tracy, was tall and slender and tanned a deep brown. Straight brown hair fell to the top of the wide concho belt that held up her jeans. Her hand was small and cool when she took Sandy's. "I've enjoyed your books," she said. The little boy, Christopher, looked about six or seven, though Sandy was a poor judge of children's ages. He had a mop of light brown hair and a lot of rambunctious energy. He stood still barely long enough to nod curtly to Sandy; then he was running off across the field to help with a second balloon, a big patchwork-quilt patterned balloon that had just started to inflate. The older child was a girl, Aurora, about thirteen, gangly and as blond as Faxon himself. She wore a *Star Wars* tee shirt, a denim jacket, and the look of benign indifference that all adolescents seem to reserve for adults who intrude on their little world.

When all the introductions were done, Faxon clapped Sandy on the shoulder and said, "And now we put you to work."

"Work?"

"Why do you think I brought you? C'mon. Give a hand with the Flying Eye." He led Sandy to the back of the pick-up. Tracy and Aurora had already started in. There was a big wicker basket, a huge fan, and the balloon itself, the gas bag all folded up, yards and yards of it. It appeared to be mostly red. All of it had to be unloaded and moved across the field to an empty spot that Christopher had already staked out for them. Faxon told Sandy what to do, and they set to work. Others showed up to help. Everybody seemed to know everybody, except for Sandy. They were all very friendly. They talked a lot about the wind. The breeze seemed mild to Sandy, but a couple of the balloonists were talking as if it were a hurricane, and thinking twice about going up.

Peter Faxon did not try to launch immediately. Once the Faxon balloon was spread out on the ground, he squinted into the wind, shrugged, and went off to help some of the others who had arrived earlier. Sandy was drafted, too. The launching procedure seemed to require a big ground crew, and it was all for one and one for all. Sandy soon caught on to the procedure. The balloons were opened on the ground, fold by fold; the basket was laid on its side in position and attached, the propane burner and tanks were locked in place. Then the ground crew grabbed hold of the sides of the bag, clutching tight to the nylon fabric and the ropes, while one or two men opened the mouth of the balloon and revved up one of those big fans and blew some air inside. When the fan was going the fabric would heave and ripple and puff up, and when it had inflated sufficiently, the pilot would kick in the gas burner, which would cough once or twice and then roar and send a long blue-white tongue of flame licking up inside the interior of the balloon, heating the air trapped within. Now Sandy understood the concern about the wind. As the bag inflated, it had a tendency to shift, struggling against his grip almost as if it were a living thing, pulling and then pushing, wiggling around in the wind. The ground crew had to hold it still; if the balloon should lurch too much to the side so that the flame from the burner actually touched the fabric, they'd have a disaster on their hands. Once, as they struggled to get up a big pumpkin-colored balloon with jack o' lantern markings, it seemed for an instant as though just that was going to happen, but everybody dug in their heels and somehow they stopped the movement. The pumpkin suddenly pushed up from the ground and stood on its basket, the flame firing straight up. Two pumpkin-auts clambered aboard, the ground crew let go, and the balloon began its ascent, leaving Sandy with rope burns across his palm and some kind of cactus thorn in his foot. He bent down and pulled it out.

Fortunately, the wind had died considerably by the time it was their turn, and Faxon got his Flying Eye launched almost without incident. "You'll be riding this time," Faxon said to Sandy. "Stay near the burner with me." There was a small bit of trouble when the burner refused to ignite on cue, but Faxon soon got it working, and everything went as before. Except this time, when the balloon popped up, Faxon was standing in the basket, waving to Sandy. "C'mon."

Sandy hesitated, looking up. Faxon's balloon was a livid scarlet. He could see how it had gotten its name. Rendered across the long, pleated vertical panels, twice as big as life, was a familiar eye insignia that Sandy recognized at once. The Eye of Mordor. Sauron's emblem in Tolkien's trilogy.

Everybody was yelling at him. He glanced around and saw that the Flying Eye was moving with the wind, pulling at the people who were try-ing to hold it down, like a big round dog pulling at its leash. "Come *on!*" Faxon was yelling again, waving. Sandy ran to him. Faxon clasped his hand and someone else put a big hand on his ass and shoved, and before he quite knew it, Sandy was in the basket beside Faxon, the ground crew had let go of them, and they were rising. The gas burner was a dull sizzling roar, but the balloon ascended so smoothly that it scarcely seemed to move at all. It really seemed as if they were standing still, while somehow the ground fell away sharply underneath them.

"What about Tracy and the kids?" Sandy said to Faxon, raising his voice to be heard over the burner.

"Chase crew," Faxon bellowed back. "They'll follow us in the truck. You can't exactly steer these things. We'll need them when we come down. Oh, don't worry, they'll get their turns. It's not as if they've never been up. They're all old hands. We've been taking the Flying Eye up once or twice a week, weather permitting, for something like five years."

Sure enough, Sandy could make out Tracy Faxon and her kids down below, climbing into the pick-up. They took off down the dirt road, more or less trailing the balloon's windblown course. But the Eye was climbing higher and faster, and the pick-up soon became a very small dot indeed. You could see the whole West Mesa from up here; the brown bare fields, the crisscrossing dirt tracks, the other balloons laid out far beneath them like brightly colored toys. Sandy glimpsed only one of the balloons that had preceded them, the jack o' lantern, way out to the east now, over the city of Albuquerque. Where the rest had gone to he couldn't imagine.

"Now you see why I had to roust you out of bed so early," Faxon was saying. "The early morning is the best time to go up. Usually there isn't much wind to fight, and the sun hasn't had the chance to pound against the ground and start sending up thermals."

"I thought thermals were good," Sandy said.

Faxon shrugged. "For sailplanes and hang-gliders, sure. They rise on the hot air. But balloons fly because the air in the envelope is hotter than the air outside. If you get caught in a thermal, you lose the temperature differential, and your lift. Which means down, down, down." He still had the propane burner going; they rose higher and higher. They were well above the orange jack o' lantern now, and drifting out over the edge of the West Mesa, caught in a gentle wind. Faxon reached up and shut off the burner.

The silence was startling. Sandy had not expected it to be so quiet. It was almost unreal, so serene and peaceful that it seemed as if he were caught in a dream. "I can't even hear the wind," he said.

"We're part of the wind now," Peter Faxon said with a smile. "So you don't hear it. Don't worry, everyone reacts the same way. You still want to be back in bed?"

"Oh, no," Sandy said. "This is great." He placed his hands gently on the side of the basket, half-afraid he'd tip them over and out if he rested his weight against it, and gazed off over the city crawling beneath their feet. The streets were starting to fill up with traffic now; Albuquerque sprawled in all directions, and the sun was brilliant on the mountains to the east. "It reminds me of LA."

Faxon bent to the cooler in the bottom of the basket, took out two sandwiches in wax paper, and offered one to Sandy. "Ham and egg," he said. "Breakfast. Actually, Albuquerque will *be* LA in ten or twenty years. Except the smog will be worse. The Sandias hold in the pollution, and they get terrific inversion layers in winter when everybody decides to light up his fireplace. And the place *grows*. They haven't learned a thing. It's a pretty ugly town, a real Taco Bell and Chicken Delight jungle, and it's going to get worse." He shrugged. "We live up in Santa Fe, which is much better. Less of a Chamber of Commerce mentality. The only problem with Santa Fe is that it's getting too fashionable. Too many people like me moving in." He smiled and took a bite from his sandwich.

"Why do you like living out here?" Sandy asked between mouthfuls of ham-and-egg-on-whole-wheat. "It seems a little strange, you taking up residence so close to the place where..."

"...where Pat got killed?" Faxon smiled. "I'm not afraid to say it. It's been a long time." He shrugged. "I don't know. It just sort of happened. When the West Mesa concert was over, we all had to stay around for a while. There were inquiries, inquests, all kinds of things. And I was in pretty bad shape. Tracy and I lived back in Pennsylvania then, had a nice old farmhouse, and a kid on the way. Aurora. But after what happened, I just couldn't stomach the idea of going back and picking up that life."

"They say you freaked out after West Mesa."

"The phrase is a little too gratingly trendy for my tastes, but the sentiment isn't far from the truth," Faxon said with a small frown. "I guess I had a breakdown of sorts. It was a pretty damn traumatic experience, Sandy. Pat Hobbins and I had been friends since we met in the fourth grade, back in Philadelphia. He beat up an older kid who was trying to steal my lunch money. Which was pretty funny when you stop to think about it, because he was something like a foot shorter than me. I was a bookworm, though, and Pat was tough. When you're a pint-sized albino in a lower-middle-class Italian neighborhood, you learn to fight, or else. Anyway, he was my oldest and best friend. We were practically brothers. I was looking at him when it happened. One minute he was so alive, radiating such energy it was incredible. Sixty thousand people were out there, hooked up to him somehow. And then it was like his head exploded. I was behind Pat and to his right. The shot came from the left, diagonally. To this day, I swear I felt it pass right by my head. I was spattered with Pat's blood. There are still stains on that white leather jacket I used to wear, the one with all the fringe. And then I was kneeling and I had Pat in my arms. I don't remember going to him, but I remember holding him, numb, looking out over the darkness, expecting another shot, watching the riot start. He died in my arms. Kind of. I mean, he was dead by the time I got to him, I guess, in a medical sense. The whole top of his skull was gone. But I could still feel his heart beating, and he was still warm, still bleeding, and he even moved a little, so it was like he was alive.

"After that, well, I just fell apart. I wanted to go home to Tracy, but I couldn't face the thought of seeing my house again, the house where I'd entertained Pat so often. The idea of performing again made me physically sick. So I just rented a motel room and holed up, and for two weeks I drank beer and watched television, wouldn't answer the door except for room service, ignored the phone entirely.

"Tracy saved me. She came out to me when she couldn't reach me by phone. When she saw the way things were, she sold the house in Pennsylvania and bought one in Santa Fe, and moved me in. She took care of me. Then Aurora was born, and we both had to take care of her. The responsibility was good for me. I couldn't face the past at all, but Tracy had gotten me to a whole new place and a whole new kind of life, and it helped. I started to function again. Tracy suggested naming the baby Patricia, for Pat. I wouldn't hear of it. I knew I couldn't take it. I was the one came up with Aurora as a name. For the dawn. A new beginning and all that. I loved the kid. I loved taking care of her. After a while I loved Santa Fe, too.

"So that's how it went. West Mesa is the place where we launch our balloon. The other . . . well, I don't dwell on that."

"You seem pretty much recovered now," Sandy said.

"Well, it's been a long time," Peter Faxon replied. He stared off toward the mountains as the wind pushed them along, his green eyes unreadable. "Five years ago, you know, I wouldn't have seen you or talked to you. I secluded myself for a long time. Living for my family. By the time I was ready to do interviews again, no one was much interested anymore." He turned and looked at Sandy with a thin quirky smile. "So what was it you wanted to talk about? Lynch?"

Sandy nodded. "That, and other things."

"Jamie Lynch and I corresponded a few times a year on business matters," Faxon said calmly, "but other than that, I'd had no contact with the man since Pat's death."

"I've talked to Maggio and Gopher John," Sandy said. "Gopher John hated Lynch. Maggio claims he liked him. What's your attitude?"

"Mixed," said Faxon. "Jamie Lynch was a rotten bastard in a lot of ways. But he was the rotten bastard who gave us our break when no one else would. He screwed us with his contract, but we were eager to be screwed when we signed it."

"Who do you think killed him?"

Faxon frowned. "I thought they got the guy who killed him? Some lumberjack or something?"

"They've made an arrest," Sandy said. "But I don't think they have the murderer."

"All I know is what I read in the papers," Faxon said. "If the lumberjack didn't do it, I don't know who did."

Sandy decided to change tacks. "Do you ever miss the old days with the Nazgûl? The fame, the money, all of it?"

Faxon gave him that quirky smile again, half-amused and half-sad. "For a long time all that was just a nightmare I was trying to escape, trying to forget. Even when I finally came to terms with it, it all seemed unreal. As if those years had been one long feverish dream. No, I don't miss it. Even when I was living it, I was always a bit uncomfortable. You commented on that yourself, Sandy, in that last piece you wrote on us for the *Hog*. I was the misfit of the group, you said. I didn't quite seem to belong, either in the Nazgûl or in rock. And you were right. Pat and Rick and Gopher John, each of them plunged in, in his own way, but there was always part of me that hung back, judging. Too intellectual, I guess. Maggio would say I was too scared. Maybe I was. The groupies always seemed bizarre to me. The drugs and the drinking seemed repugnant. The fame was a kind of insanity. The money, well, the money was nice, but I'm not hurting. We made lots and lots when we were performing, and I was smart enough to invest it well. Besides, I wrote virtually all the Nazgûl material, and I kept the publishing rights. Lynch might have taken us with the performance and recording contract, but I was adamant about keeping my songs. They were *mine*, and they still are. And now they support me. 'Napalm Love,' 'Elf Rock,' 'Blood on the Sheets'... any one of them brings in enough each year to pay the bills."

"What about the music?" Sandy said. He thought he knew, before he asked, what the answer would be.

And sure enough, Faxon's smile grew wistful. "The music," he said. Peter Faxon might have been a misfit in the rock world, but he was also the creative heart of the Nazgûl and their sound. He was the most versatile musician among them. Most of the time he played the bass, but on various Nazgûl tracks through the years, he'd switched to keyboard, to alto sax, to Cajun fiddle, once even to French horn. He could double for Hobbins on rhythm guitar. He could sing too, though his vocals were never in a class with Hobbins' or Maggio's. Most of all, he could write songs. "Yes," he said quietly, in the deep lingering silence of the sky, the ground creeping past far below them, the wicker basket creaking gently as he leaned back against it. "Yes, I do miss the music. It's part of me. It always will be."

"You were never tempted to get back into it?"

"In the early days, the thought seemed obscene to me," Faxon said. "But

later . . . well, I considered it. The idea came to me that I ought to get together a new band. A studio band, strictly. I couldn't stand the idea of tour-
ing, but I thought I could write some new material, get together some class
performers, and cut an album. Then I looked around the rock world, and I
knew it would never happen. The music had changed. I turned on the radio and it was all disco. Every song sounded like the song before. The lyrics
were sappy and dull and endlessly repetitive. I tried to write songs about
people. About life and love and pain. About politics and ideas and right
and wrong. My music was ambitious, too. I liked playing around with new
sounds. And I listened to that radio, to a top-forty station that had once
played every Nazgûl track as soon as we cut it, and I knew there was no
room for me anymore. Hell, I know I wrote some crap in my time. I'd be
the first to admit it. But I tried. I wrote music to wake the dead; what they
want now is stuff that's good to dance to. The lowest common denomina-
tor." He smiled grimly. "No thanks. A Peter Faxon comeback album would
have sunk without a trace."

"But not a Nazgûl reunion," Sandy pointed out.

"Reunions never work," Faxon said. "Look at Peter, Paul and Mary.
Look at the Moody Blues. The Beatles were smart. If they'd ever gotten
back together, it would have been feeding time for rock critics at the zoo.
You can't win in that situation; if you change your sound radically, everyone says it's not as good, and if you don't, they say you're stagnant and rep-
etitious. And if you just play the old songs instead of doing new ones, then
it's nostalgia, not music. You know the Rick Nelson song, 'Garden Party'?"

Sandy knew it. *"If memories were all I sang,"* he said, *"I'd rather drive a
truck."*

"Exactly," Faxon said. "Or in my case, a balloon."

"When I talked to Maggio in Chicago, he insisted that a Nazgûl reunion was going to happen real soon now."

Faxon frowned. "Rick is an addict."

"An addict?" Sandy said. "I knew he was hooked in the old days. I
thought he'd gotten clean."

"It's not just drugs. He has an addict personality. He's weak. He gets
hooked on anything. He can't stop himself. He's poor because he got
hooked on credit cards and spent away everything he had. He's fat now because he got hooked on food when he couldn't afford drugs anymore. He's
still hooked on little girls. And he's hopelessly addicted to dreams, in this
case to the pipedream that we're going to reassemble and it's all going to be
like it was. No way. In fact—"

"What?"

"I've never told anyone this before," Faxon said, "but I guess enough time has passed to admit it. The truth is, the Nazgûl were pretty close to busting up when West Mesa did the job for us. I doubt we would have lasted much longer in any event."

That was a shock. "Why?" Sandy said. "You were hotter than ever."

"Our music, our sales, sure. But inside we were ice cold, all eaten up by jealousy and dissension. Three of us had just about agreed to dump Maggio. He just wasn't reliable anymore. He was strung out or flying ninety percent of the time, and his playing had gone to hell. Gopher John was chafing to get out from under Lynch's thumb, and I sort of agreed with him. But I was the big problem. I was all set to walk. I wanted to break with Pat once and for all. I think that was why I took his death so hard. It was guilt. Part of me *wanted* to be rid of him, you see. And then my wish came true."

Sandy was baffled. "I don't get it. You were just saying how close you were with Hobbins."

"Like brothers," Faxon said with an ironic twist of the mouth. "You ever heard of sibling rivalry? By West Mesa, I was furious with Pat. My ego was in an uproar. He was taking my band away from me.

"I thought of the Nazgûl as *mine*. I was the leader, the driving force. I taught Pat how to play that guitar of his, back in eighth grade. In high school, I found Rick and a couple other kids and got together a band to play dances and weddings and stuff. We called ourselves Peter and the Wolves. Later on, it was Peter and the Werewolves. Pat Hobbins was just another Werewolf; I was the star. When the Tolkien trilogy got hot and everybody started calling Hobbins 'Hobbit,' I read the books and decided that we'd become the Nazgûl, but I didn't think that changed the pecking order any. I still thought I was the leader. I was the one who decided to cut Tony Regetti and take on Gopher John on drums. I wrote all our material. Until we signed with Lynch, I even did our bookings. It was my band. Except that it wasn't, not by the end.

"The thing was, Pat Hobbins had something I didn't. On stage, I was a competent, versatile performer, but that was all I was. Pat was . . . *electric* . . . hell, *nuclear* even. God knows, I was better looking than him, and I knew more about music than he ever would or could, but Pat could do things to an audience that I only dreamed about. Sex appeal, showmanship, charisma . . . whatever it was, he *had* it.

"I'd stand there and play my bass, sing my background vocals, put everything I had into my songs, and still remain trapped in his shadow. Up front, Pat would strut and pose, grinning, sneering, moving every damn second of every damn set. And *singing*! As a rhythm guitarist, he was indifferent at best, the weakest musician in the Nazgûl, but he could *sing*! He was part demon and part angel and all genius. And that was the problem.

"He dominated the Nazgûl. He knew it; everyone told him so. Of course, it went to his head. You can't blame Pat. He was a kid. We all were. He started joking around about carrying us. He suggested we re-name the group Patrick Henry Hobbins and the Nazgûl. I suggested Peter Faxon and the Nazgûl instead, and he laughed. He threw a fit when I gave Rick the lead vocal on 'Ragin','' said I did it to spite him. And he was partly right.

"Yes, I know, it all seems pretty petty now, but it was deadly serious back then. And afterward." Faxon paused and looked pensive. The balloon had lost some altitude. He turned and ignited the gas burner; a hissing, roaring gout of flame spit out, and a moment or two afterward, the Flying Eye lifted. Faxon kept the flame on.

"Afterward?" Sandy prompted. Loudly.

Faxon turned back to face him. "Even when Pat was dead, I could not accept the fact that he'd been the star. I mentioned where the shot came from, the angle of the bullet. I still swear it passed close by me. For years afterward, I told my theory to Tracy and anyone else who would listen . . . I believed firmly that the sniper had been aiming for me, and had only hit Pat by mistake when he strode into the path of the bullet. It made a certain amount of sense. I was usually stationary, while Pat was constantly moving, an impossible target. And I was the one to blame for all that subversive, suggestive music. By all rights, I should have been the victim."

"Another reason for your retirement?" Sandy suggested.

Faxon nodded. "I had no desire to be the second Kennedy. Yet, in a way, I was upset that I'd lived. Pat's death made him a martyr, seemed to confirm him as the star. I was convinced that the assassination had been politically motivated, and I wanted to believe . . . no, *needed* to believe . . . that I was the one who'd needed silencing. Here I was, the Jesus of the rock age, saying all these wise and dangerous things in my songs, and the fools had gone and nailed up one of my apostles in my place. Didn't they know that *I* was the one who should have died for their sins?" His mouth twisted down ruefully. He turned away sharply and shut off the burner. The silence of the sky wrapped itself around them once again. They had gained considerable altitude and were drifting south and east.

Sandy found himself at a loss for words, rendered awkward by Faxon's confession. "And now?" he said, finally.

Peter Faxon rubbed the back of his neck. "I got over it. Now I know the assassin wasn't political after all. Just another crazy in a world of crazies. It was a random act, and any of us could have played the victim's role. Pat just drew the short straw. And it's over, for good and all."

Sandy's lips felt dry. "No," he said tersely. "It isn't."

Faxon looked at him sharply. "What does that mean?"

"You know Lynch died on the anniversary of West Mesa. What you don't know is that the killer cut his heart out over the concert poster, while *Music to Wake the Dead* was on the stereo. I don't know what that means, but it means something. And I think the arsonist who torched Gopher John's place ties in, too. It's not over. Something is going on."

Faxon frowned. "I don't get it."

"Neither do I. Yet. I think you'd better be careful, though. I think you might be in danger."

Faxon laughed. "Come *on!* Who'd want to hurt me? I'm a family man, well on my way to being a boring old fart."

"Slozewski laughed too," Sandy said. "A couple hours later, the Gopher Hole was in flames."

Faxon scowled. "I went through years of paranoia and fear, looking over my shoulder for assassins. I'm finally out of that place. You want me to go back."

"Somebody has a grudge against the Nazgûl."

"I'm not part of the Nazgûl," Faxon insisted. "My life is Tracy and Aurora and Christopher, not Pat and Rick and Gopher John. I've practically *forgotten* about the Nazgûl."

"Oh?" said Sandy. "Then how come this balloon has the Eye of Mordor painted on its side?"

Peter Faxon leaned back against the side of the basket and crossed his arms. His mouth was suddenly tight, and his clear green eyes looked away, deliberately. "All right," he said after a pause. "All right." He sounded vaguely petulant.

"Have you ever heard of Edan Morse?" Sandy asked.

Faxon did not answer. The land rolling past below them was getting progressively more empty as they floated south of the city. "I'm going to bring us down a little," Faxon said, "start looking for a landing spot." He vented some air from the side of the balloon, and they began to sink in a series of small, bobbing increments.

"Edan Morse," Sandy repeated insistently.

Faxon turned to face him. "A promoter of some kind," he snapped. "I got a letter from him once. Big plans for a Nazgûl reunion, for a comeback tour."

"What did you do with it?"

Faxon grinned. "My wastebasket has the Eye of Mordor on it, too," he said. They had lost considerable altitude by then. Fifty feet off the ground, and drifting, the balloon seemed to be moving a lot faster. They floated over houses and roads. Sandy could see people below stopping and craning their necks to watch as the Flying Eye went by. Once it looked as though they were going to blow right into a power line that ran along the side of the road, but Faxon gave the balloon a short blast from the gas burner and they hopped over the threatening wires as neatly as you please. Then he vented more air. They passed thirty feet above a gas station, and out over a wide open field, brown and bare in the New Mexico sun. Sandy glimpsed a familiar Ford pick-up on the road that ran past the station.

"Hold on," Faxon said. "We're coming down." He maneuvered the balloon as adroitly as he used to pluck his bass. The ground was suddenly moving very fast indeed, and the bottom of the basket thumped against it and bounced. Faxon grabbed a red line and yanked and the balloon above them seemed to sag and then collapse. They went dragging along the ground as the envelope deflated. Sandy felt his teeth jar together, and he lost his footing briefly.

And then they were stopped, and the Flying Eye was just a wicker basket and a vast expanse of limp red nylon once again. Faxon was grinning. "Congratulations," he said. "You just survived your first balloon trip." He had a bottle of champagne in the cooler. He had just finished opening it when the chase crew came roaring up, huge clouds of dry dust flying from the wheels of the pick-up. They made Sandy kneel and they rubbed dirt in his hair, claiming that it and the champagne were all part of some strange balloonists' ritual. Then they drank, and loaded the Flying Eye into the truck, and drank, and laughed, and drank, and had lunch right there on the tailgate. The cooler was full of sandwiches and potato salad and cole slaw and pickles, and when the bottle of champagne had been killed, there was Dos Equis, and cans of fruit juice for the kids. It was a nice lunch.

But afterward, when they were leaving, Tracy Faxon insisted that Sandy ride up in the cab with her, while Peter and the kids balloon-sat in the back. "Peter's upset about something," she said to Sandy when she'd gotten them back on the road toward Albuquerque. She had very cool dark eyes. "What did you talk about?"

"The Nazgûl," Sandy said.

"I see," Tracy said. "No wonder."

"I'm sorry if I upset him," Sandy said. "I didn't mean to bring back bad memories."

Tracy looked over at him with a shrewd smile. "I think it's the good ones that bother him," she said.

"Peter says he doesn't miss those days."

"He says that to me, too," she said. She kept her eyes on the road. "He says it a lot. Methinks my darling doth protest too much. He's never stopped writing, you know."

"No," Sandy said. "I didn't know."

She nodded. "He has trunks full of songs and notes. At times he wanders around the house with stereos playing in every room. All the old songs, his old songs. I was pleased when he got your call. So was Peter."

"You *want* him to play again?"

"He'll never be happy until he does," she said. "I love him. We've been through a lot together. I want him to be happy."

There was nothing to say to that. Sandy sat there thinking. They did not speak again until Tracy pulled the pick-up into the parking lot of his motel, and Sandy climbed out. Then she leaned across the seat. "Nice meeting you," she said. "I'll look forward to reading your article."

The kids ignored him, but Faxon jumped down from the tailgate of the pick-up and shook his hand. "Remember what I said," Sandy told him, "even if you don't believe it. Be careful."

Faxon's eyes looked strangely furtive. "I'm always careful," he muttered, as he climbed back into the truck.

Sandy found himself thinking about those words as he reentered his darkened motel room. The drapes were still closed, and it was cold inside. Sandy pulled them back and let the sun in. He sat on the edge of his bed, pulling off his boots and reflecting that maybe Peter Faxon was a little too careful these days. The image of that trunk of unsung songs would not leave his mind. Patrick Henry Hobbins had not been the only victim of West Mesa, Sandy thought.

He lay back on the bed, his hands behind his head, and the lines of a song occurred to him.

> *Well, he came back from the war zone all intact*
> *And they told him just how lucky he had been*
>
> *But the survivor has a different kind of scar*
> *Stillborn dreams and no more hope*
> *Hooked on booze or hooked on dope*
> *The survivor has a different kind of scar*
> *Yeah, the survivor has a different kind of scar*

"The Survivor," from *Music to Wake the Dead*. A nasty song, Sandy thought. Never a big hit, but strangely prophetic when you considered that Faxon had written it in 1971. He remembered the way Patrick Henry Hobbins would deliver the final line, staring out into the audience with a frozen rictus of a smile, hesitating just long enough while Gopher John's drumming sent kind of a tremor through the crowd, and then singing, in a voice turned oddly black and cold, *Hell, there ain't none of us survived!*

TEN

**Mystic crystal revelation/
And the mind's true liberation**

On the map, it was only a short distance from the interstate to the Golden Vision Earth Community. Driving, it seemed considerably longer. The road began as a respectable two-lane blacktop, rapidly got narrower and narrower, turned first to gravel and then to dirt and finally to very rocky, bumpy dirt. Daydream didn't like it one bit. Neither did Sandy. Toward the end, he was shifting constantly as he bounced up and down hills and over canyons and arroyos and dry creek beds. It looked cold and dusty and desolate out here, although he had to admit that the mountains were gorgeous. He couldn't imagine anyone actually *living* amid this harsh, unforgiving starkness. Sandy had started to think that maybe he was lost, and was even considering trying to turn back, when he finally came to the turn-off; an even narrower dirt track marked by a big rural mailbox covered with astrological signs and a small hand-lettered board that said GOLDEN VISION.

He turned sharply and climbed a steep, windy mountain road. Daydream protested and tried to remind him that she was a sports car, not a four-wheel drive, but Sandy persisted.

Tucked neatly into a high, narrow valley with mountains rising sharply on two sides, the Golden Vision Earth Community was a sprawling sort of place dominated by a low ancient adobe house, stucco crumbling from one corner to reveal the dry bricks beneath, and a tall wooden windmill, gray and weathered, its vanes making a ratchety sound as they turned. A second, smaller house, roofless and windowless, faced the main one across a court- yard of hard-packed brown dirt, and in the center of that yard stood the biggest teepee that Sandy had ever seen. The leaves had turned on the as- pens that covered the mountainside, making the whole expanse seem golden indeed.

Sandy pulled into the yard and parked next to an old olive-drab Jeep. Nearby a blue VW mini-bus sat up on cinderblocks, surrounded by weeds and obviously long expired. When he climbed out of Daydream, Sandy could see that a large section of the south wall of the smaller adobe house had been removed. Two men and a woman were at work on it, installing long clear panes of glass. They were surrounded by adobe bricks, by a wheelbarrow of cement, by wood and hammers and nails and glass-cutting tools and putty. Two of them glanced up briefly at Sandy and went back to what they were doing. The third, a husky black man with a beard and a bald head, came walking over. "Can I help you?" he asked in a deep voice.

"I'm looking for Bambi Lassiter," Sandy said. "She's an old friend of mine."

The black man nodded. "In the teepee," he said. He pulled out a hand- kerchief and mopped some sweat from his forehead before going back to work.

Sandy ambled over to the teepee and hesitated at the entry flap, wonder- ing how you were supposed to knock on one of these things. As he was hes- itating, the flap came open and a rush of small children emerged, running and yelling. Sandy stood aside and let them pass and went inside. "Bambi?" he called.

The interior was dimly lit by light filtering down from the smokehole above and fragrant with the smell of incense. A big black potbellied stove stood in the center of the teepee, surrounded by an astonishing amount of old, battered, comfortable-looking furniture. Ragged carpet remnants in a dozen different colors covered most of the dirt floor. It all felt more spacious than Sandy would have guessed. Two women were sitting cross-legged on the floor, talking. They were both small and dark, with black hair. One of them wore jeans and a man's flannel shirt in red and blue. The other one wore a loose brown dress with a wide white collar. One wore sandals. One was barefoot. One was sewing. One was pregnant. They both looked up at Sandy. "Bambi?" he repeated uncertainly.

The pregnant one suddenly broke into a beatific smile, stood up, and came toward him with open arms. "Sandy Blair," she said warmly, hugging him with enthusiasm. The top of her head barely came up to his chin, but she was surprisingly strong for such a small woman. Sandy hugged her back, a little more tentatively.

When they broke apart, Sandy saw that the other woman had gotten to her feet and come closer. She was slightly taller than Bambi and very wiry, her black hair worn in two long braids. "This is my sister Fern," Bambi said, confusing Sandy momentarily, since he *knew* Bambi had been an only child. "Fern, this is Sandy Blair, from college. You know. I've told you about Sandy."

Sandy held out a hand. Fern took it with both of hers and held it very gently, but firmly. "The writer," she said. "Yes, I can feel it. You have very creative emanations."

"Oh," Sandy said. He grinned weakly, wondering when Fern was going to give him back his hand. Finally she let go.

"It's good to see you," Bambi said. "Come, let's sit. I get tired easily these days." She touched her stomach. "Would you like some tea?"

"Sure," Sandy said. "It's a little chilly out there. Tea would be lovely."

"Fern," Bambi said, "could you make some for us?"

Fern nodded and smiled and left the teepee.

"She has to go to the house," Bambi explained. "It's very comfortable here, but not as complete as we would like. But it's only temporary, until we've finished installing solar panels in the other building."

"Solar panels?" Sandy said. "They looked just like big windows."

Bambi smiled. "Passive solar," she said. "It's very harmonious." Pregnancy seemed to agree with her. She looked very content, and much changed from the Bambi Lassiter that Sandy had known in the old days. In college Bambi had been a short, pudgy, painfully sincere girl, the kind that is always being described as having a great personality. She had been quick to cry and quick to gush and quick to fall in love. She owned more stuffed animals than any other six people that Sandy had ever known. But she had been Maggie's roommate freshman year, and through Maggie she had met Sandy and Lark and Slum and the others, had gotten involved with politics, and then with drugs, and then with sex. Over the years Bambi had changed very dramatically, without ever really changing at all; somehow she became promiscuous without becoming less romantic, became radical without becoming less naïve, had gotten involved with violent revolutionaries of the bomb-making sort without ever giving up a single stuffed rabbit. To Sandy, Bambi Lassiter never quite made sense.

But the woman she had grown into, sitting cross-legged and very pregnant a few feet from him, smiling, seemed much more together. She looked older than she should; her face had a lot of lines and wrinkles, sun lines and wind lines and laugh lines, but it was a *good* old, somehow. Her hands rested on her knees, palms up, and Sandy could see the calluses. She carried the weight of her child a lot better than she had ever carried the weight of the Hostess Creme-filled Cupcakes to which she had been addicted in college (not Twinkies, *never* Twinkies, only the chocolate cupcakes with the squiggle of white icing and the creme inside). Bambi looked a little scuffed and worn, but more *alive* than he had ever seen her. "You look good," Sandy told her.

"Thank you," she said. "I feel good. I'm at peace, Sandy. I've found a very good life here."

"I was a little surprised when Maggie told me where you were. I didn't know that there were any communes left."

"We're still here, as you can see," Bambi said. "True, most of the new age communities founded back in the Sixties are gone. Too many of their members were never really sincere about alternative living. Of course those people don't work out. The communities that are left, like Golden Vision, are made up of people who are really truly committed to a new kind of life. We're much smaller than we were ten years ago. Once, before I came, I understand this place had thirty adult members. Now we're down to eight, plus the children. But we all love each other, and Golden Vision is very stable now. It's a wonderful place for children."

"I see," Sandy said, gazing at Bambi's stomach. "Will this be your first?"

She smiled. "My second," she said. "I have a four-year-old son named Jason. He left just before you came in."

"He nearly knocked me over," Sandy said. "Energetic."

"And imaginative," Bambi said. "All the children here are very creative. We don't have any television here, and we don't bring in newspapers. We make most of the toys for the kids ourselves. Nothing plastic is allowed. Nothing dangerous. Nothing sexist. And no toy weapons of any sort."

"Comic books?" Sandy asked.

Bambi shook her head. "Good books," she said firmly.

Sandy was bemused. "A whole tribe of kids with no idea who the Amazing Spider-Man is?"

"Children don't need violent power-fantasies. Not when they have love and music and nature. We've built a healthy, harmonious, nonviolent, noncompetitive environment for them."

"What happens when they reach school age? Don't they have trouble relating to less-sheltered peers?"

"We tutor them at home," Bambi said. "Jana has a teaching certificate and Herb has a Ph.D. That seems to satisfy the state, though we have had some hassles. But we get by."

"Sounds like you have most everything here," Sandy said.

"We're almost self-sufficient," Bambi said proudly. "We grow about half of our own food, all organic. No meat, of course. Golden Vision is strictly noncarnivore. What we can't grow, we buy in town. We need so little money that it is easy to make do. Everyone helps. Fern sews and does embroidery and she and Herb make our teas. Ray is a handyman. All sorts of people bring things up here for him to fix. He and Mitch do odd jobs in town, too, gardening and construction and things like that. Jana makes pots and little ceramic statues that we sell to tourists. Lisa does aura balancing and gives massages. She gets people from all over the state. Ed makes bracelets and torques and rings. He's very good."

"And you?"

"I do most of our baking and I take care of the kids," Bambi said. She broke into a wide smile. "I'm also a beekeeper."

"Bees?" Sandy was incredulous.

"Five hives now," Bambi said. "The best honey you ever tasted. All organic. Never heated and never strained, full of vitamins."

"You used to run screaming out of the room when a roach crawled across a wall ten feet away," Sandy said.

"Of course I did. I grew up in a little tract house in River Forest. My mother got hysterical if we had insects on the lawn, let alone inside the house. I thought all bugs were dirty and disgusting." She laughed. "I learned better here at Golden Vision. We're very close to nature. And bees and ants and spiders and even roaches are part of the harmony, the ecology, just as we are. A piece of fruit isn't any less good just because some bugs have eaten part of it, you know. I'd rather have a worm in my apple than have poisonous pesticides sprayed all over it."

"I'll pass on both," Sandy said. He looked up as Fern reentered, carrying a ceramic teapot and three handmade mugs on a big wooden tray. The tea service had roses hand-painted all over it. There was a pot of honey, too. "This is my tea and Bambi's honey," Fern said as she set down the tray. "In case you like to sweeten your tea. But it doesn't really need it."

"We don't use refined sugar," Bambi added. "It's poison."

"I don't use it either, generally," Sandy said. What he did use was Sweet 'n Low, as sort of a futile gesture at watching his waistline, but he decided not to mention that.

The tea was hot and fragrant, heavy with the scent of mint and cinnamon and some kind of flower. If he asked, Fern would no doubt tell him just what kind of flower. He didn't ask. He just sipped and smiled. "Good," he said.

"We'll be eating soon," Bambi said. "Would you like to take dinner with us, Sandy? Lisa is cooking tonight. She's a lovely cook."

"Sure," Sandy said. "Thanks. I appreciate the hospitality. You know, Bambi, you don't seem very surprised at me turning up like this."

"Maggie sent me a card and mentioned that you'd asked for my address."

Sandy grinned. "Maggie *wrote*? I'm flabbergasted."

"She said you might see Lark, too. How is he?"

"L. Stephen Ellyn has a big car and a big house and a six-figure salary and a three-piece suit, so he tells me. He also has all the alcohol that money can buy. And he's mature. He's become so damned mature he's in imminent danger of turning into Walter Cronkite."

Fern was staring at him over the lip of her mug. She put it down on the tray and said, "You sound terribly bitter, Sandy."

"Fern has good perceptions about people," Bambi said. "But I can feel it, too. Are you so unhappy? I've been going on about Golden Vision, but you haven't said anything about your own life. Tell me about it."

Sandy looked at her uncomfortably. Even though Bambi was sitting there practically oozing earth-mother empathy, she was not Maggie by any stretch of the imagination, and he found he had no great desire to bare his heart to her. Besides, he didn't even know what was in his heart to bare. "My life is OK," he said. "I've had three novels published and I'm working on a fourth. I own a house in New York and I live with a nice, sharp lady named Sharon Burnside. She's very pretty and she's good in bed and she makes more money than I do. My work is more fun than fucking a monkey."

"No," Fern said. She touched his hand lightly. "I can sense pain in you, Sandy."

"I've driven more than two thousand miles in the last couple of weeks," Sandy said. "My back is killing me, I have a permanent road buzz, I'm sick to death of cheeseburgers, I haven't been able to get anything but country-western on the radio since Kansas City, and my jockey shorts are too tight. Yes, I'm in pain. You would be, too."

Fern frowned. "Lisa could balance your aura for you," she said. "You're so tight, so full of tension and contradiction. And I can sense a blackness about you, Sandy."

"Those jockey shorts," Sandy said. "I haven't done a laundry since Chicago."

Fern stood up. "I'm sorry if I made you hostile. I was only trying to help. I'll leave you alone with Bambi." She smiled with resignation and left.

Bambi was studying him. "Do see Lisa," she said.

"My aura is fine," Sandy snapped. "I don't want it balanced. I'm used to it being all crunched up and crooked. So is Sharon. She loves my aura. If I came home with somebody else's aura, she'd never recognize me. Probably kick me out of bed, too."

Bambi shook her head. "Why must you always make fun?"

"When I was growing up, my mother said I was just a smart-mouth. I prefer to think of myself as delightfully droll."

"Your jokes are a kind of aggression, Sandy. You ought to realize that by now. When you feel threatened you lash out by turning your sense of humor on whatever you can't understand. You mock instead of accepting. You surround yourself with a shell of what you imagine is wit."

Sandy stared at her, suddenly feeling very ill at ease. "There's an uncomfortable amount of truth in that," he said carefully. But habit got the better of him, and he added, "I can't believe I'm sitting here in a teepee on top of a mountain listening to nuggets of wisdom from a guru named *Bambi*."

"See what I mean?" she said. They both smiled. "Do you remember the first time we met?" she asked.

"Freshman year?" Sandy said. "Not really."

"You came by the dorm to pick up Maggie, and she introduced us. You noted that Bambi was kind of an unusual name, and asked me how I got it. So I told you the story about how my parents had been in the movies watching Disney's *Bambi*, with my mother eight-and-a-half months pregnant, when suddenly the labor pains started and she had to rush to the hospital. I thought it was kind of a cute story. You stared at me as if I was some kind of a loon, and then told me I'd been real lucky. I walked right into it and asked why, and you said, 'Hell, they could have been watching *Dumbo!*' "

"Ouch," Sandy said.

"Ouch indeed."

"All right," Sandy said. "I'm guilty. Still, Bambi, you've got to admit that there are some things that deserve being made light of."

"Aura balancing?"

"It will do for starts," Sandy said.

"No, Sandy," she said. "You just don't understand it. You won't open yourself to it, so you'll never understand. You'd rather make light of it and reaffirm your image of yourself as shrewd and clever than try to accept and believe. If you believe, people might think you are gullible. If you believe, they might think you're a fool, that you aren't as sophisticated as you might be. That's why you're so sad and unhappy."

"I am *not* sad and unhappy," Sandy said, annoyed.

Bambi ignored him. "Your problem is that you run your life with your mind. You *think* about everything. You think when you should be feeling. Open yourself up, let your heart and your emotions and your body have their way, and you'd be a fuller, happier person, more in tune with nature, more in harmony. Believe. Trust. Accept."

"Turn off the computer, eh?" Sandy asked. "Trust the Force to zap the Deathstar?"

Bambi looked at him, baffled.

"*Star Wars*," Sandy said. "You don't know *Star Wars*?"

Bambi shook her head. "But the message is right. Computers are very sick. We shouldn't let our machines think for us. So long as you deny your feelings, you'll experience depression and anguish and all the rest. The mind cannot find truth by itself."

"Maybe not," Sandy said, "but it sure as hell can find falsehood. The idea of stumbling through life with my heart open and my bullshit detector turned off doesn't appeal to me, Bambi."

"Just because something is strange or new or too big to be compre- hended by your conscious mind, that doesn't mean it is bullshit. Look at the world, Sandy. You did once. It's a poisonous, plastic, death-worshiping society, full of war and pollution and racism and starvation and greed. And it was built with the mind, with technology, with materialist thinking and no human feeling at all. Once you rejected that world, rightly, as all of us did. Unlike Lark, you've never been able to accept it again. But you've never really found a new way of living, either . . . you reject everything."

"Such as?" Sandy said.

"Such as the Movement. You were never really totally committed, Sandy. You were always critical. Establishment journalistic ethics meant more to you than helping the cause."

"Right," said Sandy. "In other words, I wouldn't deliberately distort the facts or make up stuff when reporting a story."

"Truth is greater than facts. You've never understood that."

Sandy leaned forward, frowning. "Bullshit. I never changed my politics. I never rejected the Movement. But the Movement was pretty damn big. I rejected parts of it, yeah. The parts that had become as bad as what we were fighting against. We were supposed to *stand* for something, and Jolly Chollie Manson and the SLA had no relation to what *I* stood for."

"You rejected mind-expanding drugs, too."

"Hey!" Sandy protested. "I tried that stuff."

"You experimented. It was recreation. But you were always scared of anything that might open your being to new levels of awareness."

"I was always scared of anything that might turn my brain to small-curd cottage cheese, you mean."

"New belief systems, mysticism, meditation, transcendence . . ."

"Twelve-year-old gurus, imported superstition, self-delusion, escape, slogan-chanting yahoos. No thanks."

Bambi smiled. "You see, Sandy? You haven't changed. Your mind is still locked and rigid. It's your mind saying all this, giving orders to your feelings, to your body. Your mind is rigidly materialist, frightened, critical."

"My wisdom teeth used to be deeply spiritual, but I had them removed," Sandy said.

Bambi Lassiter sighed. "I can see that you're never going to open yourself to enlightenment. Whenever your defenses start to weaken, the jokes begin again."

"Jokes are better than mindless uncritical belief."

"No, Sandy. I love you, but you're very wrong. To be happy, to be fulfilled, you must learn to believe. To accept. Look at me." She smiled, and seemed to radiate contentment.

"Your answer would never work for me."

"Try it. Believe. Turn off your mind and turn on your feelings."

Sandy shook his head emphatically. "Believers scare me, Bambi. Sure they're happy. They're also dangerous. Look at the Moral Majority yahoos, Hitler Youth, those poor suckers in Jonestown . . . all of them good, happy believers."

Still Bambi smiled. "You're hopeless, Sandy."

"*That* you can believe."

"I love you anyway, and I wish you well." She smiled and moved off the subject. "Will you be seeing anyone else this trip?"

He nodded. "Froggy is out in LA. That's where I'm heading next. Slum is in Denver, living with his folks. I'll check in there on my swing back east."

"Give them my love," Bambi said. "Why are you doing all this? We've all been out of touch for a long time, walking our separate paths. Why this, now?"

"Hard to say," Sandy replied. "Maybe I'm looking for something. Maybe I'm just curious. And . . . well, it relates to a story I'm working on. Don't ask me how, but it does. In fact, you might be a bigger help with the story than any of the others."

"How?" she asked.

"In the old days, you went a good way beyond the rest of us when it came to tearing down society."

"Yes," she said. "A long time ago. I finally learned that society was too big and too monstrous to come down easily, and that you can't use violence to rid the world of violence."

Sandy grinned. "That was my line in the old days. What you and Lark said was that all power came out of the barrel of a gun. But that's neither here nor there. You had ties to the bomb-throwers. The Weather Underground, the Black Freedom Militia, the American Liberation Front, all of it. I need to talk to those people. Those that are left."

"That's all ancient history," Bambi said.

"Give me a name, an avenue of approach," Sandy said. "I'll take it from there."

Bambi paused and was about to answer when they were interrupted by a loud clanging. "The dinner bell," she said. She rose smoothly to her feet, with a cryptic smile, and helped Sandy up. His legs had gone to sleep. "Let me think over what you want. Perhaps I'll be able to help you."

Dinner was served in the large main house, on a long rough-hewn wooden table covered with handmade plates and platters. Everyone shared the communal meal. Sandy was introduced to the other adult members of the community, and to the children. There were six children altogether, ranging in age from a ten-year-old boy named Free to a six-month-old infant who rode in a harness on her mother's back. No one used last names. When they were seated, they all clasped hands, children and adults both, forming a huge ring around the table, and everyone stared silently at the plates, heads bowed, for a long minute. Sandy joined in, holding hands with Bambi on his right and a slender, goateed man named Mitch on his left. He felt as awkward and out of place as he always did during Christmas dinner with Sharon's parents, when her father stood up and said interminable grace over the turkey.

There was no turkey at this dinner, of course. It was strictly vegetarian; brown rice and huge platters of fresh vegetables, spiced and curried in some cases, with thick lovely homemade soup and hot, fresh-baked bread. They washed it all down with iced herbal teas and glasses of raw milk. It was enormously tasty, and the various Golden Visionaries around the table were friendly. The cook, a tall broad-shouldered woman named Lisa with the infant on her back, told him proudly that the food he had just praised had "no preservatives or chemicals at all."

Sandy had a forkful of rice halfway to his mouth, but he paused and stared at Lisa. "No chemicals? No chemicals at all."

"None at all," Lisa said.

"I ought to write this up," Sandy said. "Food made up of pure energy. Why, this could solve world hunger."

Bambi shook her head, Lisa went off to the kitchen a bit miffed, and several of the others looked at him strangely. After that, table talk was a bit more stilted.

Sandy tried to make up for the crack by volunteering to help with the dishes after dinner. They took him up on it, and he wound up laboring in the kitchen with Fern. They scraped all the leftovers into their compost pile out back, and then washed the dishes in their own homemade soap. Sandy washed and Fern dried, and he figured out straight off that the soap was definitely less mild than Palmolive, but this time he wisely kept his mouth shut and let Fern chatter amiably about literature. She was a big fan of *Stranger in a Strange Land*.

When he emerged from the kitchen, four of the adults were still seated around the big table, talking. He drifted over to join them, but one of them, the heavyset bearded black man who had talked briefly to Sandy when he arrived, got up and intercepted him. "Hey, man," he said, clapping a big rough hand on Sandy's shoulder, "let's take a little walk, OK?"

"Sure," Sandy said, uncertainly. The black guy led him outside. The sun had set a short time ago, and a chill lingering dusk was settling over the mountains. It was very still and quiet. He could hear the children playing somewhere off down the road, running and shouting, small in the distance.

"My name's Ray," the black man said. He walked slowly, his hands shoved into his pockets. "You got that?"

"Uh, sure," Sandy said.

They shuffled across the yard. Ray paused next to the old Jeep, leaned up against it, and crossed his arms. "Bambi says you want to talk to somebody with maybe some underground connections."

"Yeah," Sandy said. He studied Ray carefully. "You?"

"I ain't saying yes and I ain't saying no. Bambi says that you can be trusted, but I don't know you, so I got to be careful. Like I said, the name's Ray. But maybe that ain't always been my name. This is a nice place. I like it here. I like the people. I wouldn't like it for anything to happen that might maybe make me have to leave. You understand?"

Sandy nodded. "What group do you tie in with?"

"Me? No one. Like I said, I'm just Ray. Ray is clean, no record, nothing.

Nobody wants Ray. But let's just say I got an old, old friend who's wanted in about six states and was a real hot item for a while. The man wanted this guy something bad. And he was into just about any group you care to name, as long as they were *doing* things. This dude didn't like talk. He liked *action*. You get it? He was a real crazy dude."

"All right," Sandy said. "You know about the Lynch murder?"

Dark furrows creased the broad, balding forehead. "We don't get newspapers, man. They're full of lies and violence, give off bad emanations."

"Jamie Lynch was an old promoter and manager. He handled the Nazgûl, American Taco, the Fevre River Packet Company, and a bunch of others. Last month someone cut his heart out." He gave Ray a brief summary of the grisly details of the murder and mentioned the fire at the Gopher Hole as well.

"I remember the Nazgûl," Ray said. "For a white band, they weren't half bad. That Gopher John was a badass drummer." He frowned. "So, you think the underground offed this Lynch mothafucker?"

"I don't think anything. I'm trying to find out."

Ray tugged at his wiry black beard. "My friend was mostly involved with folks who had *political* goals, if you get what I mean. Kidnapping the man. Ripping off banks and other exploiters. Arming the ghetto. I don't see no political shit here." He scowled. "Maybe more the Manson Family style. Offing the piggies. But why Lynch?" He shrugged. "I don't think my friend knows anything could help you, man. Sorry."

Sandy nodded. "It was just a long shot. One more question?"

"Shoot."

"Edan Morse," Sandy said. "That name mean anything to you?"

For a long quiet moment, Ray just stood silently in the twilight, while Sandy watched him and waited for the familiar shrug and denial. Instead the big man turned to face him. "I done a lot of shit I'm sorry for now," he said. "This place has changed me, you know. I got my guilts, like everybody. But one thing I never done is rat on a brother, even a white one. You sure you ain't going to the man with this?"

Sandy looked at him squarely, feeling a strange electric chill creep up his spine. He was on to something at last, if he played it right. "That depends," he said. "I'll be straight with you, Ray. A lot of innocent kids died when the Gopher Hole burned. Jamie Lynch had his heart cut out of him with a knife. If I find out who did that, I'm not going to protect them. And if you've changed as much as you say you have, you won't, cither."

Ray looked troubled. "Fuck," he said. "Maybe you're right, man. Kids, huh?"

"Teenagers, anyway."

"I'm going to have a kid soon," Ray said. "I'm the daddy of the one that Bambi's hauling around." His hand clenched in a big fist and pounded very slowly against the side of the Jeep, over and over, thoughtfully, gently, deliberately. "My name stays out of this?"

"Sure."

Ray took a breath. "You got it, then, for what it's worth. Might not be much. Edan Morse is clean. Like Ray. He lives on the coast. Beverly Hills, I think. Real big money. He inherited it when he was like twenty. His parents and his big sister all died in this fire. Edan wasn't home. Funny thing, that fire. They never proved nothing, though. Edan believed in the revolution. Didn't just talk the talk either, knew how to walk the walk. He gave money to the cause. The Panthers, SDS, the Weather Underground, a hundred other groups. You needed bread in them days, there was always Edan. Later on, he was one of the guys helped start the Alfies."

"The American Liberation Front," Sandy said thoughtfully. The ALF had been a radical splinter group of the early Seventies, made up of people who thought the other groups were too moderate. Urban terrorism and assassination had been Alfie specialties.

"Edan was big in the Alfies. Not just money. He planned stuff too, gave orders, arranged for guns. But all behind the scenes, you know. He never made no speeches. The man knew that Edan was involved, but they could never make it stick. He was real careful. It's no crime to give away your money, and that's all they could ever prove about Edan. Only there's stuff the man don't know."

"Such as?"

"Edan Morse is clean, like I said. And Ray is clean. But my friend, he's not so clean. Edan had some friends too, if you're getting my drift. Victor Von Doom. Maxwell Edison. Sylvester. They were all real *good* friends of Edan's."

Sandy remembered all of those names from the old days, though he hadn't heard them in years. Maxwell Edison was the name of the guy who took credit for blowing up that school board meeting in Ohio. Victor Von Doom was said to be the top field commander of the Alfies, the one who directed all their bank robberies. And Sylvester . . . Sylvester had been on the FBI's Ten Most Wanted list for something like six years. None of them was ever apprehended. The Alfies just withered and vanished, and them with the rest. "Jesus," Sandy said.

Ray smiled. "The Alfies finally kicked him out, though. Edan was getting weird. At least, that was the word that got passed down."

"Weird?"

"Yeah. Weird. The Alfies were crazy men, maybe, but they were practical crazy men. They figured they'd bring down the system with guns and bombs and shit like that. Edan, though, started getting funny after a while. He got into a lot of occult shit. I don't know the details. Devil worship and stuff. Magic. That was too fucking much even for the Alfies. So they got rid of him, and he formed his own group. Never came to nothing, though. As far as I know, Edan is still out there on the coast, living in his house, clean as hell. His friends have all been missing for a long time."

"Well, he's not missing anymore," Sandy said. "He wants to get into the record business now. He wants to reunite the Nazgûl."

"Ain't such a bad idea," Ray said. "They made better music than what you hear on the radio these days, that's for *damn* sure."

"Thanks for your help," Sandy said.

"What help?" Ray said. "You just keep my name out of it. I don't know nothing. I just live up here real peaceful. Organic Ray, get it?" He smiled. "You better watch out, though. Edan Morse ain't the kind of guy I'd want to have mad at me."

"I'll remember that," Sandy said. He turned and walked back inside, to where Bambi and some of the others were sitting around the fireplace. "I'd like to use your phone, if I could."

"I'm sorry," said Fern. "We don't have a telephone here."

Sandy swore. "Where's the nearest one?"

"In town," Bambi said. She stood up and came over to him. "You seem upset, Sandy. Why don't you sit down and relax? We have some good dope. We grow our own. You're welcome to spend the night."

"Thanks, but no," Sandy said. "I have to get to a phone. I guess I'll be leaving."

"I'll walk you to your car," Bambi said. She took his hand. They went back outside to Daydream. Ray was still there, sitting in the Jeep with his hands behind his head, looking up at the stars. He looked immensely contented. After years on the run, thought Sandy, it must be nice.

Bambi must have noticed the look on his face. "Ray was a tortured, hunted man when he came to us for shelter," she said quietly. "We taught him a better way. He found peace here. You could do the same, Sandy. You don't need toys like this car. Just love."

Sandy sighed. "No," he said, sadly. "I can't. I won't deny that you've got something good here. For you. For Ray, maybe. But not for me. You've built yourself a pretty little shelter, but you've written off the world."

"This is the world," Bambi said. "The real world. We have food and drink and each other, the mountains and stars, clean air, peace. This is sanity."

"Maybe. But not reality. The mountains and the stars are fine. But out there is a world of pollution and murder and loud noise and neon lights and automobiles. And it's just as real as your world. More so. There are only eight of you, and there are millions of them. You're in the eye of the hurricane here, trying to pretend the storm doesn't exist, but it's out there all the same, howling." He pointed down the mountain road. "The interstate runs less than thirty miles away. It's full of semis right now. Full of oil trucks and carbon monoxide. Right by the entrance is a Chevron station and a diner that sells the greasiest cheeseburgers the world has ever known. And it's real, Bambi. It's real."

She lifted her head. "Not to us," she said. "If a tree falls in the forest and there is no one to hear, is there a sound?" Her hands rested on the bulge of her stomach. Draped in starlight, she looked austere, dignified, and infinitely serious. Sandy smiled at her and turned away, toward Daydream. He opened the door and got in and turned on the ignition before rolling down the window.

"You dream the right dreams, Bambi," he said to her, "and you're tougher than I ever would have guessed. But my money's on the world. It's too big for you."

"Nothing is too big for the human spirit," Bambi said. "It was good to see you, Sandy. Take my love with you, and go safely in light and joy."

"I'll try," Sandy said. "And you do me a favor, OK?"

"What?" she said, looking at him gravely.

Sandy pointed a finger at her and grinned. "Don't name the kid Thumper."

For a moment Bambi stared at him in horror. Then her lips curled up in a smile. And began to tremble. And her eyes sparkled. She tried to hold it in, fought, lost, and surrendered in a guffaw of sudden laughter. Then she took one step closer and made a fist. "Sandy Blair!" she said, giggling. "You are absolutely *horrible*. You're *impossible*! You're *tacky*!"

"I've never claimed otherwise," Sandy said. He waved goodbye and slipped Daydream into gear, flicking on the headlamps as he began to move. They popped up and speared out into the darkness, and Sandy started to wind his way down the mountain road carefully, a broad smile on his face.

Just around the first bend in the road, he heard the voices of the children and slowed to let them pass. Two of them went by and waved, and then, several steps behind, two more. The second pair did not wave. They were busy playing. As Sandy swung Daydream around a curve, they were outlined in the glare of the headlights clearly for an instant, and their voices floated through the open window. Bambi's son Jason had a stick in his hand. He was pointing it at the ten-year-old, Free, and shouting, "Bang, bang!" But Free kept lumbering on, arms held out in front of him. "You're *shot!*" Jason whined. "Bullets can't hurt the *Hulk!*" Free shot back, as he grabbed the younger boy.

Sandy looked back over his shoulder quickly as he passed and laughed out loud. But the laughter died in his throat, and all of a sudden he felt very sad and tired. He was going to take no pleasure in winning his bet with Bambi. The world was going to crush them.

He fumbled around and found a cassette and slid it into the tape deck, and then rushed on through the night, toward a telephone and Davie Parker, while Bob Dylan told him that the times they were a-changin'. And the terrible thing about it was, Dylan was right.

ELEVEN

One generation got old, one generation got soul/
This generation got no destination to hold

And?" Froggy asked when Sandy had finished. "What did Deputy Parker say?"

"He said he'd been waiting to hear from me. He'd gotten in touch with the FBI. They have a file on Morse a foot thick, confirming most of what my source told me. Oh, they don't have any proof, of course, or Morse would have been behind bars a long time ago. But they have a mess of suspicions. About the fire that made him sole heir to his family fortune. About the Alfies. About Sylvester. But never anything they could take to court, and since Morse and the Alfies have been quiet for a long, long time, the feds just let it slide."

"And now?" Froggy asked. They were sitting in a sushi bar in Santa Monica, perched on high stools, washing down octopus and raw fish with copious amounts of green tea.

"Parker is real excited. He's trying to get the sheriff to reopen the case. So far, he's not having a lot of luck. Meanwhile, he has warned me to stay out of it, now that things might get serious. In particular, he said I should stay away from Edan Morse."

"Will you?"

Sandy swallowed some octopus and smiled. "Hell, no. Morse has a beach house in Malibu now. Unlisted number. Took me three days to track him down, but yesterday I tried to pay him a visit. A woman answered the door and told me he wasn't home. I left my card and the number of my hotel. I can wait. I've driven too goddamn many miles to pack my bags and go home now. I want to know how this fits together."

Froggy grinned. He had a broad, flat face and fat cheeks, but when he grinned, the ends of his mouth seemed almost to touch his earlobes, and everything under his nose turned to teeth. Yellow teeth at that. "Sounds like a good story," he said. "Jared'll shit his pants when it runs somewhere else."

"That thought had occurred to me," Sandy said. He was in a good mood, for a change. His talk with Ray had been the breakthrough he needed; now he was certain that he was on to something. Besides, he felt good seeing Froggy again.

Harold "Froggy" Cohen had been Sandy's roommate for two years at Northwestern, and his friend for years after that. They'd taken to each other almost from the start. Froggy had been a short, ungainly kid, thick around the middle, with Coke-bottle glasses and dandruff in his scruffy brown hair and the thickest eyebrows Sandy had ever seen. But they'd had a pile of stuff in common. Harold Cohen came from the Bronx and Sandy from New Jersey, so they were both Eastern exiles at college. They shared a taste for New York–style pizza and Schaefer beer. They both loathed the Yankees, an attitude that Froggy admitted had gotten him beaten up more than once in his Bronx childhood. They liked most of the same music, read most of the same books, got radicalized at much the same speed, and stopped at more or less the same place. But the real bond was *Andy's Gang*, a television show both of them had watched religiously as kids.

Hosted by Andy Devine and sponsored by Buster Brown Shoes, the show had featured the adventures of Ghanga the Elephant Boy, and weekly concerts by Midnight the Cat and Squeaky the Mouse. Midnight sawed on the violin while Squeaky did tricks; it had taken Sandy a long time to twig to the fact that they weren't real live animals. But that was just the supporting cast. The real star of the show was Froggy the Gremlin.

Every week Andy Devine would say, *"Plunk your magic twanger, Froggy,"* and there'd be this puff of smoke, and in the middle of it would appear this egregious-looking rubber frog puppet, wearing a dinner jacket, a striped vest, and a bow tie. "Hiya kids, hiya, hiya, hiya," he would croak in the deepest, evilest, froggiest voice you'd ever want to hear, while rocking from side to side and grinning like the devil. And Andy would tell Froggy about this week's guest, be it Jim Nasium demonstrating exercises, Chef Pasta Fazool with a cooking lesson, or whoever, and he'd ask Froggy to promise to be good, and Froggy would make the promise solemnly while the kids chortled. And then Pasta Fazool would come out and start to show the kids how to make spaghetti. Behind him, Froggy would croak, "And then you put it in your hair, you do, you do," in that low evil voice, and sure enough the chef would do just that. All the guests were similarly suggestible, or else it was gremlin magic. All the guests were also the same actor, but as a kid Sandy didn't realize that, either. Every week would end in disaster, and Andy Devine would come rushing back out to do in Froggy, but the culprit would always vanish in a puff of smoke, to the delight of the kids. And the week following he'd return once more, promising to be good.

Froggy the Gremlin was Harold Cohen's hero. "My role model," Froggy Cohen would say after the phrase *role model* had become fashionable, "the original anarchist." The very first issue of the ratty-looking, lurid, but excitingly alive *Hedgehog* had featured a wickedly nasty fantasy by Cohen that explained the Vietnam War succinctly; Froggy the Gremlin had been visiting Nixon in the White House. "And then you drop napalm on their babies, you will, you will," Froggy would chortle, and Nixon would do just that. Nixon and Jim Nasium had much in common, Cohen pointed out.

After that smash debut, Cohen had gone on to write a column for them, called *Amerikan History*. The stories that Old Mrs. Wackerfuss didn't tell you in third grade.

But the highlight of his career had been the time when he'd challenged a Dow Chemical recruiter to a public debate. Froggy had been president of the campus SDS that year. The poor guy had accepted, and was seated at one end of a long table in his gray suit, white shirt, and blue tie when a smoke bomb went off at the other end, and Harold Cohen emerged in a tuxedo and bow tie, his face painted green. "Hiya kids, hiya, hiya, hiya," he had croaked evilly, and the audience had roared back, "Hiya, Froggy!" in unison. The Dow man was finally driven from the stage in ridicule. It had been an inspired bit of guerilla theater.

Froggy had also been the horniest human being Sandy had ever known. Despite his dandruff, his paunch, and his yellow teeth, he had been amazingly successful at it, too. Sandy, Lark, and Slum had all been in awe of him; Froggy had gotten laid more during freshman year than the three of them combined in the entire four years of college. Froggy's secret was an absolute lack of shame. He would sidle right up to a girl he'd just met, grin his ear-to-ear grin, and say, "Hey, wanna fuck?" Sandy had once accused Froggy of going radical only because women in the Movement tended to be more available. Froggy had grinned at him and said, "Hell, Sandy, *someone's* got to plunk my magic twanger!"

Sandy had stayed in touch with Froggy for a long time after they had gone their separate ways, Sandy to write and edit the *Hog* in New York and

Froggy to teach in California. Long after Sandy had lost track of Bambi and Lark, he and Froggy had still been writing, phoning, and even visiting each other, but it had finally ended with Froggy's second marriage (he'd had a disastrous two-month marriage during his junior year in college, to a high-school senior he'd met at a rally and still described as having "the face of an angel, the patience of a saint, the world's greatest tits, and the brain of Squeaky the Mouse"), to a harridan who hated all of his old friends.

Fortunately, that was all past. The first thing Froggy had said when Sandy phoned was, "Hey, don't worry about Liz. She's long gone from my doorway, though not entirely from my paycheck."

"So you're a single man again," Sandy had said.

"Nope. Married."

"Uh-oh," Sandy said. "Number three?"

"Number four," Froggy said. "Number three and I had a great thing going for two years, until she ran off with her karate instructor. But number four is terrific. Wait'll you meet her. She looks just like Andy Devine. It was love at first sight."

Sandy laughed. "Right," he said. "You want to get together for lunch?" And that was how they came to their rendezvous at the sushi bar. Froggy hadn't changed much. His cheeks seemed a little wider than before, his belly a little more pronounced, his hair a little thinner. But his teeth were just as yellow and his grin was just as broad, and it wasn't long before Sandy found himself pouring out the whole story of his cross-country odyssey.

After they finished eating, Froggy suggested a walk. "It's only a few blocks to the beach," he said. "I don't have any classes today. I teach Monday-Wednesday-Friday, and have office hours on Tuesday, but no one ever comes to my office, so I won't be missed." Sandy agreed readily, and a few minutes later they found themselves strolling along the oceanside park and descending the cliffside stairs to the beach. There was a brisk wind and an early November chill in the air, although it was still warm by New York standards. The beach was deserted. They walked along the edge of the water leisurely, talking and playing chicken with the incoming waves, headed toward the amusement pier.

Sandy found himself doing most of the talking, to appease Froggy's endless curiosity. He began by talking about Maggie and Lark and Bambi, and eventually wound up talking about himself, his own life, his books, his house, his dreams, his failures. Froggy began by making cracks but soon grew serious. They finally seated themselves a few feet from the water, Sandy sifting cold dry handfuls of sand through his fingers as he spoke, Froggy with his arms wrapped around his knees, staring through those thick Coke-bottle lenses. "For a group who spent years living in each other's hip pockets, we've drifted pretty far apart," Sandy said, "but I'm not sure any of us have found a real answer. Me included."

Froggy blew through his lips and made a rude noise. "Hey, don't go thinking we're unique, Sandy. We're just part of a so-cee-oh-*logical* phenomenon. This is Professor Doctor Harold M. Cohen talking to you now, so listen up. You and me and Lark and Bambi and all may be fucking up good, but we're making history as we do it, Sander m'boy. Once we're all safely dead, we'll be a great generation to study. Take notes, and I'll pitch wisdom atcha." He cleared his throat. "Speaking historically, I see four major causes at work here. Number one, look at the period we grew up in. Postwar America, late Forties and early Fifties. A boom time, Sandy, one of the biggest and juiciest in American history. Peace and posterity, rampant progress all around, everything getting bigger and better every day. For us, the sky was the limit. We were the generation that wanted everything, that *expected* everything. The greediest kids in history, you could say. But also the most idealistic.

"Number two, we were the first generation suckled on the tube. We grew up with *Father Knows Best* and dancing cigarettes and newscasts and, God help us all"—he rolled his eyes—"Froggy the Gremlin. From cradle on, we were immersed in a flood of information, exposed to everything under the sun. Well, the more information you get, the more contradictions you see, right? Even in the Ol' South, massa *knew* book-learnin' was no good for dem darkies, and he was *right*. The world we saw in the tube didn't always square with what our mommies and daddies and teachers had told us, and Vietnam brought that home with force. Crossbreed that little dictum with our idealism, our high expectations, and what is so very quaintly referred to as The Turmoil of the Sixties becomes inevitable.

"Third, maybe most important, was the *size* of our generation. We wanted to change the world because of one and two, and the old folks smiled and shook their heads and said every generation felt the same, that we'd grow out of it like they had. And we laughed. And raged. And knew better. We were going to be *different*, we insisted. This time it was really going to happen. But the irony is, we were *right*—we *were* different from all those generations that had gone before, because there were so fucking *many* of us. We're the baby boomers, the biggest hairiest crowd that's ever been invited to crash the party of life. All our lives American society has been busily remaking itself in our image. The suburbs were *built* to house us. Toys and diapers and baby-food had their heyday when we were using 'em. The media have licked our rosy-sweet tushes every step of the way.

When we were young, young was chic. When we got into fucking, all of a sudden you could say *fuck* in books and show tits in movies. Wait'll we get old and gray, you'll see so many senior citizen sitcoms on the tube you'll get liver spots on your eyes just watching. No wonder we thought we had the power. We'd been changing the world all along.

"Of course, our numbers have also made things harder for us. See all the young execs competing for the same promotions. Behold the vast sea of aspiring young writers and artists and filmmakers, the ravening hordes of playwrights, the teeming mass of young politicians yearning to give speeches! No one wants to sweep the floors or clean the toilet bowls or take dictation; we've all been educated to know better, but there are so many of us that most get trapped in places we don't like. Hence Maggie, feeling wasted and useless and old, ruing the day she dropped out and turned on. Lark desperately playing a money game he can't really believe in. Bambi redefining the rules so she can come out a winner. And Sandy, fretting his humble place in world lit'rature."

Froggy was enjoying himself; he worked up more and more steam with every word, and when he was finished he hopped to his feet and gave a small but flamboyant bow. Then he paused to brush sand from the seat of his baggy brown cords. "Write that in your story," he said.

"You said there were four causes," Sandy objected. "You only gave three."

"I lied," said Froggy. "It was a trick to see if you were paying attention. Hey, I do it to the kids all the time."

Sandy smiled and climbed up from the sand. "They must love you," he said. "And hate you."

"It runs about fifty-fifty," Froggy said, "but the trend is agin' me, Sander m'boy."

"Really?" Sandy was surprised. "I don't believe it. You've got to be a dynamite lecturer. And you *care*."

"About the wrong things," Froggy Cohen said. "I care about all the wrong things. Hey, Sandy, just because I can hold forth eloquently about the historical forces that have disillusioned and wounded the chilluns of Aquarius, that don't mean I'm immune to the process. I'm out of step, too." He made a rueful face, his broad rubbery features taking on a look of comic dismay. "I ascend unto my podium armed with wit and wisdom and vast stores of secret and arcane knowledge, and I spread my arms and cry out, '*Listen to me, all ye sons and daughters of Orange County Chevrolet dealers! Listen to me and I shall lead you to truth!*' And half of them stare as though I'm crazy. The other half, God help us, write it down." He clapped Sandy on the shoulder. "Come on, Sander, let's go to the pier. I'll buy you a corn dog or an ice cream, and we can ride the carousel. It's got apartments built over it, you know. I wanted to rent one once, when I first moved down from Oakland, but number three wouldn't hear of it. The woman had no poetry in her soul, I tell you. Imagine waking and sleeping to the sound of the calliope, and looking down whenever you wanted to watch the people going around and around on their pretty painted horses. Around and around and around, just like us."

"*And the seasons, they go round and round, and the painted ponies go up and down,*" Sandy quoted.

"*We're captive on the carousel of time,*" Froggy finished. "Hey, you caught me. But you'll date yourself, m'boy. Can't go around quoting Joni Mitchell these days. Besides, you're revealing your petty bourgeois inclinations, as Lark would say. Quote Yeats. Yeats is timeless and will establish your credentials as a *real* intellectual." He gave a snort of evil gremlinesque laughter as he took Sandy by the elbow and led him down the beach. "Let me tell you about this faculty party at the last college I was at. There was this vision, this angel, this luscious moist person of the opposite sex, this fair blond surfer girl, and a T.A. in history to boot, though in her case the initials had a double meaning. Ah, Sandy, you should have been there! My magic twanger grew desperate, but there I was being shut out by a man named Fowler Harrison. It was grossly unfair, you know. He was tall and devilishly handsome, with gray at his temples, and a pipe, and he was a full professor. And named *Fowler*! And you know what he was doing? He was holding fair Juliet spellbound by reciting Yeats to her! Poem after poem after poem. The human mind cannot hold so much Yeats, unless it is housed in the skull of an English prof named Fowler. And what a gorgeous voice he had! She was staring at him, like a cobra fascinated by a tall gray mongoose, so what could I do?" He looked over and winked. "Well, I joined them and listened respectfully, and when Fowler finally paused, I gushed and asked him how he could possibly remember so much. And Fowler beamed down at me and said that when he heard something beautiful he could never forget it. 'That's funny,' I says to him, 'when I hear something *awful*, I can never forget it. For instance, I live every day of my life with the accursed theme song of the *Patty Duke Show* bouncing around in my brain.' And I began to sing it, and damned if my vision didn't break into a wide smile, and laugh, and join in. Fowler turned green, and Sherry and I—no, it was Brandy, I think, or Gin, something like that—well, anyway, we moved on to *Dobie Gillis* and the *Beverly Hillbillies* and thence to bed."

"Plunk your magic twanger, Froggy," Sandy said.

"They are all so *young*, Sandy, and they bulge so against their sweaters, and I keep waiting for my temples to turn gray so they'll fall in love with me, but instead my hair is falling out." He put his lips together and made his wet, silly noise again, derisive and dismissing. "Well, that was in my callow youth. No more! I have tattooed the name of number four upon my magic twanger, and forsaken all others." They passed into the shade of the pier and ascended from sand to boardwalk. Froggy went first.

At the top they found an open stand and bought two ice cream sandwiches that tasted like chocolate-flavored cardboard. They peeled back the paper halfway and walked down to the end of the pier, over the water. "How do you feel about teaching?" Sandy asked. "Really?"

Froggy stared at him through the thick lenses. His eyes were shrewd and faintly amused, and he had a white ice cream mustache on his upper lip. "Seriously?" he asked.

"Seriously," Sandy said.

Froggy sighed. "I *love* teaching," he said. "It's my life. I love history, and in a perverse way I even love the whole ivory tower scene. And I certainly love my students." He winked. "Not often enough, but still, I do love 'em. Yet it's true, Sandy, what I said down on the beach. I'm not making it. Not really."

"How?" asked Sandy. "Why?"

Froggy balled up the paper from his ice cream sandwich, tossed it into a nearby trash can, and carefully licked his fingers one by one. When he was done, he leaned back against a piling and frowned. "I *loved* college. The atmosphere, the sense of excitement, of ferment. Those years at Northwestern changed me forever and ever. The demonstrations. The debates. The classes. Bergen Evans lecturing, making me think about just about everything in my life, though he was supposed to be teaching English lit. My history profs. Jesus, I *loved* it. I wanted to be like those teachers I'd admired. I wanted to shake kids up, to lay truth on them, to make 'em see things in a new way. I wanted to make them angry and shocked. I wanted them to argue with me. I wanted to make them *think*. Hah!

"The kids have changed, Sandy. They're not like we were. And it gets worse every year. They're *docile*. They're *practical*. They're *polite*. They don't bite. Well, hardly ever. I've been at four colleges now, never been higher than an assistant professor, so I get all the big introductory lecture courses. I used to try to do Socratic dialogues, get arguments going, controversies. Disaster. I gave that up. And no matter how outrageous I am in lecture, no one argues back. They write it all down. That business about saying there are four causes of thus-and-such, and giving only three? That's no joke, Sandy, I've really done that in class. It's about the only sure way I know to make a hand go up out there, to make someone say, 'Hey, Professor Doctor Cohen, you fucked up.' Except *they* say it politely.

"Once I was teaching a basic intro course in American history, lecture format, seventy-nine students, and I was convinced that every damn one of them had turned to stone or died out there. So I gave an entire lecture on the administration of President Samuel Tilden. His election, his accomplishments, his failures, his reelection. After it was over, exactly three kids came up and said, 'Uh, excuse me, must be some mistake, the textbook says that Rutherford Hayes became president, not Tilden.' When I fessed up to them, one of them went to the department chairman. That was my last year at that college.

"Oh, there are exceptions, of course. The kids who make it worthwhile. But so few. It's not that the others are dumb. It's not even apathy. They're just different. Products of a different time.

"You remember how we wanted courses that were more *relevant*? The new breed wants relevance too, but for them relevance means Basic and Accounting and Introduction to Advertising." He sighed. "Is it any wonder I'm a misfit? And I am, Sandy, truly I am. I'm a *good* teacher, I'm an exciting lecturer, but I move from one university to another, I've never gotten tenure and I never will. I'm a brilliant anachronism. My students give me blank stares or frightened laughs, and the deans think I'm a loon, an anarchist, a threat to the dignity of their ivy-covered halls. My God, Sandy, I tell the kids to put the spaghetti in their hair, and all they ask is how that will help them get a job!"

"I hadn't realized it was that bad," Sandy said.

Froggy grimaced. "Bad? *Bad?* I'll tell you how bad it is... *fraternities are coming back!*" He groaned theatrically, spun, and stared out over the seas. They were alone on the end of the pier. When Froggy fell silent, Sandy could hear the slap of waves against the pilings. The air was crisp with the salt smell of the ocean, and you could see the mountains curving out to the north, veiled in mist. Froggy shoved his hands deep in his pants pockets. "Fuck," he said loudly to the wind. He turned around, frowning. "I didn't mean to go on like this. Look, come over for dinner tonight, OK? I promise I won't talk so much. We'll play Nazgûl records and reminisce about Timothy Leary and I'll tell you precisely what's wrong with every one of your books. Including the dedications, none of which, by the way, have been to me. Don't think I haven't noticed, Sander m'boy. And after all I did for you." He grinned. "And you can meet Sam."

"Sam?"

"Samantha," said Froggy. "Otherwise lovingly known as Number Four. You'll like her. She won't like you, but nobody ever does, so what the hey? So what do you say?"

"I'd like to, Froggy," Sandy said, "but I have to go back to my hotel and check for messages from Edan Morse. I want to try and see him tonight, if possible."

"Sam doesn't really look like Andy Devine," Froggy said. "She won't even wear Buster Brown shoes."

"Sorry," Sandy said, smiling. "I'll see you before I leave town, though. You and Sam both. You've got my word."

"Give me some advance warning, so I can rent a tux and paint my face green," Froggy said. "We want you to feel at home." He snorted with laughter, slapped Sandy on the back, and they walked down the pier together, past the carousel and the ice cream stands, toward the city. Froggy Cohen began to talk about the history of merry-go-rounds. Sandy smiled, and listened.

TWELVE

Some are born to sweet delight/
Some are born to the endless night

The desk clerk, a plump little homunculus of a man in a gray cardigan and slippers, was engrossed in a porno novel when Sandy returned to his motel late that afternoon. "Any messages?" Sandy asked him, leaning on the desk.

The man peered at him suspiciously, obviously piqued at being disturbed. "Messages?"

"Yeah. Messages. You know. Little slips of pink paper with words written on them. From all the folks who called while I was out."

The clerk cleared his throat. "No messages," he said. He went back to his porn, and Sandy went back to his room. It was all the way around back, behind the scummy swimming pool. Sandy walked to it feeling annoyed and restless. Edan Morse should have called. He would have bet his life on it. In fact, maybe he already had. He'd left one detail out of the version he'd told Froggy: the message scrawled with a Flair on the back of the purple *Hog* card he'd left in Malibu. *I taut I taw a puddy tat,* Sandy had written. He didn't understand how Morse could afford to ignore that.

He hadn't. When Sandy reached his room, the door was ajar, and they were waiting.

There were two of them. The woman in the orange Naugahyde chair by the door rose and turned when Sandy stepped into the room. She smiled as he glanced at her, and he found his glance turning into a stare. She was striking. Tall and dark, with café-au-lait skin and ink-black hair that fell in a long jet cascade down to the small of her back. That great mass of hair made her seem smaller than she really was. Her body was taut and trim everywhere. A white halter top, knotted between high round breasts, revealed an absolutely flat and firm stomach. Her faded jeans followed the line of calf and thigh tightly. She wore a red cloth sash as a belt, and a matching red headband. Her eyes were black and deeply set and large. Her cheekbones were high and sharply defined. Her mouth looked like it belonged to someone who smiled a lot. She was altogether the most gorgeous woman Sandy had seen in years, outside of movie theaters and magazines. He could have looked at her for a long, long time, easily. But the other person in the room was enough to distract anyone, even from *her*.

He was lying on Sandy's bed. His legs, in big combat boots with a spit-shine on them, went on about a foot after the bed gave up. He was altogether the biggest man Sandy had ever seen, and never mind the movie theaters and magazines. Never mind the basketball courts, either. This guy had to be at least seven-two or seven-three, but he was wide as well as tall. He had shoulders like a comic book superhero and a huge stomach that bulged against his green muscle shirt and looked to be made of brick. He also had a bad case of sunburn, a shaved head, and one gold ring in his right ear. He looked like some bastard offspring of a mating between King Kong and Mister Clean.

Sandy stood in the doorway and looked at each of them. "Neither of you looks like a hotel maid," he said. "What are you doing in my room? How did you get in?"

"I opened your door with a lock-pick," the woman said cheerfully. "I'm good at that. We didn't know how long we'd have to wait, and I figured we might as well be comfortable." While she was talking, the man sat up on the edge of the bed, and rested hands the size of cinder blocks on thighs as thick as telephone poles.

Sandy frowned. "Who are you?" He was looking at the giant. The woman was a lot easier on the eyes, but the giant made him nervous, especially when he moved. Something that big shouldn't be able to move at all without stop-motion animation.

"That's Gortney Lyle," the woman said. "Gort. And I'm Ananda. We work for Edan Morse."

"That much I'd figured," Sandy said, turning to face her. "Pleased to meet you, Amanda." He held out his hand.

"Not Amanda," she said, obviously accustomed to the error. "*Ananda*." She took his hand, remolded his fingers into the old Movement handclasp.

It had been years since Sandy had shaken hands that way. Ananda's hand was cool and strong. She had a ridge of callus along the edge of her palm.

"I'm not going to shake hands with *him*," Sandy told her with a glance at Gort. "I type for a living." He wiggled his fingers.

Ananda laughed; Gort stood up and grunted. He had high, thick heels on his boots, and his head almost touched the ceiling. "Let's go," he said in a voice as deep as the bass on the Coasters, but a lot less musical.

"You still want to talk to Edan?" Ananda said. She held her head cocked slightly to one side as she asked, appraising him frankly. The tip of her tongue flicked out and slid across her lower lip, and she smiled.

"Uh, yeah," Sandy said. All of a sudden, he felt surprisingly unsure of himself. "Might as well. Nothing good on TV tonight."

"Nothing good on TV ever," Ananda said. "Well, get your coat or your notebook or whatever, and we'll take you to Edan. He's pretty anxious to see you, Sandy. That note you left rattled his cage a little."

Sandy grinned; it had worked after all. "Just a sec," he said. He went to the coatrack by the bathroom, walking a block or two to get around Gort in the center of the room, and traded his light windbreaker for a heavier jacket. As he shrugged into it, he caught a glimpse of himself in the big mirror over the sink. His beard had come in full and dark, and his black hair was longish and windblown. He looked pretty good, he thought. More important, he looked pretty radical. Radical enough so that Edan Morse might talk to him.

A nondescript blue van was parked outside, in the space next to Daydream. Ananda stopped to admire the car before she climbed into the van. "Nice," she said. "Yours?"

Sandy nodded, feeling vaguely pleased to have impressed her. She was the kind of woman you wanted desperately to impress. Had Froggy been here, he'd have been singing the *Patty Duke* theme already, no matter what was tattooed on his magic twanger. They stood for a moment in the fading afternoon sun and talked about his Mazda. Ananda asked a number of sharp, intelligent questions, and Sandy fielded them as best he could.

Sandy rode shotgun during the drive up to Malibu, with Ananda driving and Gort sitting silently in the back. Having Gort behind him made Sandy distinctly uncomfortable at first, but he soon got wrapped up in conversation with Ananda and managed, somehow, to forget all about the third passenger. It turned out that Ananda had read all of his books, which pleased him inordinately. And she even remembered some of his pieces from the *Hog*. "I was delighted when Edan told me who we were supposed to fetch," she told him. "I've admired you for a long time. Really. The *Hog* was so important to us back in the old days. When all the establishment rags were printing lies and distortions, twisting everything around to make us look bad, there was only the *Hog* and a few undergrounds to tell it like it really was. I've liked your books, too. I got so angry when Sarah died in *Kasey's Quest*. I cried. You never sold out, like so many of them did. You kept the faith."

"And you *like* that?" Sandy said, astonished. He laughed. "My God, you don't know what a relief it is to meet someone who doesn't want to lecture me about my immaturity!"

Ananda glanced at him with a warm, rueful smile. "They got you on the defensive, right? Don't worry about it, just hang in there. It's the same for me. My mother was a big civil rights activist once, and she used to think everything I was doing was great, but about five years back she got grandchildren on the brain. Maturity is all she talks about." She sighed and pressed her lips together. "They don't get it. I can't even think about having a child, the way the world is now. The way I see it, commitment is commitment, whether it's fashionable or not. If the Movement is dead like they say, then those of us who are left are more necessary than ever, now that all the sunshine soldiers are working for the corporations. The principles are still valid, right? The injustice is still there, people are still oppressed, war is still just as fucking unhealthy for children and other living things, right? So there's still work to be done. I couldn't live with myself if I copped out. But it does get lonely at times." She looked at him and grinned. "Another reason I wanted to meet you. The good guys are getting hard to find nowadays."

"Whoa," Sandy said. "I may be a good guy, but I ain't joined nobody's army. Least of all Edan Morse's."

Ananda shrugged. "You will, once you understand. Your heart is in the right place."

Which is more than can be said for Jamie Lynch, Sandy thought, but he didn't say it. Still, it was a disturbing thought. It wiped the smile from his face and made him a bit more wary of this breath-catchingly attractive woman who was positively radiating warmth and receptivity and good vibes. "You still consider yourself a radical?" he asked her.

She looked over at him and noted the serious look on his face. "Radical?" she said. "Shit, no. I is a *revolutionary*, massa, and the last lil' hippie chick in the whole wide world."

Sandy grinned despite himself. "At least you have a sense of humor," he said. "I never trusted revolutionaries who had no sense of humor."

"Fuck, man, these days you got to have a sense of humor. Any day now I expect to see Timothy Leary doing American Express commercials. '*I didn't need a credit card on the trips I used to take, but now, on the lecture circuit, my face won't even get me a sugar cube. That's why I carry this.*' Hell, if you don't laugh, you have to cry."

"Tell me about Edan Morse," Sandy said to her.

Her big dark eyes flicked over at him again and held his gaze, amused and confident. "You *did* taw a puddy tat, you *did*," she said wryly.

Sandy frowned. "You saw my card?"

"Sure. I'm Edan's left hand. Gort is his right. Cute little card. Edan was less amused, however. He likes to think those days are gone and forgotten."

"Aren't you taking a chance admitting all this?" Sandy asked. "Sylvester is a wanted fugitive. Suppose I went to the cops and fingered your boss."

"Well," said Ananda, "in the first place you won't. I've read enough of your writing to get a pretty good idea of what you're like. I trust you. But even if I'm wrong, it doesn't matter. Sure, Edan gets nervous when he's linked to Sylvester or Von Doom or the Alfies. You'd get nervous, too. But it isn't as though nobody suspects. The underground was always full of rumors. And I don't have to tell you how thoroughly most of the radical groups had been penetrated, which means the feds heard those rumors, too. You want to call the FBI and tell 'em about Sylvester? Just tell Edan, and he'll let you use his phone. You can't prove it. The thing of it is, what you know and I know and they know won't cut no ice unless there's proof. Edan was always careful. You want to know about Edan? That's the first thing. He's careful. He's had to be."

"Yeah?" Sandy said. "And what else is he?"

"Committed," said Ananda. "He's a great man, Sandy. Really he is. You'll see. If we'd had a few more like Edan Morse, the revolution would have come off when it should have, and this would be a better world today."

"How come the Alfies kicked this great, committed man out on his ass then?" Sandy asked, hoping to jar something loose.

"That's a distorted version of what really went down. It was Edan who washed his hands of the Alfies. They were squabbling and incompetent and fatally compromised. Fuck, I'd say about half of them were undercover cops. You know the kind—the ones who come to all the meetings and push for more and more violence so they have lots of terrorist atrocities to play up in the press. Edan had had enough of that, so he just flushed them away."

"Are you saying the infamous Sylvester turned nonviolent?"

"Edan never had any use for *meaningless* violence," Ananda replied.

"Interesting," Sandy said, "but it doesn't square with the other stories I've heard. The way I hear it, Morse got weird. Spiritual."

"That's not so far off," Ananda said calmly. "Edan has vision. Power."

Sandy felt very uncomfortable. "Oh, great."

"You sound skeptical. Fine. I was the same way at first. Who could believe all this freaky occult shit, right? Well I do, now. I've seen things. Experienced things. I don't pretend to understand it all, but I believe." She glanced at him out of the corner of her large dark eyes, and the tip of her tongue flickered across her lower lip again in a gesture both nervous and strangely erotic. "You ever seen a ghost, Sandy?" she asked.

A month ago he would have laughed at the question. But that was before his strange night in Chicago. He hesitated. "I—I'm not sure. Maybe. I think it was just a dream."

"The world is full of forces we don't understand," Ananda said cheerily. "You can deny them all you want, but that won't make them any less real. That was part of what the whole counterculture thing was about, right? Shucking off the middle-class mindset, all the preconceptions we got from Mommy and Daddy and Reverend Jones, so we could see the world like it really was. Only the preconceptions were too strong for most. But not for Edan. He's broken through."

"To what?" Sandy asked.

"I'll let him tell you," she said. "Just keep an open mind. There are more things under heaven and earth, Horatio, than are dreamt of in—"

"Gotcha," said Sandy, interrupting. They both laughed, for no apparent reason. Then there was a moment of awkward silence. Sandy sat there looking at her. He could feel a real sexual tension in the air. He tried to tell himself that Ananda was just a source, part of his story, but the attraction was undeniable. Much as he might try to look at the scenery, his eyes kept going back to her smooth bare midriff, her breasts pushing against the white halter, nipples clearly outlined, and her smile. He cleared his throat self-consciously, feeling like a high-schooler on his first date.

Ananda broke the spell by asking him what he was working on. He told her about the novel he'd abandoned on page thirty-seven. She asked him about his travels, and he talked briefly about the friends he'd looked up, and made her laugh twice with a couple of his favorite anecdotes about Froggy. Then somehow he got onto the subject of his home life. Ananda frowned when he mentioned Sharon and sighed rather theatrically. "Oh, well," she said. "Why is it the good ones are always taken, and the loose ones are always fascists?" She went on to tweak him about Sharon's profession a little. "Real estate is such an oppressive sham. I mean, think of it. Owning the *earth*! Like owning the air. It's crazy. Land should belong to everybody." But she said it with such good-humored frankness that Sandy wasn't bothered; nor did he feel any great urge to rush to Sharon's defense.

She had been talking about her own childhood in Los Angeles for a while when they finally came rolling up to Edan Morse's beach house. It was a big, sprawling place, built on two levels, with a garage underneath it. Ananda picked a garage door opener off the dash, and the rough-sawn wooden door slid up and out of their way as they approached. Lights came on simultaneously. They all climbed out of the van and Gort stretched himself and grunted. Then they went upstairs. The house was clean, modern, tastefully furnished, yet somehow disturbing. It seemed very austere to Sandy. Everything spare and functional, but the paintings on the white walls, glimpsed quickly in passing, were vivid, surreal studies of twisted faces and figures bent in pain. But that wasn't it. Something larger about the house felt *wrong*, somehow. Sandy put it down to a bad case of nerves.

Edan Morse's office looked out over the beach through a tinted plate-glass window. Out there the sun had just started to set. In front of the window stood a massive teak desk. It was the cleanest, neatest, most orderly desk Sandy had ever seen. In the middle of it was a blood-red blotter, precisely centered. There was also a gold pencil-and-pen set in a black marble stand, an antique silver dagger of unusual design, serpents coiling around the handle, an empty wooden IN basket, an empty wooden OUT basket, and a glass paperweight in the shape of a globe with a peaceful farm scene within. Shaking the paperweight would start a blizzard of fake snow, Sandy knew. His father had once had a paperweight just like that one. But there were no papers under Morse's paperweight, or anywhere else on the big desk, except in the exact center of the blotter, where someone had placed Sandy's purple calling card so squarely that the blotter seemed to frame it.

Behind the desk was a leather swivel-rocker with a high back. Morse had it turned to look out over the waves and the setting sun, but he swung around when the door closed and looked up at Sandy.

It was an uneasy moment. There were no other chairs in the room. Sandy was forced to stand in front of the desk. It reminded him of the times he'd been dragged before the principal in grade school. Gort and Ananda stood flanking him like the world's oddest brace of patrol boys. Standing and looking down on Morse should have given him some kind of psychological advantage. It didn't.

Sandy had to admit it: there was something oddly impressive about Edan Morse. At first glance, Morse was so normal it made Sandy's teeth hurt. Instead of the wild-eyed, Mansonesque, Rasputin-like character

Sandy had imagined, he saw a slender, clean-shaven, smiling man in his middle thirties. Morse wore a white turtleneck and crisp new blue jeans. His light brown hair came to a small widow's peak in the front. He had big brown eyes, a cleft in his chin, and dimples. The man who had helped found the American Liberation Front looked as though the only paramilitary group he could possibly be associated with was the Boy Scouts. For a fleeting, bizarre moment Sandy wondered whether Ray had just given him a shuck-and-jive to get rid of him.

Then he noticed Morse's jewelry, and the wholesome image cracked just a little. He wore a heavy pendant covered with astrological signs, and on his left hand was a huge silver ring with what appeared to be a dead black widow spider encased in lucite. And there was something in his eyes as well. Behind the soft brown surface warmth, something glittered briefly, and then it was gone. Sandy looked for it, and found no trace, and dropped his eyes, feeling confused. Maybe he was just seeing what he had expected to see: a fanatic. A journalist had to beware his preconceptions.

Morse's first words were innocuous enough, and they were addressed to Ananda, not Sandy. "How was your trip?" he asked.

"No problems," she replied. "Looks like it could be a nice evening. Not too chilly."

"Good," Morse said. He snapped his fingers. "Where are my manners?" he said. "Gort, get Sandy a chair, will you? The big comfortable one from the games room should do nicely."

The giant left silently and returned in short order, carrying a huge over-stuffed armchair as easily as Sandy might tote a folding bridge chair. He dumped it in the middle of the floor with a grunt. Sandy sat in it, crossed his legs, and faced Edan Morse. He had to look up now; Morse's chair was higher than his was.

They exchanged a few meaningless pleasantries, and then Morse dismissed both Gort and Ananda. When the door closed softly behind them, Morse's smile grew taut, and they got down to business. "It was not necessary to leave this sort of message for me," he said, picking up the silver dagger and using its point to tap lightly against Sandy's card. "I would have seen you in any case. Rick Maggio phoned and told me about the story you're working on. Hell, I would have contacted *you* if I'd had any idea how to find you. I *want* to talk about the Nazgûl, and my plans for them."

"Do you, now?" Sandy said. "How about Jamie Lynch? Do you want to talk about him?"

Edan Morse leaned back in the rocker, toying with the knife in his hand

and frowning. "Lynch? Why would I want to talk about that pig? I don't see what you're getting at."

"Come off it, Morse! Or should I call you Sylvester? Or Maxwell? You know fucking well what I'm getting at. Where were you the night Jamie died?"

Morse smiled thinly. "As a matter of fact, I was in Beverly Hills, at the home of an old family friend. A banker who was once close to my father. A rich, anal fascist, enormously respectable. The hour was late. I got him out of bed and stayed a long time, but he put up with it because he's chairing a local charity drive and I was giving him a check for five thousand dollars. He despises me, but I'm certain he'll remember my visit."

"So?" said Sandy. "So maybe you weren't in Maine personally, but it was still your hand at work, long distance."

"There's no possible way for you to prove that," Morse said. He smiled his dimpled, Boy Scout smile.

Sandy decided to shake him up a bit and see if the merit badges fell off. "Lynch was a very neat man. Organized. Filed all his correspondence. The cops found your letters, and carbons of his replies. They know you wanted the Nazgûl and he wouldn't give 'em up. That's motive. They have the letter where you arranged to send a representative to Lynch to talk things over, so they know why he admitted his killer. That's opportunity. It's all there."

"Then why am I sitting here, and not under arrest?" Morse said. "Come on. If these letters did exist, the killer would almost certainly have gone to Lynch's filing cabinets and removed them, leaving a few earlier letters that were essentially harmless. By all accounts, the man who killed Lynch knew what he was doing. He wouldn't leave anything obviously incriminating behind, would he?" Morse shook his head. "You're wrong. But even if you were right about me, you couldn't prove anything. Believe me. This isn't the first time I've had to defend myself against ridiculous charges. I've been under suspicion for more shit than I can remember. I've been questioned and interrogated and hassled by whole battalions of pigs, I've been beaten up by establishment goons, I've been investigated by dozens of hot young reporters, and I've been forced to testify before two grand juries. No one has ever proved me guilty of any criminal act." He leaned forward and pointed the knife at Sandy, as if for emphasis. "I'll tell you this, though—I'm not sorry that somebody offed Lynch. Like I said, the man was a pig. Filth."

"Oh?" said Sandy. "Why was that?"

"He was an exploiter, for starts. He had no talent himself. He had no creativity. He fed off the real creative spirits of our age. He leeched off the people's music, turned it into some kind of shit-eating capitalist game. He was a pusher. I've got nothing against drugs, used for the right reasons. Drugs can be very liberating. But Lynch used them to control other human beings. If you saw the house he lived in, you have an idea how much wealth he bled from the people."

Sandy gave a snort of derision. "Hell," he said. "You could have bought Lynch out of loose change, from what I hear."

Edan Morse shrugged. "So? I'm not proud of my wealth. My grand-mother and great-grandfather accumulated most of it, immorally. But at least I've done my best to use it as a force for positive change. Jamie Lynch used his money only for himself. For power. That was all he cared about, ever. Power. Control. Money, sex, love, even the music he dealt in—they all meant power to him, and nothing else. He was a pig. A Nixon with long hair. He deserved to die. If I knew who killed him, I'd certainly never turn them in. It was an execution. People's revolutionary justice."

"Jamie Lynch was a has-been rock promoter," Sandy said. "How the hell does his death help the goddamned revolution?"

"In ways you could not possibly understand," Morse replied. "It has set forces in motion, forces that will now proceed to an inevitable, inexorable conclusion. Individuals and nations alike will be swept aside. The world will be remade in justice. We will have love and peace and freedom at last, a golden age, all the things we once dreamed of." He smiled. "And you can have the inside story, Sandy. If you want it. What do you think?"

"I think you watched too many cartoons as a kid," Sandy said. "You've gone looney-tunes."

"You don't think there can be a revolution, is that it?"

"More or less," Sandy said. "On this trip of mine, I've been looking up a lot of old college friends. One of them used to be positively rabid for revo-lution. Now he works in an ad agency. He's an asshole, but he said it best. *There was never going to be no revolution,* he said."

Edan Morse looked straight at him. For a second, the strange glitter re-turned to the brown eyes, and Sandy tried to pin it down. Conviction? Fanaticism? What? "I will lay you odds," Morse said, "that you did not al-ways feel that way. Be honest with yourself. Forget what this asshole ad-man said, and look inside yourself, remember how it was. Woodstock. Kent State. Cambodia. How did you feel then?"

Sandy started to answer and stopped with his mouth open. The denial would not come. Morse had him. He *had* believed; even practical work-within-the-system Clean-for-Gene Sandy Blair, skeptic, joker, even *he* had believed for a few magic moments.

Edan Morse was watching Sandy's face. "Do you know *Julius Caesar?*" he asked. "Where Brutus says, *There is a tide in the affairs of men, which, taken at the flood, leads on to fortune; omitted, all the voyage of their life is bound in shallows and in miseries?* For us, for the Movement, that was our floodtide: Cambodia and Kent State. That was the moment we had to seize. Ever since we have drifted in our own shallows and miseries. The revolution has become a dimly remembered joke, even to us. The dream has turned to ashes." His voice was soft and sad and persuasive.

"I know the play," Sandy said. "I also know that it was that speech that led Brutus and Cassius to Philippi, and the end of *their* revolution."

"It's just a play," Morse said airily, dismissing Sandy's objection with a casual wave of the serpent-encrusted dagger he held loosely in his hand.

"Even if you're right, what difference does it make?" Sandy said. "The floodtide has passed, by your own admission. The revolutionaries have bought tract homes and three-piece suits. They'll never rise again."

"So true," said Edan Morse. "That is, unless time can somehow be turned on itself, the tide made to come again." He leaned forward intently. "Let me ask you a question. When did the Sixties end?"

"The end of '69," Sandy said, "or the end of '70, if you're a purist, because there was no—"

"Don't give me that calendar shit," Morse interrupted. "I'm talking about the spirit of an age, not when that stupid ball fell in Times Square. The Sixties began when Kennedy was assassinated and 'Nam got hot. So when they end, Sandy? When?"

Sandy shrugged. "The day Nixon resigned, maybe. Or the day Saigon fell and the war ended."

"Wrong. Too late. Our tide had begun to ebb long before that. Our momentum, our unity, the sense of destiny, of *inevitable* triumph—we had lost them all, hardly noticing when they began to bleed away, yet feeling it all the same. I've studied it. I know the moment when it changed. I *know!*"

Sandy sat very still, looking at Edan Morse, and a cold chill ripped through the marrow of his bones. Outside the sun had gone down. It was black beyond Morse, with only a thin scarlet line of light slashing across the horizon. Clouds rolled across a dark sky, above the red-tinged sea. Darkness and storm and chaos; and Morse's eyes glittered. "When?" Sandy said.

"*You* know," Morse replied. "It's written across your face. You know it in your gut. You've sensed it all along." His smile was somehow frightening. "Say it," he commanded.

"September 20th," Sandy said through dry lips. "September 20th, 1971."

"West Mesa," said Morse, "and the end of the Nazgûl." He took the silver knife in his right hand and drew it across his left palm, hard, opening a long red gash. His palm bore the scars of other markings. Blood welled from the wound and dripped down onto the blotter, leaving crimson spatters on Sandy's purple card. "It was in our blood all along," Edan Morse said in a voice of fierce conviction. "The *music*, Sandy, the *music*. It was our fuel, it was our spirit, it inflamed us and exalted us and gave us courage and purpose and truth. The songs were more than songs. They caught and shaped our minds and souls, and they summoned up something primal in the universe, and in us.

"You know the truth. We all know it, instinctively. Even the enemy. Look at how the TV networks treat the period! Marches and riots, demonstrations, elections, assassinations, Vietnam—every clip they show, they back with rock music. Something deep within them realizes that rock was a part of it all.

"The cliché is that music is a reflection of the times, but the cliché has it backward. There is *power* in music, Sandy. The songs touch us in ways deeper and wilder and more basic than words. Every army that has ever marched to war has gone to the beat of drums, humming martial music. Every revolution has had its music. Every epoch. The music defines and shapes the age.

"And in our age, the Movement exploded to the hard beat of rock, moved to it, marched to it, fucked to it, swelled to it. Drugs and sex and rock and revolution, peace and freedom. And I think the enemy understood better than we did. We were a threat to the whole rotten system, to the corrupt power and the immoral wealth. Our music had already crushed theirs, driven it from the airways and the streets and the culture, and the rest would surely follow. I think they knew that.

"And then the music died. Little by little, partly by chance and partly by design, I think. The Beatles broke up, so did a hundred other groups. The hard-edged, scary stuff was banished from the radio. The moneymen tightened their controls over the media and the record companies, and squeezed the vitality out of rock, turned our steel to marshmallow, progressively, day after day, damping our inner fires while we hardly noticed. And those who could not be bought out or broken up or retired, the loudest and most dangerous, they were killed, one after the other, in the space of a few years. Hendrix. Joplin. Jim Morrison. And finally Hobbins, finally West Mesa. The Nazgûl *were* the Sixties, more than any other group. They were young and vital and angry, they had blood in their music, and they were too big to be ignored, too committed to be co-opted. They were dangerous. They had to be silenced. No wonder the assassin was never caught."

Sandy stared at him. He wanted to laugh. He needed to laugh. But he couldn't. It wasn't funny. Edan Morse's hand dripped blood and Morse ignored it. He had passion in his voice where there should have been pain. He almost seemed to feed off the agony. To grow bigger. Stronger. His eyes were filled with slow brown fire, with absolute certainty. "And now?" Sandy said quietly.

Morse closed his bloody hand into a red fist, slowly, deliberately. "And now the hour has come round at last," he said in a voice like a preacher's. "The hour of the wolf and the serpent, the great conflagration that will destroy the house of lies. The Nazgûl will fly again. We will seize the blood-tide, and in its wake we will have a new world."

"You're crazy!" Sandy said with a conviction that he did not really feel. His rational mind was telling him that it was all insane, but there in Edan Morse's presence, looking at that pulsing red-stained fist, the world did not seem rational at all, and Morse seemed very plausible.

"No," Morse said. "The forces are aligned. Everything is come to place. Listen to the music."

"I've talked to the Nazgûl," Sandy said fervently. "All three of them. Even if all this crap was true, they'll never play together again. Oh, Maggio wants to, sure, but not Slozewski, not Faxon."

"You don't understand the situation quite so well as you think you do," Morse replied, his voice calmer now. He didn't even look at Sandy. He was staring at his bleeding hand, as if he found it vastly and endlessly fascinating. "Take Slozewski. You know about his fire. Consider the implications. His business is gone. He was underinsured and cannot rebuild. He is being sued for large sums of money he does not have. He will play when the time comes."

And then Sandy understood at last. "You weren't trying to kill him!" he blurted. "You waited until he left with me, and *then* you burned it down! To make him . . . to get him to . . ."

"You have my word, as one brother to another, as companions in the revolution—I had nothing to do with that fire." Morse reached into a pocket with his right hand, shook out a handkerchief, and wrapped it around his left to stay the flow of blood. "The fire was *inevitable*, Sandy. The fire was part of the pattern, the pattern the Nazgûl themselves foresaw. It was prophesied. Forces greater than any of us are at work."

Sandy didn't listen. "What are you going to do to Faxon? Kidnap one of his kids?"

"You don't understand. You're being thickheaded. Faxon will come around in turn. He *must*. It has been promised. The hour has come round at last, and everything will fall into place. Listen to the music."

Sandy was suddenly, furiously angry. He couldn't stand any more of this. He stood up. "What the fuck are you *talking* about?" he yelled. "Faxon wants nothing to do . . . Faxon is *past* . . ." But even as he fumbled for words, he remembered that slow balloon ride over Albuquerque, and Tracy's words in the truck afterward, and his denial rang hollow. "Wait a minute," he said. "What the fuck difference does Faxon make? You're nuts and I'm nuts for sitting here listening to you. So what if you get Faxon and Slozewski? That's only three out of four. And that fourth dude is going to be real fucking hard to convince." Sandy was shouting now, as if the volume of his denial lent weight and truth to it. "Strain your little memory for a sec, and you may be able to recall that Patrick Henry Hobbins *died* in 1971. He got half his head blown away by a high-powered rifle, and he never did sing worth a shit after that. How do you figure on getting around that?"

Edan Morse was astoundingly calm. "Death is not always so formidable an obstacle as you might imagine," he said. He rose and walked quickly around his desk and over to the door. He opened it, turned, and beckoned Sandy with a wave of his maimed hand. The handkerchief had turned red. Numbly Sandy walked to the door.

In the living room, Ananda sat on a couch talking to a short, slim man in denim whose back was to Sandy. "Pat?" Edan Morse said.

Patrick Henry Hobbins turned, got up off the couch, looked at each of them in turn, and said, "Yeah?"

THIRTEEN

And I come back to find the stars misplaced/
And the smell of a world that has burned

A noise, a soft footfall, and suddenly Sandy was awake, his heart pounding. He was naked and cold under a thin sheet on a wide king-size bed. The room was strange to him. He peered through the dimness at a fireplace, wood-paneled walls, smelled the salt of the sea, and felt dizzy and disoriented. Then he rose unsteadily and pulled back the heavy curtain beside the bed. Pale chilly light flooded the room. Beyond a pair of sliding glass doors was a patio deck and a gray, cold beach, wisps of fog curling around the deck railing and lying heavily on the sea.

Then Sandy remembered, vaguely. He was in the guest room of Edan Morse's beach house. Yes. But how . . . ?

While he stood there, squinting and frowning, the door behind him opened and Ananda came walking in. "Morning," she said cheerfully. "Thought I heard you moving around. We've got coffee and fresh orange juice, and I make the meanest waffle you ever tasted. Learned at Mommy's knee. Want to try one?" She was wearing a white tee shirt and the bottom half of a blue bikini. She looked as though she'd come straight from a morning swim. Her hair was wrapped up in a fluffy brown towel, and the tee shirt was sopping wet and clinging to her, emphasizing those incredible breasts. Her nipples were large and hard.

Sandy stood looking at her and realized that her nipples weren't the only things that were large and hard. He was suddenly very conscious of his nudity. He turned away from her slightly, trying to keep his cool. "Uh," he said eloquently. "Good morning."

Ananda grinned and walked over to him, her small bare feet leaving wet footprints on the parquet floor. "Hey," she said, "why so shy?" She caught him under the chin and gently turned his face toward hers. "I saw it all last night, right?" Her mouth was slightly open and she did that little thing with her tongue, flicking it across her lower lip. "Liked it, too," she added.

His erection throbbed, and Sandy looked from her to the bed and back again. "You mean you . . . I . . . us?"

Ananda gave him a mock scowl. "You don't remember? I'm hurt. I thought I was better than *that*." She kissed him lightly. "Well, we'll just have to try it again, I guess. And again and again and again until I get it right. I is a greedy lil' girl, massa."

"*Jesus*," Sandy muttered. He walked back across the door, sat on the edge of the bed, and cradled his head in his hands. "I don't remember *any-thing*. Well, hardly anything." He glanced up at her; she was standing there, one hip cocked, smiling fondly at him with vast amusement in her eyes. "What happened last night?" he asked her. "I mean, besides you and me. Us. You know."

"I know you need that coffee," Ananda said, "and that waffle, too. Why don't you take a shower while I whip 'em up? There's a couple of robes in the wardrobe. All different sizes. You should be able to find one that fits." She turned on her heel and pattered out. He stared at her trim curved ass as she left, and groaned.

The shower helped. He got it good and hot at first and scrubbed himself thoroughly, then wrenched it all the way over to the cold to blast the cob-webs off his memory. He emerged shivering, with beads of water in his beard, feeling a little closer to human. In the heavy wardrobe he found a thick green robe with white peace symbols all over it, and slipped it on. It was very warm. He sat on the bed, drying his hair and trying to remember.

Yet what he remembered most vividly were his nightmares.

They crowded his head now, refusing to fade as dreams ought to fade with the coming of the dawn, and Sandy knew they would be with him for a long time to come.

He had seen Sharon in the night, staring at him, her face still, her eyes cold behind her tinted glasses. As he'd watched, frost rimed over her glasses and crept up her cheeks until her whole face had turned to ice. Then it cracked and blew away.

He remembered papers fluttering in the wind, turning and rising, away and away, paper after paper. One paper in particular, half-covered with writing, twisting as it rose up into a storm-lashed purple sky. He had watched it go with a strange bittersweet feeling.

He heard Jared laughing at him, nastily, his great belly shaking with the force of it.

He was with Slum, talking to Slum, looking at Slum. Except that Slum was different; the beard and the great nimbus of hair were gone and he was gaunt and hollow-cheeked, and dressed neatly in white clothes, but his smile was tentative and his blue eyes were pale and watery and full of fear. And he began to scream, very suddenly, over and over, and his thin hands clawed at the empty air in front of him.

He dreamed of a candlelight parade he'd once marched in, walking through endless dark, windy, rain-swept streets with a small candle in his hand, holding it cupped between his fingers so the wind could not snuff the tiny flame. Others marched with him, before and behind, and they emerged in some vast field beneath a high white building on a hill. There were thousands of them, each with a candle; everywhere the flames burned, small brave stars in a sea of night, winking, shivering, held in frail cupped hands. Up above the stars in the night sky flickered like a million more candles. And then, suddenly, the stars changed. They were not candles. They were eyes. A million yellow slitted eyes. Watching. As they watched the darkness yawned, and gray faceless shapes in blue and khaki rushed in, and the candles fell and died.

But the longest dream, and the one he recalled most vividly, was one he had dreamed before, that terrible night in Chicago. Yet this time it had been longer, more real, more detailed. In some huge dark hall, the dance went on forever. The Nazgûl were up on stage, playing the "Armageddon/ Resurrection Rag" again, but they were hideous. Gopher John was gray and horribly burned, and ash flew from him as he played. Maggio's sneer had become satanic, and his chest crawled with maggots. Faxon's face was serene and handsome on one side and bleeding from a hundred grisly slashes on the other. And in front Hobbins stood, twice as large as life yet somehow insubstantial. Sandy could see through him, to the back of the stage, where a naked woman had been nailed up to a great X-shaped cross. She was a thin, big-eyed child-woman, and she was screaming in anguish as blood dripped from her nipples and ran out her vagina and down her legs. Her voice was strangely familiar, but none of the dancers paid her any mind. Froggy was there, dancing with a blond and trying to feel her up. Maggie and Lark danced together, around and around. Bambi sat on the sidelines, surrounded by children, waiting for a partner. Burning men and corpses and flayed women moved through the press of dancers. And Sandy was shouting at them, warning them of the coming bloodtide, but none of them would hear.

Ananda broke him from the grisly reverie when she returned with a tray bearing a hot, fragrant pot of black coffee, two cups, plus orange juice and waffles. The smell was heavenly, and Sandy suddenly realized that he was ravenous. "Want to go outside?" she asked him. "The sun's burning off the fog, and it's getting nice and warm."

Sandy nodded absently, got up, and opened the sliding glass doors for her. There were a white iron table and three chairs out there. Ananda set down the tray and Sandy settled into a chair. She poured him a cup of coffee, and he took a good healthy swallow of it before she even had time to serve the waffle.

She did make good waffles. He drowned his in butter and maple syrup—*real* maple syrup, the one-hundred-percent kind that costs the gross national product of Ecuador—and found that after a few bites he felt much better. He looked up at her. "Did I get drunk last night, or what?" he said. "I don't have a hangover, but I sure as hell had some weird dreams."

"Not dreams," Ananda said seriously. "Visions."

Sandy scowled. "Visions?"

"Don't you remember any of it?" she asked.

"I remember my little conference with your boss real well," Sandy said. "He took that motherfucking knife and slashed his palm halfway to the bone and bled all over the goddamned desk. It was one hell of a memorable conversational gambit, I'll tell you that much. It didn't bother him, either."

"Edan has learned disciplines that can banish pain," Ananda said. "He's taught me a few of them, but I'm not as good as he is. I can will away the pain of a toothache or a bruise, but Edan can withstand anything if he chooses to."

Sandy could believe her. He knew damn well that the hand had more nerves than any other part of the body, except the genitals. And Morse had cut *deep*. A normal man would have been in agony. "But *why*?" Sandy demanded. "What was the point of it?"

"For the blood," she said in all seriousness. "He needs the blood for the visions. But not only that. He wants your help, Sandy, he wants you to understand. That gesture showed you he isn't a fake or a liar, right?"

"No," Sandy said curtly. "It only showed me he's a fucking masochist, and a nut." He took another bite out of his waffle and was washing it down with some coffee when he caught sight of a figure walking along the beach, off in the distance. A big dog followed at his heels, romping and barking. The man had his jeans rolled up to his knees to walk in the cold surf. His hair was long and white in the sun. And suddenly it all came rushing back to Sandy. He almost dropped his coffee cup. "The kid!" he said. "*Hobbins!*"

Ananda smiled. "You were pretty wrought up by your talk with Edan. I heard you shouting through the wall. When the door opened you looked like you wanted to hit somebody. And then you saw Pat, and you *really* freaked out. I thought your eyes were going to pop out of your head."

The wind gusted off the sea, and Sandy shivered with cold. "Yeah? Well, I thought I was going to *die*! I almost shit my pants. Talk about seeing a ghost! I saw the film clips of Hobbins' death a dozen times, saw him lying there bloody in Faxon's arms with half his head gone and that microphone still clutched in his hand, went to his *funeral*, and then suddenly Morse opens the door and there he is, small as life, looking like he ain't aged a day since West Mesa." Sandy held his head in his hands and sighed. "You *bet* I was shook. Your boss shouldn't do things like that. That kid looks enough like Pat Hobbins to be his fucking *clone*. If you spring him on Faxon the way you sprung him on me, you'll give the guy a nervous breakdown."

Sandy was still unsteady, remembering it, but little by little the knots in his stomach untied. The kid *wasn't* Hobbins, of course. That had become clear the minute he'd opened his mouth and said a few words. He *looked* just like Hobbins, and his voice had roughly the same timbre and tone, and even the same kind of Philadelphia accent. But the personality was totally different, obviously different. The real Patrick Henry Hobbins had had most of the traits that so often seem to come with genius and fame and vast success early in life: when Sandy had interviewed him, he had been cock-sure, arrogant, loud and opinionated and often derisive. He'd had an enormous ego. But the kid was none of those things. He was soft-spoken and deferential, painfully polite, shy. Four times he had said he hoped he was good enough for the Nazgûl, and Edan Morse and Ananda had had to reassure him.

Larry Richmond. That was the kid's real name, as he'd admitted when Sandy questioned him. He'd been born in Bethlehem, Pennsylvania, where his father worked in a steel mill, but had moved to Philly in his early teens, after his father's death. That explained the accent. Like Hobbins, he was an albino, and short, and had been mocked and beaten frequently for his differences from the norm. Unlike Hobbins, he had been frightened instead of toughened by those childhood torments. Patrick Henry Hobbins was his hero. As Larry put it, "There aren't many albino role models, you know. The Hobbit was the big one." So naturally Richmond learned to play the guitar and sing, and naturally he formed a band as soon as he was able, and naturally they specialized in doing Nazgûl material. Larry Richmond sang well enough so that he was even able to make a career out of it, of sorts; he became a teenaged Hobbins imitator.

And then Edan Morse found him.

The rest had been Morse's doing. Richmond had borne only a superficial similarity to Hobbins, a likeness of coloration and size that he had played on and bolstered with clever costuming and a little makeup. But cosmetic surgery, paid for by Morse, had completed nature's work and made the likeness almost supernatural. Three operations, Larry said proudly. In between, and afterward, the kid stayed in Morse's beach house, learning a role. He spent six hours a day immersed in the Nazgûl: listening to their albums over and over, watching film and videotape of their concerts, studying every Hobbins move and intonation. He took voice lessons so as to sing more like Hobbins. He took dance class and gymnastics so as to move like Hobbins. He read every word ever written about his idol, including the complete back files of *Hedgehog* and *Rolling Stone* and *Crawdaddy*. He was a big fan of Sandy's.

The hell of it was, he was kind of a nice kid. And Edan Morse, like a man obsessed, was trying to obliterate him. In Morse's house, Larry Richmond did not exist. The kid was called "Hobbins" or "Pat" or "Hobbit," and Larry himself admitted ruefully, with a nervous little laugh and a glance at his host, that he now answered to those names a hell of a lot faster than to the one he'd been born with.

Sandy sat back in his chair, his coffee cooling in front of him, watching Larry Richmond come toward them up the beach. He was half-walking, half-running, playing with the dog, a big crazed golden retriever. The dog was yapping and barking and running circles around him, splashing water and spraying sand everywhere, and Larry was grinning and shouting commands to the animal, commands that the big dog seemed to blithely ignore. Richmond's hair, long and white and silky, moved with the wind and the motion of his running, and Sandy felt once again as if he were seeing a ghost. A pale pink-eyed ghost.

"I still think it stinks," he said to Ananda across the table. "Hobbins is dead. The kid should live his own life. Morse is making him over into some kind of grotesque parody. It's a sick joke."

"So you said last night," Ananda replied, "but I thought we'd talked you around."

Sandy grimaced. "You still haven't told me what happened last night. I remember meeting Larry—"

"Pat," Ananda corrected.

"*Larry*," Sandy insisted. "I interviewed him for a while, and when I finally got the whole story out of him I told Morse what I thought of it. Which wasn't much. And then..." He rubbed the back of his neck. "And then it gets all fuzzy."

"You remember drinking?" she said.

"Uh, yeah. And no. I remember, when I first saw Richmond, I was pretty shaken. Morse made me a drink. Scotch on the rocks. I sipped it as I talked to Larry." He shook his head. "And then?"

"Then you had another one," Ananda said. "And another one after that. You sat around talking to Edan and Pat and me, and drinking, and after a while you got pretty happy." She grinned. "Pretty horny, too. Edan went off to take care of his hand, Pat went to bed, and I finally led you into the bedroom and tucked you in. You were very drunk, and a little stoned from some hash I'd dug out, and silly, and lecherous. If you weren't having a good time, you sure as hell put on a fine act."

Sandy remembered none of it. It was disturbing. It wasn't like him to get that plastered, although come to think of it, he had been drinking too damn much this whole trip. It *certainly* wasn't like him to forget going to bed with Ananda—she was nothing if not memorable. "I feel like a fool," he said. "And a lout as well." Despite his long-standing open relationship with Sharon, he felt vaguely guilty, as if he'd betrayed her in some sense. Maybe that was the meaning of the icy image of her face that had troubled his sleep; his own unease come to haunt him. He also felt obscurely cheated; bad enough to sin and feel guilty, worse when you can't even recall the fun you'd had.

Ananda was remarkably understanding. "You're cute when you're drunk," she said lightly. "Don't worry about it." She turned toward the beach and waved to Richmond.

Richmond saw her, waved back, and came trotting their way, the dog bounding at his heels. He climbed up to the deck, breathing hard, and collapsed into the third chair. "Hi," he said. "Boy, I'm hungry. Can I have your leftovers?"

Sandy had eaten one waffle and part of a second; he pushed the portion that remained, cold and soggy with syrup, over to Richmond, and the kid wolfed it down eagerly. The dog, meanwhile, kept running around and around the table, stuck in a doggy orbit about them all. Finally Richmond said, "Hey, boy, hey, calm down. Sit, Bal, sit." The dog paused for a second and shook itself, spraying Sandy with saltwater and sand. Then it sat, and Larry Richmond gave it a piece of waffle. It gulped it down, then peered around and looked at Sandy suspiciously. It sniffed him, seemed to find him objectionable, and barked. Like most dogs, it had terminal halitosis. It barked again. "He likes you," Richmond said.

"Oh, great," Sandy said. "What does he do if he doesn't like someone? Tear out their throat?"

"He growls," Richmond said. He ruffled the top of the dog's head. "Down, boy. Lie, Bal, lie." The dog gave Sandy one final bark for good measure, flailed around frenetically with its tail, and stretched out on the deck. "Good Bal," Richmond said.

"Bal?" Sandy asked.

Richmond smiled shyly. "Balrog," he admitted. "I was really into that Tolkien stuff, you know, on account of Hobbins. Bal and I been partners for six years now. I raised him from a pup. We go everywhere together." He leaned over and patted the dog's head. "Don't we, boy? Huh, don't we?" Bal barked happily in affirmation.

Sandy frowned. "Are you really going to go through with this insanity?" he asked Richmond. "The Hobbins impersonation, I mean?"

Richmond gave him a look of innocent puzzlement. "Sure," he said. "I mean, why not? Mister Blair, you got to understand, that was what I was doing anyway. Mister Morse has just fixed it so I get to do it better. I'd be pretty dumb to pass on a chance like this. I do my best, you know, but I know I'm not the singer Pat Hobbins was, and I never will be. The only way I can make it at all is by taking advantage of what I've got. And now I'm going to get a chance to sing and play with the Nazgûl. You don't know how much that means to me. The *Nazgûl*! I mean, *wow*, you know? I used to dream of just meeting those guys, and now I'm going to be in a band with them." He got up. "I got to go shower and get dressed. Good talking to you, Mister Blair. I hope you write us up good. Thanks for the waffle." He slapped his thigh. "Heel, Bal, heel." The dog rose and followed him inside.

Sandy found Ananda studying him. "Will you?" she asked. "Write them up good?"

"I may not write them up at all," Sandy replied. "In the first place, I still don't really believe in this reunion. In the second place, I doubt that I'll be covering it. I don't think I *want* to cover it." He leaned forward and put his elbows on the table and peered at her intently. "Ananda, your boss is *weird*, and so is that giant geek of a bodyguard he keeps around. I don't know what you're doing hanging around with them."

She smiled. "What's a nice girl like me doing in a place like this, right? My part, Sandy, that's what I'm doing. That's what you ought to be doing, too. As for Edan, are you still so skeptical?"

"I'll admit he had me going last night," Sandy said. "It all seemed very real. He can be persuasive, no doubt of it. But in the cold light of day, it all seems very silly. The man is deranged. He mutilates himself on a regular basis, it seems, and he has traded in the violent revolutionary set for a lunatic pipedream of some kind of rock 'n' roll armageddon. Come *on*, Ananda!"

"I don't know what I can say, or how much I *should* say. If you're not part of the solution, you're part of the problem, right? If you aren't with us, you're an enemy, and there are things an enemy ought not to be told." She leaned forward and licked her lips nervously. "But I like you, Sandy. I hope you know that. Really. I don't get so close so fast to just anybody, you know? So I want to try. For your sake and mine and for the sake of the world, I want to make you see." She cocked her head thoughtfully to one side and looked at him. "If Edan has no power, how do you explain what happened to you in Chicago?"

Sandy suddenly had gooseflesh creeping up both arms. He shivered and pulled back from her, still unwilling to accept. "Chicago?" he said. "What do you mean?"

"You visited Maggio in Chicago and talked to him," Ananda said patiently. "Rick called Edan as soon as he got home that night, to tell him all about it. Edan decided right then that you could be useful to us, or that you could be a danger. So he decided to influence you, to test you. He . . . he cut himself, as he always does, to begin the ceremony. Across thousands of miles, he touched you. You felt his power. You can't deny it, can you? That night in Chicago, something strange happened to you."

Sandy was sitting very straight in his chair, staring at her. He could feel his heart pounding in his chest. The silence and the tension were palpable. He opened his mouth to reply, hesitated, fell silent, and looked away. He couldn't bear her serious, somehow scary, eyes. Finally he forced himself to look back. "Yes," he said, in a low voice. "A dream, I thought. Strange. I was at the Hilton, and suddenly it was 1968 again. The convention. The demonstrations, the police going nuts, the rioting. All of it. I walked through it. It was like it was happening all over again, only it was different too, it was spooky. Sometimes I was part of it and sometimes I was like a ghost. The people were faceless, frightening. I thought it was just a nightmare, but I changed hotel rooms during the dream and woke in a different room."

Ananda nodded. "You touched the past. It might have been the future just as easily. Edan says the past and the future are the same thing, in a way, and that either is just as malleable. It is only our mindsets that lock us in rigidly to the moment, right? But Edan has broken through. In a very limited way. With visions." She reached across the table and took hold of Sandy's hand and squeezed it. "Sandy, *believe* me! It *can* happen! It *will*! It *must*! Edan says there is power in blood, and power in belief, and power in the music. And forces are at work now, forces bigger than any of us can understand, and they will bring the blood and the belief and the music all together, and the walls will come *down*, Sandy, they will, and the past will become the future and the future will become the past, and we can seize the moment and change what was and what is and what will be. We can do it, right? And it's for the cause, Sandy. It's the only way. We'll end racism and sexism and oppression, get rid of war and crime and violence and injustice, we'll remake the whole fucking *world*! But we all have to play our roles. And you have to *believe*."

For one eternal moment, the wind shuddered through Sandy and he felt the warmth and the strength of Ananda's hand around his own and heard the conviction in her voice and remembered the blood flowing from Edan Morse's hand and the glitter in his eyes and the faceless ghosts in the streets of Chicago, and he was convinced. For one eternal moment; but then the wind blew again, and it all flew away and faded. He extricated his hand. "No," he said.

Ananda looked at him, puzzled, defiant. "You felt it yourself. You admitted it."

"I had a strange dream," Sandy said. "I didn't know how you could possibly know about it, so you had me going for a second. Only I figured it out." He smiled. "I *told* you about it, didn't I? Last night, in bed."

"No."

"Yes," Sandy insisted. "What else could it be? I admit that I don't remember telling you about it, but I don't remember going to bed with you either, so I can hardly be expected to recall all the pillow talk. Sometimes I have a very big mouth. Good try, but no cigar."

Ananda sighed. "Have it your way," she said. "You're wrong, but I'm not going to be able to convince you, I can see that now. OK. You'll still get convinced, and when you do you'll come back to us. Just remember the things you saw in the night. And think about what I've said, and what Edan told you yesterday."

"Let me give you some advice, 'Nanda. Cut yourself loose from Morse, and do it now. This whole scheme is insanity. And Morse is dangerous. He denies it, but I know he's responsible for Jamie Lynch's murder and probably for the Gopher Hole fire, and there's no way of telling what he might do tomorrow. You're a nice lady, and I know you sincerely want to make things better out there, but this isn't the way, believe me."

Ananda was looking at him with her large dark eyes, and for an instant the expression there was strange, somehow alien. Then she smiled and shook her long black hair and her eyes lit with amusement. "It's the *only* way," she said. "And you are wrong about Edan. He did not have Lynch killed and he did not have the Gopher Hole burned. Take my word for it."

"I wish I could." He stood up. "I've got to get going. Suppose you show me where my clothes are and drive me back to Santa Monica?"

Ananda nodded and led him back inside. When Sandy shrugged out of the heavy robe and started to dress, she moved close to him and draped her arms lightly around his neck. "Sure you don't have time for a quickie?" She smiled. "This time, you could pay close attention. There might be a pop quiz afterward."

She was warm and tempting as she pressed lightly against him, but the fire had gone out, and Sandy shook his head. "I can't," he said. "I've got to go."

Ananda disengaged and gave him a mock scowl. "You can't trust anyone over thirty," she said. Then she hit him with a towel.

But later, much later, after he had dressed and she'd driven him back to his motel, Ananda leaned out of the van and gave him a quick kiss on the forehead and said, "Take care of yourself. I'm going to be seeing you again, right?"

"I'm not so sure about that," Sandy said.

"Oh, yes I am. You don't know it, but I do. You'll be back." She grinned, "Meanwhile, keep on truckin'." She revved up the van, backed out, waved at him one last time, and shot off down the street. Sandy went back to his room. He was cold inside, and empty, and anxious to be off. He started to pack.

FOURTEEN

**Flashing for the warriors whose strength is not to fight/
Flashing for the refugees on the unarmed road of flight**

In the high mountains of western Colorado, Sandy ran into the first onslaught of winter. Cold winds hammered at Daydream and shivered through her door cracks, and a thin powdering of snow covered some of the roads and forced him to slow down. It took him longer than anticipated to get to Denver, and longer still to find the Byrne estate, though he had been there once before, a long time ago.

It was an imposing place, occupying a block all its own, sealed off from the grunge of the city by a ten-foot-high wrought iron fence that ended in an intimidating row of black spearheads. Behind the encircling barrier were thickets of old trees that obscured the view of the house from the street, so common eyes might not peer at the Byrnes at play. Behind the trees were broad green lawns, carefully tended flower beds, and four lean and nasty Dobermans that roamed the grounds freely and liked to lunch on unwelcome visitors. The house itself was big, white, and vulgar, with four tall columns in front that gave it the look of an old plantation house. The only thing needed to complete the image was a shuffling darkie or two, and no doubt the lack was deeply felt. There was, Sandy remembered, a lawn statue of a black jockey out front, which Slum's father in his infinite charm liked to pat and call "Jigaboo Jim."

Inside, the Byrne house was full of dead animal heads, antique furniture, and guns. It smelled of pipe smoke and money. Northwestern had been an expensive school, but of Sandy's college chums, only Jefferson Davis Byrne—Slum—had come from real wealth. Maggie had been on full scholarship till she dropped out, Sandy himself had a partial scholarship and a work-study job and a student loan, while Froggy Cohen and Bambi Lassiter and Lark Ellyn had all hailed from affluent upper-middle-class environs. Only Jefferson Davis Byrne had arrived freshman year driving his own Corvette Stingray.

Sandy parked Daydream on the cold, sunny street across from the big double gate fronting the drive, got out and walked around the car and stood there a moment, looking up at the house and remembering. It had been Christmas of sophomore year, and Slum had invited Sandy to come for the holidays, and Sandy had accepted. One of the biggest mistakes of his life. The real irony of it was that he had accepted mostly so he could meet Slum's father. Even then Sandy had wanted to be a writer, and the head of the Byrne clan was a very successful writer indeed, even though Sandy found his books sexist, racist, and semiliterate. Sandy's opinion made damn little difference, however. Joseph William Byrne was the author of an endless series of big, fat, steamy, bloody novels about mercenaries, all of them full of explicit gore and manly martial virtue and cheerful rape. Every one of them was at least six hundred pages long and had a one-word title. The best of them had dominated the bestseller list for months at a time, though they were the sort of books that no one would ever admit to reading. The worst of them still outsold *Copping Out*, Sandy's most successful book, by a factor of about four to one. In the trade they called him "Butcher" Byrne, and he was proud of the nickname.

Sandy had met him only once, for that long-ago Christmas visit, but once had been enough. His memories were vivid. Butcher Byrne had been tall and wide, with iron-gray hair and horn-rimmed glasses. His bearing was rigor-mortis-erect. He smoked a pipe, and claimed to carry a knife inside his heavy black boot. He favored khaki bush jackets with belts and pocket snaps and strange little colored ribbons. Sandy suspected that he had epaulettes on his undershirts. His voice boomed and echoed like artillery fire, and he brooked no interruptions. He had four Dobermans outside and a big black German shepherd inside and all of them were attack-trained. He had five sons, Slum being the third in the succession, and would have liked to attack-train them as well. He had no daughters, but he did have very firm opinions about the female role in society. He had very firm opinions about most everything, in fact, but his favorite topics were war, politics, and writing. Sandy made the mistake of mentioning his literary aspirations, and for two days he received Butcher Byrne's Famous Writers'

Course. The heart of the course seemed to be how well Butcher's books sold, and how much royalty money he collected. "I cry all the way to the bank," he told Sandy, eight or nine times, while dismissing his bad reviews. He was just a "storyteller," Butcher said. Forget about that "art" stuff. "A crock of human excrement," he said loudly. Despite the fact that Butcher could describe the way human brains looked on a wall after being splattered by a rifle bullet, the word *shit* was not in his vocabulary, and was not heard in his home.

Given Butcher's character and the nature of home life in what Sandy had promptly dubbed "Fort Byrne," it was no surprise that Jefferson Davis' rebellion, when it came, had taken him all the way to Slumhood, and made him the antithesis of everything his father stood for, and the embodiment of everything his father loathed. What *was* surprising was that Slum would return here, to Fort Byrne, after all the bitterness and all the renunciations. The last Sandy had heard of him, Slum had been a draft exile in Canada, back around 1973 or so.

Hands shoved deep into his pockets, Sandy crossed the street and started up the drive, keeping a wary eye out for Dobermans and wondering whether Butcher had mellowed or whether Slum had somehow changed into a kind of ghastly echo of his father. The Dobermans did not appear. Maybe it was too cold for them; there was a real snap in the air, and most of the trees were bare now. Sandy climbed the porch, past the jockey statue, and pressed the doorbell, half-expecting the chimes to play *Charge!* A raucous buzz was all he got.

There were no servants. Never had been. Butcher could easily have afforded servants, but he had a deep distrust of what he called "inferior genetic material," and wouldn't allow any in his castle. The youth who opened the door had a face that gave Sandy a start. It might have been Jefferson Davis Byrne himself, as he had looked that first day Sandy had seen him behind the wheel of that red Corvette.

Sandy remembered that Jeff Byrne very well. A tall, skinny, gangling sort, all elbows and knees and awkwardness, always bumping into things and knocking them over. Life in Butcher's shadow had left him quiet and deferential, and apology always on his lips. Shy and painfully insecure, he sported a crew cut, a hundred wide ties, and lots of double-breasted sports jackets. He studied very hard for fear his grades would be poor, and took Rush Week in dead earnest, terrified that he'd fail to pledge a good fraternity.

Then Maggie had gotten hold of him, and the change had begun. She'd been seeing Jeff even before she started going with Sandy; in fact, they'd met each other through her, and for a year or two they'd managed to share her attentions without rancor or jealousy. But Maggie had done more than take Jeff Byrne's virginity; she'd given him some self-confidence for the first time in his life, and planted the seeds of his revolt. Once started, the metamorphosis snowballed, and Jeff seemed to change into Slum as fast as Lon Chaney, Jr., changed into the Wolfman.

In October he went to his first foreign film, and ate Chinese food (or "gook slop" as Butcher so endearingly called it) with Maggie afterward. In November he went to hear a radical speaker, and smoked his first marijuana cigarette. In December he signed a petition against the war, and took part in a student power rally.

By February he had quit his fraternity. By March he had a beard growing, and his hair was getting wilder and wilder. He never trimmed the beard or cut the hair as long as Sandy knew him. Eventually the beard became a gnarled red-brown thicket covering half his chest, while his hair stood out a foot from his head in all directions. His bangs hung down across his face and his whiskers crept up his cheeks so that you could scarcely see a face there, just a tiny little mouth smiling gently and two bright blue eyes behind a hirsute veil.

In April Maggie taught him to sew, and he sat down and made up his Slum Suit, sewing all of his neckties but one into a weird crazy-quilt knee-length poncho of a hundred different colors and patterns. He was very proud of it; he said he'd taken his neckties, a symbol of repression, and made them over into a bright and flagrant flag of freedom. Just about the time Butcher Byrne was paying his staggering income taxes that year, his son donned his amazing poncho. He wore it every day for the rest of his college career. The lone necktie he had saved—a skinny electric-blue tie on which he hand-painted the words "Souvenir of Guam"—he wore loosely tied around his neck, the ends wildly uneven.

In May he bought a block of hashish the size of a cornerstone and gave free samples to every guy in the dorm. It made him real popular. In June he told Butcher that he wasn't coming home for the summer, painted his Corvette green and purple and wrote FUCK LBJ on its hood, and took off with Maggie for a summer on the road.

He returned in the fall riding a red-white-and-blue motortrike, with Maggie sitting behind him. He had flowers threaded through his beard and a faded porkpie hat on top of his head, and he was Slum, then and forever. Still quiet and gentle, he liked to sit in his room and eat endless trays of hash brownies that he baked himself. He bought three kittens (Butcher said cats were "fairy pets") and named them Shit, Piss, and Corruption. He hired a couple of guys to go to his classes and take his tests. He burned all his boots and his feet got hard with calluses and crusty-black with dirt. He smiled a lot and laughed uproariously at TV sitcoms and got fat from all those brownies, so that his Slum Suit bound tight around his belly. And that was what he'd been like, in December of sophomore year, when he took Sandy home to meet Butcher. The expression on Butcher's face when they sailed up the drive on Slum's motortrike had almost made the week of rancor worthwhile.

"Yes?" asked the kid in the doorway. "What can I do for you?" Sandy realized he'd been standing there dumbly, staring. The kid was about seventeen or eighteen, in an alligator shirt and designer jeans, and he looked so much like Jeff Byrne had once looked that it hurt.

But it wasn't Slum, of course; it was a brother, the youngest brother. "I'm Sandy Blair," he said. "I was a good friend of your brother Jeff, in college. And you're . . . Dave, is it?"

"Doug," the youth corrected. "I don't remember you."

"You were pretty young the last time we met," Sandy said. "Four or five, maybe." He remembered an energetic boy with a loud voice and a lot of toy guns. Doug, yes, of course the name was Doug. Douglas MacArthur Byrne. He'd owned a huge water gun shaped like a tommy-gun, and he used to like to hit Sandy and Slum in the crotch so it'd look as if they'd wet their pants. "Is your brother here? I'd like to see him."

"Jeff?" the kid asked uncertainly.

"Yeah. He's the only Byrne brother I know."

Doug looked uncertain. "Well, I don't know." He frowned. "Well, I guess you should come in." Ushering Sandy inside, he led him through a foyer to a large, stiffly formal sort of room full of gun racks and trophy cases. "Wait here," he said. "I'll get Jane."

Sandy had no idea who Jane was. Maybe Slum's mother, he thought. He had met her, of course—a plump little mouse of a woman with faded blond hair and frightened eyes—but as he recalled it, her name had been "Mrs. Joseph William Byrne," or sometimes just "Mother."

While he waited, Sandy wandered around the room, which reminded him a bit of a museum or a war memorial. Above the fireplace was the centerpiece: a long, wide slate mantel absolutely covered with Butcher's trophies, forty or fifty years' worth. Shooting trophies, military medals on black felt, testimonial plaques from various lodges, dog show awards, and no less than three citations as "Father of the Year" from something called the Patriotic League: 1954, 1957, and 1962. On the wall above the trophies were Butcher's degrees and a big oil portrait of the man himself, circa

World War II. He wore a captain's bars, and bombs were exploding in the terrain behind him, while Messerschmitts screamed overhead. Sandy wondered how many Messerschmitts they'd had on the Georgia army base where Captain Joseph William Byrne had actually spent all of his war years, according to Slum.

There were no literary prizes among Butcher's trophies, but the bookcases built into the wall on either side of the hearth were jammed with his novels, each of them hand-bound in black leather.

Elsewhere in the room, each of the Byrne sons had his own portrait and trophy case. The eldest son, Joseph William Byrne, Jr., had won almost as many trophies as Dad. His portrait showed a fortyish man with a hard, seamed face, wearing a uniform and oak leaves. He was career military, Sandy remembered. Across from it was a case done up all in black, full of personal effects as well as prizes, including a few scraps of uniform. The portrait was black-bordered and showed a young man wearing a green beret and squinting into the sun. Robert Lee Byrne had been one of the first Americans in 'Nam, and one of the first casualties as well.

Doug's trophy case was packed with baseball and basketball prizes. The fourth brother, George Patton Byrne, was more of a football player. His portrait showed him in West Point gray.

Slum's case was almost empty. A row of honor roll pins, two small chess trophies, and even one pathetic plastic victory cup for winning a three-legged race at a VFW picnic in 1957. His portrait had obviously been painted from a high-school graduation photo.

He was staring at it when he heard footsteps. "Hello," a woman's voice said. "You must be Mister Blair. I'm Jane Dennison."

She wasn't Slum's mother, that was for sure. She was a slender, brisk, handsome woman of about thirty-five, with short brown hair and nails trimmed to the quick. She gave Sandy a peremptory handshake and led him to a chair. Then she sat opposite him, crossed her legs, and said, "What can I do for you?"

"Damned if I know," Sandy said. "I want to see Slum. Jeff. That's what I told Doug, and he went and fetched you."

"I see," she said. "Why do you want to see Jeff?"

"No special reason. We're friends. We go back to college. I was traveling through and thought I'd see how he was doing. What's the problem here? And who are you? A housekeeper, Slum's girlfriend, what?"

She pressed her lips together primly. "I am Jeff's nurse," she said. "Mister Blair, you claim to be Jeff's friend, but you have obviously been out of touch with him for some time. Might I ask you when you last saw him?"

"A long time ago," Sandy admitted. "It was either '72 or '73. Up in Canada." He remembered the visit well. Slum had been in exile for almost two years at that point. Having dropped out of college at the beginning of his junior year, he'd lost his draft deferment, and his efforts to get conscientious objector status had been denied, though they had caused Butcher to disown him. "I ain't gonna shoot no one," Slum had said stubbornly. "I used to get sick when Butcher made me shoot deer when I was a kid. He even made me shoot this cat I'd brought home with me once, and I wet my pants. I sure as hell ain't shooting no people." And so he'd hit the road for Canada. Maggie had thrown him a big farewell party, and hundreds of friends had come to see him off. He'd sat on a raised platform under a HELL NO, SLUM WON'T GO! banner, beaming, and they'd given him a standing ovation. Froggy had jumped up on a table and toasted him as one of "the *real* heroes of this war" and "the gutsiest member of the Byrne clan."

Slum wound up in a farmhouse in Nova Scotia with three other American draft exiles, and when the *Hog* sent Sandy up that way to cover the baby seal slaughter, he'd taken some time off for a visit. He'd liked the friend he'd found up north. The beard and the wild hair were still there, but he'd traded in his Slum Suit for plain denim work clothes, his fat had turned to muscle, and his dopester phase was obviously behind him. One day Sandy had helped him shingle a roof. He remembered the deft, agile way Slum had handled himself, the way he drove a nail with three sure swift hammer blows while Sandy needed a dozen and usually bent the sucker, his simple pride in doing a good job. He had seemed robust, very self-assured, growing and happy. Sandy had left with the promise to visit again, soon, but of course he never had.

"Canada," Jane Dennison was saying. "Well, that was quite a long time ago, Mister Blair. Jeff returned from Canada in March of 1974, when his mother died. He wished to attend the funeral. Of course, the authorities were watching for him, and Jeff was apprehended and sent to prison for draft evasion. He spent just over two years in a federal penitentiary, and I'm afraid the experience was a shattering one for him. He has had severe psychological problems ever since."

"What kind of problems?" Sandy demanded. He was suddenly angry. Angry at the nurse for laying the bad news on him. Angry at Slum, for not writing, not trying to get in touch. Damn it, he could have helped, could have mounted a campaign in the *Hog*, could have done *something*. Most of all he was angry at himself for falling out of touch and letting all this happen behind his back.

"Chronic depression," the nurse said, "and episodes of psychotic vio-lence."

"*Violence?*" Sandy said. "That's impossible. Slum was as gentle a soul as I ever knew."

"I assure you, Jeff is as capable of violent behavior as anyone. He has been institutionalized twice, Mister Blair, and has received a full course of electroshock therapy, but his problems persist. So you see, under the cir-cumstances, it would not be in Jeff's best interests for you to talk to him. While he is happy enough much of the time, he is easily disturbed, and I'm afraid that seeing you would be most likely to touch off an episode. I'm sure you don't want that."

Sandy stared at her. "What the hell are you talking about? I'm his friend. He'll be glad to see me."

"Perhaps part of him will, but another part will be badly upset. You rep-resent the very period of life that he most needs to forget, the period in which he first began acting irrationally and assumed the identity of 'Slum,' as you call him. It would be much better for him not to be reminded of those years."

"Those were the happiest years of his life," Sandy said. "This doesn't make sense to me. I want to see Slum."

"The fact that you continue to call him by that nickname tells me that you cannot be trusted to speak to him," she said stiffly. "If you were truly his friend, you would understand that."

"I don't think you know what you're talking about."

Jane Dennison uncrossed her legs and stood up. "I do not intend to sit here and listen to a layman question my professional competence. I'm afraid I cannot permit you to see Jeff. Doug will show you out, or perhaps you can find the way yourself?"

Sandy stood up and faced her, scowling. "Yeah," he said, "I can find the way, but I sure as hell don't intend to. Not until I see Slum, or Jeff, or what-ever the fuck you want to call him."

"That is not your decision to make, Mister Blair, it is mine, and I assure you that you will not change my mind with vulgar language. Must I have you evicted?"

"Yeah, I guess you must," Sandy said sharply. He stalked past her, quickly, out into the foyer, and looked around as he heard her hurrying af-ter him. Upstairs, he thought. The bedrooms were upstairs, and that was where he'd find Slum. He darted to the wide curved stair and bounded up the steps two at a time. Down below he heard Jane Dennison calling loudly for Doug. "SLUM!" he shouted, moving down the corridor and opening doors as he went. The thick carpet absorbed the sound of his voice, and he had to shout louder. "SLUM! Where the fuck are you? *SLUM!*"

All the way at the end of the hall, a door opened. A tall, painfully thin man in tennis clothes stood there blinking. He was beardless and shorn and looked older than his years. "Sandy?" he said wonderingly. "Is it really you, Sandy?" His face, long and hollow-cheeked, broke into a tremulous smile. "*Sandy!*" He beamed.

Sandy took two quick steps, stopped, and almost stumbled. Slum's appearance hit him like a physical blow. The severity of his face. The faded, watery look of his eyes. The very gauntness of him. And his clothes. Tennis clothes. White clothes. So very white. *The dream,* Sandy thought, with a tremor of sudden irrational fear. But then Slum came toward him and hugged him fiercely, and the moment passed as Sandy found himself hugging back as hard as he could.

"You look…" Sandy started. He was going to say, "good," but he found he couldn't stomach the lie. "…uh…different," he finished.

Slum smiled warily. "I know *that*, Sandy," he said. "Come on." He led him down the hall to a large bedroom full of light and settled into a lotus position on the floor while Sandy sat in an armchair. "How did you get past Butcher?" Slum asked.

"I didn't see Butcher. Just your brother Doug and some dragon lady who calls herself Jane Dennison. She didn't want me to see you. I pushed past her and came up anyway."

"We had better talk fast, then. Dennison is probably phoning Butcher right now. He must be at his club, or out to lunch. Otherwise he'd have set the dogs on you." Again that quick, shaky smile, a smile full of fear, as if Slum knew he was smiling at the wrong thing and would shortly be punished for it. "But he'll get back fast when he hears from her, and then you'll get your ass kicked out."

"What *is* this? You can't have visitors? Don't you have anything to say about it?"

"No," said Slum.

Sandy scowled. "She says you're crazy. Chronic depression. Psychotic violence. Is it true? You gone nuts on me, Slum?"

Slum looked down at his thin, bony hands, and giggled. "Crazy," he said. "I guess I am." He giggled again. Sandy didn't like that giggle one bit. "I'm legally incompetent. Butcher had me declared legally incompetent. So that does make me crazy, I guess." He looked up at Sandy, and the little smile faded. His mouth trembled, and for a moment it looked as though he was going to cry. "Sandy, I *am*... disturbed. I was real down after I got out of prison. Chronic depression, they called it. They put me in a mental place, gave me electroshock. Therapy, they call it therapy. And Sandy, ever since...well, maybe I'm not so depressed, but it's like I'm scared, scared they'll do the shock thing again. And I don't remember things. Things I ought to remember. It's like part of my mind is *gone*. So I guess they're right. I'm crazy. But it's *their* fault, Sandy. It's *Butcher's* fault." He wrapped his arms around himself and trembled violently.

Sandy felt himself getting more and more angry, but he tried to hold it in check. "What about these psychotic episodes?" he asked. "Are you really *violent?*"

"After I got out of the hospital the first time and came home, I tried to leave. I wanted to go back to Canada. Butcher wouldn't let me, so I pulled a knife on him. Kitchen knife. He just walked up and took it away from me and slapped me across the face, told me he knew I was too yellow to use it. He was right, too. That was one of my episodes. Sometimes I get mad and throw things. Last week I smashed Butcher's Father of the Year cup for 1964. It's out being repaired. I'm a dangerous maniac, Sandy. A dangerous violent *incompetent* maniac. I even got to use an electric shaver." He forced a smile. "It's real good to see you, Sandy. How's the old gang? Do you still see them?"

"I haven't," Sandy said. "Not for a long time. But just recently, I've been seeing them all, one by one, driving across the country. That's why I'm here."

"How's Maggie?" Slum asked. "If you see her again, tell her I think of her a lot, OK?" He looked down at his hands again. "I haven't been with a woman since prison. I'm impotent. I don't know if it was the electroshock or the time in jail. Jail was pretty bad. I got raped a bunch of times. It was like it broke something inside me, something strong, that made me *me*. Rape can do that to you."

Sandy was aghast. "I don't *believe* it! What kind of place were you in? I thought draft evaders got sent to clean little minimum security places where things like that didn't happen."

Slum smiled. "No, that's for the Watergate guys. Oh, maybe some draft dodgers got minimum security, but they didn't have Butcher for a father. I can't prove it, but I think he was the one did it to me. The judge was an old fraternity buddy of his. Butcher didn't want me coddled, thought some hard time would do me good. I spent my time in a maximum security institution, until I freaked out." He frowned. "When I tell people, when I say that Butcher was the one that did it, they say it just shows how incompetent

I am. Paranoid. Blaming my father for everything. He's the one who turned me in to the police too, when I came back to Mother's funeral."

"Are you *sure*? Not even Butcher—"

"Oh, he's admitted it. I was a criminal. I had to face up to my crime like a man, take the consequences of my actions. The consequences were about a hundred million cocks up my ass, I guess. At the end I didn't even struggle." Now he did have tears in his eyes. "Sandy, why didn't you come visit? Or write me at least? It was really bad in there, Sandy, I could have used a few friends. I kept hoping that you or Maggie or Froggy would show up. I would even have been glad to see Lark, even though he would have called me a dumbshit. Why didn't any of you *come*?" His voice got shrill toward the end.

"Because we didn't know," Sandy said. "Were we supposed to read minds, or what? Until a few weeks ago, I thought you were still in Canada. Why didn't you write when you got into trouble?"

Slum stared. His mouth opened and closed again soundlessly. Then he threw back his head and laughed. "Oh, oh, oh, oh," he said in a high, hysterical voice. "Oh, oh, that's *funny*, oh, so funny, oh, oh." He wiped tears from his cheek with the back of his hand. "Sandy," he said, "I wrote you, oh, three, four times. I wrote Bambi and Froggy too, and even Lark. I wrote Ted and Melody and Anne, everybody I could think of. I wrote Maggie once a week for half a year, until I finally gave up."

"I don't get it," Sandy said. "I never got any letters, and I'm sure the others didn't, either. They would have called. Even Lark."

Slum laughed again. "What a joke!" he said. "Of *course* you didn't get any letters. Butcher must have had them intercepted. Paid somebody off. The warden, some guards, maybe even someone in the post office, who the hell knows. Maybe all of them. Butcher could afford it. He didn't want me to associate with you. Not with any of you. You were all bad influences. You turned his son into a commie dope-fiend faggot. He'll tell you so once he gets home. I was a coward already, he knows that, but I wasn't a commie dope-fiend faggot until I got to college and fell in with you bad sorts. Oh, I was so *stupid*. I *am* incompetent. I should have known. I'm not near paranoid enough, not yet. You can't be paranoid enough with Butcher around. I thought what he wanted me to think, that you just didn't care, that you'd never really been my friends at all." He balled his hands into fists. "Sandy, I want to kill that man. My shrink says that's very sick, but I want to do it. I wish I had the guts to do it. We got enough weapons around here. Shotguns, rifles, pistols. He's even got an Uzi and an old bazooka down in the basement." Slum grabbed an imaginary machine gun and sprayed the room with invisible bullets. "Boom boom boom boom," he announced loudly. "Blow his fucking head right off, just like in his books. Piss on his coffin. And then rape Miss Dennison. If I could get it up. Shove it right up her ass, that's where she deserves it." He giggled. "I told you, Sandy, they're right."

Sandy remembered a tall gangling freshman who kept knocking things over and apologizing. He remembered a heavy, hairy sophomore in a suit of a hundred colors, smiling as he listened to Donovan sing "Atlantis" over and over, sitting very still for fear of disturbing the kitten asleep in his lap. He remembered an exile, bearded and muscular, driving nails with smooth precision. He wanted to gag.

Downstairs he heard a door slam, and a huge familiar voice boomed, "*Where is he?*" A female voice answered, shrill but too soft for Sandy to catch the words, and two pairs of footsteps started up the stairs.

"You're in trouble now," Slum said. "He'll threaten to sic the dog on you, and then promise to shoot you himself. Watch and see. Butcher is as predictable as his plots."

It was only a moment before Butcher Byrne appeared in the doorway of his son's room, but Sandy had time to stand and cross his arms and feed his fury. Joseph William Byrne had grown older. His hard leathery face was scored by deep wrinkles and frown lines, and the iron-gray hair was mostly white. He had traded his horn rims for silver aviator frames, and his bush jacket was made of leather instead of khaki. But it still had epaulettes. "Mister Blair," he said loudly, "you are trespassing in my house. You will re-move yourself. Now."

"I'm visiting my friend," Sandy said. "Slum, you want me to leave?"

Slum smiled. "Of course not."

"My son Jefferson is under psychiatric care thanks to friends like your-self. He doesn't know what's best for him. Your visit may already have set his treatment back months or even years. *You* did this to him, Blair. You and your Jew roommate and that shanty-Irish slut he got involved with. Well, Jefferson is finished with all of you. I have seen to that."

"Yeah, I know," said Sandy. "Interfering with the mails is a federal rap, Butcher."

"Do you intend to leave peacefully or not?" Byrne said.

"Not," said Sandy.

Butcher actually smiled at that. "Good. I have several dogs on the grounds. All I need do is whistle, and they will see to your permanent re-moval. Or I could simply shoot you."

Slum laughed. "Told you so."

"Do I get my choice?" Sandy asked. "Butcher, you know, you're a real crock of shit."

Byrne purpled. A big vein in his forehead began to throb, like a thick blue worm in a feeding frenzy. "If you're trying to shock me, save your breath. I served in the military, you know—"

"I never would have guessed," Sandy said.

"—and in the barracks I heard all the four-letter words you know and quite a few others besides. So spare me your vulgar vocabulary."

"You want vocabulary? Here's a few words for you, then. Sadist. That's a good one. Anal-retentive prick. Bastard. Psychotic. Hack. Fascist. Put them all together and they spell BUTCHER."

Byrne's vein looked about to burst. "I will not stand here and be called a fascist by a cheap little peacenik punk," he roared. "I defended this country against the Nazis, I'll have you know!"

"Oh, yeah. Single-handedly saved all the peanut fields in Georgia from the blitzkrieg, the way I hear it. Whoop-de-do."

"You realize that you and I have the same publisher, Blair? And that I can end your career with a phone call?"

"Don't trouble yourself, I'm ending it myself."

Butcher Byrne turned around. Jane Dennison and his son Doug were standing in the door behind him, watching the show. "Douglas, bring me my shotgun," Butcher said.

"Yes, sir," Doug replied. He vanished.

"You'd better leave," Slum said. "He'll shoot you, Sandy. He will. And call you a trespasser."

Sandy turned. "I'll leave, if you'll come with me."

Slum shook his head. "I can't," he muttered, averting his eyes. "It wouldn't help. Butcher would just call the cops, and they'd drag me back, maybe shut me up in that mental place again. I'm incompetent."

"Like shit you are," Sandy said. "All right, then. Stay. But I'm going to get a lawyer, Slum. We're going to get you free of this, I promise."

"Hire all the lawyers you want, Mister Blair," said Butcher Byrne. "I assure you that I can afford to hire better ones. You won't take my son from me again." Douglas reentered the room carrying a double-barreled shotgun. Butcher accepted it from him wordlessly, cracked it to check that it was loaded, then closed it up again and pointed it at Sandy. "Your choice, Blair. You begin walking right now, or I pull the trigger."

The mouth of the shotgun, only a few feet away, loomed vastly large. Sandy trembled. Butcher looked deadly earnest. But something inside him, some rage, some stubbornness, some wild courage, would not permit

Sandy to back down. He fell back on the only defense he had ever really perfected: words. "Violence is the last resort of the incompetent," he said with an insolence he did not really feel. "You shoot me and you're in deep shit, asshole."

Butcher sighted along the barrel very carefully, squinting, and for an instant Sandy thought it was all over. And then, behind him, Slum shouted: "NO!" and something came whizzing over Sandy's shoulder—a book, thrown hard. Butcher ducked, but too slowly. The book caught him square across the temple, staggering him. The shotgun came down, and he raised a hand to his forehead, blinking. Then he smiled. "Not bad, Jefferson," he said. "Maybe I'll make a man of you yet."

Slum was on his feet, glaring from wild eyes, teeth bared. "I'll *kill* you, you fucker, you FUCKER!" he screamed. He lunged toward his father.

But Sandy got in the way, and grabbed him. "No, don't."

"Let me *go*," Slum said, struggling. "He would have *shot* you. He would have."

"Maybe," said Sandy, wrenching Slum backward and planting himself firmly in the way. "But if you kill him you become what he is. That's what he wants. That's what he wanted all along—to make you over in his image. You don't need that. You're *better* than him. You're the one who had the guts to say *no*, more guts than any of your brothers ever had. Don't throw it away. If you hit him, he wins."

Slum slumped back against the wall, his rage ebbing until he simply looked confused. "I don't know," he muttered. He put a hand to his face. "I just don't know."

Jane Dennison came across the room with brisk strides, carrying a medical bag of some sort. "See what you've done," she said coldly to Sandy. "I *told* you this would trigger an episode." She took Slum gently by the hand. "It's time for your medicine, Jeff."

Slum wrenched his arm free and backed away from her. "I don't need no medicine." He held up his hands as if to ward her off. "Stay away." But Dennison ignored him. Methodically, she extracted a hypodermic from her bag, loaded it. "No!" Slum insisted, more loudly. Dennison took his arm, swabbed it with alcohol. He cringed but did not fight.

"This is just something to calm you down, Jeff," the nurse said, but when the needle neared his vein, Slum screamed. Sandy felt a sick horror, and moved toward them, but before he could interfere Butcher caught him from behind. Slum screamed and cried. He was still screaming as Butcher and Doug together pulled Sandy from the room.

Outside, the door closed behind them. Joseph William Byrne smirked.

"He would never have touched me, Blair. I didn't need your little sermon. Jefferson is a coward. He's always been a coward, since he was a little boy. Sometimes I don't think he's mine at all. But he bears my name, and he won't disgrace it any more than he has."

"*Disgrace?*" Sandy said shrilly. He was so angry he thought he might choke, but there were tears in his eyes as well. He fought desperately to hold them back, unwilling to give Butcher the satisfaction of seeing him cry. "What kind of miserable excuse for a human being *are* you? He's your *son*! You ought to be *proud* of him!"

"Proud of what? Cowardice? He threw away every advantage I gave him, and when his country called him, he ran. His mother died of the shame. There's not an ounce of courage in him."

"Like hell," Sandy said. "You think it took *guts* to go to 'Nam? Hell, it was easy. Just go along, do what's expected of you, follow orders. It takes a hell of a lot more courage to do what Slum did—to stand up alone, to follow his own conscience. More courage and more brains and more fucking morality. He made the hard choice, gave up his family and friends and country for something bigger than any of them. You think that was *easy*? Especially for him, for a goddamned *Byrne*? What did you want?"

"I wanted him to be a man, to do his duty."

"A *man*?" Sandy said savagely. "He is a man, you asshole. A man who did his own thinking and stood up for what he believed. All you wanted was a martinet. If he'd gone to 'Nam and napalmed a few villages, brought back a few gook ears, you'd have thought that was terrific, even if he only went because he was scared of you. And maybe he would have died. That would have been better, right? Then you could have had two black-bordered portraits downstairs instead of just one."

The vein in Butcher's forehead was going wild again. "My son Robert gave his life for this country, and I won't have his memory blasphemed by your foul mouth, Blair."

"*Shit!*" Sandy said. The tears had come at last, and he was screaming. "It's *Slum* who's the hero, not your precious Robert! It don't take no courage to kill, you bloody fucker. A machine can take orders, and all it takes to stand in front of a bullet and die is a mess of bad luck. You stupid *evil* man, you—"

The shotgun was still in Butcher's hands, and the man's face had turned a deep stormcloud purple. The gun came up so fast that Sandy never saw it move. The stock caught him hard across the face, snapping his head around, sending him stumbling. He went down and sat up spitting blood. He'd bitten his tongue, and the whole left side of his face tingled from the blow. Butcher was standing over him, the shotgun pointed down. "One more word and you're dead meat."

"Is that a line from one of your shit-ass books?" Sandy spat.

That was when Doug took a hand. He grabbed his father by the shoulder and gently drew him back. "No, Dad," was all he said, but it seemed to be enough. Butcher stared at Sandy with a terrible loathing for a long minute, then spun and stalked off down the hall.

Doug helped Sandy to his feet. "You better get out of here, Mister," he said. "Butcher doesn't cool down, he just gets madder and madder. He didn't like what you said about Bobby."

"I noticed," Sandy said ruefully. He touched the side of his face. It was already tender. He was going to have an awful bruise, and was probably lucky not to have lost any teeth. "I'm going," he said. Doug walked him to the door.

But out on the porch, Sandy turned to face the youngest Byrne boy one more time. He looked so much like Slum had. "You got to understand," he said with sudden urgency. "Slum's a *good* man. Your father's wrong. There was an awful lot of love in Slum. And he was brave. That's the important thing. Yeah, he was uncertain, insecure, scared of a lot of stuff. Your father especially. But he always faced those fears, and that's what courage really amounts to. Being scared and going on anyhow. Do you understand that? Do you understand why Slum went to Canada? Do you?"

Douglas MacArthur Byrne leaned back against one of the pillars and studied Sandy out of cool, clear eyes, full of all the certainty of adolescence. He looked so achingly familiar, and yet so terribly different. Finally he crossed his arms. "Guys like you make me mad," he said in a flat alien voice. "It was on account of guys like you that we lost in 'Nam, and got kicked around by piss-ant Iranians. I know why Jeffy went to Canada all right. Jeffy went to Canada 'cause Jeffy is a wimp."

It drew no blood, but it hurt about a hundred times as much as the blow from Butcher's shotgun.

FIFTEEN

Home, where my thought's escaping/
Home, where my music's playing/
Home, where my love lies waiting, silently for me

By the time he left Denver, headed northeast on 1–76, the left side of his face was swollen and aching. If he was lucky his beard would disguise the worst of the discoloration, but the pain would just have to be borne. It wasn't too hard. His anger helped. He was mad enough so that hurting became just another goad to his rage. His thoughts were fevered; thunderclouds that filled his head with black fantasies and impossible plans.

He crossed the flat emptiness of eastern Colorado scarcely seeing it, conscious only of the miles rolling by, the cold wind outside, the blare of the radio, and of his anger. He drove fast, driven by his rage and feeding it with speed. Daydream became a low-slung bronze bullet in the passing lane, shooting past cars, trucks, wobbling U-Hauls, swerving right only when some slower-moving speeder blocked the left lane. The speedometer crept up: seventy-five, eighty, eighty-five. And Sandy, fuming, pushed her still faster, and thought of Butcher Byrne. He was full of wrath and full of schemes. He would hire lawyers, get Slum free. He would talk Jared into exposing Butcher in the *Hog*. He would write nasty reviews of Byrne's books. He would do something, anything, everything. It was an outrage, a crime. Slum might be helpless, but Sandy wasn't. He would get justice.

The road became a white-line blur; and somehow that fed the fantasies. Behind the wheel of Daydream, he had power. He could taste it, feel it, see visible proof of it all around him as he passed everything in sight. There is something about a fast car that does that. With a steering wheel in his hands and an accelerator under his foot, even the world's biggest loser becomes briefly competent. In a world that so often frustrated one and left one feeling helpless to change anything, do anything, affect *anything*, the car was still subject to one's will. A tank of gas, an open highway, and a box full of tapes was enough to give Sandy an illusion of confidence, to make him feel effective.

But the mood broke up near the Nebraska border, where I-76 fed into I-80. Gas was running low by that point, and the Denver oldies station that Sandy had tuned to had disintegrated into static. The interstate swung around in a long wide curve; Daydream took it at just over eighty, hugging the road. And then Sandy saw the police car up ahead. But it was too late; they'd radared him already, and one of the cops was waving him over.

He screeched to a stop on the shoulder, rolled down his window, and accepted the ticket in a sullen silence. The cop looked a bit concerned as he handed back the license. "You OK, Mister?" he asked. "You don't look too good."

Sandy touched the side of his face. It hurt. "It's nothing," he said. "Guess I could use an ice-pack, though."

The cop nodded. "And slow it down."

He stayed just under sixty all the way to the next rest stop, where he pulled off. A full tank of gas for Daydream, and some ice for his face—the pudgy waitress took pity on him—while he drank three cups of coffee and ate half a slice of blueberry pie. It was getting dark outside while Sandy lingered, and as the daylight faded his righteous anger was fading too.

It was all a delusion, he thought. You speed along, confident, competent, and they stop you. They are always waiting down the road somewhere, with lights and sirens and guns, always waiting to stop you, and there's nothing you can do about it, no matter how many Burt Reynolds pictures you've seen. And there was nothing he could do about Butcher Byrne either. He could hire a lawyer, and Butcher would hire a better one, a whole battalion of them, and Butcher could win. Justice didn't mean anything in the courts. He could spring Slum loose violently, and Butcher would have him arrested. He could write something, and get sued for libel. What the hell was the use? The power was all on the other side.

The ice helped his bruised face, a little. He couldn't finish the pie, but he had the waitress fill his thermos with hot black coffee, and he bought a jumbo bottle of No-Doz in the shop next to the restaurant. Sandy swallowed a handful after he'd settled back into the driver's seat. He hunted up and down the band but couldn't find a decent radio station. It was all country-western and religious stuff. Finally he gave up in disgust, rooted through his box of tapes, and slammed some Doors into the tape-deck. Then he turned on his lights—the Mazda's concealed headlights rose up out of the hood like machine guns popping out of James Bond's Aston-Martin, and there were times when Sandy found himself wishing they *were* machine guns—and pulled back onto the highway.

Nebraska was even flatter and more boring than eastern Colorado, and it went on forever and forever. I-80 was heavily traveled, but Sandy paid little attention to the other traffic. This time he stayed in the right-hand lane, cruising at or just above the legal limit, depressed, lost in thought, high on caffeine and low on hope. Jim Morrison was asking someone to light his fire, but Sandy felt as though his own fire was out for good. The trip, the story, everything seemed to have turned to ashes in his mouth.

The Butcher Byrnes of the world went on and on, and sometimes they seemed to win all of the pots. Slum went to prison, got raped, got tortured with electroshock, and Richard Nixon went free to live out his days in comfort and luxury. The Watergate conspirators wrote books and made fortunes on the lecture circuit, but Bobby Kennedy was still dead, would *always* be dead.

Just before he'd gotten himself hit, he'd called Butcher an evil man. The hell of it was, he couldn't even be sure of that anymore. Butcher no doubt figured Sandy for the evil one. Edan Morse said that Jamie Lynch deserved execution. Others would say the same of Edan Morse. Sandy saw their faces up ahead of him, dim visions in the night, drifting between the road and the stars, just beyond the reach of his headlights. Other faces seemed to join them: friends, enemies, public figures, crowding and jostling one another. Gutless Jared Patterson, who'd sold out friends and principles for a buck. Rick Maggio, fat and bitter, hurting so much he had to pass on the pain to those around him. Charlie Manson and Richard Nixon, arms wrapped around each other; was one any better or worse than the other, really?

He saw them all. The young Guardsmen at Kent State faced off against the SLA. The soldiers at My Lai danced with the Alfies. The well-dressed gentlemen from Dow Chemical who made their nice profit from napalm deplored the actions of the ragged black scum who burned down the ghettos during blackouts. The pushers, the assassins, the slumlords, all the faceless little men and women who thought that good and evil didn't apply to *them*, the ones who were just getting by, the ones who read their Bible and did the work of the Lord, the ones who had to be practical, the ones who took orders, who only worked here, who were just carrying out company policy. And their reflections, their opposites, the ones who lived for a cause and died for a cause and killed for a cause, who were blind to the gray of human souls and the red of human blood. Once Sandy had been able to tell them apart, the good guys and the bad guys; now they all looked alike to him.

He drove on. Watched the stars, watched the road, watched the faces. He hurt. Ahead of him, the faces seemed to come together, melting into one another, writhing and shifting as they coalesced. The Dow men and the slumlords and the Kent State Guardsmen fused into one vision, teeming. Nixon marched in front of them, side by side with Butcher Byrne. The SLA and the looters and the pushers formed a second army, with Manson and Edan Morse at its head. Jared Patterson hesitated and went right; Rick Maggio wavered and finally floated left. The armies blurred and shifted, and finally there were only two faces, only two, staring at each other: Edan Morse and Joseph William Byrne. They seemed as distinct as night and day, as white and black. And then, a heartbeat later, Sandy found that he could not tell them apart at all. The same face, he thought. *They have the same face.*

Nebraska went on and on. Semis rumbled past him, the wind of their passage shaking Daydream like slaps from some insolent giant. The sky was empty but for a million stars looking down on him like a host of yellow eyes, watching, weighing. Jim Morrison sang on. Jim Morrison had died for our sins, like Joplin, like Hendrix, like Bobby Kennedy and John Lennon. Like Patrick Henry Hobbins. Jim Morrison was singing about the end.

Sandy pulled over on the shoulder and let the traffic scream past while he fumbled in his glove compartment for some aspirin. He found the bottle, shook out two tablets into his hand, then another two. He dry-swallowed the four of them, harsh and powdery in the back of his mouth, with a taste like crumbled brick. Then he took another couple No-Doz, washing them down with a mouthful of coffee from his thermos. The coffee burned his mouth, and his head was buzzing from all the caffeine. He slammed through the gears quickly as he pulled back onto the road, trying to build speed fast as he slid into the traffic once more. A big tractor-trailer, coming up quickly, didn't think it was fast enough; the driver sounded his air-horn angrily and blinded him with a flick of his brights before finally shifting over to the passing lane. "*You fucker!*" Sandy shouted after him, but his windows were closed and the truck was gone already.

The Doors tape had started to repeat. Sandy hit the eject button and popped it out.

"Good move, Blair. I was getting tired of that. Besides, you were dating yourself."

Sandy glanced over. In the dimness of the passenger seat: a mocking smile, a raised eyebrow. "Lark?" he said.

"Steve," the other corrected. "You got to change, Blair. Times change, people change. Give it up."

"Like you?"

"Sounds good to me."

"You're a phony, Lark."

"What a joke! I'm not even *real* and you're telling me I'm a phony! And the name is Steve."

"I liked you better as Lark," said Sandy. "Though I never liked you much even then."

"That's because I was always smarter than you. Of course I was a fake. You think the world gives a gold-plated shit about sincerity, Blair? You're no better than me, and no worse. You can't do diddly-shit in this world, Blair, and neither can I. So why tear ourselves up about it? Get drunk, get laid, get rich. He who dies with the most toys wins."

"Fuck off, Lark."

"Steve. Where do you think you're going, Blair?"

"Home. I'm going home."

Lark laughed at him. "Sucker. You're the one who's supposed to be the big-shot writer. You can't go home again, Blair, you ought to know that. You got yourself a hot-shit sports car, but that only means you're going nowhere *fast*."

Sandy reached over toward the passenger compartment. It was empty, except for the box with all his tapes. He pulled one out at random, pushed it into the tape deck. Simon and Garfunkel.

Time, see what's become of me, they sang.

"See what's become of all of us," Sandy said aloud.

"Sander m'boy, that's your problem," Froggy replied. "You have seen, and it hasn't exactly made your day, has it? Hasn't warmed the cockles of your heart?"

"My heart does not have cockles," Sandy said.

Froggy made his wet, rude noise. "Quit trying to be funny. Around me you're just another straight man, and you know it."

"Lark says to give it up."

"Misery loves company, as someone unbearably trite said once. And you're talking about Lark. This is a lad who used to tell every girl he met that romantic love was just a bourgeois plot to distract us from the revolution. Then he'd bitch because he never got laid."

Sandy smiled. "Still. He's right. What can I do, really? Can't change the goddamned world. Can't do anything to help Slum. I don't think I've been much help to Jamie Lynch, either."

"Detectives seldom are. Didn't you ever notice that whenever Charlie Chan set out to solve a murder, six more people were dead before he found the killer?" He laughed. "You want to win *all* the time? No way. Nine out of ten sweet things what I invited to plunk my magic twanger preferred to slap my smiling face. How do you think I got this nice rosy complexion? Slaps, Sander m'boy, hundreds and millyums of *slaps*!" Froggy rolled his eyes. "But the tenth, ah, the *tenth*. Moist lips and heaving bosoms, laughter and strawberry wine, poetry and potato chips, and such ankles, such *ankles*, my friend! There's always a tenth out there, a secret tenth with genitals cleverly concealed beneath her clothing, with lust in her heart, willing to put the spaghetti in her hair if only someone will ask. That's what life *is*, Sander m'boy—the search for the secret tenth."

"My cockles aren't warming, Froggy. Butcher Byrne is no secret tenth. If you ask him to put the spaghetti in his hair, he'll shoot your fucking head off."

"Froggy the Gremlin could handle him," said Froggy the Cohen.

"A rubber puppet in a kid's show. Canceled. Gone. Forgotten." Sandy's voice was bitter.

Froggy gasped in horror. "Don't say that! He'll live *forever* in the minds and hearts of his countrymen. Froggy was magic!"

"I don't believe in magic," Sandy said.

Bambi Lassiter sighed with gentle disapproval. "No. You don't believe in anything. That's the cause of your pain, Sandy. You shut out the light that might illuminate your life, you refuse to accept. You question everything, reject everything. It will be your downfall. The time is coming when you will have to believe, believe or go mad. You know that, Sandy. You've tasted it already. In Chicago. In Denver. Slum was just as you'd dreamed him, wasn't he? White. Gaunt. Screaming."

"Coincidence," Sandy said, "or else...I don't know, I knew he was living at home with Butcher, somehow my subconscious must have made the assumption..."

"You're reaching, Sandy. The world is larger than your mind can grasp. Sooner or later you'll have to admit it. Strange things are afoot."

"Fucking A," Sandy said.

"You know what's happening, Sandy. Deep inside, in some primal instinctive way, you understand. You can see the shape of it already. It's true. It's *true*, Sandy. But you won't understand consciously until you accept that it's possible. And you *have* to understand. You know that, too. There are choices to be made. Important choices." Her voice faded to a whisper and was gone.

Slum was hovering in front of the car, floating in a lotus position between the beams of the headlights, receding as fast as Daydream plunged toward him. He was wearing his Slum Suit, old and tattered now, and he had two kittens in his lap and dandelions behind his ears. His smile was full of reproach. "You left me alone," he said. "I almost beat him, almost made it. I only needed a little help, and you weren't there."

"I didn't *know*," Sandy said in an agonized voice.

"Too busy with your own life, I guess. You let me down."

"Slum, I'll hire lawyers, I swear. We'll get you away from him somehow. Froggy will help out, I know it. And Maggie. We love you."

"Not enough," said Slum, with a hapless shrug. "I'm sorry. I don't mean to get on your case. Only it's too late now. I knocked it over, and it broke. I'm sorry, it was my fault. I broke it. Only it was my mind, Sandy, it was my mind, and now it's too late."

"*Slum!*" Sandy shouted, as the figure began to waver and fade.

"It's too damn late," Slum said, and as he did all his hair fell out and curled up in sudden smoke, and the colors faded from his Slum Suit, and he was gaunt and pale-eyed with a machine gun in his hand, giggling. He laughed and sprayed the windshield. The bullets hit and shattered, and Sandy cringed.

It had begun to rain. Freezing rain.

A winter's day, in a deep and dark December, Simon and Garfunkel sang. *I am alone.*

"No," Maggie said. He felt her gentle touch on his arm. "You have Sharon. Go back to her, love. That's what it's all about. You're not a rock, you never will be. You hurt, you love, you care. Go home and cry for Slum and remember him like he was and love him. It's all you can do."

"It's not enough," Sandy said.

"No, it's not," Maggie said. "It never is. That makes you angry, doesn't it? Makes you want to cry, huh?" Her hand went to his knee, a light phantom touch that brushed the inside of his thigh. "That's why I loved you, Sandy. You could cry for the things you couldn't fix."

"And all this time I thought it was my bod you were after."

She laughed. "That too. We had a groovy thing going." Or was it the tape deck that said that?

"Does it have to be past tense? Cleveland isn't too far off 80. I could stop. We could—"

Something light and cool on his lips, silencing him. "No, love," she said. "I wish it could be. But we're past now. Like history, huh? We blew it somehow. Your visit was lovely, but there are too many ghosts between us. We'd only spoil what we had once. Let it die. Go home to your Sharon and love her."

Sandy looked over. Maggie was half-transparent, and her face was wet with silent tears. "You're afraid," he said wonderingly. "You were never afraid of anything."

She nodded. "I've been hurt too much, Sandy. I'm not the girl I was, love. I don't want to hurt anymore. Don't push."

Her tears brought the pain back, sharply. He felt moisture gather in the corners of his own eyes. "You were the best of us all," he said. "You touched us, changed us, led us. You had so much spirit, so goddamned much love. Joy. You always had joy. They couldn't put it out. It made me crazy, inflamed Froggy, infected Slum, lit up everyone around you. And it's gone now, isn't it? I felt it that night in Cleveland. Tears and desperation. Loneliness. You, of all people, lonely. And worse, too wounded to break free."

She shrugged. "I tend my garden."

"*Candide*," Sandy said.

"So I'm not original. Sue me. Oh, don't look so sad, love. Please. It's just time, and a little hard luck. Maybe if I had it to do over again things would come out better, huh? For you and me? But I don't. Maybe they'd come out worse, anyhow. The wounds don't heal, Sandy. Leave the scabs alone. Go back to your realtor in Brooklyn, and do your best. That's all any of us can do."

The rain pattered against the windshield as Daydream plunged through the night. It was late now, and most of the other traffic had pulled in somewhere for the night. Black fields rushed by on either side, full of shorn corn and hidden missile silos. The road was slick. Sandy gripped the wheel hard, and there was a dryness at the back of his mouth. He could feel Maggie fading, the last of his fever dreams drifting away from him. "What if it wasn't?" he said.

"Huh?" she asked. She seemed just a little more solid when he glanced over at the passenger's seat.

"What if it *wasn't* all we could do," Sandy said. "What if there was something else, some way to have a second shot at it, to bring it all back, to do it over. To put Lark in denim again, and give Slum back his sanity, and you your joy."

"But there isn't, love," Maggie whispered.

Simon and Garfunkel were singing about a most peculiar man. Sandy punched the eject button. The music stopped suddenly, and the cassette came popping out of the tape deck. "There's a cassette in the box there. The Nazgûl. Give it to me."

"The Nazgûl?" Maggie asked.

"I've driven thousands of miles, listening to my tapes or the radio every foot of the way, and I haven't played any Nazgûl since the case began. I think I was scared to. Bambi was right. I did understand. I saw the shape of it a long time ago. I've just been afraid to admit it. The tape?"

No answer. The silence was heavy. Rain and road noise. Sandy waited a long minute with his hand out, before he remembered that she wasn't really there at all. None of them had been there, not really. And yet they were; they would always be with him. He reached into the box, and came up with the right tape on the first try, as if something had put it in his hand.

The Nazgûl. *Music to Wake the Dead.*

He slammed it into the waiting slot and turned up the volume. The music filled the interior of the car, drowning out the rain and the sound of tires against slick wet pavement. The teakettle whine of descending bombs, the hammering of drums, and Hobbins' voice.

Baby, you cut my heart out! Baby, you made me bleeeed!

"Jamie Lynch got his heart cut out on top of a desk, with the West Mesa concert poster underneath him. A poster. A broadsheet. You get it." Then he was quiet, while Hobbins sang of love, loyalty, and betrayal, and Maggio's guitar cried anguish.

See the ash man, gray and shaken, too powdery to cry,

began the second cut. The background vocals were saying, *Ashes, ashes, all fall down,* over and over again. Maggio went wild on guitar. The music was a living thing, full of crackle and heat. In the bridge Gopher John did a long drum solo. Sandy dug out the No-Doz, swallowed another handful. No sleep tonight. Just driving. Just music. No sleep and no dreams, he'd had enough of dreaming. *Ashes, ashes, all fall down*, the lyrics went, the four voices of the Nazgûl blending into one terrible whole, full of hurt and loss and passion gone to cinders.

"Next up," Sandy announced as the third song began, "Richard Maggio and his fabulous trained *angst*."

Yes, I'm ragin'!

RAGIN'!

The growl of Maggio's voice, the rumble of Faxon's base, the drums, the guitar, the rage all melted into the whine of Daydream's tires, the smooth hum of her rotary engine. This time Sandy didn't hear out the song. He stabbed the fast forward, held it as the tape spun. Just long enough. Then it was Hobbins singing again, the hard beat behind him.

The survivor has a different kind of scar.
YEAH! The survivor has a dif—

Fast forward again, whirring, spinning. "I think I knew by the time I left Albuquerque," Sandy said, "but when I saw Morse, talked to him, the outline became really unmistakable. *Listen to the music*, he said. Two or three times. What the fuck did that mean? And something else. He kept saying that the hour was at hand for his revolution, that the time had come. Only he didn't say it like that. His phrasing was very precise. *The hour has come round at last*, he kept saying. A very familiar phrase, that."

Was it Maggie's voice he heard, a whisper above the road noise, above the sound of the tape skittering forward? Or only the caffeine buzzing in his head? "Yeats," it said.

"Yes and no," Sandy said. "Words by William Butler Yeats, music by Peter Faxon. Here." He released the fast forward in the middle of the song.

Things fall apart, the Nazgûl promised. *The centre cannot hold!* Acid frenzy. Discords. Chaos drums. Feedback. Singing like the wailing of the damned. An Irish poet spinning in his grave and sixty thousand kids leaping to their feet, clapping their hands, dancing, shouting. *He's coming!* cried the vocals behind the poem. *He's COMING!* shouted the crowd. Again and again. Something wild and beautiful and chilling.

Mere anarchy is loosed upon the world,
The blood-dimmed tide is loosed, and—

Eject: sudden quiet settling like a veil, a shroud, a grave-cloth. "The best lack all conviction," Sandy said, "while the worst are full of passionate intensity." He pulled the cassette loose. "Larry Richmond, the new Hobbins, reborn in surgery and the mind of Edan Morse. But he was born in Bethlehem. A steel town in Pennsylvania. Bethlehem." He glanced down at the label on the tape.

SIDE ONE
1. BLOOD ON THE SHEET	2:07
2. ASH MAN (ASHES, ASHES)	5:09
3. RAGIN'	3:01
4. THE SURVIVOR	3:15
5. WHAT ROUGH BEAST	2:02
6. PRELUDE TO MADNESS	5:23

SIDE TWO
1. THE ARMAGEDDON/RESURRECTION RAG	23:14

"The Rag was the best thing the Nazgûl ever did," Sandy said. "That was the song they were singing at West Mesa when Hobbins was shot." He put the tape back in, upside down, pushed the rewind until he hit the leader, and then let it play.

Later it would pick up speed, Sandy knew. Later it would grow fevered and insistent, the backbeat would crawl under your flesh and become one with your blood, the guitars and the bass would move faster and faster, the drumming would turn satanic, and you would hear chords like Hendrix used to play, impossible licks, sounds that made you wonder just how many instruments they *had* up there, and lyrics that made you angry, lyrics that made you sad, lyrics that conjured visions from the night. Later. Later. But the beginning of it was slow, slow and mournful and almost quiet, a whisper of guitar strings, a gentle rain upon the drums.

> *This is the land all causes lead to,*
> *This is the land where the mushrooms grow.*

And Sandy hit the eject, stopped it before it had even gotten started, suddenly afraid. Afraid of what? Afraid to put a name to the thing he was afraid of. "Music to wake the dead," he said to Maggie. But she wasn't there. He was alone, hurting, tired, amid rain and darkness and the Nebraska winter night.

SIXTEEN

**Is there anything a man don't stand to lose?/
When the devil wants to take it all away?**

New York had tasted its first snow of the season, and the streets of Brooklyn were filthy with wet brown slush. Sandy drove slowly to avoid skids, but Daydream's wheels still sent up a spray as she wound her way home. The hour was late enough so that few pedestrians were abroad, but one bag lady on Flatbush Avenue, splashed by his passage, hurled curses after him. "Welcome home," Sandy muttered.

He parked the Mazda in his rented garage, opened the hatchback to remove his suitcase, and started the two-block trudge toward home. The slush soaked through his boots and left his feet wet and cold, so he hurried. He had been driving all day; exhaustion had set in, and he wanted to be home. It seemed as though he had been away for years.

The brownstone was dark. Sandy set the suitcase just inside the door and fumbled for the light. The hallway looked strange at first. There was a new rug, he saw dully, and Sharon had moved the tall bookcase that used to stand in the living room, moved it to the hall and filled it with glass figurines. He wondered what she'd done with all of his paperbacks. Tossed them in some box, probably. She'd frequently complained that the cheap paperbacks made the living room look tacky.

"*Sharon!*" he called. "It's me." He started up the stairs. Near the top he took them two at a time, turned to their bedroom, flicked on the lights. She'd heard him call. She was sitting up in bed. So was the man next to her.

Sandy blinked, sighed, tried to keep his composure. "Hello, Don," he said.

The man was thick-bodied, blond, florid. Lots of hair on his chest. A forty-ish jock just beginning to go to fat, but a real up-and-comer in the realty business, Sharon said. Sandy was still annoyed. He'd thought she had better taste.

"Uh," Don said. He turned a little redder than he was already. "Uh, hello, Sandy. How was your trip?"

"More fun than fucking a monkey," Sandy said, a little too sharply.

Sharon picked up her glasses from the nightstand and put them on. Her hair was rumpled by sleep, and the lace nightgown she was wearing had bunched up on her. She smoothed it out, frowning. "No need to get sarcastic with Don," she said to Sandy. "We're not monogamous, you know, and you didn't even give me a hint as to when you'd be home."

"I didn't know," Sandy said. "And I've been distracted."

"I'll bet," Sharon said dryly. "You could have called ahead, you know. Say from Jersey. Given me a little warning."

"Yeah," Sandy said. Hey, Penelope, this is your old man Odysseus coming home at last, time to clear out the suitors, he thought. He sat down on the edge of the bed. "Well, what now?" he asked. "Anyone for a game of Monopoly?"

Sharon turned to Don. "You better go home, honey," she said. "Sandy and I have a lot of things to settle."

"I understand," Don said. He crinkled up his face with what Sandy thought was excruciating cuteness, kissed Sharon on the tip of her nose, and got up to dress. He wore striped boxer shorts and had flabby thighs, and somehow that made Sandy even angrier. Neither he nor Sharon spoke until they heard the door close downstairs. Then Sandy pulled off his boots and turned to face her, crossing his legs and leaning back against the foot of the bed. The brass bedpost dug into his back.

"Well?" said Sharon. Her face was very composed. She made no effort to touch him.

"What can I say?" Sandy said. "I suppose I ought to be grateful that he hasn't moved in yet. Christ, though. *Don!* Of all people!"

"Don't pass judgments, Sandy. You have no right. He's an attractive, intelligent man. He's attentive and responsible and we have a lot in common."

"Do you love him?" Sandy asked.

"Not especially, but I'm comfortable with him, which is more than I can say about you. You've been away a long time, Sandy. You didn't write, you seldom called. I've had a lot of time to think about us."

"I don't like the sound of that," Sandy said. "Please, Sharon. Not right now."

"Waiting won't make it any easier. I want to get this over with. Let's make it clean and civilized if we can."

Sandy suddenly had an awful headache. He rubbed his temple. "Sharon," he said, "don't do this to me now. Please. I'm asking as nice as I can. The trip, the story . . . it's turning into some kind of fucking nightmare. It's surreal. I need to talk to you about it. I can't handle any more grief at the moment, you know? I need you right now. I need somebody who cares."

"But I don't, Sandy," she said calmly. She didn't even have the grace to look sad. "You need somebody, but it isn't me. We have to face the truth. It's over between us. It's been going bad for a long time. I think it's only been inertia keeping us together."

"You're mad at me for taking off like I did—" he started.

"I was," she admitted, "but not for long. That was the problem. When you'd been gone a while, I wasn't angry anymore. I was . . . I just felt *nothing*. I didn't miss you, Sandy. Not at all."

"Terrific."

"I'm sorry if I'm hurting you, but this has to be said. How many women did you sleep with this trip?"

"One and a half," Sandy said. "The half I don't remember. Seems to defeat the whole point. Why?"

Sharon shrugged. "I just wanted to know. To see if I'd care. I don't. When we started with the open relationship, back in the beginning, I always cared. I tried not to be jealous, but I always was, just a little. Nothing I couldn't control. I think I liked it a little, knowing that you were attractive to other women and still came home to me, but that tiny bit of insecurity was still there. Now it's gone. You could have said fifty and I wouldn't have given a damn. I don't hate you, Sandy. I don't dislike you, even. There's not enough feeling left to dislike you. You just don't matter."

Sandy winced. "You have a great touch for this kind of thing, lady. The least you could do is tell me I'll always be a cherished friend."

"But you won't be, Sandy," she said. "Lovers get together for the weirdest reasons, like we did, but friends have to have something in common. You and I live in different worlds. We march to different drummers."

"Linda Ronstadt and the Stone Poneys," Sandy said sullenly.

"What?" Sharon frowned at him, then sighed. "No, Sandy. It was Thoreau or Rousseau or somebody like that. See what I mean? We don't speak the same language and we don't sing the same songs. And we won't,

ever. I don't love Don, but maybe I could, eventually. I want to give the relationship time to grow."

"Fuck," said Sandy. He thought he ought to cry but he had no tears left.
Maybe he'd used them up on Slum and Butcher Byrne. More, he knew
that Sharon was right. It had been a hard trip, but not because he'd missed
her. He'd hardly thought of her. Still, that didn't prevent him from feeling
abandoned. "Do you have to be so damn cold about it?" he said accusingly.
"We meant something to each other once. We could at least end it with a
little passion."

"To what end? I'm trying to keep this civilized. We're both mature
adults who tried something and it didn't—"

"Screw maturity," Sandy said. He stood up and scowled. "I have had it
up to *here* with maturity. Goddamn it, call me a shithead, throw something
at me, yell! Cry, damn it! We've been together for almost two years. I deserve at least a few fucking tears, don't I?"

"I don't want to cry," Sharon said briskly. "Let's take care of the sticky details, shall we? You're just back from a long trip, so you can stay here
tonight. I'll go over to Don's. But I'd like to keep this house, if you don't ob-
ject. I'll buy your half. At a fair price. We both know how much the place
has appreciated. I can only give you ten thousand dollars right now, but I'll
pay the rest in installments. How does that sound?"

Sandy wanted to scream. "I don't *care* about that stuff," he said. "We
made love half a million times. We shared . . . laughs, dreams, all that shit.
That's what matters. Cry, dammit!"

"You don't care about the money now, but you will," Sharon said. She
got out of bed and crossed the room, began to dress. When she pulled her
nightgown over her head, Sandy found himself looking too hard at a body
he would never hold again. There was something about the fact that she
was lost to him that made her more attractive than ever. As she dressed it
was as though she was armoring herself against him, covering her last vul-
nerabilities. She pulled on a pair of pale blue panties, slipped into a matching bra, fastened it. Then faded jeans and a pristine white tee shirt. Blue
and white. Like ice.

"Sharon," Sandy said, in a voice faintly edged by desperation, "you're
scaring the hell out of me. I had a dream about this. Your face turned to ice.
You're making it come true. Don't. Please. Leave me if you want, go to Don,
but don't do it like this. Show some emotion. Please. I'm begging you!"

She pulled out an overnight bag and began to pack her work clothes.
"You're being juvenile, Sandy," she said without looking up. "I don't care
about your dreams."

He had to make her cry, he thought wildly. He had to make her rage. "Remember the time we made love in the bedroom of that boring party on the Upper East Side? And the guy came in to get his coat? Remember?"

She ignored him and went on packing.

"Remember the week in Mexico? The party I threw for you when you turned thirty? Remember how we both bawled like kids when E.T. phoned home?"

Sharon zipped shut her bag, shouldered it, and gave Sandy a brief look, a chilly look with only the faintest hint of emotion in it. And that emotion was pity. She started for the door.

Sandy followed her downstairs. "Remember the kitten I bought for you? The one that got run over after he got out through the open window? Remember the ERA rallies we went to together?" Sharon took her coat off the hook. "Remember when your father was sick? I stayed with you then. All the funny gifts you used to get me? You have to—"

But she didn't have to. She didn't even care enough to slam the door. It closed with a small, terribly final click, a click like the sound an icicle might make, falling to shatter on the ground.

Blue-white, and frost on her glasses, Sandy thought.

He stood on the stairs for a long time, too tired to walk back upstairs, too uncertain to go elsewhere. Finally he wandered into the kitchen. Two six-packs of Schaefer were stacked in the refrigerator. He started to pull loose a can, then thought better of it. Instead he grabbed both six-packs and lugged them into the living room.

Sharon had been playing the stereo. The dust cover was still up. He had told her a hundred thousand times to keep the dust cover down, but she never listened. Suddenly furious, he took her Donna Summer album off the turntable and flung it across the room. It bounced off the wall hard, leaving a deep gouge in the plaster.

He didn't think he could handle the Nazgûl right now. He searched through his record collection, pulled out some early Beatles, and placed one disc carefully on the turntable. He set it to repeat indefinitely, and turned the volume up. Then he stretched out on the couch and cracked the first beer.

The next morning he woke up with an awful headache, a litter of beer cans all around him, and John, Paul, George, and Ringo still singing their hearts out, over and over and over. He winced, pushed himself off the couch, killed the music. He didn't remember falling asleep.

He showered, made himself some strong coffee, drank two big tumblers of orange juice and ate a stale jelly doughnut that Sharon had left in the fridge. He tried not to think. Upstairs he found himself staring at the clothing in his closet. He had been wearing the same clothes repeatedly for so long, washing them in so many dingy coin Laundromats, that he'd almost forgotten that he owned anything else. It seemed a stranger's wardrobe. Finally he chose a pair of black cords and a comfortable, faded cotton shirt with a camouflage pattern. Maggie had given him that shirt, he remembered.

Sharon had piled all his mail on his desk in his office. Sandy rifled through it desultorily until he came to the letter from Alan Vanderbeck. It could have been a royalty check, of course, but somehow he knew that it wasn't even before he opened it. He ripped off the end of the envelope and shook out the letter.

Dear Sander,

I've been giving a lot of thought to our association of late. In view of the directions that your literary career is now taking, I'm no longer sure that I'm the proper man to represent your interests. It might be best for both of us if

Sandy crumpled the letter in his hand and lofted it toward his wastebasket. It missed and rolled across the floor to join a pile of discarded pages from his novel.

Page thirty-seven was still in his typewriter. He rolled it out. The paper was permanently curled by now. Sandy flattened it ineffectually and put it in the box with the rest of the book. He took the box downstairs with him, donned his heavy blue peacoat, and headed for the subway with the novel under his arm.

Hedgehog had its offices in the Village, just off Washington Square. Sandy paused on the stairs, looking at the door he had passed through so many times. This used to be home once. And now?

"Can I help you?" the receptionist asked when he stepped inside. She was no one he'd known, nor did she recognize him.

"I used to edit this rag," Sandy said. "I want to see Jared."

"Who shall I say—"

"Don't bother," he interrupted. "I know the way." He went up the stairs, ignoring her protests. He ignored Jared's personal receptionist as well, and walked right into his office.

It had been years since Sandy had seen Jared Patterson in the flesh. There was a lot more flesh. Jared was sitting behind a big desk, looking through some layout sheets. He was wearing a navy-blue leisure suit, an open-collared pastel shirt, and three gold chains around his neck. Already the suit was too small, binding visibly under the arms. Jared had always been overweight, but now he was gross. He looked up at Sandy, startled, and then smiled. "Sandy!" he said, pushing his work aside and leaning back in his huge swivel chair. "What a treat! How long has it been?"

"About seventy or eighty pounds," Sandy said. He crossed the room and sat down. The receptionist came in, but Jared waved her away. "I want to talk to you about the Nazgûl story," Sandy said. "It's bigger than we could have imagined, Jared."

"You mean the Lynch story, Sandy old chum, and you're too late. We've already done our thing on that. I warned you." He leaned over and punched his intercom. "Betsy, bring in the issue before last, willya honey? You know, the one with that hinky painting on the cover, all the hobbits and shit."

She brought it in and gave it to Jared. Jared smirked and handed it across the desk to Sandy. "Sorry, pal," he said, "but you can't say I didn't warn you. I really wanted you to do this one for us, Sandy, but you had to go and be stubborn. Like you can see, we hadda cover it without you."

The front page of the tabloid, under the *Hog* logo, had an old photo of Jamie Lynch superimposed over a garish fantasy landscape. Hobbits clustered around his feet, and overhead record albums sailed the pink skies like a flock of flying saucers. The caption read, *Who Killed Sauron?*

The story developed that theme. The staff writer had learned that Hobbins had called Jamie Lynch "Sauron," and he'd taken that and run with it, right into the ground. Pages of Tolkienesque bullshit. Maine became the Shire, Paul Lebeque an unlikely Frodo. Sandy was awestruck. "I can't believe you'd run this shit," he said.

Jared Patterson shrugged. "Hey, when you finked out on us, we needed something fast. Don't blame me, Sandy. It's on your own head."

Sandy kept his temper with an effort. "Jared, listen to me. This moronic tripe doesn't begin to tell the real story."

Jared smiled. "All right already, tell me the real story."

"First, Lebeque didn't do it. I'm positive about that. I suspect the real killer was a radical goon named Gortney Lyle, but I can't prove that yet. Whether it was Lyle or not, the killer acted at the command of one Edan Morse, of the old Alfie high command."

"Sounds juicy, if you got facts," Jared admitted. "So why'd the Alfies want to kill Lynch?"

"Not the Alfies, just Morse." Sandy hesitated. "It's crazy, Jared, but I believe it. God help me, but I do. It all has to do with the Nazgûl. They cut an album called *Music to Wake the Dead* just before West Mesa. You remember it?"

"Platinum," said Jared. "Sure I remember, I'm no dummy. This is my business."

"Morse *wants* to wake the dead," Sandy said. It all came out then. He started talking about each cut on the album, and what it meant, and about tides, and about visions coming true. Jared listened with a broad smile on his face, and suddenly he could hold it in no longer. He laughed. He laughed again. He began to roar with laughter, clutching at his gut, shaking in his big swivel chair. Sandy waited it all out patiently; he had known it was coming. Finally, when Jared had subsided and was wiping a little trickle of saliva from his chin, Sandy said, "That was in the vision, too. You, laughing. Will you let me write the story?"

"And you call *our* piece shit?" Jared said. "Sandy, you need a shrink. I can recommend a few good ones, if you can handle their fees."

"You won't print it?" Sandy said with iron certainty.

"Does the pope shit in the woods?" Jared said. "Fuck no, we won't print it. This ain't the *National Enquirer*, Sandy. You're talking libel, besides. That dumb Canuck's the killer."

Sandy stood up. "I knew it was hopeless before I came here, but I had to try. Funny thing about seeing the future. At first you try like hell to change what you've seen. And then you kind of get worn down, and you find yourself just going through the motions, tracing out the patterns. The Nazgûl are getting back together, Jared. Wait and see. The Nazgûl are getting back together and they're going to play 'The Armageddon Rag,' and God help us all." He started for the door.

"Hey, Sandy," Jared called after him.

Sandy turned. "Yeah?"

"You'll be the first one we call when the Martians land!" Jared promised, guffawing.

Sandy frowned and waited for him to finish. "I'm glad you're in such a good humor," he said finally. "Until I walked in here and saw you, I thought the blue whale was an endangered species."

He walked down the stairs and out into the slush. He had no stomach for the subway now, and besides, there was one penultimate gesture to make. He hailed a cab and gave his Brooklyn address.

As they were speeding across the Brooklyn Bridge, Sandy opened the box in his lap, rolled down the window, and fed the first page of his novel to the cold wind. "Hey!" the cabbie protested.

"Drive," said Sandy. "If we get stopped for littering I'll pay the fine and double your tip." He let go of page two. Page three. And on and on. Page thirty-seven he hesitated over. It was still a little curled. Sandy reread the final sentence, still half complete. Then he shrugged and flipped the page out the window. As he'd expected, the wind got hold of it. Instead of skittering along the ground like the other pages, it rose and rose, higher and higher, until it vanished somewhere against the gray sky and the rooftops of Brooklyn. Sandy watched it climb through the rear window.

"You must be a writer," the cabbie said.

Sandy laughed. "Yeah," he admitted.

"I knew it. Scattering pages to the wind and all that."

"Only a gesture," Sandy said. "I have a carbon copy at home in my drawer."

"Oh," said the cabbie. That seemed to stop conversation.

Back in his office, he found a message on his answering machine. Sharon had phoned. If he was ready to behave like an adult, she was prepared to meet him to discuss the terms of their separation. Sandy erased the tape, sat down, thought for a moment, and then placed a call to Davie Parker in Maine.

"Listen to me," Sandy said when he got the deputy on the line. "You're my last fucking chance. Lebeque is innocent."

"Notch don't buy it, Blair," Parker said.

"I talked to Edan Morse," Sandy said. "He *is* behind it. Believe me."

"I told you to stay away from Morse," Parker replied, annoyed. "We've got our own investigation under way and you're going to foul it up."

"Morse has an alibi for the night Lynch died, but I'll give you odds I know who the real killer was. A man named Gortney Lyle, acting on Morse's orders. I don't know where you'd fly to get to Maine, but you ought to check with the airlines. Gort probably flew in from LA and rented a car. I hope he did. If he drove all the way, it'd be hell to prove. But if he flew, even under an assumed name, you'll find people who remember him. He shaves his head and wears a gold earring and he's got a terrible sunburn. Now maybe he was covered with hair when he killed Lynch, and maybe he didn't put on the earring and get the sunburn until after, but that doesn't matter. They'll still remember him. He's *big*, Parker."

"Lots of big men out there, Blair," Parker said dubiously.

"Not like Gort," Sandy said. "We're talking well over seven feet, and wide, too. We're talking jumbo-sized Mean Joe Greene. Hell, we're talking Mighty Joe Young. I bet he flew first class. I don't think a guy his size could fit in a coach seat. If he did, the guy next to him had one goddamned memorable flight."

"Interesting," Parker said. "Strong, you figure?"

"He looks like he could arm wrestle a steam shovel."

"Hmmmm," said Parker. "That would answer some questions. It isn't *easy* to pull a man's heart out of his chest. You have to get through the rib cage. Surgeons cut the ribs, I think, but our killer just smashed them. Gortney Lyle, you say?" He sighed. "Notch is going to have kittens, but I guess I better check this out."

"You do that little thing," Sandy said. "After that, you're on your own. I won't be calling anymore. I don't even know why I'm telling you this much, except that I made you a promise. I've got a thing about promises."

"I'm not sure I like the sound of that."

"You wouldn't be willing to bust a guy in Denver for me, would you?" Sandy asked. "It's a child-abuse case. The child's about thirty-five."

"What are you talking about?"

"I didn't think so," Sandy said. "Well, I've got a lot of thinking to do about all of this. For starts I'm going to try and figure out what side I'm on. And Parker . . ."

"Yes?"

"Don't get too attached to this decade. It may end sooner than you think." Sandy placed the receiver carefully back in its cradle.

SEVENTEEN

And in my hour of darkness/
She is standing right in front of me

Came the snows and the freezing rains, the iron-gray months of winter, and Sandy moved through them like a sleepwalker, going through the motions, yet somehow unable to interest himself in the details of everyday living, waiting, waiting for something to happen, waiting for something he could scarcely begin to articulate.

He moved to a rundown, roach-infested, one-bedroom apartment in the East Village, above a used-record store. That seemed strangely appropriate. The bathroom window had a long diagonal crack, and the cold winds shivered through and chilled the porcelain and the chipped tiles until they felt like ice on his bare skin. Sandy never did get around to bitching at his landlord; he just closed the bathroom door.

Sharon kept at him, and he finally let her buy him lunch and divide up their life. She'd already drawn up papers on their brownstone; Sandy signed without reading them, and accepted her check for ten thousand dollars, folding it and jamming it down in a pocket of his jeans, where it stayed for nearly a month until he ran short of cash and remembered to deposit it. They split the bank accounts down the middle. Sandy demanded and got the stereo. Sharon insisted that he take half of the furniture as well, the older, scuffed, funky half. And so shortly his apartment was jammed with about four times as much junk as it could comfortably hold, and Sandy had to wend his way through a labyrinth of boxes and empty bookcases and bureaus piled on top of one another to reach the mattress he slept on (Sharon had wanted their bed).

He survived the holiday in a numb gray haze, seldom leaving his apartment. It was as if the world had retreated from him, leaving him in a small bubble of solitude. Or perhaps he had retreated from the world. A few friends got his address through Sharon and came by to cheer him up, but he met their pep talks with a sullen stubbornness, and after a while they stopped coming. He kept meaning to try and get a new agent, but he never got around to it. He kept meaning to try and make a new start on his novel, but he never got around to that, either.

Sharon brought him mail from time to time, wrinkling her nose at the state of his apartment and trying so hard to be civilized that it drove Sandy to bitter sarcasms. There was a long, funny, rambling letter from Froggy, reproaching him for skipping town before meeting Number Four and asking for a report on the Nazgûl story and Edan Morse. Bambi sent a short, warm letter, and enclosed a snapshot of herself breast-feeding her newborn daughter, Azure. And there was a telegram from Davie Parker, too. Short, brusque, and to the point. NO INDICATION THAT LYLE OR ANYONE FITTING HIS DESCRIPTION TRAVELED TO MAINE IN SEPTEMBER, it said.

For a time, Sandy could hardly bear to read his mail, let alone answer it. He did not want to think about himself or his life, and the thought of reporting on it to his friends was too painful to consider. He did not want to think about much of anything, in fact. He found himself a connection in the neighborhood and scored a big block of hash and a couple of nickel bags of third-rate pot. Weeks passed with Sandy sitting on his mattress, getting stoned every day and watching lots of TV. He'd picked up an old black-and-white portable in a secondhand store down the block. With the money Sharon had paid him for the house, he could have afforded one of those big-screen color projection systems, but somehow the little set with its built-in rabbit-ears and its flickering picture full of snow and ghosts belonged in this apartment in a way that an expensive new set never could. Sandy grew very familiar with the plots and characters of a half-dozen daytime soap operas, and shouted out answers to the moronic contestants on the game shows, but the highlight of his day was always the *Leave It to Beaver* rerun. "Where have you gone, Eddie Haskell?" he muttered.

It could not last, though. It did not last. Sandy had been a writer for too long, and the writing was too much a part of him, too deeply ingrained. Words were his defense, his addiction, the means through which he sorted and rationalized and justified his actions and experiences, the way he made sense of the world and gave his life whatever rough meaning it possessed.

Ultimately, whatever might happen to him, he would try to understand it through his words. And finally the words came, breaking through even when he was stoned and drunk, distracting him from Beaver and Wally and Lumpy Rutherford, filling him with restlessness. The words came, and there was nothing for Sandy to do but put them down on paper.

That was in January. January was his month for writing letters. He turned off the TV for good, plugged in his typewriter, and bought a few yellow legal pads. His letters were long, discursive, confused. They were letters to himself as much as to those addressed. Some of them he wrote over and over, repeatedly, trying to get to the heart of things, never quite succeeding.

The letter he wrote Maggie was twenty pages long, even though he knew she'd probably never answer it. It had to be long. It was full of groping, full of confusion, full of hurt.

His letter to Froggy was even longer and more rambling. He wrote about Edan Morse and the Nazgûl and *Music to Wake the Dead*, trying to make sense of it by putting words on paper, but failing. He wrote about sex and love and old TV theme songs. He wrote about Alan Vanderbeck and Sharon and his writing, and he wrote a lot about his car.

He felt driven to write to Bambi as well, feeling somehow closer to her now than he ever had before, feeling as if he had a new insight into a place that she had been once. He said so, after telling her a little about his troubles.

He started a letter to Slum but found he had no appetite for it. He knew damn well that Butcher or Jane Dennison would screen all of Slum's mail, and the chances of anything Sandy wrote getting through were nil, so there didn't seem to be much point.

Not that it really mattered. When the letters to Maggie, Froggy, and Bambi were done, he sealed each of them in an envelope, stamped them and addressed them, but never quite got to the point of mailing them. After a while, he realized that he had never intended to mail them. Mailing them wasn't the point. Writing them was the point.

And having written them, Sandy finally felt ready to reenter the world. He started by seeing an attorney about Slum. The man promised to look into the situation and see what could be done, but he was not very encouraging. Sandy began reading newspapers again, even the *Hog*, wondering how long it would be before he came across the announcement of a Nazgûl reunion, dreading the day and yet looking forward to it as well. He even cleaned up his apartment a little, getting rid of about half his furniture and taking his books out of the cardboard cartons and placing them in his bookcases.

By the time Lincoln's birthday rolled around, Sandy had done a lot of thinking. He had two choices. He could pretend that everything that had happened since the day of Lynch's murder had been a bad dream, forget it all, and set about rebuilding his life and his career like a sane, rational person. Or he could take a hand once again, play it out to its conclusion.

It was no choice at all, not really. He felt like a moth that had just sighted the Great Chicago Fire. He went to his record cabinet, slid out *Music to Wake the Dead*, and placed it on the stereo.

In the months that followed, Sandy played the album so often that eventually he had to hunt up a replacement copy in the record shop downstairs, since his was getting so badly worn. The more he listened to the music, the more certain he grew. The only thing that didn't seem quite to fit was the final cut on Side 1, "Prelude to Madness." The title was plain enough, but the lyrics were disconnected, cryptic. *Right is wrong, black is white, who the hell's got the justice tonight?* the song said. *Wolfman looked into his mirror and Lon Chaney looked back out*, said another line. The chorus went, *Queens beat aces every time, yeah! Dead man's hand, dead man's hand! And Charlie is the joker in the deck.* But who the hell was Charlie?

He played "Prelude to Madness" more than any other cut, wondering what it was talking about, trying to make sense of it. But it never quite jelled.

He played "The Armageddon Rag" hardly at all. That one he thought he understood damn well, and the understanding made him nervous.

In March the dreams began again.

Some of them, Sandy thought, were just ordinary nightmares. He dreamed of Sharon dressed in ice, her skin blue with the cold, her glasses rimed by frost. He dreamed of Maggie weeping. Butcher Byrne stalked his nights, shotgun in hand, hunting him, and at the end of *that* recurrent dream, Sandy would see his own head mounted on the wall of Fort Byrne, between a moose and a large bear. He would wake shaking and sweating, deathly cold under all his worn blankets.

But it was the other dreams that scared him, the ones that were not ordinary. He could recognize them now, he thought. He could feel the difference between the visions conjured up by his own troubled subconscious and the ones sent to him, somehow, by Edan Morse. There was something *alien* about these other dreams. They were vivid and fevered, always in full color, yet less chaotic than his own dreams.

He dreamed a lot of war. He had never gone to war, never known war, but the dreams seemed very real to him. He was in Vietnam, and the silver jets screamed overhead and the napalm fell, and he felt its searing kiss on his body, burning, burning, an agony that lasted half the night. He was a nun in El Salvador, and the death squads came, and they raped him over and over again, sodomized him, took him two and three at a time, mouth, anus, vagina, until finally they brought out knives and put the cold steel in all the places where their flesh had gone. He was somewhere in the Middle East, working in an oil field, and the paratroopers came down, and he grabbed a gun and tried to fight but he was an engineer, not a soldier, and he caught a bullet square in his gut and it took him hours to die.

But there were good dreams, too. Sometimes it was Ananda who came to him in the night, her dark eyes glowing, her soft brown skin glistening with oil. She would smile for him and mount him and do things to him that you can only do in dreams, until the dawn came and he cried out and woke to wet, stained sheets.

And, always, he dreamed of the music. Waking or sleeping, it was with him. The Nazgûl in a hall as vast as the night, the broken people dancing, the yellow eyes above, his warnings unheard over the loud beat of the rock, Gopher John burning, Maggio rotting, Faxon slashed and bleeding, and Hobbins shrieking and writhing like a man possessed, and behind them the thin bleeding woman on the great X-shaped cross, the darkness gathering, the air full of fear and sex and joy and the metallic taste of blood. Each time the dream came, the sense of awful imminence was greater, until finally came one night in April when he dreamed the dream and woke to the sound of his own scream. He sat up in darkness, hyperventilating, damp with sweat, thinking *something's wrong*. The dream had been too vivid to bear. He could still hear the music; melancholy and full of threat, as if a storm were gathering, the guitars in pain, the cadence of the drums almost martial, enough to set the blood rushing in his skull. On a darkling plain beyond, the armies gathered, good and evil. *This is the day we all arrive at*, Hobbins sang, *this is the day we choose*. The rhythm quickened, the battle began, armageddon, the great storm, *soulstorm* said the lyric, and the four Nazgûl became as one, *Kill your brother, kill your friend, kill yourself!* In the Rag, *all the dead look just like you*, one line promised. And they fought on. Dead or alive, it made no difference on armageddon day.

How long he sat in the dark, waiting for the sound to fade. How long he sat breathing heavily, trying to calm himself. How long he sat and listened before he knew the truth. It was real. The music was real. Not a part of his dream, no, not at all.

In the other room, someone had turned on his stereo, and the Nazgûl were performing "The Armageddon Rag."

Sandy felt the fear pass through him, swift and cold and thin as an ice pick. He rose from the mattress, unsteady in the darkness, and went to the door.

The only light came from his amp; the dim red eye of its ON light, the pale band of the radio stations he never listened to. The darkness was full of music. She was sitting in the old overstuffed rocker by the window, but she rose when Sandy entered.

He went to his stereo, hit the reject button. The song ended abruptly, with Hobbins in mid-word, the final broken chord lingering in the still cold air of his apartment. Sandy breathed a little easier, and shivered. She had opened the door to his bathroom, and a chill had seeped in everywhere. He closed it and turned to face her. "I've dreamed of you," he said.

She came closer. "I know." Her arms went around his neck. She pulled him down to her, kissed him. Her mouth opened, and her tongue pushed at the unyielding wall of his teeth. She drew back, her eyes wide and questioning. "What's wrong?"

"Nothing," Sandy said. He trembled. "Everything."

Her face was as smooth as a pool of still water, with hidden depths below. "We have unfinished business," she said.

Sandy was strangely nervous. He felt as he had felt years before, the very first time, with Maggie. He was a boy again, and a frightened boy at that. He wanted her, wanted her terribly, and yet he said, "I'm not sure."

"I am," Ananda whispered, and she took his hand and led him back into the bedroom.

He had been hard since he'd seen her seated in the living room, but it was a strange sort of erection, as much fear as lust. He felt very passive. His head was full of Sharon and Maggie and armageddon.

But Ananda was a master exorcist. "This time you'll remember," she promised. It was like the dreams. She undid her blouse, popped the snap on her jeans and peeled them off, and straddled him wearing nothing but her panties. She did that little thing with her tongue. Her body was lithe and slender, with the long hard muscles of a swimmer. She had high firm breasts with nipples the color of dark chocolate that hardened instantly when Sandy brushed them with his fingers. Her hair was a fine black cascade that trailed across his face and chest as she kissed his mouth, his nipples, his navel, and finally took him in her mouth. For years she teased him, tongued him, brought him right to the brink and then drew him back, smiling, tongue flicking across her lips.

And when the games finally stopped, when she finally stripped off her panties and mounted him, she talked to him. Small jokes, whispered endearments, little gasps and cries of pleasure, urgent four-letter instructions. And somehow that made it better; more exciting, more personal. He thought only fleetingly of Sharon, who had always been silent when they made love, as if somehow he shut off her personality when he thrust into her. She would move with him, and sometimes groan, but never talk, and in that sense she was a stranger during lovemaking, in that sense she was only a body. But Ananda was *there*, always there, with him every step of the way, and her mind and her wit and her words made her body more erotic and intense than it could possibly be alone. When Sandy came, it was not just an orgasm, but an orgasm inside Ananda, which was different somehow. He was very conscious of her, of her smile and her cries. And then she came, moving on top of him wildly, her head thrown back, gasping, her hair whipping back and forth as she shook, a dark flush spreading across her breasts. Sandy could feel her contractions, one after the other, ebbing slowly.

Finally he pulled her down against him, hugged her, kissed her. She licked his ear. When he laughed she rolled off, smiling, and said, "Good enough for government work, right?" Then she padded into the bathroom and returned with a damp, warm washcloth whose touch was incredibly soothing. "Say something," she told him.

But in the short time she had left him, the darkness had crept back into the room and settled over the mattress, and Sandy was no longer smiling. "You're the only good thing in any of the dreams," he said. "The rest of it scares me."

Ananda settled down next to him. "Tell me about it," she whispered.

He did. When he was done, she sighed. "Ugly," she agreed. "But only dreams, for you. Other people lived those dreams, or will. I think maybe the oil field war is something yet to come."

"Yes," Sandy said. He had felt the same way. The planes had looked oddly futuristic in that one.

"I think you understand, Sandy. Deep down. That's where it all comes from, deep down. Edan just brings it forth. So you knew all along. Those are the things we're fighting against. War, oppression, injustice. The dreams were sent to remind you."

"What about the concert dream?" he said.

"I think you misinterpret that one. Or maybe not. Maybe you're just telling yourself that there's an ugly time ahead, right? That's true. Remember, the Rag has two parts, with the long bridge between, but before we reach the resurrection we have to pass through the fire."

"Armageddon," Sandy said. "The bloodtide. It's a nightmare."

"No," said Ananda, "the world around us is the nightmare."

"And you're the dream?" he said.

She kissed him lightly. "That's the nicest thing you've said yet."

"How did you find me?" Sandy asked.

"Got your address through the *Hog*. Your realtor gave me the next clue. Nice lady, if you like dyed hair and fingernail polish. What happened?"

"It turned out our ideas on real property were just too diverse," Sandy said. "She wanted a luxury condominium in order to maximize long-term capital gains, and I wanted a sugar shack to boogie-woogie in."

"I'm glad," Ananda said. She ran a languid hand up his body so softly it made him tremble.

"Why are you here?" he said. "I don't have that much natural charm, I know that damn well."

"You underestimate yourself," she said, "but you're right. Edan sent me to get you. The deal is set. The Nazgûl are back together. They're down in Philadelphia right now, rehearsing secretly. Edan told me to fetch you down."

"Why?" Sandy demanded. "What's his interest in me?"

"He wants you with us. You have talents we need."

"Talents?"

She sat up in bed, shook her black hair. "When the hour comes, we must raise an army. They must come to hear the Nazgûl play, come in the hundreds and the thousands. You can do that. You write. You understand the media, you have access to it. Edan wants you to travel with the band, to handle all the publicity for the tour. He said I could tell you to name your own fee."

That was a curve ball that Sandy had never anticipated. "Is that why you're here?" he said sharply. "Are you part of my fee?"

She frowned, and crossed her arms against her high, beautiful breasts. "Edan doesn't tell me who to sleep with," she said. "After a crack like that, I ought to spit in your face and leave, right? But I won't. I'm going to forget you said that. There are more important things at stake here than your feelings or mine. Remember your dreams. Think of the stakes."

Think of the stakes. *I tend my garden*, Maggie said with weary resignation. She looked old and beaten; robbed of their animation, her features were almost homely. *What a frigging laugh*, Lark jeered. Had he always been such a bitter, empty man? *Believe*, counseled Bambi, *believe and you'll be happy*. Believe in Jesus or in pyramid power, in vegetarianism or love or the Democrats, it was all the same. Contentment built on sand, with a tidal wave onrushing. Froggy snorted with laughter. *We coulda been a contender,* he said. *Only they said, "Kids, it ain't your decade." It ain't our decade! We coulda changed the world, we coulda been something. Instead of bums. Which is what we are. Bums with spaghetti in our hair.* How many wives had it been now? How many colleges? *It's too late,* Slum said with downcast eyes. *I'm incompetent. It's too late.* But what if it wasn't? Edan Morse and Butcher Byrne, who was white and who was black? Round and round it spun, and the painted ponies went up and down, and everyone's getting old but Mama Cass. Think of the stakes. Think of the stakes.

Ananda took his hand. Hers was smaller, cool and firm, her nails cut short, almost to the quick. His thumb traced the hard ridge of callus on the outside of her palm and little finger, in a gesture both tender and confused. "I know the stakes better than you can possibly imagine," he said quietly.

She smiled. "Then you're with us, right?"

Sandy stared at her. "You know, I don't even know your last name."

"Caine, but I never use it," she said. "Why does that matter?"

"Maybe it doesn't," Sandy said wearily.

"Well?" Ananda demanded. "If you're not part of the solution, you're part of the problem. Which is it, writer-man?"

He sat up. "I want to see it go down. I want to see it for myself. I think Edan's a fucking murderer, but these days it's hard to see who isn't, so maybe it doesn't matter. I'm going to be part of it anyway, so what the fuck, I might as well get paid for it. Tell Morse I'll do his PR for him."

Ananda touched his cheek lightly. "Welcome to the war," she said, and Sandy took her and kissed her hungrily, and they made love again. He was on top this time, and he rode her hard for what seemed like hours, slamming into her over and over with an almost desperate force while she moved beneath him and cried out and urged him on. It seemed a dark, terrible sort of lovemaking, and for a while Sandy thought it might last forever, that he would never come, never. But when the orgasm finally arrived for him, it was explosive, a sudden spasm of release that drove all thought from his mind. There was nothing but sensation, the throbbing in his loins, her heat wrapped hard around him, and perhaps, far off in the back of his head, a dim and distant crescendo of drums.

Afterward, Ananda slept, but Sandy found himself tossing and turning. He had visions of Jamie Lynch with a gaping hole in his chest, staring out at him from blind eyes. He heard the screams of children burning in the Gopher Hole, and smelled the smoke. Finally he rose and dressed and went out into the cold, leaving Ananda in bed.

Two blocks away, there was a small candy store that stayed open all night. It was still an hour before dawn when he got there, but a half-dozen customers were seated at the soda fountain, drinking coffee and leafing through the early edition of the *Daily News*. Sandy went past them, back to where the telephone was squeezed in behind the pinball machines. He had never gotten around to having one installed in his apartment. He fished in his pocket, came up with a handful of change, fed the phone and dialed.

After a dozen rings, Jared Patterson's groggy voice came on. "Who... wha? Jeez, wha time is it? Who's it there? What?"

"Just me, Jared," Sandy said. "I wanted to tell you that the Martians have landed. And guess what? I'm their press agent."

EIGHTEEN

**Look what they've done to my song, ma!/
Look what they've done to my song!**

t was an old neighborhood movie palace in a run-down section of Philadelphia, a Thirties relic that had been closed for more than a decade now, heavy with decay and faded charm. The marquee had six rows of neon tubing, three above and three below the blank gray area where movie titles would have been displayed. All the lights were gone or broken. Underneath was a ticket-seller's booth as ornate as something from *Arabian Nights*, its glass cracked and boarded over, set in the middle of a tiled outer lobby with a third of the tiles gone. The doors to the inner lobby were boarded up as well, and padlocked.

He parked Daydream in the alley beside the theater, and they both climbed out. "This way," said Ananda. She led him around back, to one of the fire exits with its big double steel doors, old red paint flaking off the metal. Gort was there, leaning against the brick wall and reading Sartre. He looked up and grunted at their approach.

Sandy flashed him a peace sign. "Klaatu borada nicto, Gort," he said.

Gort glowered. "Real original. I hate that fucking joke. Everybody makes the same stupid fucking joke." He went back to Sartre and let them pass.

Inside, they crossed a short corridor and pushed through a heavy velvet drapery, moth-eaten and covered with dust, its maroon faded almost to gray. They passed under an arched doorway into the dimly lit auditorium.

When his eyes adjusted, Sandy saw a sea of rotting empty seats, a wide deserted balcony, vaguely Moorish decor, a ceiling painted with stars and clouds, and a stage strewn with sound equipment. Two huge speakers stood by the wings, cables snaked everywhere, and back by the ancient screen was a set of drums painted with a familiar black-and-red pattern. Gopher John was already seated among them, wolfing down a sandwich. Sandy spotted Rick Maggio and Larry Richmond as well. Richmond was seated on the edge of the stage, looking small and lonely in a way that would have been impossible for Patrick Henry Hobbins, his eyes closed as he did what looked like isometrics. Maggio was off in the back surrounded by a knot of people, most of them of the female persuasion. Sandy heard his loud, snorting laughter. Already the Nazgûl seemed to have captured a sizable number of drones, groupies, gophers, and hangers-on; Sandy saw at least a dozen people he didn't know. "Where's Faxon?" he asked.

"There." Ananda pointed to the front row, where Peter Faxon sat on the aisle, concentrating on some papers in his lap. They went toward him.

Faxon seemed surprised to see him. "Blair," he said. He set his papers aside and stood up, and they shook hands. "What are you doing here?"

"I could ask you the same question," Sandy said.

Faxon smiled thinly. "Don't bother, I've been asking it myself. Sometimes I don't *know* what I'm doing here." He shook his head. "It's all your fault. After our talk, I got to brooding a lot. Maybe I realized how much I missed it all. But it was Tracy who really made up my mind. She came up to me one day last month, planted her hands on her hips, and said, 'I can't take it anymore. You want it and you know you want it, so pick up the phone and call before you drive us all crazy.' Next thing I knew, here I was."

"Here," Sandy said. He glanced around. Rotting seats, dust, faded draperies, probably lots of roaches and rats. "Terrific rehearsal hall," he said. "Was the city dump booked, or what?"

Faxon laughed. "Blame Morse. Still, I don't mind too much. Nostalgia. This was where it all began, Blair."

"Make it Sandy, please. What do you mean?"

"This was the first place Nazgûl ever played. We were still Peter and the Werewolves then. We'd done a lot of weddings and high-school dances, a few clubs, and we were getting quite a local following. This place was already in trouble, and it was catering to the teen crowd, showing a lot of horror flicks and beach pictures, whatever the management thought might draw 'em in. Finally they got the idea of doing a live rock show, with all local talent. Local talent came cheap. We were the headliners. Our first concert was up on that stage, right there." He nodded. "We'd been hashing over the name change for a while, and that seemed a hell of an auspicious moment for it, so when they brought us out, we were the Nazgûl for the first time, and we did a lot of brand-new stuff. The kids loved it, so the theater started booking us regularly. We did six shows, one a month for half a year. At the last one, a guy named Lynch came backstage afterward with a bottle of champagne, a block of hash the size of a brick, and a contract."

"The place has come down a little in the world," Sandy commented.

"Haven't we all?" Faxon said.

"So," Sandy asked. "How long you been at it?"

"Couple of weeks."

"And? How's it going?"

Faxon grimaced. "Let's just say we got a few kinks to work out."

"It's all that new material," Ananda said, "that's the problem."

The comment clearly annoyed Faxon. "The new material is what this whole gig is *about*," he said sharply. "I told you, I'm willing to throw in a few of the old songs for the hell of it, because they'll expect it, but the act is going to be built around my new stuff, or it's going to be built around somebody else besides me. You got that?"

Ananda put up her hands and smiled disarmingly. "Hey, I'm just the messenger girl, Peter, take it easy!"

Faxon scowled. "Sorry, but you know how I feel. If Morse doesn't like it, let him whistle up his surgeons and make a nice docile plastic Faxon for himself."

"Ouch," Sandy said. "Sounds like you have some reservations about Richmond."

Peter Faxon turned back to him, frowning. "He's a nice kid and he tries hard, but he ain't Pat and he never will be. And I think the whole surgery bit is ghoulish. They warned me ahead of time, but I still had a weird couple of minutes when I met him."

"And now?"

"Oh, hell, the feeling doesn't last. I knew Pat Hobbins better than anybody, and this kid isn't remotely like him. He even has a *dog*, for Chrissakes!"

"So?" Sandy said.

"Pat *hated* dogs. He was mauled by a German shepherd when he was a kid, had to go through the full rabies treatment, and after that he was always scared of dogs. They could smell the fear on him, and they'd growl at him and bare their teeth. If Pat had had his way, they would have gassed every dog in the world. But Richmond takes that neurotic pooch everywhere."

He pointed, and sure enough, Sandy saw Balrog off to the side of the auditorium, his leash tied to an ornate column. "And that's just for starts. I got nothing against the kid. It's hard to dislike someone who worships you. But I sure wish Morse had gotten us a singer instead of a dime-store plastic Hobbins."

"I take it you're not worried that Richmond is going to dominate your band the way Hobbins did?" Sandy asked.

Faxon laughed. "I wish. Larry Richmond couldn't dominate the Pillsbury Dough-Boy." He glanced at his watch and sighed. "Well, it's about that time. Have a seat, Sandy, and give a listen while I make atonement for all my sins. I warn you, it might be painful." He put two fingers in his mouth and whistled, and all heads turned in his direction. "Enough fucking off," he announced loudly. "Let's do it again."

Sandy and Ananda settled into seats in the front row, along with a dozen other spectators. A few sound men took their positions, and one by one the Nazgûl got ready. Behind the drums, Gopher John washed down the last bite of his sandwich with a swallow of beer and grabbed his sticks. They were Pro Mark 2Bs, big, long, fat, heavy sticks, marching band sticks, mean-looking sticks, but they seemed almost fragile in his huge, knuckly hands. Though still clean-shaven and gaunt, he was wearing jeans and a loose-fitting purple shirt, and he looked a lot more like Gopher John than had the pin-striped businessman Sandy had interviewed in Camden an eternity ago.

Maggio came on stage with a cigarette in his mouth, his belly bouncing under a blood-red Nazgûl tee shirt that was at least fifteen years old and two sizes too small. After a long final drag, he dropped the cigarette to the stage, ground it out underfoot, and picked up his guitar, the same familiar Fender Telecaster he had played in the old days. He started to tune it, and muttered "Fuck" loudly into his microphone.

Larry Richmond, in crisp new blue jeans and an embroidered denim shirt, stood in front, his Gibson SG already tuned, his boots polished and gleaming, his white hair falling softly to his shoulders. He licked his lips anxiously.

Finally there was Peter Faxon, blond and handsome, with a stern, businesslike look on his face as he slipped on his bass, a darkly gleaming metallic black Rickenbacker. He tuned it as the sound man fiddled, and when he got the nod at last, he turned to the others and said, "All right, here we go again. Let's try 'Sins.' And, Rick, it would be real nice if you could try to sing the same words as the rest of us, you know?"

"Hey, fuck you, Peter," Maggio snapped.

Down in the front row, Sandy's hand found Ananda's. He felt as nervous as Larry Richmond looked. For more than half a year now he had been chasing the chimera that was the Nazgûl, playing their old songs over and over until he knew them all by heart, obsessed by the music and the meanings. And it had all been leading up to this. Here in this ruin of a theater where the music had begun, it was about to begin again. The long silence was now to be broken once and forever, the tide was about to turn, the rage and the love and the dreams that they had lost were about to be summoned back to them, and the true and terrifying voice of the Sixties was going to be heard once more in the land. The Nazgûl were taking flight.

Maggio's Fender whispered softly, almost gently, and Richmond came in flawlessly behind him with the sweeter sound of the Gibson. Gopher John laid down a tentative beat on snare and bass, and Richmond began to sing.

Oh, lately I been thinking on my sins

"Sins," was almost a ballad, the music deceptively soft although the lyrics were wickedly double-edged. The Nazgûl followed it with "Goin' to the Junkyard," a feverish hard-rocker about trashed lives, with a hot, heavy baseline and a chorus that said, *Everybody's goin' to the junkyard!* Maggio switched to a red, rocket-shaped Gibson Firebird for that one, and grabbed for some piercing, distorted chords that sounded like a busload of schoolkids caught in a metal compactor. He went back to his Fender for "Good Ol' Days," a little bit of kick-ass country rock that featured Faxon on Cajun fiddle.

"Dogfood" had the kind of trenchant political lyrics Sandy hadn't heard in a decade, all about Pekinese getting the gout while kids starved to death in Asia. "Visions in the Dark" was cryptic, dreamlike, with a sound like a bastard child of acid rock and heavy metal that was really big brother to them both. It had a drum solo for Gopher John and a few bits of guitar work in it that only Hendrix and Clapton and the old Rick Maggio could possibly have handled, lots of fast intricate chords, screams of pain that sent Maggio to his Wah-Wah pedal, dark wavery echoes, black on black, that needed lots of Echo-plex and phase shifting.

Maggio sang lead on "Cupcakes," another loud hard-driving piece of rock with pointedly feminist lyrics. His ground-glass macho voice was made for the song, although its ironies were probably lost on him. Faxon went to keyboard for "The Things That I Remember," a bittersweet love song, and to synthesizer for "Flying Wing" with its promise of transcendence among the stars. "Dying of the Light" was Faxon swiping Dylan Thomas, and none of the Nazgûl was going gently into that good night.

They wound up with "Wednesday's Child," a long wild number with an endless bridge during which the drums went airhammer mad and the guitars screamed and clawed and Faxon's Ricky went down and down and down. It ought to have been a goddamned *apocalypse* of a song, the sort of song that gets the audience to its feet, that drags 'em up kicking and hollering, that makes 'em shriek and shake and lights up their blood like it was gasoline hungry for a match. It ought to have been the kind of song that goes on for fifteen, twenty minutes at a concert, and nearly starts a riot, or a war.

It wasn't.

Not the way they did it.

In the front row of the old theater, Sandy was very conscious of the faint smell of mold, and of the bedbugs in the seat beneath him. When he should have been lost in the music, he found himself thinking of decay, on stage and off. At first he was excited and afraid, but as song followed song, numbness set in ... and finally a strange cool feeling that was both relief and disappointment.

All the fears that had so obsessed him that winter seemed very faraway and foolish now as Sandy sat in the rotted-out old movie house and watched three middle-aged men and a green kid try to recapture a magic that was long gone, a sound and a promise and a spell that had passed from the world forever in 1971 when a bullet came screaming out of the night to write a message in blood, a message that said THE END. Edan Morse and all his talk of power in music and the tide that must come again and hours coming round at last seemed pathetically self-deluded all of a sudden. Sandy found himself thinking that it was no wonder that Jared had laughed at him. He deserved to be laughed at. He felt like laughing himself, but instead he just ground his teeth together grimly and continued to listen.

It wasn't the songs. All the material was new, every single song, and while some of it was obviously less good than the rest, nearly all of it was still nine cuts above the stuff you heard on AM radio these days. Faxon hadn't lost his touch. He was still eclectic, unpredictable, and sharp as hell. The characteristic sound was still unmistakably *Nazgûl*; fast, driven, with a hard, heavy beat, complex muscial lines, lyrics that meant something. It was mean music, but not mean in the way so much punk was mean; the points were razor-edged and threatening but never nihilistic, the violence was an evil, not a good, and something in the music itself partook, not of chaos, but of a kind of new, resurgent order. It wasn't even that Faxon had dated himself, or stood still. These songs were not rehashes of the old Nazgûl hits—they were evolved, they were ghostly musical phantoms of what the Nazgûl would have sounded like in 1972 and 1973 and 1974 if West Mesa had never happened. The best of them were as good as anything the Nazgûl had ever done. In the old days, "Goin' to the Junkyard" and "Wednesday's Child," for sure, would have had top ten, with a bullet, within a week of release. And maybe some of the others as well.

No, it wasn't the songs. It was the band. The Nazgûl had lost it.

Faxon gave the most credible performance, maybe because he had lived with the material for so very long. His bass and his voice were sure and steady, and he was never less than professional on the other instruments he took up during the course of the rehearsal. But he was seldom *more* than professional, either. The fierce concentration that had so often marked his features in the old days, as he sweated blood to keep up with the more naturally gifted musicians in the group, had been replaced by a look of embarrassed frustration. The edge was off. He was competent; no more, no less.

Rick Maggio was more and less, in turns. Faxon's pointed comment at the beginning of the set had been on target: more than once, Maggio seemed to be having trouble remembering his lyrics. Sandy noticed him faking it on both "Dogfood" and "Flying Wing," and on "Visions in the Dark" he got so wrapped up in his guitar playing that he forgot to fake it and actually sang a different line than the other three, bringing the song to a screeching halt and initiating a brief, ugly exchange between him and Faxon. To give him credit, though, he did know all the words to "Cupcakes," and he sang it with energetic, evil glee. On lead guitar, his skill seemed to come and go. The wild, difficult parts of "Visions in the Dark" would have been tough sledding for him even in the old days, before drugs had ruined him; now they were way beyond him, but Maggio did his best. Sandy saw him sweating, and once or twice he was almost there, and for a line or two his fingers would almost conjure up the old brilliance, *almost*, closer and closer...and then he would fumble, and the moment would be gone. He managed very nicely on "Wednesday's Child," was impossibly leaden on "Good Ol' Days," and seemed an almost total stranger to what he was supposed to be playing on "The Things That I Remember." By the end of the rehearsal, his tee shirt was soaked with sweat and his face was a dead fish-belly white, and *ugly*.

If Maggio was erratic, Gopher John Slozewski was just off. Maggio had at least had his bar bands to keep him in shape; Gopher John had simply been out of it for too long. His drum solo on "Visions in the Dark" was lack-luster, he seemed simply unable to sustain the kind of wild frenetic drum-ming that "Wednesday's Child" needed during its bridge, he stumbled more than once and often seemed to be playing a half-beat behind the rest of the band and struggling madly to catch up, as if his reflexes had simply grown too damn slow for the kind of music that had once been his trade-mark. At the end of "Wednesday's Child" he tossed his stick up in the air. It was an old bit of business that Sandy had seen him do a hundred times in the old days. Lots of rock drummers used similar flourishes, tossing up a stick and then catching it again; Gopher John's claim to fame was that he threw *his* stick higher than anybody else, and caught it without looking as it came down right in his hand just in time for him to smash the hell out of his cymbals. Today the stick went up and up, turning end to end against the old movie screen . . . and finally came down ten feet away, in front of Faxon. Gopher John didn't even seem to have the energy to scowl. He looked tired and confused, as if he could not quite grasp why everything was going so terribly wrong.

And then there was the kid. The ghost that wasn't. The other three might eventually jell; with time, their old skills might be recaptured. But Faxon had been right about Larry Richmond; he was not Patrick Henry Hobbins and he never would be. He looked like Hobbins, dressed like him, he did his best to ape all of Hobbins' stage mannerisms, but it was awkward, self-conscious parody at most. The kid actually wasn't half-bad on rhythm guitar. If anything, his playing was a cut above that of the real Hobbins. But he just did not have it as lead singer. His voice sounded a lot like Hobbins' when he spoke, but when he sang it seemed weak, washed-out, straining. The hard-rockers demanded a certain explosive verbal energy of the lead singer that Richmond couldn't supply; the softer songs cried out for a voice that could wring emotion from the lyrics, and Richmond's best efforts sounded hollow and fake. He didn't have the range, he didn't have the power, he didn't have the *anger* to sing like Patrick Henry Hobbins had once sung. All he did have was white hair, a familiar face, and a denim suit, and it wasn't enough.

It was no damned good, and they all knew it. The Nazgûl, Sandy, Ananda, and everyone else in the theater. When the last chord had faded away, Peter Faxon took off his bass, made a disgusted face, and walked off backstage without a word to anyone, visibly fuming. Maggio said, "Fuck you too, asshole," after him and stomped away in the opposite direction. Gopher John got off his throne wearily and went over to pick up his stick. And Larry Richmond spied Sandy and leaped off the stage, grinning. "Hi," he said cheerfully. "I saw you halfway through the set." He stuck out his hand. "Remember me?" he asked inanely. "We met in Malibu. I'm Pat Hobbins."

Sandy took the hand but shook his head. "No, you're not."

Richmond looked hurt. The expression was somehow incongruous on that pale face that was so much like Hobbins'. "You didn't like us?"

"Some of the songs have promise," Sandy said carefully, trying to be kind. He didn't think Richmond half-realized how bad they had been. "You're going to need a lot of practice, though."

Richmond nodded, but he seemed aggrieved. "Yeah. We'd sound a lot better if only Peter wasn't so stubborn, though. We ought to be doing the old stuff. That's the stuff I know. We do a lot better on the old stuff. Well, we'll get the hang of it." He looked around, and smiled. One of the gophers was walking toward him with his dog. "Hey," Richmond said. "Balrog liked it, anyhow. Didn't you, boy? Didn't you, huh?" He knelt and ruffled the top of the dog's head and batted him playfully, and Balrog barked happily in affirmation. "Hey, that's right, Bal, we did good, huh? Soundin' better and better, huh, Bal?" Richmond grinned up at Sandy and Ananda. "Bal's my toughest critic," he said. "If he don't like the way I'm singing, he starts barking during the set. You heard how quiet he was, didn't you?"

Sandy nodded. "Not a single bark."

Richmond stood up. "See? Well, you got to excuse me, Mister Blair. Got to take Bal for a walk. Catch you later, right? Hey, what are you doing here anyhow? You going to write us up for the *Hog*?"

"In a manner of speaking. I'm your new flack."

"*Great!*" Richmond said with enthusiasm. "Well, see you at the next rehearsal, then." He trotted off up the aisle, the dog running at his heels.

Sandy turned to Ananda. "Not if I can help it," he said. "Christ, the kid thinks his dog is a rock critic! They're going to tear him to pieces, 'Nanda."

Ananda's face was grim, but she didn't seem to have heard Sandy's comment. "I have to talk to Edan," she said.

"Where is he?"

"At the hotel. The Bellevue-Stratford."

"Let's go, then," Sandy said. "I've got a few things to say to Morse myself."

They drove to the hotel in silence. Ananda's mind was elsewhere, and the rehearsal seemed to have angered her, somehow. Sandy didn't feel much like talking himself. They pulled up in front and Sandy lugged his suitcase from the hatch. "I'm going to check in," he said. "I'll meet you in Morse's room. What's the number?"

She told him and headed for the elevators while Sandy went to the desk. It was ten minutes later, after he'd stashed his suitcase in his room and hung up a few of his shirts, that he walked down two flights and knocked on the door of Edan Morse's suite.

Ananda opened the door for him. She still looked furious, and said nothing. Edan Morse was seated by a window on the other side of the room, looking markedly less Boy-Scoutish than he had in Malibu. He had started to cultivate a beard, and it was coming in dark and full, covering his dimples and the little cleft in his chin. He seemed leaner as well, as if he were losing weight, and there was just the slightest hint of circles under his eyes. A heavy silver pendant with a complex spider-and-snake design hung against his black turtleneck. The brown eyes glittered as he swung to face Sandy. "So. You have elected to join us, then."

"I don't know if I'd go that far," Sandy said.

Edan Morse frowned. "If you don't believe in what we're doing, why are you here?"

"You tell me. You're the magic man."

Morse steepled his hands under his chin and regarded Sandy with those dark brown eyes. "Three possibilities," he said after a pause. "One, you know this is going to be a hell of a big story, and you want in on it. Two, you wanted into 'Nanda's pants again. Three, you're doing it for the money."

"Four," Sandy said, "all of the above."

"And you know what, Blair? I don't care. As long as you do your job, I could care less about your motivations."

"Let's talk about this job I'm supposed to do," Sandy said. He strode across the room and took the chair opposite Morse. "You just heard about the rehearsal from Ananda, I'd guess. You don't need a PR man. You need a new band. Maybe you should forget about the Nazgûl and reunite the Beatles instead. Get Paul, George, and Ringo, and make yourself a clever plastic John Lennon. Only make damn sure he can sing better than Larry Richmond."

"I don't know any Larry Richmond," Morse said flatly. "When the time comes, Patrick Henry Hobbins will give the best performance of his life." He smiled. "Or death. You can count on it."

Sandy leaned back and made a rude noise. He didn't do it as well as Froggy, but it got the message across anyway.

"Skepticism is a healthy attitude for a citizen of this pig society," Morse said, "but you take it too far."

"I heard them play today," Sandy snapped. "You didn't."

Edan Morse shrugged. "Stay away from the rehearsals, then. You have

no business being there in any case. And you have work to do. I want people to know that the Nazgûl are coming back. I want to have excitement,
anticipation. I want the audiences to be ready. Can you do that?"

"Sure," said Sandy, "but..."

"No buts. Do it, Blair. And do it soon. I've already set up their first concert. Chicago. The Civic Auditorium. June 12th."

Sandy frowned. "That's barely six weeks away," he said.

"Can't you do it?"

"*I* can do it," he said, "but the Nazgûl can't. They won't be ready in six
weeks. They might not be ready in six goddamned years, the way they
sounded today."

"They'll be ready. And it's not important anyway. This is only a prelimi-
nary. There will be other concerts, more crucial ones."

The way he said it sent a shiver down Sandy's spine. "I've listened to the
music," he said. "That's what lies behind this all. *Music to Wake the Dead.*
You think it has some kind of, I don't know, *power.*"

Edan Morse smiled thinly and said nothing.

"I almost believed you, too. But this afternoon it all fell to pieces. The
Rag is only a song."

"Is it?" Morse asked.

"Yes," Sandy said. "And the rest of that album came true only because
you *made* it come true. You killed Jamie Lynch, or had Gort do it, or somebody else. Because of the lyrics. Because you're nuts."

"Do I have to deny that again? You still don't understand. What really
happened was that Peter Faxon, back in 1971, saw the shape of Lynch's
death and wrote a song about it. You refuse to face the truth. The *music*
made it happen. Or maybe you could say it was fated to happen and the
music predicted it. But it was an accident, an accident that fortuitously ad-
vanced our cause."

"And the Gopher Hole fire? Was that another accident?"

"Yes. Part of the pattern."

"An accident that fortuitously sealed the emergency exits? No, Morse.
Someone wanted people to burn in that fire, wanted people to die.
Someone who wanted a song to come true, someone who'd bought the
delusion that blood has power. And plastic explosive doesn't accidentally
find its way into too many taverns in Camden."

"Plastic explosive?" Morse shrugged. "Did I deny that it was arson? No.
Only that I was the arsonist. I had nothing to do with that fire."

Ananda had listened in silence to the whole exchange, but now she
spoke up. "Edan's telling the truth," she said. "I've known him a long time

and I know what he's capable of. He'd lie to the man, he'd lie to protect the cause, but he's straight with our own. You are one of our own, aren't you?"

Sandy hesitated. "I guess," he said. He looked at Morse, who was turning the big silver ring on his finger and staring at the black widow caught inside. "If I could really believe that you had nothing to do with Lynch, or the fire."

"What you believe is your own goddamned lookout," Morse snapped impatiently. "To tell the truth, I'm getting fucking tired of you and your questions and your relentless middle-class rationality. You're not worth this much trouble, Blair. Maybe you ought to just go home and write some nice little novels about defeat and despair."

"No," Sandy said quickly. Too quickly, perhaps; his urgency was showing. It was important for him to stay with the Nazgûl, he knew; it was vital that he see it through. But why? Did he believe or not? Was he still a reporter/detective, infiltrating the enemy, hoping to find some proof of Morse's involvement in the Lynch murder? Or was he one of them, a part of this fever-dream vision of the old days come again? When the time came, would he stop them or help them to succeed? He didn't even know himself. But he knew he couldn't go home again. He had no home . . . unless it was the past. "I'm staying," he told Edan Morse. "I'll do your goddamned PR."

"Good," Morse said. "Then do it, Blair, and let's have no more of this pointless squabbling." Something in his face softened a little then. For an instant he looked almost tired, as though the weight of all this was getting to be too much for him, and his voice sounded vaguely troubled and very human as he said, "Look, we want the same things, really. I'm not so different from you, Sandy. You think I don't have doubts? Sometimes I just want to chuck the whole fucking thing and go enjoy my money like a good little capitalist pig. You have to keep the goal in sight, no matter how hard it is."

"The revolution?" Sandy said.

"Is only a means to an end, and the end is a better world. For everybody. It's the only way, Sandy. Yesterday fused with today. We'll wake a lost vision. *They* will, rather. The Nazgûl. A dead spirit will be reborn to sweep across the land." Morse stood up suddenly. "You'll see," he said. "Everything is going to fall into place, and you'll see." He offered Sandy his hand in the Movement handclasp.

Sandy took it. He couldn't think of a reason to refuse. Morse clasped him hard. "Peace," he said, with an ironic twist to his mouth.

A slow wet trickle ran between Sandy's thumb and index finger. He drew his hand away suddenly. His palm was smeared with blood. "You're cut," he said to Morse.

"No," Morse said, but even as he spoke he was staring at his hand. A wash of bright red blood was seeping across his palm and running down his finger. Morse looked at it with something like horror on his face. "No, I can't..." he said.

"One of your old knife cuts must have come open," Sandy said.

"Yes, that's it," Ananda put in quickly.

Edan Morse stared at her. "The wrong hand. I never cut my right hand, 'Nanda. It was always the left. Always." He held up his left hand for them to see. It was crisscrossed with a dozen old scars, and a few not so old. But it was dry, while the right hand was bleeding. "What the *hell* is happening?" Morse said in a shaky voice.

"You must have cut yourself, Edan," Ananda said. "That's all. C'mon, we'll bandage it up and everything'll be fine, right?" She went to him and put her arms around him, and looked over her shoulder at Sandy. "You better go," she said. "I'll give Edan a hand. See you up in the room, love."

Sandy went to the door slowly. As he stepped into the hall, he was still looking down at his own hand and the smear of Morse's blood drying rapidly on his skin. Something was wrong, he thought. Something was very, very wrong.

NINETEEN

Purple haze all in my brain/
Lately things they don't seem the same/
Acting funny, but I don't know why

The incident of Morse's bleeding hand troubled Sandy deeply that night, but in the weeks that followed it was never mentioned, and after a few days he simply put it out of his mind. He was kept so busy by his PR work that it was easy to do. With so little time before the concert in Chicago, his work was cut out for him.

He would have preferred to start slowly; a few rumors floated to the right gossip columns, a whispering campaign in the industry, maybe a planted retrospective or two to remind people who the Nazgûl had been. But there was no time for that kind of strategy, which meant that Sandy had to go for the big splash. There was only one sure way he knew to get the kind of play he wanted. He phoned *Hedgehog*.

Jared was derisive at first; Sandy was smooth and a touch obsequious. He knew where all of Jared's buttons were located, and he pushed them. He was suitably mysterious, and dropped plenty of hints about what a blockbuster story this was going to be. He used the word "exclusive" a lot. He promised that he would never phone Jared at home again, not no way, not no how, not ever as long as they both should live, not for no reason whatsoever, solemnly on his mother's grave. Finally he got what he wanted: the cover.

Then Sandy called *Time, Newsweek,* and *Rolling Stone* and made the same deal with each of them. They were more of a challenge, since he didn't have quite as good an "in," but eventually all of them came around. After all, it was a damned big story, and they were getting an exclusive.

"Well," Sandy told Ananda the night *Time* finally, grudgingly, agreed to his terms, "I've just kissed off any chance of a career in public relations. When all these exclusives come out simultaneously, I'll lose every fucking bit of credibility I've got, and a lot that I haven't got. Not to mention that I'll never get a good review from any of them."

"You knew the job was dangerous when you took it," Ananda said.

"Why do all my women always quote Superchicken?" Sandy bitched. He brightened. "Oh, well. It'll be worth it just to watch Jared turn chartreuse. The way I figure the publication schedules, his exclusive will come out fourth." He smiled. "Froggy the Gremlin would be proud of me," he added.

Sandy handled each of the reporters the same way. They got interviews with Maggio, Faxon, and Slozewski. They got to photograph the trio to their heart's content, on stage and off. But they were not allowed to attend a rehearsal, and Larry Richmond was kept very carefully out of sight. Of course, it drove them nuts.

"But what about *Hobbins?*" They would ask the question of everyone: Sandy, the Nazgûl, the gophers, the groupies. "Do you have a new lead singer?"

"Yes and no," was the answer everyone was instructed to give.

"What does that mean?"

"We can't reveal all the details right now. Come to Chicago."

"You got to give me something!"

"OK. There will be a fourth Nazgûl. A new lead singer, or an old one. Depends on how you look at it. And it will be somebody big. The last person in the world that you'd expect."

"Can you tell me off-the-record?"

"Sorry." Regretful shake of the head.

"Will you nod if I guess it?"

Cryptic smile.

"Last person I'd expect, eh? Hmmm. Rod Stewart? No? Mick Jagger? Elton John? Shit. Bruce Springsteen? That's it, right? No? Fuck. Somebody big, you said? I don't know. Paul McCartney?"

The reporter from *Time*, a sarcastic fellow, got bored with the guessing game the fastest. "I know," he said finally. "It's Elvis."

"You're warm," Sandy told him with amusement, and then would say no more.

Art directors' minds work alike, as Sandy knew damn well. Within one four-day period in the middle of May, the exclusives all hit the stands. *Newsweek* used an old concert photo of the Nazgûl on its cover, with a big red question superimposed over the Hobbins figure. *Rolling Stone* went with a rehearsal photo of Faxon, Maggio, and Slozewski, with a shadow man drawn in their midst holding a microphone. The shadow had a very Hobbinsesque stance. The *Hog* used new photographs of the old Nazgûl as well, but they put in a morgue photo of Hobbins to complete the group; then put a big red crosshairs over the Hobbins figure, *and* a red question mark at the center of the crosshairs, *and* four of Tolkien's Nazgûl wheeling around above the band. "Real fucking subtle, Jared," Sandy commented. *Time* welshed on him and went with a cover about the troubles in Africa, but they did have the Nazgûl peering out from under the flap in the upper right-hand corner. "Can't trust anyone these days," Sandy said.

The mystery of Patrick Henry Hobbins dominated all four stories, as Sandy had known it would. In fact, he had counted on it. It was just the right touch to whet the public interest. The old Nazgûl fans would come out in any event, but by playing it this way he had ensured that the curious would pack into the Civic Auditorium as well.

The writers had played more or less the same notes all the way down the line. Lots of then-and-now photographs. The rise and fall of the group's first incarnation. The horror of West Mesa. The killer who was never caught. Peter Faxon as one of the great creative forces in rock history. Peter Faxon's breakdown. The post-Nazgûl careers of Slozewski and Maggio. Maggio and the drugs. Slozewski's nightclub and the recent tragic fire. Paul Lebeque, who had made the reunion possible by ("allegedly") killing Jamie Lynch.

Only the tone of the pieces and the writing skill differed greatly. The *Hog's* story, Sandy was a bit sad to note, was the worst. Jared's reporter had recapitulated too damn much puffery; if Sandy had been her editor, she would have been out on her cute little ass. The *Rolling Stone* story had the most meat to it, and *Time* was the most cynical. Was it frustrated creativity or simple financial desperation that had pushed the Nazgûl back together? *Time* asked. And could they possibly hit it again in an era when musical tastes had changed so markedly, when the charts were dominated by groups like Styx, Journey, and REO Speedwagon, groups whose sound was the antithesis of everything the Nazgûl had symbolized in rock? *Time* didn't think so. Sandy didn't really think so either, but he tried his best to keep his doubts to himself.

Not that it mattered. The atmosphere of doubt and gloom and impending catastrophe that hung over the Nazgûl rehearsals was thick enough to cut with a chain saw, and it grew worse instead of better as the Chicago concert drew closer. Sandy attended a few more sessions, just to see what was happening, and left feeling depressed and tired. There was some improvement, to be sure. Under the whiplash of Faxon's tongue, Maggio was growing steadier on lead guitar, and had finally learned all the lyrics to all the songs. And Gopher John's drumming had gotten dramatically better as he shed years of rust and began picking up a few of his old moves again. But no matter how proficient they might be, Richmond was still standing there in front, and Richmond grew no better. He was already trying as hard as he could, but the only one who thought his best sufficient was Balrog. "Maybe we should play dog shows," Faxon said glumly after one especially trying set.

Sandy saw almost nothing of Edan Morse during those weeks. Morse preferred to deal with the band through Ananda and the omnipresent Gort. That was fine with Sandy; Morse and his bleeding hands gave him the creeps. Ananda was much more congenial company.

They were living together now, sharing a hotel room and a bed. Sandy wasn't sure how that had happened. They had never discussed the subject of their relationship, really—it was more of a case of falling into it. Not that he minded. The more he got to know Ananda, the more she intrigued him.

They seemed to spend an awful lot of time in bed. It wasn't just sex, although the sex was an important part of it. 'Nanda was as sensuous and uninhibited as any woman he'd ever known. She had more than a touch of Maggie's craziness; he was never quite sure what she'd think of next, but he found that he usually enjoyed it. Once, after a particularly wild night, he smiled down at her and said, "Any second now I'm going to wake up and discover that this is all a wet dream."

They talked a lot in bed, too. Once or twice they gabbed the night away, and Sandy staggered off to work yawning—yet somehow exhilarated. Ananda was a terrific listener. He told her about the breakup with Sharon, and the very telling made the hurt fade. With Ananda curled up in his arms, warm and smiling, losing Sharon seemed unimportant. They had never had that much in common anyway, Sandy was forced to admit.

He told her about Maggie too, and about all the other women who'd come and gone in his life and his bed. He told her all his favorite anecdotes about Froggy, and she laughed with him. He told her about Slum and Butcher and she shared his rage. They spoke about his novels, and how much the writing meant to him. About the old days in the Movement and on the *Hog*. They talked about movies and comic books and politics and music. They almost always seemed to agree, and even when they didn't, Sandy found none of the derision in Ananda that had been so much a part of his relationship with Sharon.

"Why is it that I always seem to be the one doing the talking?" he said to her one night, after he'd been holding forth for some time. "What about you?"

She sat up in bed, cross-legged and gorgeously naked, and grinning at him. "What about me?" she said.

"Tell me about yourself. You know, where you grew up, your family, your old boyfriends, all the usual stuff."

"Uh-oh," she said with mock alarm. "He wants to hear all about my checkered past. Where should I start? The brothel in Cairo? My years with the circus? You want to know why I flunked out of astronaut training?"

Sandy hit her with a pillow. "Cut it out," he groused. "Fess up!"

"I was born at a very early age," Ananda said with a straight face. "My parents are in the metal business. My mother irons and my father steals."

He slugged her again, growling, and she slipped to one side, grabbed a pillow of her own, and hit back. For a minute or two they whaled away at each other, cursing and laughing, and then Sandy lost his pillow and it turned into a wrestling match, and in no time at all to lovemaking. That was the end of conversation for that particular night.

But Sandy persisted, and finally he did get Ananda to open up about her past. She was an Air Force brat, she told him. Her father was an NCO and a martinet; he'd disowned her about ten years ago and she hadn't seen him since. An only child, she had grown up on a dozen different bases, at home and abroad; a troubled, lonely, friendless childhood that had left her with a deep, abiding hatred of all things military.

Sandy had believed it all for about a week, until Ananda happened to mention her sister one night. "Sister?" he said. "What sister?"

And it came out that none of it was true. Actually, she told him, she was the youngest of three. She did not like to talk about her family. She'd never known her father. Her mother said that he was a sailor, and that was about all she knew of him. She'd never gotten on with her two half-sisters. The oldest had become a working girl, like Ma. The youngest had gotten mixed up with a bad bunch in school, had gotten hooked on drugs, and had OD'd at seventeen.

Sandy was properly sympathetic, but a little dubious this time. It was not the last story he got from her, by any means. Ananda was nothing if not inventive. She had been forced to drop out of high school, she told him once. No, not really—she'd gone to Berkeley on a scholarship and graduated with honors. Except, really, she'd been expelled for her part in the turmoil on campus. Her major had been in journalism. No, English. No, history. Or film. At least on Tuesdays. Her mother was dead. Her father was dead. They were both alive, a nice old couple living peacefully in San Diego. No, they'd moved to Africa ten years ago, where there was less stigma attached to interracial marriage. Ananda had figured it was more important to stay and fight. They'd been so poor she'd been forced to do a few porno films as a teenager. But she'd been a virgin until she met Edan. Edan had been her common-law husband once, but it broke up a long time ago. Edan and she had never been lovers. She'd never been arrested. She'd spent eighteen months in prison. As a kid, she'd been in and out of reform school a dozen times. She was the homeliest kid in her class. She was a high-school cheerleader. She was a high-school radical. Her real name was Sarah. Or maybe Cynthia. Or Jane.

"You realize," Sandy said to her at last, "that all this is more than a tad contradictory."

Ananda only smiled. "Consistency is the hobgoblin of small minds. I am large, right? I contain multitudes."

"You sure do," he agreed. But by then it had begun to bother him. "Look, 'Nanda, I'm getting the feeling you don't really trust me. I don't like it. Why can't you give it to me straight?"

"I thought you liked women of mystery?" she said playfully.

"Damn it!" Sandy snapped. "Cut it out!"

That wiped the smile from her face. She crossed her arms over her breasts and regarded him soberly. "All right," she said. "You want serious, I'll be serious. You're pressing me, Sandy, and I don't like it."

"Why?"

"Maybe because I like *you*."

"That makes absolutely no sense."

"No? Well, it makes sense to me. I know what kind of life I've lived, even if you don't. Some of it—well, let's just say I've done a few things I'm not too wildly proud of. And a few others that I *am* proud of that you might not approve of. We haven't known each other all that long, Sandy. I like you a lot, and I think you like me...but I'm nervous, too. Scared. Maybe if you really knew all about me, you wouldn't like me so much. I'm afraid."

"I think you ought to give me a chance."

"Maybe I will," Ananda said quietly. She reached out and took his hand. "But not now. Not so soon. There's too much going on, and it's all happening too fast. Gimme some time. Don't force things. Let them grow."

"And what do we do in the meantime?" he said.

Ananda grinned at him. "We go right on having a good time. Getting to know each other. Enjoying each other. Right?"

"I guess," he said, reluctantly. He didn't like it. But neither did he want to press too hard and risk losing her. He didn't think he could take that, after everything else.

"Good," she said. "Then it's settled."

It was their only serious disagreement. Otherwise, they got on famously. Ananda was everything Sandy might have asked for; quick and intelligent, attractive, erotic, supportive, funny. She believed passionately in all the old, unfashionable ideals that Sandy had once believed in too. In her company, he found all those old beliefs coming back, as if he had never put them aside at all. With Ananda taking up so much of life and time and energy, it was almost possible for Sandy to forget his nightmares, forget Morse's bloody hand and Jamie Lynch and the ominous echoes of *Music to Wake the Dead*. It all seemed a little silly now. Whatever strange dreams Morse might be dreaming, it was clear that the Nazgûl themselves knew nothing of them. They were only men, four musicians each struggling with his own problems, his own destiny.

And struggle they did. "I don't want to be here," Gopher John told Sandy one night in the Bellevue-Stratford bar. "If it hadn't been for that fire, I'd be gone. It's not working. We oughta leave the memories alone. We used to be good. The best. The fucking *best*. We're going to shit it all up with this comeback." His voice was bitter. "But what choice do I have? No fucking choice at all that I can see." He glowered and finished the beer and called for another. Slozewski was drinking a lot of beer lately. Too much. Already his face was puffy under the heavy black beard that he was regrowing for the concert. And a small potbelly was pushing at his belt.

Peter Faxon was not as open about his frustration, but Sandy knew that he was hurting as well. Tracy Faxon visited on three occasions during that period, and the last time she looked quite upset. "I'm worried for him," she told Sandy privately just before she left to fly back to New Mexico. "He's frightened about Chicago. Badly. He won't let me attend, you know, me or the kids. He just says he doesn't want us there. He says I ought to go to a movie that night, or take the kids up in the balloon, but he doesn't want us in Chicago. He won't even talk about it, and that's not like Peter. I know what it means. He can't say it out loud, but he thinks he's going to fail, and fail badly, and he can't stand the idea of me seeing it. Sandy, you seem like a decent enough guy. Watch him for me. Call me if things get rough. I don't want anything to happen to him. Not again. He couldn't take it again."

Even Rick Maggio did not seem happy with his dream come true. Chicago's Civic Auditorium was a far cry from the Come On Inn, but Maggio had a frightened, desperate edge to him nonetheless, like a man trying to enjoy all the vice he possibly could today because he knew it was all going to be gone tomorrow. He felt up every woman in the sound crew and hangers-on, propositioned most of them, screwed about half, and gave the world long, rambling accounts of his sexual exploits on the morning after. Since he never seemed to bed the same woman twice, before long he was going further and further afield for his lays, and the girls were getting younger and younger. Sandy encountered him in a hotel corridor one night, with his arm around a black girl who couldn't have been more than fourteen, and even Maggio had the grace to look briefly embarrassed before he forced a lascivious grin and asked Sandy if he wanted sloppy seconds.

Maggio also talked about the stringent diet he was on, and to be sure he was losing weight dramatically. Only the "diet" was a fraud. What Maggio was dieting on was speed. He managed to keep it secret until the day that Faxon surprised him in the men's room of the theater between sets, and Maggio spilled black beauties all over the tiled floor. The argument that ensued almost killed the Nazgûl reunion right then and there. Sandy was talking to Slozewski when they heard the yelling. They came running, along with a half-dozen others.

Maggio was red-faced and screaming, on his knees, scrambling to pick up the pills as he shrieked epithets at Faxon. Faxon said nothing at all in reply; he just stood there in front of the urinals, looking down at his lead guitarist with a face like death. When Maggio had gotten all the black beauties, he got to his feet again and went on yelling. "You ain't got no fucking *right*, man! Who the fuck you think you *are*? I don't take orders from you, you hear, you hear, nobody tells me what the fuck to do, nobody, and especially not *you*!" He glared at Sandy and Slozewski and the rest of them. "Bug off, creeps," he said. "This is between me and the fucking big shot here, the goddamned wimp big shot. It ain't none of your fucking business, you hear? You're all against me anyway, don't think I don't know it. I get all the pussy and you assholes are jealous, so fucking jealous you drool. You too, Faxon. Especially you. You been after me all along. You and your big house and your goddamned publishing rights, and you left me with shit. WITH SHIT! And the fucking Nazgûl wouldn't have been nothin' without me, *nothin'*, you hear?"

"Rick..." Gopher John began tentatively.

"Shut up, Polack," Maggio snapped. "This is none of your business, man. You got that? You're too fucking dumb to understand anyhow. So I take a few pills? What the fuck? I got it under control, man, you hear? *I got it under control!* It's just for my weight, man, just to get my fucking *weight* down, I can't go out there looking like this, you hear, you assholes, you *hear*? You'd like me to play like some goddamned hippo, right? That way you figure maybe you'd get some of that prime nooky, right? Well, forget it, assholes, it ain't going to happen, I got it under control." He looked at each of them in turn. "Fuck you," he said. "Fuck you all." Then he stomped out of the men's room.

"He really has it under control, doesn't he?" Faxon said to the rest of them after Maggio had left. He turned to the urinal behind him, took his piss in silence, then zipped up calmly and walked out of the room and the theater. He didn't come back for two days, and Sandy was left wondering whether it was over. Finally, on the third day, Faxon returned. "Gopher John needs the money and I need the music," he told Sandy with a cold, still face. "It's going to be a disaster, but I can't live the rest of my life without making the attempt."

"And Maggio?" Sandy asked.

"I don't care," Faxon said curtly. "He used to be my friend once, but that was a long time ago, and now I find that I just don't give a fuck. If the band fails it won't matter anyway, and if we make it, we'll just get a replacement for Rick when he kills himself. That shouldn't take long."

From then on, Maggio did his drugs openly, defiantly, taking a couple of black beauties before every session, a couple more afterward, and God knows how many when he was alone. The fat melted away, sure enough, and so did large hunks of his personality. He and Faxon scarcely spoke anymore, and relations between him and Slozewski also deteriorated steadily, until they almost came to blows over one of Maggio's endless Polish jokes. Even Larry Richmond, deferential as he was, began to get pissed with the way Maggio treated him like dirt and ordered him around. "If only he *was* Hobbit," Gopher John told Sandy after one bad afternoon, full of rancor and sniping. "Hobbit could always keep Rick in line . . . well, better'n anybody else could, anyway."

Sandy tried to avoid the rehearsals as much as he could. It was easy enough to do. Once the story of the Nazgûl reunion broke, his phones were constantly ringing with reporters wanting facts and interviews, old friends of the band wanting messages delivered, and parasites wanting free tickets. Besides, coordinating the local publicity in Chicago was a full-time job in and of itself. He had press kits to prepare, ads to place, a poster to design and print up, stories to feed to the local media.

But work was not the real reason that kept him away. It was painful for him to hear the Nazgûl sounding so bad, and the atmosphere in the decaying Philadelphia theater seemed to grow more poisonous every time he dropped by.

There were more and more people at the rehearsals, an army of strangers, many of whom made Sandy uncomfortable. The publicity that Sandy had planned had done its share, and Edan Morse had done the rest; together they produced an ever-swelling number of followers who wanted a piece of the Nazgûl. It was a very mixed crowd. There were groupies, of course, though not as many as Maggio would have liked, and not as pretty. Most of them were just groupies, a few still innocent and awestruck, a lot more looking faded and worn and badly used, one or two real burnouts with ravaged bodies and empty eyes. Yet there were some others . . . brusque and cold ones, too quiet, dangerous and somehow frightening.

You saw the same strange mix all the way down the line. The head sound man was a short, square black man who had worked for the Nazgûl in the old days; he was good-humored and competent, as were his two assistants, though the rehearsals seemed to be doing a damn good job of grinding away his spirits. But Reynard (that was the only name he used), the light man, was brought in by Morse, and he struck Sandy as very strange; gaunt almost to the point of emaciation, his thin hair badly combed, his pants ragged and baggy, the pocket of his short-sleeved shirt always full of Flairs in a dozen different colors. Reynard was a whiz at lighting, but his manner seemed to swing between icy hostility and manic sarcasm. The road manager was a veteran hired for his experience, and he did his job well enough, but the roadies were like no other roadies Sandy had ever encountered. They were quiet, distant, humorless. They never got drunk, never got stoned. One of the women had snakes tattooed on both arms, curling around from wrist to shoulder. One of the men wore silvered sunglasses everywhere and carried a nunchaku. The rest of them could have blended right in at a Jaycees convention, they were so gratingly normal. But when Gort gave them an order—Gort had been put in charge of the roadies— they obeyed with an almost military precision. They gave Sandy a fluttery, cold feeling in the pit of his stomach, and he didn't think he was alone in that. Even Maggio never hit on the female roadies, although a couple of them were quite attractive. Faxon called them the "orcs" and Sandy knew he was harking back to Tolkien, not to the long-defunct Nazgûl fan club.

Ten days before Chicago, Sandy had a brief discussion with Ananda about the orcs. "They're Edan's people, aren't they?" he asked her. "Alfies or worse? That's why they seem so damned, I don't know . . . disciplined, I guess."

She smiled. "So? I'm one of Edan's people too, remember?"

"Not like them. There's something wrong with them, 'Nanda. I think they're hearing things on the Jim Jones/Charlie Manson wavelength, if you know what I mean. I think they'd do anything Gort told them to do. *Anything*."

"They would."

"And that doesn't bother you?"

"They're soldiers," she told him. "When you're in a war, you need soldiers. War changes people. You know what it did to the grunts in 'Nam. Fighting the war at home wasn't any easier, right? Sometimes it was harder. Daddy was one of the enemies, and Mommy, and all your teachers and maybe even your playmates. They don't trust you, Sandy. That's why they're cold. Give it time, right?"

"This is a rock concert, not the Battle of the Bulge," Sandy said to her. But he broke off the conversation then and there, feeling uncomfortable. It wasn't his only moment of discomfort. More than once he woke up in the middle of the night in his room at the Bellevue-Stratford, feeling troubled by dreams he could not remember, wondering what the hell he was doing here, why he was involved in all of this. It would always be impossible to get back to sleep on those nights. Often he would dress quietly, in the dark to keep from waking Ananda, and go out to find an all-night coffee shop somewhere, where he could sit and stare down at the brown, muddy coffee and grope for a reflection there, hoping to see a bearded face he scarcely remembered, a face he had abandoned and changed a long time ago. All his ghosts would squeeze into the booth with him, and he would see them smiling at him across the formica, hear the clamor of their debate. Sandy would drink his coffee in silence and stare out the plate-glass windows at the darkness sighing through the city streets.

The sleepless nights came more frequently as time ran down on him. One week before the scheduled comeback concert, they finally closed up the Philadelphia theater. The instruments and all the massive new sound equipment and the roadies and friends and groupies and sound crew and light crew piled into a bus and a semi for the trip to Chicago. Maggio, Slozewski, and Larry Richmond flew out. Faxon was supposed to fly with them, for a final week of rehearsal in Chicago, but instead he announced that he was taking a plane to New Mexico to see his family. "If we don't have it now, we're never going to have it," he said, leaving unspoken the thing that everyone knew: they *didn't* have it. "Don't worry, I'll be back in time for the gig. Just don't ask me *why*."

Sandy and Ananda drove in Daydream. He cut loose from the bus and the semi as soon as he could by the simple expedient of flooring his gas pedal and leaving them far behind. He had had too much time with all of it, and he wanted to be alone. Ananda, who had been attending the rehearsals regularly, had been unusually quiet during the last week in Philadelphia, but on the road her spirit came back to her. She was playful, lively, erotic. They made a silly game of making love in every state along the way, and whenever he expressed doubts or forebodings, she was there to talk or joke him out of it. She was good to have along.

He did think of visiting Maggie when they passed by Cleveland, but somehow, with Ananda along, it didn't seem like a good idea, though he had never known Maggie to be jealous.

When they reached Chicago, Sandy was careful to stay away from the Conrad Hilton. He checked into the big new Hyatt Regency, a tall modern goliath of a hotel that had not even been dreamed of in 1968. Even at the last minute . . . or especially at the last minute . . . there were a million things to do. Sandy did them. Doing them took so much energy that he had none left for worry.

But on the last night, the dream came once again.

The hall, the vast dark hall. But it was not a hall, Sandy saw; they were outdoors, under the stars, spreading stars like yellow eyes. There were the Nazgûl, bathed in flickering dancing light, red light, dull violet light, white light that made them burn and shimmer, black light that made them brighter still. Each was as Sandy had seen him before. Gopher John was burned, Faxon was still-faced and bleeding, Maggio's whole body seemed ripe with pustulence and decay. And in front was Hobbins moving. *Hobbins*, not Larry Richmond, the real, the original, the dead Patrick Henry Hobbins himself, singing as only he could sing. He was vast, taller than the others, the three mere humans, the living; he was tall enough to brush the terrible black sky, and he was translucent, burning with a furious inner light. He was singing "The Armageddon Rag." Behind the stage was the big rough X-shaped cross, and the naked woman nailed to it, bleeding. They had pulled off her nipples with pincers and the blood ran down her chest. Another thin red trickle crossed the whiteness of her thighs, flowing from her vagina, from somewhere deep inside her. Her eyes had been put out; she twisted her head and screamed and looked out at the dance from empty, bleeding sockets. She was familiar, he sensed. He knew her, knew her somehow, this wasted child-woman. He knew the sound of her screams, knew the look in those blind bloody eyes, knew the sad, pathetic motions of the thin body. But how? Where? It would not come clear. Behind her were the demons, all around them were the demons, dark shapes writhing in greater darkness, slitted yellow eyes, red red mouths, breath like fire. But on the dance floor the people boogied on, lost in the magic of Hobbins' voice, lost in the spell of the Nazgûl. Sandy ran from one to another, shaking them, hitting them, trying to make them listen. Froggy grinned at him and made a joke. Lark told him his politics were incorrect. Bambi said he had to believe, to believe in the promises. The promises were beautiful. Ananda was there too, dancing wildly, laughing. She was naked and her dance was maddeningly erotic. But she stopped when Sandy came near. "It's all right," she said, and she did that thing with her tongue, slipping it across her lower lip, so quickly, so enticingly. "Don't fight it. Come." And she took his hand and tried to draw him into the dance. But as she pulled him he saw Edan Morse, off to the side, standing alone and looking at his hands. His hands were bleeding. He held them up and they dripped black, viscous blood. "This isn't right," Morse said. "This isn't right."

"NO!" Sandy screamed, and he sat up in bed, shaking. For an instant it had seemed so real. Then it faded, and it was just a dream again, and he thought he would have another black, sleepless night. But his shout had woken Ananda, and she put a gentle hand on his shoulder, drew him back and down. "I had the dream," he said.

"Don't think of it," she said. She took his hand and put it on her breast. It was warm and alive, and Sandy felt her nipple grow erect under his palm. "This is no night for bad dreams," Ananda whispered. She kissed him and ran her hand down along his spine. "It's all right," she said. "Don't fight it. Come." He was already hard, and she opened her legs for him, and she was very wet and very warm, and he entered her and found his comfort there, found his warmth and solace, found shelter from the storm. "Come," she whispered to him as they moved together, "come, come, come, come." And finally he did.

TWENTY

And we'll go dancing baby and then you'll see/
How the magic's in the music and the music's in me

Between the Hyatt and the Civic Auditorium lay the streets the ghosts had walked on his last visit to Chicago, the streets where the battles had swirled on a hot, humid night like this in 1968, but tonight they flowed with a different kind of excitement, the normal Loop traffic swelled by a steady stream of couples moving south from the parking garages to the theater, to hear the Nazgûl play. Sandy made the walk alone, since Ananda had been down there all afternoon. He felt very much a part of the crowds streaming toward the concert. They were all strangers, but he knew them, the men and the women in jeans and tee shirts and the ones in denim suits, the ones who came in cabs and the ones who piled out of ancient VW minibuses, the ones whose hair was styled and the few who still wore it long. It would be an older crowd than those at most rock concerts, he knew, full of people like himself, full of Bambis and Froggys and Slums, come together in celebration after too many years apart, come together once more to hear some memories... or maybe, just maybe, because they were lost, and looking for something.

The street outside the theater was a zoo. Taxis pulled up one after another, discharging fares. Cars cruised past slowly, with women hanging out the windows shouting to see if anyone had extra tickets, stopping dead when one of the scalpers came sidling up. The concert was a sell-out, had been a sell-out within hours of the moment tickets went on sale. Already the double line of concert-goers stretched around the block. Sandy saw a lot of beards still, a few headbands, here and there a fringed vest. There was one woman with waist-long red hair whose chest was covered with buttons; buttons for candidates and causes and bands that had been forgotten for years, with slogans that no one ever chanted anymore. Sandy smelled grass as he pushed through the crowd. He counted a lot of Nazgûl tee shirts; the famous blue Dead Hobbit tee shirt from the 1969 tour, the dead-black shirt (washed-out now), with nothing on it but four pairs of red eyes, that had been given away to promote the Black Album, the common blood-red printed shirt with its white lettering and line drawing, and of course the new shirt Sandy had helped design, a deep purple, the color of an old bruise, with silver lettering that said THE NAZGÛL FLY AGAIN over a transfer showing a black rider etched in silhouette against a swollen red sun.

He flashed his pass at the door and was admitted. Backstage was the normal preperformance chaos multiplied by about a factor of ten. Everyone seemed to be running somewhere and shouting. He found Ananda back with the band. They were sitting amid the confusion and trying to look calm. Rick Maggio was smoking a joint, his feet up on a chair. He was still porcine, though he'd dropped about forty pounds and the strain was showing in his eyes. A cute blond was sitting in a lotus position at his feet, like a faithful dog, and every once in a while Maggio would give her a little pat on the head, and she would look back and repay him with a crooked red-lipped smile. Gopher John was sucking a beer and scowling at himself in a mirror. He was wearing an old tie-dyed smock that he must have dug out of the bottom of the closet he'd thrown it in fifteen years ago, and his beard had come in full and fierce, making his face look rounder than it was. Larry Richmond wore a red denim suit and a black shirt. His long white hair was freshly washed and brushed, and it looked pale as ice, like a frozen waterfall. He was putting in the contact lenses that would change his pinkish eyes to a vivid, piercing, demonic red. Balrog was asleep at his feet.

"Where's Faxon?" Sandy asked.

Ananda shrugged. "He's been running around all day, checking the lights and giving Reynard a hard time, bitching at Gort, supervising the sound check. Wants to do everything himself. I don't know—"

Faxon came in the door, frowning. "They're letting 'em in now," he said. "Packed house. This is it." He looked at the other three Nazgûl. "The rehearsals may not have been the best, but that was for practice and this is for real. If we don't pull it together tonight, it's over. You got that? All of you? Rick?"

"Don't sweat it, man," Maggio said. "We're cool. It's goin' down smooth as baby shit, I guaran-fucking-*tee* it. Biggest fucking comeback in the history of rock and roll. Don't get all uptight."

Sandy could tell that Faxon was controlling his temper with an effort. Real tension showed in every line of those handsome surfer-boy features. "If you fuck up, Rick," Faxon said carefully, "I'm going to come across the stage and shove my bass up your fucking ass. Is that clear enough for you?" He smiled. "So who's uptight? Not me. John, Pat, how you doing?"

"I'm a little nervous," Richmond admitted. You could see the anxiety all over his face, Sandy thought. He'd never looked less like Pat Hobbins than he did right now, scared as he was.

"You'd be a freak if you weren't nervous," Faxon said. "Don't fret it, kid. You'll be okay." His voice didn't really believe it. "All right, we all know how it's going to go. We'll open with 'Napalm Love' for old times' sake, and then get into the new stuff. The sound's real good out there. This place has terrific acoustics."

"We know, Peter," Gopher John said with a small smile. "We played here in '71, remember? Take it easy."

Faxon grinned self-consciously. "Well, then," he said. He looked at his watch. "We got about an hour before we go on. Let's get our asses next door. Morse has set up a hell of a spread. Booze, wine, beer, enough food to feed the entire Polish army. It's already full of celebrity types. Lots of designer jeans and gold chains, and all the media too, of course. Sandy says we're supposed to mingle and make nice."

"Fuck that shit," Maggio said. "I'm staying right here and gettin' me some head." He patted the girl at his feet and she smiled for him again.

"Suit yourself," Sandy put in. "It's Larry they're going to be interested in, anyway."

"Ah, fuck," said Maggio. He got to his feet, as Sandy had figured he would. "Whattahell, I might as well get me a few brews and talk to them jerks. C'mon, baby." She followed him from the room in much the same way that Balrog followed Richmond.

Sandy left the preshow party early. It was too crowded and smoky and hot for him, and he was getting more and more nervous as the moment of truth neared. Out in the auditorium, most of the seats were filled, and the crowd was buzzing noisily and starting to get restless. The darkened stage, with instruments and sound equipment all set up, looked pregnant with possibilities. He was standing looking out at it when Ananda appeared silently at his side and took him by the arm.

"Look at them," Sandy said, nodding at the tiers of seats, at the balconies, at the blur of faces.

"What am I supposed to see?"

"Me," said Sandy. "Me, writ large. Us, our generation, the class of 1970. This isn't a rock concert, it's a convention for aging hippies and co-opted radicals. Why the hell are they all here?"

"Because they took the wrong road a long time ago," Ananda said with unexpected vehemence. Her voice was dead earnest, her eyes dark and lambent. "They lost something, just like you did. They betrayed everything they stood for, abandoned it, changed into their goddamned mommies and daddies only half-knowing it. And now the world is shitting on them like it shit on their parents, and they don't like it. They know in their guts now as well as their heads what a stinking world this is, and they know they could have changed it, but they blew it. So now they want to get back. They want to get back to the time when they counted, when they still believed in something, when there was still a little hope that their lives would actually mean something. And music is the only road, Sandy, the only road back. Right?"

Sandy smiled. "I wish I knew," he said. The lines of a song occurred to him. "*We are stardust, we are golden, and we've got to get ourselves back to the garden,*" he said.

"Exactly."

"What if there never was a garden, 'Nanda? What if there never was a garden at all?"

She never got to answer. Suddenly they were surrounded by people, noise, commotion as the party backstage broke up and spilled itself into the wings. And a moment later, out in the auditorium, all the house lights died on cue.

You could feel the stillness, the sense of expectation. You could hear the conversations perish. You could touch the pulse of the crowd, the fluttery excited beat of the mass heart in that darkness. You could catch the scent of hope and fear.

Dark silence for a long moment.

Then the announcer's voice filled the breathless quiet. "LADIES AND GENTLEMEN, FOR THE FIRST TIME SINCE 1971...THE NAZGÛL!"

Three flaming red spots lanced down and touched the pitch-black stage, and there they stood as they had stood so often in concerts long past, long past but not forgotten. Rick Maggio grinned and drew his long, hard nails across his Telecaster, leaning on his Wah-Wah pedal to send a wild scream of distortion out to challenge the night. Gopher John, scowling behind the red-and-black drums, eased into a tremulous roll on his floor tom.

Peter Faxon stood with his bass against him like a shield against the world, his face still and expressionless. He tuned the Rickenbacker as coolly as if he were alone in his room.

The crowd came to its feet, cheering, clapping, whistling, stamping, screaming its approval. The shouts all melted together into one loud, incoherent noise, a thunder of welcome that went on and on and on, the din of it drowning the faint sound of Gopher John's drum roll, the deep vibrations of Faxon's bass, the stabbing whine of Maggio's guitar. The sound built and built until it seemed as though it might never end, as if the band might never get to play at all . . . and then, like the voice of God himself booming out of heaven, came the voice of Larry Richmond with the words of Patrick Henry Hobbins, the words that ought to have been inscribed on Hobbins' tombstone. *"All right kids,"* the voice said, cutting through the din like a knife, *"let's rock till our ears bleed!"*

The white spot flashed on, incredibly brilliant, nova hot, a shining shaft angling through the dimness, alive with dust. It came alive and it came down and it caught him, and there he was walking around the drums, there he was, his white hair shining in that light, his clothes as black and shiny as sin and as red as doom, his eyes burning, there he was, there he was, strapping on the guitar, moving to the microphone, there he was, there he was, it was impossible, he was gone and buried, it couldn't be, but there he was, Patrick Henry Hobbins, there he was, the Hobbit himself, in person, on stage, back from the goddamned *dead*.

The applause dwindled and stopped. For an endless moment, the hall was filled with the silence of disbelief. The faithful stood there and gaped, unable to believe their eyes. Someone off in the back screamed hysterically. And then the cheering began again, twice as loud as before, so wild and fevered and hoarse that it threatened to rip the roof off the auditorium. The Nazgûl basked in it. One by one, Sandy saw them smile. It had been a long time, a long, *long* time.

It was Peter Faxon who came to his senses first and broke the spell. He lifted his head, grinning, and said, "Hey, you wanna hear some rock and roll?" The audience screamed back at him as one, and slowly the cheering staggered to a halt. The Nazgûl looked at one another. Maggio laid into the sizzling opening riff of "Napalm Love," the crowd recognized it and screamed, Richmond's rhythm guitar picked up the song and filled in behind Maggio, ringing the contrasts, and then came the bass and the drums, the quickening tempo, and the crowd screamed louder still, and Larry Richmond tossed back his long white hair with a jerk of his head and gave 'em the opening lyric:

Hey baby, what's that in the skyyyyy?!

Maggio's cement-mixer and whiskey voice provided the answer:

It's loooooove!

And then they were into it full-force, the guitars screaming together, Slozewski scowling away, Richmond moving from one Hobbins pose to another, boogying, posturing, pounding his Gibson as he gave his best to Faxon's acid lyrics.

For a few minutes, the crowd seemed to love it. Most of them were still standing, shaking, shouting. One woman up front climbed up on her seat and began to dance. When the Nazgûl got to the first chorus, a hundred voices or so sang out *Oooooh, napalm! Oooooh my napalm love!* just as thousands had sung it out once at concerts and demonstrations and May Day parades.

Richmond gave it his best, his goddamned best...

Yeah, it's hot because I love ya!
Oh, it burns because we love ya!

...but even with the audience alive and frenetic and wanting it, even with them ready, even with Maggio playing lead like he hadn't played in years, even with the bass driving and ominous, even with all the memories on his side, Richmond's best just wasn't good enough. Sandy would have been hard put to say exactly when the change began, but begin it did. Slowly, person by person, the audience seemed to realize that it wasn't Hobbins they were hearing, but a clever plastic simulacrum who couldn't sing nearly as well. One by one they began to sit down and make themselves comfortable. The second chorus drew a much weaker response. Maggio and Faxon tried hard during the bridge, jamming at each other, laying it down hard and hot as they could, and that seemed to help a little, but only until Richmond began to sing again. The closing chorus was sung by the band, with damn few voices from the crowd helping out. The dancing woman had climbed down off her seat. The applause was healthy, warm, respectful... but tentative somehow.

Now the audience was waiting. Now they weren't sure anymore.

"And that was one of the old songs," Sandy said numbly to Ananda. "They're in trouble."

"Napalm Love" should have gotten the concert off explosively and pushed the energy level in the hall up several notches, so the Nazgûl followed it with "Sins," one of the softer of the new songs. It was a bad mistake. The unfamiliar song evoked no memories in the crowd, tugged no emotional chords, and its relative quietness made the deficiencies in Richmond's Hobbit imitation all that more conspicuous. He did his best, as always, and he still looked a lot like Hobbins up there, he had all the gestures and motions down pat . . . but the audience was only lukewarm.

Gopher John wasn't the only one scowling when the number was over; Faxon didn't look too happy either, and Maggio was already damp with sweat. They went from "Sins" to "Goin' to the Junkyard," with its loud, slamming, relentless beat and catchy tagline. Catchy it might have been in theory, but no one in this audience caught it. And that was maybe the best of the new songs, Sandy thought. Standing there in the wings, holding Ananda's hand, he felt a curious mixture of emotions. Whatever mad dreams Edan Morse might have had about a rock 'n' roll armageddon were dying there on the stage, and Sandy felt a certain amount of relief at that . . . yet, at the same time, he found that he was disappointed, more than a little sad.

"Flying Wing" crashed and burned. "Dying of the Light" died, and by then you could actually taste the restlessness in the hall. Everyone was seated. The first Nazgûl concert since 1971, a packed house, and they wouldn't get out of their goddamned seats; it was almost tragic. The response seemed to weaken with every song the band performed. After "Dying of the Light," Maggio actually snarled into his microphone, "Hey man, any of you fuckers awake out there? We're playing some *rock*, man."

"No you're not!" a heckler shouted out.

Faxon gave Maggio a long desperate look. " 'Visions in the Dark,' " he said. That picked things up a little. Gopher John really got into the drum solo, and there were whistles and screams of approval from the house, and Maggio was credible if not inspired on the tricky guitar bits, triggering a few shouts of his own. The applause was a little warmer afterward. But mixed in with it came the voice of the heckler again. "*Do the old stuff!*" he shouted. A couple of other voices picked up the cry. "Rage for us, Rick!" one kid yelled out, and a woman shouted, "We want the Rag! Give us the Rag!"

Larry Richmond turned around to look at Faxon. Faxon was frowning again. "Anybody out there like cupcakes?" he asked.

No response.

Maggio grinned anyway, and Richmond turned around with a damp, frightened look on his face, and the Nazgûl slammed into "Cupcakes" hard as they could.

"Flop sweat," Sandy said. "They were going to save 'Cupcakes' to open the second set."

"The natives are restless," Ananda replied.

"So let 'em eat cake," Sandy said glumly.

With Maggio singing lead, his voice rasping over Faxon's pointed lyrics, and with Richmond concentrating everything he had on his guitar playing, and Gopher John almost exploding behind his drums, "Cupcakes" went down pretty well. After Slozewski's final lingering swell off his cymbals had closed it, a few people even got to their feet, and one voice called out, "Right on, man! Right on, baby!" But there were other voices, too, shouting for old favorites, shouting for "Elf Rock" and "This Black Week" and "Ragin'" and "The Armageddon Rag."

By then the band was clearly exhausted. "We're going to take a little break," Faxon said. "Don't go away, we'll be back." He unslung his bass wearily and headed offstage, followed by the others.

They were snapping at one another by the time they passed Sandy and Ananda. "It's no fucking *good*, man," Maggio was saying loudly to anybody who would listen. "The songs ain't worth shit, and that little pinhead kid can't sing. It's no fucking *good*."

Sandy followed them backstage, along with Ananda and about a dozen other people. Faxon chased most of them out of the room with a single semicoherent growl, but he let Sandy and Ananda remain. Gopher John sat down heavily and opened a beer. Maggio fumbled some black pills out of his pocket—three of them—swallowed them, and washed them down with Jack Daniel's straight from the bottle. Larry Richmond just sat staring at his feet, looking as if he wanted to die. Faxon leaned back against the door and regarded them all sourly. "So what are we going to do?" he asked.

"The kid can't hack it," Maggio said. "I'll sing lead, man. Save our fucking ass. You heard 'em when I did 'Cupcakes,' they loved it, they fucking *loved* it."

"I did my best," Richmond said. His voice made Sandy think he was about to break into tears. "I thought I sounded pretty good." Balrog came padding across the room and put his head in Richmond's lap, and Richmond petted him absently, and smiled a wan smile.

"You tried," Faxon said, "we all tried. But it's not working."

"Let me sing lead," Maggio repeated.

Faxon rounded on him angrily. "Fuck off, Rick! You can barely remember the backup vocals you're supposed to be singing, you sure as hell don't know the lead parts."

"I know the old songs, man," Maggio said. "That's what we oughta be doin' anyhow, big shot. They liked 'Napalm Love,' didn't they? Bunch o' friggin' assholes." He took another swig from his Jack Daniel's bottle.

"He's right," Gopher John said.

Faxon looked at him in astonishment. "You, too?"

Gopher John scowled. "I don't like it either, Peter. The new stuff is terrific, yeah, but it ain't going over. These people came here on account of who we were. We got to give them what they came to hear. That don't mean we got to drop the new songs entirely. But maybe we ought to introduce them gradually, you know? Not hit them with a whole mess of music they never heard before all at once."

"Damn it, no," Faxon said forcefully.

"Mister Faxon," Richmond said, "I can do the old stuff better. I know I can. I've been singing those songs for years, and I studied the way that Hobbit did them, every word, every move. I can come real close, I know I can. The new songs, well, like John says, they're real good songs and all, but Hobbit never did them so I can't be sure how *I* ought to do them, you know?"

Faxon looked at the three of them in turn, and then swung to face Sandy and Ananda. "I know what you think, 'Nanda," he said. "What's your opinion, Sandy?"

"You won't like it," Sandy said reluctantly.

Faxon frowned. "Go ahead."

"They're right," Sandy told him. He hated to say it, knowing how much the new material meant to Faxon, and how badly he wanted to avoid turning the comeback into a nostalgia trip, but it was the truth nonetheless. "I don't say the old songs would save the show. But they'd help, sure. These people all came here with heads full of memories. They were on your side to start with—"

"Like a fucking bitch in heat," Maggio said. "I never seen no crowd wanted it so bad, and we blew it."

"Yeah," said Sandy. "When you do the old stuff, you remind them of the first time they got laid, maybe, or the time they dropped acid and had this really great trip, or the time they saw you in concert in 1969, or how you sounded on their old stereo the first time they bought your album, or what it was like singing Nazgûl songs at the demonstrations. Evokes good memories. So it helps. The new stuff has to rise or fall as music, and it's been falling."

Peter Faxon shoved his hands into his pockets, looking royally pissed. "It looks as though I'm outvoted," he said. "All right. We're not going to drop the new material entirely, I won't stand for that, but we'll mix it up a little more second set."

"Who sings lead?" Maggio demanded.

"Larry," said Faxon. "You'll open with 'Ragin'' and he'll take it from there."

"He'll fuck it up, man, I guaran-fucking-*tee* it."

Richmond finally got angry. "Screw you, Maggio," he said.

Maggio laughed at him. "Whoaaaa," he said. "I'm scared, look at my knees shake, the little wimp kid is getting his temper up."

"I ought to . . ." Richmond started, balling a fist.

Maggio jumped up. "C'mon, kid. Try it. I just want to see you try it." He sneered.

"*Cut it out!*" Faxon screamed.

Maggio turned on him. "You gonna make me, big shot? Huh? That it? You gonna make me cut it out? Gonna make me leave the kid alone? What is it, the little queer give you blow jobs when we're not around, is that it? That why you're stickin' up for him, huh?"

Ananda let go of Sandy's hand and walked between them. She looked straight at Maggio and said, "*I'm* going to make you cut it out, Rick. Do you want me to call Edan about this?"

"Shit no," Maggio said. He sat down very suddenly, and picked up the Jack Daniel's. "No one can take a little fucking joke anymore," he muttered. "No goddamned sense of humor."

"Thank you," Faxon said to Ananda. Sandy was looking at her with a certain amount of astonishment. "Now," Faxon was saying, "we'll give them 'Ragin'' to start with, and alternate old and new stuff from there. I'm going to talk to Malcolm, up the sound of the instruments a little. The vocals are the weak point, so maybe if we overpower 'em we'll be all right. We'll close with 'Wednesday's Child.'"

"Wrong," snapped Maggio. "We wanna get called back for a fucking encore, don't we? No way that's gonna happen if we close with the new shit, man."

"Damn you, Rick—" Faxon began.

Gopher John Slozewski stopped him before he got started. "Take it easy, Peter. I hate to say it, but Maggio's right. You know he is. Save 'Wednesday's Child' for the encore, if we get one. Close with something they know."

Faxon looked close to meltdown, but he kept it under control. "All right," he said helplessly. "What'll it be, then?"

"The Rag," Maggio suggested.

"No," said Faxon. "Too long, too complicated, and we haven't rehearsed it. We're not ready for the Rag. Something simpler."

"How about 'What Rough Beast'?" Gopher John said.

Faxon thought a moment and nodded wearily. "OK," he said. "If that doesn't get them off their asses, nothing will. Can you do it, Larry?"

"Sure," Richmond said, brightening. "I've done it hundreds of times. You ought to call me Pat, though. Mister Morse says that everybody should call me Pat."

"Fuck Mister Morse," Maggio said gleefully.

"Get Reynard in here," Faxon said to Ananda as he collapsed into a chair. "I've got to talk to him about the lighting." She nodded and departed.

It was some twenty minutes when the band returned to the stage. They moved desultorily, and the restive crowd greeted them with scattered polite applause. The house lights went down again, and the Nazgûl spent a moment or two tuning. All of the energy seemed to have drained out of them, except for Maggio, who was wired on speed and grinning like a maniac.

"You know something, suckers?" he growled into the microphone when Faxon had given him the nod. "You assholes made me *mad* last set!"

A few whoops of pleasure greeted this declaration, and one or two loud voices shouted back the straight line: "How mad *are* you, Rick?"

"Shit, man," said Maggio. "I'm positively *ragin'*!" Slozewski's sticks stuttered across snares and toms to underline his words, the guitars seized the opening bars angrily, and Maggio ripped into it.

> Ain't gonna take it easy
> Won't go along no more
> Tired of getting stepped on
> When I'm down here on the floor

The crowd was trying damned hard to have a good time, Sandy thought. At the chorus, a hundred voices screamed out *"Ragin'!"* A few couples popped out of their seats and started dancing in the aisles, and there were whistles and shouts of encouragement. The Nazgûl seemed to feed on it. The music picked up, and Maggio sounded madder and madder as he plunged on. His Telecaster roared with anguish and frustration, with the helpless desperate rage that ran through every line of the song.

Sandy could feel it filling him, inflaming him. "That's good," he said to Ananda, loud enough to be heard over the music. "That sounds almost like the old Nazgûl." She nodded agreement.

The crowd felt it, too. More of them were up now, and when the Nazgûl hit the second chorus, half the audience raged along with Rick. He sneered at them, as he had sneered in the old days; he sneered and sweated and his fingers tortured the strings of his guitar and he spat poison at them, at all of them, at all the world. And they loved it! The roar that greeted the final chorus was deafening, overwhelming even the music pouring through the stack of huge amplifiers. Maggio ended the song with a primal scream, guitars screaming along with him, Slozewski's drums exploding into an orgasm of hard-driven sound, the lights flashing red to white to red to white to red to white in a strobelike fury, and the crowd ate it up. The applause went on and on, and there were shouts of "Yeah, man!" and "Do it!" and things less intelligible, mixed with more whistles and foot-stomping. For one song, at least, the Nazgûl had broken through, and the audience was with them again.

Maggio was drenched when he finished, his tee shirt turned a darker shade of red under the arms, and all down the chest in a wide V, but he was smiling. Faxon was less sure of the victory. He licked his lips nervously, and he and Gopher John laid down a real heavy bottom on bass and drums to lead into "Dogfood."

Before the song was half over, the hall was dead again. Sandy stood there and watched it die, watched the dancers find their seats, watched the gap between listeners and performers yawn ever larger. The Nazgûl could see it, too. You could read it on their faces. Larry Richmond looked as though he might break down at any moment, but somehow he staggered to the end of the song. There were a few catcalls mixed in with the weak applause.

From then it went from bad to worse.

Even Peter Faxon had had enough; he abandoned the new material entirely after "Dogfood" and tried to win back the affections and enthusiasm of the house with the safe stuff, the old familiar hits. He called for "Elf Rock" next, the very first Nazgûl smash, off of *Hot Wind out of Mordor,* a silly bubble-gum sort of song that Faxon had come to hate despite its popularity, or maybe because of it, but Richmond couldn't summon up enough innocent teenaged bounce to do the song justice, and "Dogfood" had left him so shook that he actually screwed up and forgot an entire verse on "Elf Rock." The others covered for him, but the audience knew the song, and they shouted out their disappointment. Lots of booing afterward.

"This Black Week" had been the big hit off the Black Album; it was a long song, nearly ten minutes long on the album and often twice that when the Nazgûl did it live. It had seven distinct parts, a different sound and color for every day of the week, opening with an almost dolorous beat and a wash of glum blue illumination and Larry Richmond singing:

Monday is a blue day, baby, Monday is the pits

Once it would have been a sure crowd-pleaser, but not with Richmond singing the Hobbins part. Sandy noticed a couple leaving during Wednesday, and a few more people drifting out by the time the Nazgûl got to Saturday.

When that sad endless week had ended, Sandy could look at the Nazgûl and taste their despair. Larry Richmond stood like a lost little kid, his red denim and black silk a pathetic mask that couldn't disguise what a fraud he was. Maggio was still sweating and looking miserable, too conscious of his flab to remove his shirt. Instead he took something from his pocket and swallowed it. Gopher John slumped over his drums wearily, like a man who'd rather be off somewhere in a pin-striped suit, hobnobbing with his fellow Chamber of Commerce members. And Peter Faxon was in pain. It was no use. Faxon decided to cut short the agony, no doubt, and called for "What Rough Beast" to close the debacle.

The clean, searing acid of the opening licks came over wavery and half-hearted. The drums plodded when they should have pounded. Larry Richmond sang the opening lyric in a high, strained voice.

Turning and turning in the widening gyre

And Faxon, Maggio, Slozewski chorused:

He's coming!

And Richmond said:

The falcon cannot hear the falconer

And again the Nazgûl promised:

He's coming!

Richmond frowned down at his guitar, coaxed a building counterpoint out of it to follow Maggio's lead, tossed back his white hair, sang:

Things fall apart! The centre can—

And then he jerked.

For an instant Sandy thought there had been some kind of terrible accident, a short somewhere in the Gibson or the cords that had sent a surge of power back through the singer's body. The kid seemed to spasm wildly for a second. He broke off the lyric and looked dazed. The hostile crowd stirred unpleasantly.

And then a slow wicked smile spread across Larry Richmond's face, a smile that was arrogant and smooth and hauntingly familiar. He shook out that long hair again, immune to the discontent out there, contemptuous of it. "*Yeah!*" he shouted, in a voice that filled the auditorium. He pounded the Gibson, grinned at the discord, and went right back into the song.

> *Things fall apart, yeah! The centre canNOT hold!*

The other Nazgûl had stopped playing. Sandy saw Maggio and Faxon trade looks before they picked up the thread again.

> *He's coming!*

They seemed to sing it a little harder than before.

> *Mere anarchy is loosed upon the world!*
> *That blood-dimmed tide is loosed, and*
>   *everywhere the innocents are drowned!*

came the prophecy, and it came in a voice that seared and sizzled through the sound system, the great stack of Marshall amplifiers, that crackled down the aisles like ball lightning and went straight for the bone marrow, a voice rich as fine wine and astringent as vinegar, a voice that laced the bubble of indifference in the auditorium and let it bleed out onto the floor.

> *He's coming!*

cried the Nazgûl, and a few voices took up the cry, a few hands clapped, a few fists jabbed at the air.

> *The best lack all conviction, while the worst*
> *YEAH! They're full of passion, and intensity*

Maggio seemed to wake up as if from a long dream, and suddenly the lead guitar crackled with energy. Feedback came snarling and hissing over the sound system, a vast curling serpent loose in the hall, a living thing that screamed its ominous displeasure.

He's COMING!

roared a hundred voices hoarsely, and the fists slammed upward, and Larry Richmond opened his mouth and grinned and postured and leered at them as he sang.

Surely some revelation is at hand?
YEAH! Surely it's at hand!

Gopher John's drumming went mad then. He scowled with concentration, his big red hands became a blur, the bass drum shuddered and the cymbals rang and clashed and mocked all hope, and Slozewski's big deep voice joined a thousand others with the call:

HE'S COMING!

Hobbins looked over at his drummer, grinned wickedly, spun around and leaped three feet in the air, his finger jabbing out at the crowd, a knife of flesh. His eyes burned and sparkled, red as the pit, and his voice seemed on fire as well.

Surely the Second Coming is at hand?
YEAH! What else could it be!

Faxon's face had gone white and blank, but his fingers moved with the sure certainty of old over the strings of his Rickenbacker, and low booming notes melted into the current of music, notes that were as deep as God clearing his throat, as threatening as the first rumble of an earthquake, as true and terrible as a mushroom cloud.

HE'S COMING!!!
HE'S COMING!!!!
HE'S COMING!!!!!

The entire crowd was on its feet now, screaming, singing, shoving its centipede fists into the air, arms smashing upward again and again and again like the piledriver of some great dark engine, with a rhythm that was oiled and sexual.

"*He's COMING!*" Sandy shouted with the rest, his fist giving mute testimony to the force and fury of that truth.

Hobbins swiveled and shielded his eyes against the flashing lights from above, the silent cacophony that imprisoned band and singer. Peering out into the darkness, he saw something, and he cried:

> *The Second Coming, YEAH! But what's this thing I see?*
> > *HE'S COMING!*
> *What vast image comes troubling my night?*
> > *HE'S COMING!*
> *Somewhere in the sands of the desert*
> > *HE'S COMING!*
> *A shape with lion body and the head of a man!*
> > *HE'S COMING!*
> *A gaze blank and pitiless as the sun!*
> > *HE'S COMING!*
> > *HE'S COMING!!!*
> > *HE'S COMING!!!!!*

Maggio danced wildly across the stage, like a man shocked by cattle prods, but he was grinning and sneering all the while, and his guitar spit acid, belched flame. He ripped at the strings frenetically, and the chords flew like razors. Hobbins turned to face him, glowering, clawing his own instrument. The notes burned back and forth as they jammed at each other. People were standing on their chairs, clapping their hands over their heads, writhing to the music, shaking, fucking the air with their fists.

> *HE'S COMING!*
> *HE'S COMING!!!*
> *YEAH! HE'S*
> *COOOOMING!!!*

Maggio sneered and his Telecaster was a hissing cobra that swayed and stalked and sparked. Hobbins glowered back and his Gibson was a mongoose, wild and darting and lightning-fast, with a sound full of tiny sharpened teeth. Bass and drums gave them a bottom heavy as an avalanche, and drove them both to battle frenzy. Five minutes the jam went on. Ten min-

utes. Fifteen. The crowd was screaming, the crowd was electric, the crowd
was hysterical.

> HE'S COMING!
> OH, HE'S
> COMING!!!
> YEAH, HE'S
> COOOOMING!!!

And Maggio struck and killed and Hobbins staggered back, grinning,
reeling, gave a wild banshee scream that hurt the ears, leaped in the air and
spun and pointed at the audience again.

> It's moving its slow thighs, while all about it
> Reel shadows of indignant desert birds
> The darkness drops again, but now I know
>   Yeah baby, how I know!
>   HE'S COMING!
>
> Oh yes, I know, I know
> That twenty centuries of stony sleep
> Were vexed to nightmare by a rockin' cradle
>   Oh, a rocknrollin' cradle!

And the Nazgûl sang behind him, and the crowd as well, and they sang,
"He's coming, he's coming, he's coming, he's coming, he's coming he's com-
ing he's cominghe'scominghescominghescominghescominghescominghes..." until it
became a low mutter loud as thunder.

Patrick Henry Hobbins held up his hand for quiet, and every sound in
the hall died instantly. The chanting ceased. The drums and guitars were
silent. The lights went out. In the darkness his voice was plaintive and
afraid.

> Oh, what rough beast,
>   its hour come round at last
>   Slouches towards Bethlehem to be born?

In the echoing stillness that followed those lines, a single small spotlight
came on, illuminating only Hobbins' face, still and white. A long breathless
pause. Then he smiled.

"*I'm coming*," he said softly, and the light blinked out.

An instant later the house lights and stage lights all came on at once in a single blinding burst of illumination, and the crowd in the hall went crazy wild, shrieking, stomping, whistling, jumping around, dancing across the seats. The ovation lasted for a good five minutes before it even started to wane. The Nazgûl stood dazed, every one of them looking as if he'd been poleaxed except for Hobbins, who had on his old cocksure smile.

People were shouting for an encore, and when the noise had finally died away enough to hear, Peter Faxon leaned forward, smiling, and said, "Shall we give 'em 'Wednesday's Child' now?"

A burst of renewed cheering greeted his words, but Hobbins just glanced at him and shook his head and turned to the audience, holding up his hands for silence. He got it. "You been a real good crowd, girls and boys," he said cheerfully. Gopher John, smiling, went *boom-boom-ba-boom* on the drums in the pause between sentences, and tossed his stick up in the air. Thousands of eyes watched it sail upward, end over end, before it finally began to descend. "Now," said Hobbins, "bug off and leave us alone." The stick landed square in Slozewski's outstretched hand, he looked at it wonderingly for a second and brought it down on his cymbals in a final deafening shot.

The crowd was still cheering and whistling as the Nazgûl left the stage.

They looked drained, all except for Hobbins...no, not Hobbins, *Richmond*, Sandy reminded himself. But he looked like Hobbins, with the swaggering arrogance of his walk, the graceful way he held his head, the music of his laughter. And he had *sung* like Hobbins, at least once. Sandy felt a little dizzy himself. He found himself following the Nazgûl backstage.

The place was packed when they got back there. Everyone was crowding around the band, slapping them, congratulating them. Maggio was loud and boisterous, squeezing every breast in reach as he pushed through the crush. Gopher John just looked confused. Faxon was pale and quiet. And Larry Richmond positively radiated self-satisfaction. Joints were going from hand to hand, bottles were being upended, a few lines of coke had been laid out on the big table next to what remained of the food. The noise was loud enough to give Sandy a headache. He got himself a screwdriver and tried to make his way through the press to Faxon or Richmond.

Rrrrrrrrrrrrrrrrrrrrrr.

The sound killed the party babble dead. People shifted uneasily, backing away from something, and suddenly Sandy found himself on the edge of a clear space in the crowd, a few feet from Larry Richmond.

Rrrrrrrrrrrrrrrrrrrrrr.

It was a low, threatening sort of growl, enough to raise the hairs on the back of your neck. Richmond was standing with a bottle of beer in his hand, looking even whiter than usual. His mouth was open. So was Balrog's. The dog's teeth were bared, his lips drawn back, his tail very still. A nervous gopher held the end of his leash and was tugging at it ineffectually while simultaneously trying to back off toward the corner. The growl went on and on.

"Fucking *dog!*" snarled Richmond. Richmond?

Balrog leaped.

TWENTY-ONE

Like a rat in a maze the path before me lies/
And the pattern never alters, until the rat dies

T he dog's leap ended with a jolt when he came up hard against the restraint of his leash, but the force of it was enough to send the frightened gopher stumbling to his knees, and when the boy fell, he let go his grasp. A second later, Balrog was free, getting his legs under him once again, snarling, his muscles bunching for another leap. Like the rest, Sandy stood frozen with surprise and horror.

Then a huge shadow passed quickly in front of him. Gort moved faster than Sandy ever could have imagined. When Balrog went for Richmond once again, the big man was already in between them, and he caught the animal with both hands in mid-air, and slammed him to one side hard. The dog bounced off the wall, landed on the table and knocked bottles of booze every which way as he scrambled to his feet, and then Gort was on him once again, cuffing him solidly across the muzzle. Balrog yelped in shock and pain, and tried to back off, snarling and snapping. Gort caught the end of his leash, looped it around the dog's throat, and tightened it. Balrog whimpered, and all the fury seemed to bleed right out of him. He let fly with a sudden stream of urine, all over the canapés. Gort pulled the loop tighter and the dog struggled ineffectually. For a moment it looked as though the big man was going to strangle the animal to death, right there in front of everyone.

Then Larry Richmond cried out, "No! Leave him alone!"

Richmond's voice seemed to shatter the trance. All at once everyone was saying something or moving to help; the room exploded with noise and motion once again. Gort grunted and let up a little, and Balrog whined his relief. Richmond shouldered past Gort and wrapped his arms around the animal's sides protectively. "Hey, boy," he said, "easy, Bal. It's okay, boy, I'm here, it's okay." Balrog's flanks were heaving and he was panting wildly, but as Richmond talked to him and ruffled his fur and patted him, the dog's tail rose and finally began to wag.

Gort stepped back with a disgusted noise, turned, and beckoned to two of the roadies. "You. And you. Take the damn dog out back and tie him up."

"No!" Richmond shouted. "Bal stays here! With me!"

Ananda came forward and took him by the shoulders. "He'll be all right, Pat. He can't stay here. He just pissed all over the food, right? The excitement must have been too much for him. All the noise. All the strangers. You don't want him to hurt anybody, do you?"

"Well, no," Richmond said reluctantly.

"Then let them take him out back," Ananda said. She gathered up the leash and handed it to a roadie. "Why don't you go with them, Pat, get him settled down? And then come back and party." She smiled. "You've got a lot to celebrate, right?"

"Well, okay, I guess," Richmond said. With Richmond along to soothe and cajole, the dog exited docilely enough in the company of two of Gort's underlings.

Sandy looked around. Ananda had pulled Gort aside and they were talking in low, private tones. Elsewhere the party was gathering steam again, with half the people talking about the performance and half about the crazy dog. Peter Faxon was leaning up against the wall, alone, staring speculatively at the door through which Richmond had just left. He had filled a big water tumbler with ice cubes and Chivas Regal, and most of it was already gone. Sandy headed toward him. "Good show," he said when he got there. "What do you think got into the dog?"

Faxon studied him, sipping the Chivas, and frowned. "Nothing," he said brusquely. "The question is, what got into Richmond?"

Sandy met Faxon's clear green eyes, and knew that those eyes were seeing right through him. "I think you know the answer to that already," Sandy said.

"Sure," said Faxon. "Only the answer is impossible." He finished his Chivas, looked around for a gopher, and sent him for a refill.

"Whatever it was, the dog scared it right back out of him," Sandy said when Faxon had a glass in hand once again.

Faxon took a big healthy swallow. A lot of his ice cubes had melted, and what he was swallowing was mostly Scotch. He drank like a man who badly wanted to get plastered. "It wasn't a good show," he said. "It was a terrible show, right up until the end. And then something happened. I could *feel* it up there. Richmond *changed*. And when he changed, it changed the rest of us, too." He snapped his fingers. "We were the Nazgûl again. For one song, it was like the old days. The music was alive, and you could feel the energy pouring off the crowd. I couldn't believe it was happening. Everything we wanted, everything we'd been trying for all night, and in all those weeks of practice, all of a sudden it was *there*. And you know what? It scared me. It scared the living piss out of me." He swallowed some more Chivas and looked pensive. "But I want it again, Sandy. I know that much. Whatever the hell happened up there tonight, I want it to happen again."

"I have a feeling it will," Sandy said.

Peter Faxon set his empty glass aside. "I have to go call Tracy and tell her how it went," he said. "Damned if I know what I'm going to say, though."

On his way out, Faxon passed Larry Richmond, who was just coming back. He stopped and clapped the kid on the shoulder and said a few words, and Richmond smiled. The minute Faxon left, Richmond was mobbed by well-wishers, groupies, and members of the crew. He was grinning like a six-year-old on Christmas morning who has just discovered Santa Claus dead in his living room and is only now realizing that he gets *all* the toys for the whole damn world. Gopher John had his acolytes too, buzzing around him like a swarm of fat happy horseflies and fetching him bottles of beer to join the growing pile of empties at his feet. And Maggio was sprawled in a big chair as if it were a throne. He was laughing raucously and talking a waterfall of words, the volume rising and falling so that Sandy, all the way across the room, caught only strange disconnected snatches. He had a girl in his lap already, and his free hand was up her blouse, roaming around. Another girl, even younger and prettier, was sitting on the arm of his chair, and he was paying more attention to her than to the one he was fondling. The blond who had been with him at the preshow party was five feet away, looking resentful.

Sandy got himself another screwdriver and drifted from one knot of people to another, listening, infrequently venturing a comment or two. He didn't feel much like talking, somehow. The excitement was contagious, but he seemed to be immune, disconnected. Maybe he understood too much. He wandered around looking for Ananda, but she seemed to have left, along with Gort. Finally, when he was on his fourth or fifth screwdriver and the vodka had given the room a nice mellow haze, he found himself standing in front of Larry Richmond, staring at Patrick Henry Hobbins' face. "How did it feel?" Sandy heard himself ask.

"It was great!" Richmond said with enthusiasm. He started babbling away about how wonderful it was to play with the Nazgûl.

"No," Sandy said abruptly. "I mean, the last song, how did *that* feel? When it changed. You jumped, you know. Like you got a shock or something. You jumped and you broke off the song."

"Yeah, I know," Richmond said with a bit of discomfiture in his voice. "It wasn't a shock, though. I mean, not like electricity, you know? It was like . . . I don't know, I was getting into the lyrics, you know, and all of a sudden . . . it was like a *chill*, maybe . . . no, worse than a chill . . . it was like somebody had come up behind me and slid an ice cube down my back. A real cold feeling, going all through me. Weird, huh?"

"Weird," Sandy agreed.

"I recovered though," Richmond said happily. "It was only an instant there, and then I came right back."

"You were terrific," Sandy agreed. "Sang till their ears bled, all right."

Larry Richmond smiled uncertainly. "Everybody up yelling and screaming and dancing, I mean, *wow*! It was wild, wasn't it? That's never happened to me before, you know. But everybody says it was wild."

Sandy felt a little chill himself, crawling along his own spine. "Everybody *says*? Don't you remember, Larry?"

"Pat," the kid corrected automatically. He was a good kid and he did what Morse told him. He smiled weakly, as if to apologize to Sandy for having corrected him. "Sure I remember," he said. "Still, I gotta admit, the excitement and all . . . it's kind of fuzzy, you know? I guess I was really into the music then. It's like I was in a daze all during the close, you know, it really leaves you feeling weak and kind of blurred-out around the edges. I didn't really get my head together again until Bal got crazy."

"I think we were all feeling a little blurred-out," Sandy said, but he was thinking that the kid had absolutely no idea what had happened to him out there. The dog knew, but not the master. "What now?"

"The tour," Richmond said, beaming.

"Tour?"

"Sure. Hasn't Mister Morse told you yet? He's been setting it all up. A big national tour, coast-to-coast. Then maybe we'll cut a new album, he says, but the tour first, to get people excited again."

"Of course," Sandy said. "A national tour. Yeah, sure. You'll be part of it, of course."

Richmond seemed puzzled. "Well, yeah, sure. I mean, why not?"

"Nothing," Sandy said, "nothing at all." He smiled weakly. "I've had too much vodka, I think. Need some fresh air. 'Scuse me." He turned away abruptly and headed for the door. When he glanced back over his shoulder, Richmond was still standing there, looking baffled.

He groped down a hall, found a men's room, splashed some water on his face. It made him feel a little less dizzy, but he did want some air, he thought. He went out the back door. One of the roadies was there, the man with the silver mirrored shades. He stared at Sandy and said not a word. Balrog was there too, tied up just outside the door. He barked, and Sandy patted his head before making his way to the street.

A few people still lingered in front of the auditorium, and there was light traffic on the sidewalk. Sandy ignored it, leaned back against the wall, savoring the cool night air. It was what Richmond wanted, he thought to himself. The kid had lived his life wanting nothing so much as to be Pat Hobbins, and now he was going to get—

"Sandy?" said a small, scared voice at his elbow.

He turned, stared, felt a strange small sense of disorientation, of déjà vu. The teenaged girl standing there looking at him seemed oddly familiar, but in his half-drunk haze he couldn't place her. She was short and thin, flat-chested under a Nazgûl tee shirt at least three sizes too large for her. Her hand pulled at his sleeve, and there were rings on every one of her fingers. Her face was streaked with green where her eye makeup had run, and the big brown eyes looked as though they were going to start spilling tears again at any moment. "I know you," Sandy said.

She smiled weakly. "I'm glad you remember. I'm Francie."

"Francie?" Sandy said. Then it came back to him. Maggio and the Come On Inn. "Sure," he said. "You were with Rick." But there was something wrong, he thought doggedly. He remembered her all right, remembered her from that night, from that first interview with Maggio, but that wasn't it, or at least that wasn't *all* of it. He knew her from somewhere else as well, recognized her from . . . from where?

"I used to be Rick's old lady," Francie said. "I want to see him, Sandy. I want to see him so bad. He never even sent me tickets or nothin' and they wouldn't let me in, even though I tried to tell 'em who I was." Her voice was plaintive. "We lived together for almost two years, and he just up and left and he didn't even write or phone or send tickets. I was sure he was goin' to call when he got back to Chicago, you know? Bring me to the show and all. But he didn't."

Sandy was still trying to figure out where he had seen her besides the

Come On Inn, but nothing was coming. "I'm sorry," he said. "They've all been very busy. Maybe he just forgot."

"Can you get me in to see Rick?" she asked hopefully. "Or at least tell him I'm here? Please? I need to see him bad, Sandy. I love him. He's my old man, you know?"

Sandy thought of Maggio inside, surrounded by his groupies. He knew damn well that the last thing in the world the guitarist would want right now would be for his old skinny girlfriend to pop up, teary and full of re-proaches. "Look," Sandy said, "I don't think...I mean, the show just ended, everybody's a little flaky right now, drunk and tired and crazy. I don't think this would be a good time, but I tell you what. We'll be in Chicago for another day or so, at least. You come by the hotel tomorrow morning and I'll take you in to see Rick, OK?"

"Please," Francie repeated, her voice pleading. "I need to see him now. I don't care if he's with somebody else, Sandy. It don't bother me none. I know he is. Rick is like that, you know? He don't mean nothing bad by it, it's just the way he is, and he needs girls. I'm used to it. Really. He used to have me fix him up with my girlfriends, when I could. He liked three-ways, you know?" She forced a smile. "It won't hurt me any. I just got to see him. Please."

Sandy still wasn't sure whether he could believe her, but she sounded so pathetic, and Maggio had treated her so damned shabbily, both at the Come On Inn and now, that he found himself getting angry on her behalf. "I told you once that you were more than he deserves," he said. "You are."

"I just want to take care of him. He's not a bad guy, he just needs some-body to take care of him. Will you help me?"

"Yeah," Sandy said. He took her hand. "Come with me. We'll go in the back way." The dude with the mirror shades might try to keep her out, but with Sandy along he had damn well better not try too hard.

"Thank you," Francie said as they walked around back. She squeezed Sandy's hand.

It was very dark by the back door. Very dark and very quiet. The roadie was gone. "Fuck," Sandy said. "The door's locked." He made a fist and pounded. "*Open up in there!*" he yelled.

No one answered. Finally, after a good three minutes of knocking, Sandy said, "I don't think they can hear us over that damned party. Screw it. We'll have to go back around front." He turned away in disgust and started down the alley, Francie following.

Sandy had taken four steps when his boot came down on something wet, the heel skidded out from under him, and he flailed and went down hard, scraping his hand and ripping the hell out of the seat of his jeans. He managed to land in some garbage too. It was wet and warm and there were lots of flies. "God *damn!*" Sandy said unsteadily. "What the hell is…" He groped, felt fur and warm wetness between his fingers, sucked in his breath, struggled to his feet.

Francie made a small whimpery sound and backed off. "*Blood,*" she said.

Sandy looked down and felt sick. He wanted to vomit. He could feel it rising in his throat, gagging him; he fought to keep it down. Waves of dizziness washed over him. He forced himself to kneel and look at it close up.

Blood. Lots of blood. Lying there near the garbage cans, covered with flies and still warm, was Balrog. Or what remained of Balrog. The dog's throat had been cut open, and he was lying in a spreading pool of his own blood.

Sandy reached out a tentative hand to touch the dog's head, the fly-covered staring blind eyes. The head moved easily, at an impossible angle. A huge raw wet mouth opened in his neck, and fresh blood washed out. Francie screamed.

Whoever had done this was *strong,* Sandy thought numbly. Had severed neck muscles, tendons, and flesh in a single clean stroke, slicing right down to the bone, almost removing the dog's head. Francie screamed again, more loudly.

Sandy got to his feet, dizzy. Francie was sucking in breath between screams and then screaming again. Someone was running down the alley. Francie pressed back against the bricks, curled up small, her ring-covered hands in front of her face. Screaming. Screaming. She had a high thin scream, full of shock and almost unthinkable pain, and as she screamed it again and again, Sandy found himself regarding her with a sudden mounting horror that dwarfed what he had felt for the poor mutilated dog. He recognized that scream. He knew that goddamned scream. And now he knew why Francie had seemed so eerily familiar.

He had met her at the Come On Inn, all right.

But he had seen her again after that, not once but several times. He had seen her and he had heard her screaming. He had seen her in his dreams, at a concert, naked and bleeding and nailed to a great X-shaped cross.

TWENTY-TWO

When logic and proportion have fallen sloppy dead/
And the white knight's talking backwards

And next...and next...Sandy didn't remember. He didn't re-member stumbling away from the dog's remains, didn't remember being sick, didn't remember the door opening and all the people rushing out. Everything was a haze of blood and vodka. Francie saw Maggio stumble out into the night and she ran to him, crying, and threw her arms around him. He looked perplexed at first. Then he smiled, oddly, almost kindly, and returned her embrace. There was shouting, shoving, questions and screams. A policeman was barking orders; no one was paying attention. Sandy found he could not take it. He started to back off down the alley, away from the noise, away from the blood. Larry Richmond emerged, and the crowd made way for him. When Richmond saw Balrog, he went hyster-ical. Someone was holding him and shaking him when Sandy turned his back on it and moved off down the street. He began to trot, only half-aware of his destination.

Dark streets, still crowded. His pants were torn, his palm was scraped, and his hands were covered with blood. His shirt-front was damp with spat-ters of orange juice and vodka that he'd brought back up. People shied away from him when they saw him coming. Sandy hardly noticed. He moved faster.

He heard footsteps on the sidewalk behind him, the light steps of some-one running. Sudden irrational fear overwhelmed him, and he bolted, trying to get away, running, running. She caught him anyway. She was faster than he was. She caught him by the shoulder and spun him around and he saw that it was Ananda, it was only Ananda. He trembled and grabbed her and pulled her as hard as he could, holding her, clinging to her, his anchor in an ocean of blood and darkness. She stroked his hair. "Easy," she said, "easy, love. It's all right. It's all right."

Sandy pushed away from her. "No," he said. "No, it's not. They killed the dog. Cut its throat. And they're going to kill her, too."

"Who?"

"Francie," he said. "Maggio's old lady. Francie. They're going to nail her up, and . . ." He couldn't go on.

"I don't know what you're talking about," Ananda said. "Where are you running to?"

"I don't know," Sandy said. But he did. Suddenly he knew just where he had been going. "I'm going to see Morse. I'm going to talk to Morse."

"I'll go with you," Ananda told him, and her hand was in his, cool and firm, its ridge of callus and short-clipped nails very familiar to him now. She paid no attention to the blood on his hand, took no notice of his trembling. She walked beside him, and her very presence seemed to drive away the shadows.

It was late. Sandy knew it was late. Gort opened the door to Edan Morse's suite, looked at them, and said, "It's late."

Sandy wanted to tell him to fuck off, but the words got caught in his throat and it was Ananda who spoke. "Wake him up," she said crisply. "It's important."

Gort studied Sandy's torn, soiled clothing, grunted, and ushered them in. "Wait," he said in that deep, threatening voice. He pointed them at a couch and left for a bedroom.

Edan Morse emerged looking as wretched as Sandy felt. It had been several weeks since Sandy had seen him; the change was astonishing. Morse's face was drawn and bloodless, his tan had faded, and his dimples were no longer in evidence, covered by a growth of scraggly brown beard. His eyes had that fanatical gleam to them, but they were tired as well, surrounded by the heavy dark circles of a man who hadn't been sleeping well. He was dressed in a black satin robe. "What is it?" he demanded as he sat down in the big chair facing the couch.

Sandy held out his hands. "I . . . the dog." His voice was thick. "They butchered the dog. Richmond's dog."

Morse feigned astonishment. "You know anything about this, 'Nanda?"

"Mirrors was out watching the dog. He went inside for a couple minutes to bum some cigarettes. Somebody did the job while he was gone."

"Gort," Sandy said suddenly, glaring at the big man.

"Hey, fuck that shit," Gort grumbled. "I been here with Edan for hours. Hell, if I wanted to kill the dog I could of done it at the party, when the fucker went nuts."

"It's *wrong*," Sandy blurted. He pushed his hair back out of his eyes. "The dog, Francie, what happened tonight at the concert... it's all, I don't know... wrong. Morse, I'm quitting. I want out."

"Why?"

That was a question Sandy couldn't answer. He hadn't come here intending to say what he had just said; he wasn't sure why he had come here. He wasn't very sure of anything. His head was swimming. Morse's features seemed to blur, as if they were going in and out of focus. "The blood," Sandy said. "All the blood."

Ananda reached over and put a hand on his knee. "He's drunk, Edan," she said. "He doesn't know what he's saying."

"No," Sandy insisted. "I *do* ... it's just... I can't take it anymore. All the blood. I don't belong here."

"Oh?" Morse said coldly. "Where do you belong, then?"

Where did he belong? Where indeed? If not with Morse and the Nazgûl, if not with Ananda, then *where*? It was all gone. Maggie and Sharon and all the women in between, the *Hedgehog*, his books, his agent, his house. All gone. And no one cared anymore, about him, them, anything. Of course he belonged here. There was nowhere else for him. "Edan, I'm afraid," Sandy heard himself say. "I don't understand what's going down; it makes no sense, but it scares me. And all the blood... Lynch, the Gopher Hole, the dog... it's not worth it."

"I don't like blood any more than you do," Morse said. "But there is a price to be paid here. I pay as much of it as I can myself." He held out his palm, crisscrossed with white scars, deep and terrible scars. "Maybe not enough. I don't know. I try. There has never been a truly bloodless revolution. The price has to be paid."

"To *what*?" Sandy said hoarsely. "Who killed the dog, dammit? Who ripped out Lynch's heart?"

"It doesn't matter."

"WHO?" Sandy screamed. "Or *what*? That's the right question, isn't it? *What*, not who! Some ... thing ... some force. I can't believe it, but it's true, isn't it?"

"You can't believe it, and that's your problem. The time for rationality has passed. You know that. You've heard the music. Why do you keep fighting it? This is the last cut on the first side. This is the—"

"—prelude to madness," Sandy finished for him. "Yeah, I get it. The dead man picked up his hand tonight, didn't he?"

Edan Morse smiled and said nothing.

Sandy felt a terrible coldness in the room. One of the windows behind Morse was open, and the curtains were stirring slightly in the wind, but the warm June breeze had suddenly become frigid. Out there in the night sky, above the black towers with their jeweled lights, were stars like a million yellow eyes. They would never look away. Sandy shivered, and he knew somewhere, deep within him, that Morse's master was with them now, called up by the music and the blood and the dying, staring at him now. "Close the window," he said.

"Do it, Gort," Morse snapped. As the big man went to obey, Morse leaned forward. "You don't approve," he said.

"You don't know what you're doing," Sandy said.

"Oh, but I do. We've tried it all before, you and I, haven't we? You tried elections, and newspapers, and persuasion, and compromise. I tried assassinations and riots and violence. None of it worked, did it? This is all that's left, Blair. This is our last chance."

"It's not worth it."

Morse stared at him, but it was Ananda who answered. She reached over and touched Sandy's face and turned it to face her own. "You're wrong," she said.

"No—" he began.

"Yes," she said harshly. "Listen to me. Not *worth* it? Sandy, some lunatic kills a dog, and you say it's not *worth* it? A *dog*? Look around you. Look at the way the world is going. We have a raging nuclear arms race that could turn into a holocaust at any moment. We got the Ayatollah and we got Falwell and we used to have Jim Jones, and they're really all the same, right? We got a fucking government that doesn't give a shit about poverty and hunger or human misery. Brushfire wars everywhere, and we're running out of resources, running out of energy, running out of hope. We're poisoning the air, the water, and the earth. We got genocide in the Middle East, racism and sexism at home, xenophobia and hatred on all sides. We face a future of grinding poverty, economic chaos, and iron repression in a new fascist police state, and we don't even have the strength to oppose it, because we've lost our courage, we've turned cynical and selfish. We're beaten, we're lost, and we're damned. We have *got* to change things. We have got to get back what we lost, and this is the only way to do it—tear down the whole rotting, stinking system and start over again, smarter and better. It's worth it. I'd kill every fucking dog in the whole fucking world if that was what it took, and it'd *still* be worth it!" Her face was flushed and impassioned. The big dark eyes, so often playful, were angry now. The shining black hair that Sandy liked to stroke swayed as she shook her head in fury. She was breathing hard, and under her pale blue sweater, her breasts rose and fell with each breath. The wry, ironic smile was gone, replaced by a tight-lipped defiance, and the teasing way she so often held her head now seemed somehow like a challenge. Sandy had a sudden frightening feeling that he didn't really know her at all. But she was all he had left, and he knew, dully, amid his confusion, that if he said the wrong thing now, Ananda too would retreat from him forever.

"I just . . ." He could not find the words, did not know what they should be. She was right of course, everything she said was true, and yet, and yet . . .

"We *need* you, Sandy," Ananda said with sudden gentleness. She touched him lightly on the arm. "*I* need you."

"Need me," he repeated. "For what?"

Edan Morse turned and snapped his fingers. "Gort, get me a copy of the schedule."

The giant grunted, went to the desk just beyond the bedroom door, returned with a crisp sheet of white paper. He handed it to Sandy.

It was the tour that Richmond had mentioned; neat columns of photocopied type, dates and times, cities and auditoriums. It began in New York City and snaked west, zigzagging north and south as it went: Pittsburgh, Detroit, Cincinnati, Minneapolis, St. Louis, Houston, Kansas City, Denver. But it was the final date that Sandy read aloud. "Albuquerque," he said. "West Mesa. September 20th." He folded the schedule into crisp quarters with a deliberate precision and shoved it deep into his back pocket. "No west coast dates."

"Of course not. Those dates were canceled after the assassination. It would be pointless to book anything after West Mesa."

"This is why you need me?"

"You'll make a public announcement at a press conference in a day or two. Then you'll orchestrate the national media blitz."

"It won't happen," Sandy said, desperately hoping that was so. "One look at that schedule and Faxon is going to recognize the itinerary. You think he wants to dance those steps again? You really think he'll play another West Mesa concert? On *that* date? For that matter, you think the local authorities will allow it?"

Morse smiled grimly. "The permits are already in hand and the advance work well begun. Money can accomplish wonders. You underestimate the sheer corruption of this society. It will all come together. On that date, at that place, the forces will be immense. The time, the place, the music, the people, the *belief.* When the Nazgûl sing it will all fuse together. Past and present and future. They'll perform the entire album, just as they did in 1971, and this time they will finish the Rag, sing it all the way through, sing up armageddon and give us our resurrection. Patrick Henry Hobbins will live again, the Movement will live again, and this time we will seize our tide." His scarred hand made a fist and pounded softly against the arm of his chair, over and over, rhythmically.

"But it will only happen if we all keep the faith, right?" said Ananda. "We all have roles to play, Sandy. You're important. If you leave us, *they* may win again."

Sandy felt lost and confused. "I want the same things you want," he told them. "I want to go back as much as any of you, want to try it all again and get it right this time. I want it for myself, and for . . . for some friends of mine, people you wouldn't know. But the *blood* . . . I don't want any more. Francie, in my dreams, she . . . I don't want her hurt, you hear?"

"Who's Francie?" Morse asked.

"One of Rick's lady friends," Ananda said. "She was with him when he found the dog tonight."

"Very well," Morse said. "I'll prove to you that I don't want bloodshed any more than you do, Blair." He turned to Gort. "Find this girl. Take care of her. Guard her. If anybody tries to hurt her, blow the fucker away. Got it?"

Gort cracked his knuckles. "No sweat."

"Terrific," Sandy said. "You just assigned the head butcher to guard the lamb."

Gort said, "Get off my case. I'm tired of you, Blair."

"That's the best I can do," Morse said. "Trust me or not, I don't give a flying fuck. But make up your mind."

"If you're not part of the solution, you're part of the problem," Ananda said. She had taken her hand away. Her features were chilly and full of judgments waiting to be made.

"It's going down, Blair," Morse said. "With you or without you. It's going to happen, whether you approve or disapprove. There's going to be blood, ours or theirs or both. Armageddon, brother. Believe it. Resurrection. All you got to decide is whose side you're on. Commit yourself, Blair, one way or the other. What's it going to be? Us or them?"

His face was iron, unyielding, gray, cold. His words were sudden hammer blows, driving Sandy back, nailing him to the wall. The room was spinning. They were all watching him, Morse, Ananda, Gort. He forced himself to his feet unsteadily. "I . . . I don't know." He put a hand to his brow. Everything was so thick, so stuffy. He was trapped and suffocating. "Give me a minute," he said.

"You have a minute," Edan Morse said. Gort grunted and cracked his knuckles threateningly.

"I need some air," Sandy said. He went to the window, the window that Gort had closed. Their eyes were still on him. He put his palm to the glass. It was cold, almost icy. June, and yet the window burned with cold. Sandy held his hand against it, and the chill crept up his arm, the pain stabbed through his fingertips. Beyond the thin pane of glass was darkness. All the eyes were on him, on both sides of the glass. Beyond the window was a cold wind and the lights of a black alien city, where ignorant armies still fought by night, still, *still*, after all these years. He saw the Kent State Guardsmen raise their rifles and fire, and the students fell. He saw the napalm drop from the sky. He heard the chanting, stared at gas-masked glassy-eyed visages of the enemy, saw the small candles wink out one by one.

Faces swam before him, taking shape from chaos, mouths wide with pain. Faces from the newspapers, faces from television, faces from the past. There was Bobby, his head all bloody. There was King, his dream shattered by a bullet. There was Nixon, and in his eyes Sandy saw the reflections of a Redskins game, saw them blocking and tackling while thousands marched past outside, unheeded.

Maggie was out there in the night, a soft smile on her lips. She said nothing, but her eyes were sad. Froggy was at the window, grinning. "Plunk my magic twanger, Sandy," he croaked. "Go on, do it. You can, you can." Lark was there, headband and mocking smile and all, and he said, "I always knew you didn't have it, Blair. The revolution failed because of weak sisters like you." Bambi looked at him solemnly and said, "You have to *believe*, you have to believe in something." And finally there was Slum, resplendent in his Slum Suit, all those uptight ties sewn together into something wild and free and gorgeous, with his great beard crawling down his chest, his smile stoned and gentle. "Let me in, Sandy," he said in that quiet, apologetic voice of his. "Let me in, please. I don't want to be dead. I don't want to be incompetent. Let me in." And he raised his hand and Sandy saw he had a hammer there.

Chaos roiled beyond that pane, chaos and turmoil and blood and anger. But on this side of the glass was nothing. On this side of the glass it was dead and stifling and Sandy could not find air to breathe. Out there the wind was fresh and cold, and out there his friends were waiting, with flowers and dreams and hope. Beyond the pane. Beyond the pain.

Slum raised the hammer high. Edan Morse said, "Your minute is up, Blair."

Sandy opened the window.

TWENTY-THREE

Come hear Uncle John's band, playing to the tide/
Come with me or go alone, he's come to take his children home

On the road. New York. Pittsburgh. Detroit. Cincinnati. Minneapolis. St. Louis. Houston. Kansas City. *And the Nazgûl spread their dark wings across the land,* Sandy wrote in a press release.

On the road, all the cities blurred together, days and weeks and months melted into one seamless sleepless whole. On the road it was all cheap food and driving and noise and crowded rooms, it was all motel suites that looked alike, television sets that played endlessly with no one watching, drugs and booze and strangers and pointless arguments, and music, music most of all, songs that haunted the damp hot nights and echoed deafeningly through the concert halls.

On the road it was always night.

On the road it was always hot. July was torrid, August was unbearable, Labor Day came in glowering and sizzling, the air-conditioning never worked well enough, and the parties were always too packed. But the bus and the trucks rolled on, Sandy rolling after them, Daydream burning up the roads, all the old songs repeating on the tape deck and whispering in his head. A dazed time, a crazed time, months turned crimson with the bright flushed heat of fever.

New York burned clear, New York was Shea Stadium. The Nazgûl had kicked off their 1971 tour at Shea, and to Shea they returned. They had filled it then, but now, so many years later, with the mystery of Larry

Richmond debunked in the press and the reviews from Chicago mixed (*Hedgehog* had torn them apart), the ballpark was only half-packed. Still, that was almost thirty thousand people, thirty thousand old fans under a hot July night, the band looking small in the infield. It was Chicago all over again. The *new* songs, Faxon insisted, and he was their leader, and though the quarrel went on and on backstage, in the end it was he who called the shots. So they played "Visions in the Dark" and Maggio milked his axe for every sound that was in it, and Gopher John rode his snares and toms with rim shot after rim shot and broke a stick on the hardest, maddest solo he'd played in years, but Richmond sang lead in his small voice and the crowd stayed cool. And they did "Wednesday's Child" with the sound cranked up all the way so the stack of Marshalls trembled and thundered and filled the humid Long Island night. But the night swallowed Larry Richmond's vocal, swallowed every last bit of it and gave nothing back, and the crowd was tired and indifferent. The Nazgûl sang "Goin' to the Junkyard" and "Good Ol' Days" and "Sins," and at last Faxon saw it clear. When he called for the old songs, Richmond nodded and Maggio grinned wickedly and Gopher John scowled and slammed down the lead-in to "Blood on the Sheets." And it happened, as Sandy had known it would; as all of them had known. *Baby, you cut my heart out,* Richmond sang, but by the time he reached *heart* it was not Richmond at all, it was Hobbins, Hobbins back to sing again. The crowd stirred restlessly, uncertainly, and then the excitement began to build. By the end of the song they were on their feet, charged with some power none of them could have explained. They screamed and they shouted and danced in the aisles, and the Nazgûl blasted them with sound and blistered them with raw emotion. Hobbins sang a half-dozen songs, and for an encore they did a fifteen-minute version of "What Rough Beast" and Gopher John tossed his stick twenty feet in the air, rattled it off the front teeth of the stars and caught it again.

On the road was an empty highway wet and shiny with rain, the sound of his wheels on slick pavement, the lights of the other vehicles lost behind him, the speedometer pushing eighty, Ananda asleep in the seat beside him. Sandy turned on the radio, found an all-night station, but it was top-forty music, gutless, soulless, commercial as the age. He turned it off and drove faster. Somewhere in the night ahead was West Mesa, and the sweet sound of the past.

Detroit (or was it Cincinnati?) was wolfing down cheeseburgers with Gopher John Slozewski in an all-night coffee shop after the concert. Gopher John ate ravenously; four burgers, a triple order of fries. "Nightmares," he confessed, in a heavy, weary voice. "I dream 'bout that fire allatime. Yeah.

Alla fuckin' time. Kids burnin' up. Screaming. They say I locked the fire exits. Fucking lie, Sandy, fucking lie. I never would of." He smiled. "It's good on stage. The drumming. The music puts out the flames in my head."

Cincinnati (or was it Minneapolis?) was the Pop-Tarts, a raucous all-girl nostalgia band who opened for them in white shorts and halter tops, and played a bunch of old songs and whipped the crowd into a horny, whistling fit so the Nazgûl could come out and play some more old songs at them. Backstage afterward, the party got wild and then violent, and Sandy drank too much and passed out, and woke in a chair when everything was over. Maggio was the only one of the Nazgûl left by then. He was comatose and the dark-haired big-breasted bass player from the Pop-Tarts was sucking drunkenly on his limp cock. The television was playing. Cable news; Sandy watched it blearily until a familiar face appeared. He knew that man, he thought, but he couldn't remember where or why, and the words from the screen didn't make sense. Maggio moaned and stirred a little and Sandy saw he was starting to get hard. The commentator was talking about someone named Paul Lebeque, about to go on trial in Maine. But who the hell was Paul Lebeque? Maggio sat up, patted the Pop-Tart on the head, said, "Good, baby, oh, good."

On the road they were always drunk, or stoned, or horny.

St. Louis was Houston was Pittsburgh was Cincinnati. The new songs failed and old ones worked, the old ones made the crowds come alive. And each night, when they did some cut off *Music to Wake the Dead*, Patrick Henry Hobbins sang with them again. But only for those songs. On the new material it was still Richmond, poor timid plastic Larry. Even when they tried material from *Napalm*, or *Hot Wind out of Mordor*, or the Black Album, they were stuck with Richmond. Only *Music to Wake the Dead* woke Hobbins. Peter Faxon fought every step of the way, rewrote the new material, reworked the act over and over again, and failed, and failed, and failed. Richmond couldn't carry it; they needed Hobbins. With each performance, the balance shifted a bit more. Drop "Sins" in Detroit, do "Survivor" instead. Jettison "Good Ol' Days" come St. Louis (or was it Minneapolis?), play with "Napalm Love" for a while, end up with "Ash Man" rocking 'em in Kansas City. Axe the new songs, sing the old, don't argue with success.

On the road you need the applause, the shouts, the whistles, the love of the crowds.

On the road Francie traveled with the band. She was Maggio's old lady again, at least in name, and she was up on stage near him during the concerts, swaying and boogying to the music, smiling a small, sad, vacant smile, her big eyes still a little lost. Rick seemed oddly tender with her now.

From New York through St. Louis, he went through groupies faster than ever, and talked endlessly about each new conquest. Francie took it all, the blow-jobs and the three-ways, and when he passed out or wound down she would sit by him, stroking his long greasy hair, smiling at him as gently as a mother at a wild, unruly, but much-beloved son. She knew that she was real to him, she told Sandy once, while the others were only passing dreams, faces and names and mouths that changed from city to city. Francie was with Rick always. And Gort, huge and quiet, was never far from Francie.

On the road it was always midnight. On the last leg of interstate heading into Minneapolis, Sandy pushed on the radio, the power antennae rose with a crackle of static, and the music filled Daydream. Between two smarmy contemporary hits, the DJ said, "Now for a blast from the past . . . or maybe the future, right?" and he played "Napalm Love," the long version recorded in concert but never used on any Nazgûl album.

And the Nazgûl spread their dark wings across the land, and the tribes gathered, Sandy thought, and so they did. Each night he watched the crowds swell and seethe and change. They came in middle-aged and just a bit frayed around the edges, came in wearing designer jeans and jewelry, drawn by their memories, by the echoes of the songs they had marched to, fucked to, dropped acid to, sung along with, and believed in during the Sixties. They went out younger somehow, full of an energy that was almost tangible, a power that crackled; they went out smiling and whistling, holding hands like kids again, and often as not the jeans seemed faded afterward, cheap and worn and stained, with flower patches and peace symbols ironed on to cover up the holes. At Minneapolis (or was it St. Louis?) he counted twenty headbands, five tie-dyed shirts, one pair of granny glasses. The concerts lasted hours, but could human hair really grow that far, that fast? Then why did the women's hair seem so long and clean and straight coming out, flowing down and down, stirring in the wind, when it had seemed so shagged and styled and curled coming in?

On the road anything seemed possible, and everything was real. In St. Louis Sandy thought he recognized a face he'd seen in Pittsburgh, right up front. In Houston he was sure of it, of that face and of a dozen more. They were following the band; the pudgy woman who always stripped down to the buff and danced slowly to even the fastest songs, her eyes closed, and the tall, stringy, goateed guy who always had a joint dangling from his lip, the bikers, the gaggle of hippies out-of-time, the fellow who was hairy as a werewolf but wore a three-piece violet Edwardian suit, the sultry sloe-eyed knockout with the silver-blond hair. Night after night, city after city. In Kansas City he could have sworn he saw Lark out there in the crowd, throwing his fist in the air and shouting, "He's *coming!*" with all the others, one vast roar of prophecy and promise.

On the road all the faces seem familiar.

Kansas City was Houston was St. Louis, and they lived and moved and traveled in their own lost world, in the eye of a rock 'n' roll hurricane, in the midst of gathering force. By St. Louis (or was it Houston?) they were national news again, the mixed reviews from Chicago now forgotten. Dan Rather talked about the Nazgûl on the *CBS Evening News*, *Time* finally delivered on the cover they had promised months before, *Hedgehog* did a second cover, much better than the first, to feature a twenty-page article called "The Impossible Comeback Flight," even though Sandy never returned any of Jared's calls. Two encores in Minneapolis (or was it St. Louis?), and in Houston the crowd wouldn't *let* them leave the stage, and Hobbins danced and sang like a man possessed (what else?) and drove them on and on, and they ran out of material and kept going anyway, playing "What Rough Beast" with an endless jam in the middle, until the cries of *"He's coming!"* brought the police screaming in to shut down the show. There was shouting, curses, rocks thrown, arrests made, two tear gas canisters thrown to disperse the crowd. The Nazgûl played on through all of it, and when the Houston cops finally whipped out nightsticks and formed a battle line, the crowd charged and overwhelmed them, while the Nazgûl struck up "Ragin'."

And the Nazgûl spread their dark wings across the land and the free peoples gathered and they raised their banners of old, with love and joy and righteous anger, Sandy wrote in the statement he released to the media after the Houston "police riot." But he thought twice and crossed it out before release. Already you could see the polarization beginning. Some Texas politicians wanted the band indicted for inciting a riot, there was agitation in Kansas City and Denver and Albuquerque to ban the three remaining concerts, and an Alabama television evangelist called rock a communist, satanist plot. But rushing north through the darkness to beat dawn to Kansas City, Sandy told Ananda to turn on the radio. She found a big Dallas top-forty station, but they were playing "This Black Week," and they followed it with "Blood on the Sheets" and "Napalm Love" and "What Rough Beast," a solid hour of Nazgûl hits, one after another, and at the end the DJ said, "I want to thank all of you who called in. We'll keep playing the Nazgûl as long as you keep calling, boys and girls, and keep sending the money. And remember, all the filthy lucre goes to the legal defense fund for the Houston Eighteen." Ananda made a fist, pounded the dash, and whooped with gleeful laughter.

Kansas City was fifty thousand people under the stars, and music that lasted half the night, encore after encore after encore. The Nazgûl opened with "Wednesday's Child"—Faxon still hoped—and later, when they were really hot, they did "Goin' to the Junkyard" just for the hell of it, and the crowd was so moist and ready and hopped-up that they almost bought both of them, despite Richmond, but that night especially it was Patrick Henry Hobbins from start to finish, almost, dominating the stage, dominating the crowd, making them howl and clap and stomp their feet, driving the music even higher and louder. Out in that sea of people were all six members of American Taco, Jamie Lynch's other world-class band, disbanded since 1975, but Hobbins spotted them and called them up on stage, and for almost an hour the two bands battled each other as they had warred in days of old, and even the egregious Todd Oliver of the Tacos, dressed in a paisley shirt and silver-gray stovepipe hat instead of the silver lamé jumpsuit he wore with Glisten, seemed to rise to the occasion and remember what rock and roll was all about. The battle of the bands ended with Oliver and Hobbins strutting across the stage and singing an insane duet while Maggio traded hot licks with the Tacos' lead guitarist. Then the others left, and the Nazgûl shut it down with a rousing, chaotic, thunderous version of "Prelude to Madness."

But Kansas City was also Larry Richmond going crazy in his room back at their hotel. Sandy was padding down the corridor in search of a Pepsi when he heard a noise. The door was ajar; he hesitated a moment and opened it. Richmond stood against the window with balled fists, his white face reddened by hysterical tears. A lamp had been knocked over; it lay on the carpet, the base shattered and the shade torn, but the bulb still alight, giving the room an unnatural bleak cast. There were too many shadows in all the wrong places, and a glare of light from below. Peter Faxon stood a few feet from Richmond, talking him down in a calm, reasoned voice. "Take it easy, Larry," he was saying. "It's OK. Too many pills, that's all."

"I don't *do* pills," Richmond said shrilly. His eyes, pale with fear, found Sandy. "I *don't!*" he insisted.

"You took a whole handful in the middle of the first set," Faxon said. "That's why you're so crazy now." He raised his hands, palms out, in a gesture that said calm, calm, calm.

"No," Richmond said, petulant as a child. "No, no, no, no, no. I *didn't!* I don't do...don't..."

"You tell him," Faxon said to Sandy.

Sandy nodded slowly. "Uppers, I think."

Larry Richmond screamed and kicked the fallen lamp as hard as he could. It spun around, and the shadows shifted sickeningly. Then Richmond collapsed on the sofa, sobbing. "I don't remember," he said loudly. "I don't remember it, I don't remember anything. What's happening to me, what's *happening*?"

"Give me a hand," Faxon said. He and Sandy laid the kid out on the couch, covered him with a blanket, tried to calm him down. "It's strain," Faxon said in the even tones of one who knows. "You've been under a lot of strain. The travel, the shows. You're not used to it. Hell, none of us ever get used to it. Look what's happening to Rick and John. John's eating too much, drinking too much. Rick's freaking out on drugs. And both of them are old hands at this. You're having a breakdown, maybe. A nervous breakdown. Big fucking deal. You'll get through it. Only two more shows to do, and then we've all got a long rest coming. We'll cut a new album after West Mesa and go home and sleep for a year. Don't worry about it. You hear? Don't worry." He forced a smile. "And you're singing better every damn night, too."

Faxon's words seemed to take the edge off Richmond's fear, and at the last comment, the kid actually smiled a bit. "I am?" he said. "No shit?"

"No shit," Faxon said.

But a minute later, when they closed the door behind them and stood together in the hall, Faxon turned to Sandy and said, in a tone vastly less cheerful, "Do you really believe the bill of goods I just sold him in there?"

"Why?"

"I don't," Faxon said. "Come with me. I want to talk."

They went back to Faxon's room, and Faxon got a couple of beers out of his refrigerator, opened them, and sat down with a grim, hard look on his face. "You know why he went crazy?"

"I can guess," Sandy said.

"Someone mentioned American Taco, how great the whole thing had been. Richmond didn't remember. Not a bit of it. He didn't even know the Tacos had been in the crowd tonight, much less that we'd jammed with them. He remembers less with each goddamned show, but up to now he's been lying to himself. He remembers less, but he sounds better. Why is that, I wonder?"

"Why are you asking me?" Sandy said.

Faxon's green eyes were bright and piercing. "Because I think you know a hell of a lot more than you let on. Don't bullshit me, Sandy. We're both too smart to play those games. You're a part of this. I don't know how or why, but you are. For me, it all started when we went up in the Flying Eye together, and you dug up a hell of a lot of memories and feelings that I'd buried a long time back. So don't play the innocent with me. Tell me what the fuck is going on here."

"You wouldn't believe it if I did."

Peter Faxon laughed. "Try me. Right now I'd believe anything. You don't get up on that stage night after night. I do. I can feel it, see it, hear it. Sometimes—" He hesitated, took a swig from his beer bottle, and frowned. "I swear, I get the weirdest feelings up there. Back in St. Louis, I was playing, wrapped up in the music, not paying much attention to the crowd, and then I looked up... it was in the middle of 'Prelude to Madness,' I think... and the whole fucking hall was full of candles. Thousands of candles out there in the dark. It was like I'd been transported back in time fifteen years. Then I blinked, and they were gone." He shook his head. "I get a horrible *cold* feeling sometimes, too. It's all I can do to keep my teeth from chattering. Mostly I get it when I look over and see Pat there, singing. *Pat!* Not Richmond. Yeah, they look alike, but I knew Pat Hobbins better'n his mother did, and believe me, I can tell the difference." He hesitated, drank some more beer. "It *is* Pat, isn't it?" he asked, with a shrewd tilt of his head.

"You ought to know," Sandy replied. "You wrote the music."

"The music?"

"*Music to Wake the Dead,*" Sandy said.

"Crazy," Faxon muttered. "It can't be happening."

"It is," Sandy said. "Don't lie to yourself. You believe it as much as I do. Larry Richmond doesn't remember the concerts because, for the most part, he isn't there."

"Pat," Faxon whispered. "I knew it. I could feel it."

Sandy said nothing.

"It's got to be... I don't know... psychological, right? Split personality. I've heard of things like that. An actor who does the same role so often he wigs out and starts thinking he *is* the character he's playing. That's got to be it. There are two people inside Richmond's body—the kid, and this pseudo-Hobbins. Up on stage, the kid can't do it, so Hobbins takes over."

"Plausible," Sandy said. "Believe that if you want to. You and I both know it isn't so."

"So what's the alternative?" Faxon snapped. "Possession? Possession from beyond the grave?"

Sandy suddenly felt very tired. The beer tasted sour in his mouth. He nodded wearily.

"Impossible," Faxon said. "I don't believe it."

"You *can't* believe it," Sandy said.

"Why?"

"Because you're a decent man, Peter, and if you believed it, you'd have to stop it, wouldn't you? You said it in Chicago, backstage, the first time it happened—you don't *want* it to stop. Do you?"

Peter Faxon looked away, frowning.

"*Do* you?" Sandy insisted.

Faxon's head snapped around. "No," he said, his mouth tight. "*No.*" He grimaced. "Jesus. What am I saying?"

"The truth," Sandy said. "Which is more than you gave to Richmond, isn't it? Why lie to him? Why the false reassurances? Unless you wanted it to go on."

Faxon was staring at the floor now. His eyes had taken on a haunted, frightened cast. "It's not just the sound, Sandy, not just the music. It's Pat. He was...he was my brother, my best friend, another side of myself...I hated him at times, but I loved him, too. When I see him up there, just a few feet away, it rips me apart. I want to go to him, hug him, *talk* to him again. I *want* him back. Yes. But he fades. Every damned time, when the show is over, he fades, and it's Richmond again." He looked up, looked Sandy in the eye. "But not after West Mesa, right? That's what we are all heading for. Morse, you, me. West Mesa and...and..."

" 'The Armageddon Rag,' " Sandy said quietly.

Peter Faxon nodded. "Get out of here, Blair," he said. "I need to be alone with myself for a while. Get the hell out of here."

Sandy stood up and moved toward the door, understanding full well what Faxon was going through. But when his hand was on the doorknob, Faxon stopped him. "One more question."

"Yeah?" Sandy said.

"I know why I don't stop it. I want Pat back. Maybe I damn myself by saying so, but I value Pat more than a dozen Larry Richmonds. But what about you, Blair? Why are you going along?"

That was a hard question to answer this late at night, so close to the closing number. "You're not the only one who loves a ghost," Sandy said.

Peter Faxon nodded and looked away, and Sandy made his exit. But out in the hall, when the door snicked shut behind him, his parting words seemed to echo hollowly above the nearby hum of icemaker and Pepsi machine. Wrong, Sandy thought dully, wrong, wrong, *wrong*. For after all, his ghosts were not dead, only changed, and maybe that only made it hurt the more, yet somehow it made a difference.

Back in his room, he woke Ananda from her sleep, and she looked at him and smiled and kissed him and they made a swift and violent sort of love, and from her body Sandy took his reassurance, and in her arms he found his comfort.

On the road Ananda was always close to him, and her closeness made it all right.

On the road there is no room for doubt.

TWENTY-FOUR

Heard the singers playin', how we cheered for more!/
The crowd then rushed together, tryin' to keep warm

Long before the Nazgûl reached Denver, the crowds had arrived. The concert had been sold out a month before, but that did not deter them. They came in campers and trailers, in brand-new Porsches and weathered old Beetles, in pick-up trucks and panel trucks and chartreuse school buses. They came by the hundreds and the thousands and they poured into Red Rocks Park in the foothills west of the city, hard up against the mountains. They camped in the mountains, in the hills, in the amphitheater itself, slept in their vehicles, in sleeping bags, in yurts and tents and teepees, all erected illegally. They gathered around illegal fires and played guitars and passed illegal joints and sang old songs, ignoring park rangers and police and concert security equally.

A week before the show, the newspapers brimmed with furor and agitation. There was talk of sending in an army of cops to clear out the squatters, there were calls for the National Guard; serious consideration was given to canceling the concert, banning it, moving it. The amphitheater was a gorgeous place, a bowl of pale crimson stone, tier after tier of ascending seats carved from the mountain, walled on three sides by weathered cliffs and tall columns of rock, but low in the east so that, beyond the stage, the lights of Denver shone in the distance . . . yet, though it was capable of seating nine thousand, it was far too small for the hordes who had trekked to

Denver to hear the resurgent Nazgûl. Red Rocks would be destroyed, claimed those who wanted the show stopped; a major riot was predicted.

Edan Morse worked to defuse the situation, with the help of cooler heads among the local authorities, those who recalled the example of Houston. He asked permission to erect sound towers all through the surrounding parkland so that those outside could hear the show. Permission was granted. He doubled the size of his security, doubled it again, finally increased it to almost a thousand. The authorities went along; Morse assembled a small personal army. He signed a binding pledge making the Nazgûl responsible for all damages, and agreeing to pay the massive clean-up bill afterward.

Sandy himself released the final announcement to the press. The West Mesa concert, Morse swore, would be completely free. Only ten days off, it promised plenty of room for everyone, good sound, an easy view of the band. Go to Albuquerque, Morse told them, and thousands took him up on the suggestion. The others remained. On the day of the concert, the police estimated that there were thirty thousand of them.

Sandy and Ananda left for the show four hours early and still had their problems getting there. The roads were jammed with traffic, all of it crawling in the same direction. The shoulders were lined with cars, either stalled or parked. They had to abandon Daydream three miles from the site, when the snarled road became totally impassable. Sandy found room to pull her off, and they walked the rest of the way, the two of them part of a river of humanity streaming up the road. The chaos was infused with a curious light-headedness, a sense of joy, of holiday. Everyone seemed friendly. Six-packs were cracked freely, cans given over to anyone who looked thirsty. Strangers talked to one another happily, shared joints, turned into friends in no time at all. Frisbees went sailing through the late afternoon air.

Closer to the amphitheater, the throngs grew denser and more testy. The road narrowed, the rocks rose around them as redly as promised, the pilgrims were pushed closer together, and tempers began to fray. Still they streamed on, pressed up against one another until the flow had a life of its own. Sandy could not have turned back then even if he'd wanted to. Up near the entrance to the theater itself, the crowd was a solid hard-packed mass churning with frustration, disappointment, and more than a little claustrophobia. Those who had tickets swore as they tried to push to the front; others pushed back.

Sandy glimpsed one of Morse's security force, a big blond woman wearing a crimson armband with a black Nazgûl insignia emblazoned upon it. "Tickets," she was shouting, "tickets. Tickets come with me." She was carrying what looked like a sawed-off baseball bat, and using it adroitly to clear a path through the press. Three or four sweaty, grinning ticketholders trailed in her wake.

"Here," Ananda shouted when the woman came close. They traded nods of recognition, and she and Sandy shoved through to the woman's side and were given an escort up to the gate.

They were in sight of the barrier when a tall, fat black man in a dashiki called out to Ananda. "Hey, babes," he yelled in a slurred, drunken voice. "Hey, mama, help me out. Get me inside, sister." Ananda ignored him; they tried to shoulder past, but the going was slow. The man pushed up next to her. "Hey, tits," he said, "I'll do ya better'n that white boy." Sandy, boxed in, was helpless to intervene as the man put a big meaty arm around Ananda and squeezed a breast roughly. "Hey, mama, be nice to me. I'm gonna—"

He never finished. Ananda moved, moved *fast*, a deft half-turn that freed her from his grasp, an elbow that took away his breath, and then a hard sharp slam upward, her arm a piston, her palm open. She mashed his nose with the heel of her hand and a thin line of blood ran down from one nostril. Then he collapsed, or began to . . . the crowd pressed so close on all sides that he barely had room enough to sag, but his blood-smeared face and suddenly vacant eyes sent his neighbors pushing away, and inch by inch the heavy body in green-and-black vanished, sinking to the hard dusty ground.

The security line was manned by at least twenty of Morse's people, in the bright crimson armbands. Mirrors was in charge, twin suns shining off his silvered sunglasses. Ananda jerked a thumb back at the man she had felled. "Get him out of there," she said.

"We'll take care of it," Mirrors said.

They passed beyond the line to the lip of the amphitheater. It was crowded even there, but at least there was room to breathe. "Jesus," Sandy said, glancing back, "what'd you *do* to him, 'Nanda?"

"Broke his fucking pig nose for him," she said.

"His nose," Sandy echoed, stunned. He remembered the glimpse he'd had of the swift, sure blow. The flat palm. The crunch at impact. The trickle of blood. "The way he went down," Sandy said. "I mean, he didn't even make a sound . . ."

"Mirrors will take care of it."

"You could *kill* someone with that kind of blow," Sandy said.

Ananda regarded him innocently. "Oh? Well, he started it, right? No one grabs me unless I want to be grabbed." She smiled and took Sandy's hand. "And you're the only one I want grabbing me these days. End of discussion. Come on."

Red Rocks was crammed solid with human flesh. Even the aisles were full, and people were sitting and climbing all over the tall encircling rocks. Down in front, a small section had been roped off, and another knot of security men were keeping it clear. Sandy saw Gort among them, his sunburned shaven head looming above all the rest. They climbed down, trying not to step on anyone. Gort grunted at them and lifted Ananda over the rope. "Fucking zoo, ain't it?" he said.

"Wait till West Mesa," Sandy told him.

Maggio was there, pacing, talking in an excited babble. When he saw Sandy, he came over. "Hey, man, this is wild. Whattaya think? We didn't get no draw like this even in '71. Fuck, no. This is gonna be one hell of a show, I guaran-fucking-tee it." He laughed.

"Is that so?" Sandy said. His mind was on other things. On the big man, falling silently, the bright colors of the dashiki lost in the human sea. On the blood from his shattered nose. On Ananda's hand in his; the long, strong fingers, the nails cut to the quick, the familiar ridge of callus along the edge of little finger and palm. He felt disquieted.

"Fuck yes," Maggio was saying. "Reynard's gonna do some freaky stuff with the lights, man. Fireworks and shit, out over there." He jabbed a finger at Denver. "And the music, man. Gonna be all solid tonight. No weak spots, baby, I guaran-fucking-tee it."

That got Sandy's attention. "What? What do you mean?"

Maggio grinned. "Ain't you heard, man? Leader-man finally got the shit outta his ears and listened to me. No more of that new junk."

"And that's not all," Edan Morse said. "Tonight the Nagzûl are going to perform the Rag. Right, Rick?"

"You got it." He held out his palm. "Gimme some skin, man."

"I . . . no," Morse said. He held up his hands. Both of them were bandaged.

"Fuck it," Maggio said. He spied Francie, turned, and left them.

Sandy was staring at Morse. He had spoken to Morse on the phone frequently in the past two weeks, but this was the first time he'd seen him since Chicago. But for the voice, he might never have recognized him. Morse looked ravaged. The eyes were all glitter and obsession, sunk in deep pits in a face that was nothing but skin pulled tightly over jutting bones. He wore a pale cotton gauze shirt that did nothing to conceal the cadaverous condition of his body. His beard had gone wild and scraggly, but his hair seemed to be falling out. Around his neck were a dozen heavy pendants and chains, and their weight seemed almost too much for him. Morse leaned over and kissed Ananda, smiled crookedly, and took a seat next to her.

"What the hell is wrong with you?" Sandy blurted.

"Nothing," Morse said. "It's under control. It's all under control."

"You look like you ought to be in a hospital. Why are you here, anyway? You've never bothered to come to a concert before."

"Tonight's going to be different," Morse said.

"Why?" Sandy demanded. "What is ..."

"You'll see," Morse said, his voice strained. He leaned over to Ananda and began to talk to her in low, private tones.

Dismissed, Sandy found himself gazing at the empty stage, the waiting instruments, and Denver beyond. Slum was down there somewhere, he thought, locked in a house that had become a prison, locked in the cage of his own despair. He found himself fantasizing. He saw himself ascend the stage, deliver a long harangue into the open mike, and they all came together to follow him, all thirty thousand of them, cheering and whistling and singing, marching behind him down the city streets to Fort Byrne, overwhelming Butcher and his guns and his dogs. Slum came out to join them, and with each step he took he changed. His face filled out, his hair grew, his clothes melted and reshaped themselves and flowered in a hundred bright colors, and when he embraced Sandy, he was whole again, and young, and strong.

Sandy put the dream aside, pressed the button on his watch for the time. An hour till showtime, the readout told him.

An hour and a half later, the shadows of late afternoon had begun to lengthen appreciably, and the amphitheater was full to bursting, and restless. Someone began clapping. "We want the show," he called. Others took up the chant. "We want, the SHOW, we, want, the SHOW, we, want, the SHOW." Clap clap clap-CLAP. "We, want, the SHOW!" They clapped and chanted for ten minutes, the volume of the sound growing until Sandy realized that the call had been taken up even beyond the tiers of seats, that they were chanting it out in the park as well, and all along the road.

The surrounding stone was a vivid, livid red with the light of sunset, and the impatient, chanting faces were red as well. The lights of Denver were starting to come on, and the far eastern horizon was a band of blue-black darkness. "We, want, the SHOW. We, want, the SHOW. We, want, the SHOW. We, want, the SHOW." The mountain itself seemed to vibrate in time to the claps.

They let it go on and on, let it continue for another twenty minutes at least, building and building until it seemed impossible for it to build any more. By then Denver was a grid of lights to the east, a vast field of stars caught and tamed and ordered and set against the encroaching blackness. The mountains to the west were towering black teeth, their tips outlined blood-red and suffused with the glow of sunset. Clouds were massing to the west above the mountains, an ominous wall of churning black and scarlet; Sandy didn't like the looks of that.

"We want, the SHOW. We, want, the SHOW. We, want, the SHOW. We, want, the ... *oohhhhhh!*"

The whistle of a skyrocket knifed through the tumult; it exploded off to the east, and a pinwheel of red and orange spun against the night, turning the chant to a sigh of appreciation and awe. More skyrockets followed, one, two, three, four; booms shattered the rhythm of the clapping, broke it, scattered it. Fireworks lit the night. All eyes turned upward. Among the fading showers of trailing fire, a phoenix suddenly sprang into view, a burning yellow phoenix with wings greater than the city beneath, and eyes like hot red coals.

"THIS IS THE HOUR," the PA boomed.

They had taken the stage while the crowd was staring upward; now they stood silent and still as shadows, holding their instruments, indistinct in the dimness.

"THIS IS THE DAY," the PA said.

A few lights came on; low red lights that illuminated them from below, that made the stage a murky scarlet pool.

"THIS IS THE YEAR," the PA promised.

Another skyrocket shrieked up, closer and louder than the others, and it burst overhead and spread a brilliant white umbrella over all of them, flaring so bright for a second that it washed away the darkness entirely. From the west came a low rumble from the gathering storm.

"OF THE NAZGÛL!" screamed the PA, and a thousand people screamed along with it, and then five thousand, and then more and more as the excitement rippled outward and flowed over the rim of the amphitheater and washed through the darkened park beyond. And the stage lights all came up at once, a blinding flare of illumination in a dozen different colors, and drums and bass and guitar all sounded together, a great hammer blow of music that smashed out at crowd and mountains and storm. White hair shining, black denim suit drinking in light, Patrick Henry Hobbins sang:

Hey baby, what's that in the skyyyy?!

And there *was* something up there, a silver shape that knifed through the darkness, glittering; behind it spread a rippling sheet of fire, a flaming aurora that curtained off Denver. A handful of people flinched away from its fury, but the rest screamed, whistled, went crazy. Maggio was growling back at Hobbins now, voice hoarse and lascivious.

It's looooooove!

And the music came burning off the stage, faint martial airs magnified and twisted and distorted into new shapes, the lead guitar as hot as the jellied gasoline it invoked, the bass alive with the rumble of approaching bombers, the sound gone to smoke and fire, delivered against the crackling backdrop of the wounded red sky. Hobbins' voice was pure hot, sweaty sex, and when he hit the chorus the crowd sang with him:

Oooooh, napalm! Oooooh my napalm love!

And then he stood alone again, but his voice echoed for miles.

Yeah, it's hot because I love ya!
Oh, it burns because we love ya!

Filled with an emotion for which he had no words, an emotion that went beyond the music, Sandy leaned over toward Ananda. "It's Hobbins!" he shouted in her ear, yelling to make himself heard. She nodded at him absently. She didn't understand, he thought: "Napalm Love" was off *Napalm*, not *Music to Wake the Dead*. It should have been Larry Richmond. But it wasn't. Tonight it was Hobbins from the first.

From the first, and until the last.

When the song was over, Hobbins smiled and asked, "Are your ears bleeding yet?"

"Fuck NOOOOOO!" thousands of voices screamed back.

"Just have to play *louder* then," Hobbins said, and he led them into "This Black Week." The fireworks veiled and slashed the sky behind him, blue, then green, then red, a different color for each verse of the song, and the stage lights shifted with the pyrotechnics above, and the music changed, too. When he hit Black Sunday, the amphitheater was singing along, swaying from side to side, clapping its uncounted hands. Edan Morse, eyes closed, beat a soft time against his knee with one bandaged hand. Even Gort, standing and scowling at the foot of the stage, moved slightly to the music.

The first set was one hit after another, all the old songs off the old albums, the first four albums. They did "Elf Rock" and "Cold Black Water" from *Hot Wind Out of Mordor*, "Crazy Cara" off *Nazgûl*, and "Jackhammer Blues" and "Poison Henry" and "Schuylkill River" off the Black Album and wound up with the long, long version of "Makin' War!" off *Napalm*. Maggio caught fire and went up into the seats, his Telecaster shrieking, while the audience echoed the band. "*Makin' war!*" they sang, "*Makin' war, makin' war, makin' war, war, WAR!*" but it was a kind of love they were making, it was all passion, and when Maggio finally broke off the endless jam, he was drenched in sweat. Faxon's Ricky and Hobbins' Gibson led him back to the stage and the closing verse, and Gopher John closed it off with some riffs that made it seem he was out to flay his drums, and Red Rocks came to its feet screaming, and the applause was a long rolling thunder.

But when it died, as all thunders do, another deeper rumble came behind it. Sandy craned around and saw the storm, closer now, black and threatening. Lightning flashed in the distance, against the mountains. The horizon was a vast wall of inky blackness about to fall on them. As Sandy watched, the clouds lit from within.

People were on their feet, stretching, moving around during the short break. Sandy got to his feet as Gort approached. "Faxon wants to cut short the second set," he reported.

Morse looked startled. "What? Why?"

The big man jerked a huge thumb toward the west. "He's scared of the thunderstorm."

"No," Morse said, agitated. "No, absolutely not. They have to finish the show. They have . . . they have . . ." He reeled, and his face went pale. "Dizzy," he muttered. "I got to sit down." He almost collapsed back into his seat.

"I'll talk to him," Ananda said crisply. She followed Gort through the milling crowd. Sandy came after them, quickly, but not quickly enough. The argument was already in progress when he got there.

"NO!" Faxon was shouting. "Absolutely not! Are you crazy, or what?" He pointed. "That storm's going to be on us any minute now."

"What's a little rain?" Ananda said. "They played in the rain at Woodstock, right?"

"Rain? Are you kidding? *Look* at that! I've been staring at it all show, and it's not going to be any drizzle, 'Nanda. That's a major-league thunderstorm out there. Lightning and electrical instruments don't mix."

"Scared, leader-man?" Maggio put in from the side. "Not me. I'm playing."

Faxon looked harassed and outnumbered, but he wasn't about to give up the argument. Then Hobbins came pushing through a bunch of roadies. "We're going on," he said. "You hear me, Peter? We're playing."

"No," Faxon said, but weakly. He was pale and edgy.

"Yes," Hobbins snapped. "Who the fuck's the star here, anyway?" They were all staring at him now. His tone had been light, bantering, but behind the joke was steely self-confidence, iron certainty. He would have his way, the tone said; he always did. It was Hobbins talking, not Richmond.

"*Pat*," Faxon said. "It is you."

"Jesus H. Tapdancing Christ," blurted Maggio, his mouth sagging open.

"Pleased to meet you," Hobbins said. "I see you guessed my name."

Peter Faxon put himself back together with a visible effort. "If we're going to play, let's get on with it," he said. "Before the storm front gets here and we all get electrocuted."

"Fine," Hobbins said. "*I'm* ready. We do the new album in order."

"You got it," Faxon said. They started to break up, but as the others walked away, Sandy took a few steps forward and caught Hobbins by the shoulder. "What?" the singer snapped.

"The others don't understand," Sandy said. "Not even Faxon. They're only tools of...of Morse, or whoever's behind this. But you, *you* understand. Don't you?"

The eyes glittered scarlet; the thin mouth twisted into a mocking sardonic smile. "What if I do?"

"Armageddon," Sandy said. "The final battle. The ultimate confrontation between good and evil. That's what armageddon is supposed to be. Right?"

Hobbins lifted a pale white eyebrow, said nothing.

"Which side are we?" Sandy demanded. "*Which side are we?*"

"That's one you got to work out yourself, friend. This ain't like in Tolkien, is it?" He started to move away.

"Wait," Sandy called out after him.

Hobbins turned back, shook his head. "Sorry, Charlie. Got me some music to play." He made a thumbs-up gesture. "Listen to the tune, bro', just listen to the tune."

Ananda and Gort had listened to the whole exchange. When Sandy turned back, he thought he saw a strange, wary light in Ananda's dark eyes, but she reached out and took his hand anyway. "Come on," she said. They went back to their seats.

Reynard sent up another rocket, a whistler that pierced the night with a high, shrill scream, singing counterpoint to the rumble of the approaching storm. Gopher John laid down the backbeat, the guitars sent their sharp notes skirling, cutting, and Hobbins hit it:

Baby, you cut my heart out!
Baby, you made me bleeeed!

The first rains came just as "Blood on the Sheets" was winding down, tiny drops of coldness that wet the skin and chilled the soul. It came down harder and faster during "Ash Man," but it failed to dampen the enthusiasm of the crowd. One of the skyrockets fizzled, but the spirit in Red Rocks continued to mount. The dark passed overhead, swallowing up the stars, churning above them like the sea of chaos.

Rick Maggio stepped forward. He was sneering; his old, familiar, contemptuous sneer. He was soaking wet. "Fuck it," he roared into the microphone. He stripped off his sodden tee shirt, balled it up, tossed it into the crowd. Women screamed and fought for it. Maggio's ribs were outlined clearly; his body looked sallow and sick, and everywhere his skin was crawling with acne. It glistened wetly in the downpour. "I'm *wet*," he said into the mike, and he touched his strings and stepped on his Wah-Wah pedal to underline the point. "When I get wet, I get fuckin' MAAAD!" he said.

"How mad *are* you?" the crowd shrieked.

"Why, I'm absolutely positively RAGIN'!" Maggio shouted, and just as he did, a sheet of lightning crackled overhead, the clap of thunder coming right on top of it, the wash of purple-blue light turning night to day. Maggio blinked up, and grinned. "Holy shit," he said. "Looks like I'm not the only one who's pissed."

The crowd roared with laughter, Maggio hit his guitar, and music slammed into them.

Ain't gonna take it easy
Won't go along no more

Francie climbed up on the stage, started dancing to the music, her eyes closed, swaying back and forth in front of the band. She was drenched too, like all of them. Her long thin hair was plastered to her face, and her wide, dark nipples showed clearly through the wet tee shirt. The audience followed her lead, climbing, dancing, clapping their hands.

'Cause I'm ragin'!

Maggio sang it, and thousands echoed him.

RAGIN'!

they cried. More lightning splintered overhead. A web of light flickered over the mountains behind them, touching down once, twice, three times. Thunder came rolling, and the sound system crackled with static for an instant, drowning out the music. Then the song came flooding back, louder than ever.

Hobbins took over again and delivered a soft, poignant rendition of "Survivor," then grinned at them all savagely, flipped his mass of white hair back—water ran down it freely, and it looked to be almighty heavy now— and spread his arms and looked up and sang:

   Turning and turning in the widening gyre

And the Nazgûl whispered *He's coming!* loud as midnight.

   The falcon cannot hear the falconer

sang Hobbins, and Sandy heard the skyrocket go off, saw it struggling against the pouring rain, saw the fire trailing and hissing behind it, saw it climb into the jet-dark clouds...and then the lightning caught it, a great jagged blue-white bolt that burned the eyes, and then another, and another, and another, until for an instant it seemed as though four spidery electric arms held the rocket still against the darkness. It exploded. For an eyeblink a falcon shape wheeled against the sky, but it was shattered, distorted into something hideous and grim, and then it was gone entirely.

   He's coming!

Faxon looked as white-faced as Hobbins, but his bass had never sounded better. The electrical storm was crackling and snarling all around them, sending unpredictable static into the sound system, but somehow Maggio was using it all, playing around it, weaving it into the song. Time and time again the thunderclaps came booming down just as Gopher John struck his bass drum with his foot stick.

   The best lack all conviction

sang Hobbins, and he looked at Sandy, his red eyes burning deep into the soul.

> while the worst,
>
> OH! They're full of passion, and intensity!

His gaze shifted, just a little, and who was he staring at now, at Morse? at Gort? at Ananda?

Lightning smashed against a high outcropping of rock. A woman seated a few feet away screamed shrilly, her voice, unamplified, small and weak in the night. The rest of the crowd laughed, clapped, pointed. Hobbins waved a fist at the storm. Thirty thousand voices shouted *"HE'S COMING!"* as one. *"Yeah!"* sang Hobbins. Faxon was blank-faced, concentrating, Maggio was sneering, Gopher John wore his fiercest scowl, and hit, and hit, and hit.

Sandy was very wet, very cold, very afraid. He took Ananda's hand. It felt cold and slimy in the rain, the edge of callus hard and sharp.

> Oh, what vast image comes troubling my night?
>
> HE'S COMING!

Ananda's face was lost, her eyes alive with music and unseen visions, her lips parted as if in rapture. Beyond her, Edan Morse slumped with his eyes closed. His bandaged hands rested on his knees, the bandages turned a pale pinkish red. The rain was washing thin sheets of blood down his legs. His cotton shirt was plastered to his skin by the downpour, and over his heart the gauze had turned pink. As Sandy watched, the spot darkened and grew.

> A *gaze as blank and pitiless as the sun!*

Above the stage, it seemed as though some vast shape were forming among the clouds, a huge black face with glowing eyes, lightning flashing in its open mouth.

> HE'S COMING!
>
> HE'S COMING!!!
>
> YEAH, HE'S COMING!!!

Chanting. Clapping. Rain pouring down. Lightning all around. Thunder and drumming. Chanting. Clapping. Patrick Henry Hobbins

sang verse after verse, his words filling the park and booming off the mountains. When he asked the last question, the lights went down, and there
came an ear-piercing boom from the sky above. A long lightning strike
slashed the far horizon, and the crowd—and Sandy too—fell deadly silent
for a moment as all the lights in Denver went out.

In the dark, someone had given Hobbins a candle. He lit it in the rain,
held it under his chin, grinned. The sound system crackled back to life.
"*I'm coming*," he told them. "Hell, I'm almost here." Denver blinked, went
out again, and lit back up in welcome.

Hysteria that went on and on.

Just when Sandy thought it was never going to end, the Nazgûl struck
up the music once more, and slid into "Prelude to Madness." The number
was full of chaotic instrumentals, full of feedback and echo, full of discords
that rattled the fillings in your mouth, yet after the frenzy of "What Rough
Beast," it seemed almost soothing.

> *Right is wrong, black is white,*
> *Who the fuck's got the justice tonight?*

Sandy heard Edan Morse gasp and cry aloud. He looked over. Morse
was holding up his hands. "No," he screeched. "This isn't right, no, *no*." He
turned to Ananda, plucked at her arm, smeared blood on her rain-
drenched sleeve. "Help me," he cried. His shirt was soaked through with
blood, his voice thin with fear. People were staring.

> *I hear laughter in all the wrong places*
> *See color in all the white spaces*

Morse staggered to his feet, shrieking, waving his bloody hands. Ananda
rose with him, arms on his shoulders, trying to keep him calm. Rain ran
down their faces. Gort saw the struggle and began to fight his way through
the dancers who swarmed before the stage.

> *Queens beat aces every time, yeah!*
> *Dead man's hand, dead man's hand!*
> *And Charlie is the joker in the deck!*

Sandy was trying to make his way to Ananda's side, to help with Morse,
but they had moved away from him and the crowd was getting wild. He
shoved into someone, muttered an apology, staggered back as the man

spun and swung on him. Someone else hit him from the side. The music went on and on.

"I'm *bleeding!*" Morse screamed shrilly, his voice loud enough to be heard even above the music. "What's *happening* to me?" Sandy glimpsed him taking a wild swing at Ananda. His hand connected with a soft wet sound, and left a smear of blood on her cheek. The rain washed it away. And then Gort was there, looming above the crowd. He swept people aside with his massive arms, cradled Morse protectively. Morse shouted something up at him, and Gort caught him under the arms, lifted, hoisted him to a wide, broad shoulder. He began to fight his way out, bulling through the crowd on sheer size and muscle, Morse on his back. The dancers eddied around him, oblivious.

Sandy reached Ananda. She'd been knocked down in the struggle. He gave her a hand, pulled her to her feet. "You all right?" he asked.

Maggio played a long, wavery, insane riff that prickled at the nerve endings; Faxon's bass sounded way way down, almost at the threshold of hearing. Hobbins sang the final chorus.

> *Queens beat aces every time, yeah!*
> *Dead man's hand, dead man's hand!*
> *And Charlie is the joker in the deck!*

Her knee was bloody, the pants leg torn, but she dismissed it. "Just a scrape," she said.

Sandy tried to shout a question at her, but it was no good. Gopher John was playing the final drum solo of "Prelude to Madness," and right in the middle of it, it slowed and shuddered and changed into something else, into the opening of another song.

The crowd screamed.

Thunder rumbled dimly, way off, as if the storm were passing.

Hobbins looked at them all with his red, red eyes, smiled knowingly, and sang.

> *This is the land all causes lead to,*
> *This is the land where the mushrooms grow.*

And in the sky behind him, above the lights of Denver, you could see them growing; towering ghostly images, blue and purple and poisonous below, and above as white-hot and brilliant as the sun, flowering and spreading their seed, so more sprouted all around them, mushroom after mushroom, horizon to horizon. The dancers froze in step, gasped, held their breaths. The world was silent and waiting. Even the storm stilled, while the Nazgûl sang.

> *To the battleground I'm coming,*
> *Oh, don't you hear the drumming?*
> *They're playing the armageddon rag, oh!*
> *Playin' the armageddon rag!*

And the drumming was there, the bass drum sounding deep in the blood, the toms whispering in a slow-building martial rhythm that called out, inflamed, conjured. Gopher John scowled and looked down and his big hands moved faster and faster, and each lick was a bullet, each rim shot a rattling artillery shell.

> *This is the day we all arrive at,*
> *This is the day we choose.*

Hobbins had started the song in a sad, almost gentle voice, but with each word his anger seemed to build, and around him the storm was gathering force again. Another distant lightning strike shattered the brief stillness, and as the thunder died the Nazgûl were singing:

> *Well, I'm here to make things right,*
> *To fight the last good fight,*
> *And they're playing the armageddon rag, oh!*
> *Playin' the armageddon rag!*

Bare-chested, wet, ravaged, sneering, Rick Maggio let his fingers fly across the strings of his Fender, and the music blasted out of the amps in a sizzling barrage, and Faxon and Hobbins fired back, in a jam turned firefight, each of them grimacing, moving with small wary steps to face one another, lines blistering back and forth for long minutes until Maggio knifed it dead with a long, anguished scream of feedback. The bass drum pounded, the bottom was a solid living viscous thing, the beat moved faster and faster still, and the crowd began to clap in time. Hobbins took charge again.

> *This is the day of SOULSTORM, baby!*
> *The day all debts come due!*

Remember the things you done to me,
while I'm doing 'em to YOU!

He made a fist, jammed it in the air. A thousand other fists echoed the gesture. Others were clapping, clapping, clapping, thirty thousand pairs of hands slamming together in noisy unison. Sandy was clapping, too. Hobbins sang ice and fire and deliverance, Maggio's guitar turned rabid and demonic, Faxon's bass was a steady fatal cannonfire, Gopher John was lost in a holocaust of drumming, and the sky was a deep bruised purple-black, alive with flashing fire. All the old ghosts rose up like mists, mocking. Faceless men swarmed from elevators, swinging bloody clubs. Daley's ugly jowls twisted with hate, Nixon squirmed and lied, Butcher Byrne brought down that shotgun once more. The clouds were full of bayonets and flowers gone to war. Churning armies swirled and fought with rifles that spat lightning and cracked like thunder. The dead rose up to fight again. Distortion. Death. Feedback. Blood. Echoes. Ghosts. Lyrics. Screams. Old times old wounds old enemies they've done us wrong all we wanted was peace old bitterness fixed convention unhearing ears blindness stupidity greed don't believe in killing got no choice war for peace kill for love kill kill kill kill KILL.

The song reached a howling crescendo, instruments all keening to a fine razor edge, holding it, searing, driving, and Hobbins sang:

Kill your brother, YEAH!
    That sucker done you wrong.
Kill your friend, goddamned traitor
    Just listen to the song
They're playing the armageddon rag!
Kill your brother, kill your friend, kill yourself!
    Cause you're a killer too
    All the dead look just like you
When they're playin' the armageddon rag!
YEAH! They're playin' that armageddon rag!

He delivered the line looking straight at Sandy, his eyes scarlet and sardonic, and Sandy remembered what Hobbins had said to him during the break. The Nazgûl flew through the long bridge, soaring, singing, slowing bit by bit until they hit the opening bar of the "Resurrection" verses, and Hobbins turned away from Sandy at last and sang:

This is the day we've dreamed about,
  This is the land where the flowers grow.

But there were no flowers in the sky above him, only darkness and lightning, and the rain was still coming down steadily, and the furor was dying little by little, and suddenly Sandy felt very cold. He turned to Ananda. In her face he saw something that frightened him, but he turned her toward him anyway. "On armageddon day," Sandy said, "both armies will think they fight for good. And both of them will be wrong." But the music was still too loud, and she could not hear him, and her eyes, like all the eyes around him, were hard and shiny as black ice.

TWENTY-FIVE

She was practiced at the art of deception/
Well, I could tell by her blood-stained hands

Sandy woke from an exhausted, nightmare-ridden sleep in early afternoon the third or fourth time that the maid came knocking on the door of his room at the Hilton. "Come back later!" he screamed at her through the chained door, his voice full of irrational fury. He tried but could not get back to sleep, so instead he phoned down to room service.

The coffee tasted too bitter, the orange juice too acidic, but it was probably his mood, not the liquids themselves. He forced himself to eat the pancakes and sausages, and turned on a reading lamp to study the Denver papers. Ananda was still asleep, so he kept the curtains shut.

ROCK RIOT AT RED ROCKS! the *Rocky Mountain News* proclaimed alliteratively; ROCK FANS RAVAGE PARK, said the *Denver Post* in big bright red banner-headline type. Page one in both papers, with plenty of photographs.

Sandy swallowed some coffee and leafed through the stories, wincing at some of the pictures. Cold dead campfires dotted the face of the park like sores, mountains of beer cans and cigarette butts and broken bottles had been left behind, and even the red rocks themselves bore scarred witness to the passing of an army. The *News* had three pages of photos of the spray-can graffiti. Peace symbols everywhere, large and small. Slogans old and new. And, ominously, in a dozen different colors, in letters ten inches and ten feet high, lines from the songs themselves. "*Ragin'!*" scrawled blood red in a wavering, jagged hand, and underlined three times. *"He's coming!"* sprayed a hundred times; *"He's here"* just once or twice. *"Oh, can't you hear the drumming?"* one person had asked, while another—in great black letters on the seats of the amphitheater itself—said, *"Dance to the Rag!"*

The newspaper text was even grimmer, concentrating on the mob scene that followed the end of the performance. Massive traffic tie-ups, more than forty minor accidents, two major ones. Scuffles between fans and nearby homeowners, between fans and police, between police and Morse's security force. A cop car stoned, its windshield broken. A stalled Mercedes overturned and spray-painted in psychedelic colors. Fistfights, singing, drinking, broken windows, broken bones, broken teeth, a dozen miscellaneous arrests. And six deaths. Three dead in a fiery automobile collision, one woman killed when she fell almost a hundred feet while climbing on the rocks, one youth struck by lightning in a sound tower, and one man killed in a fight. LeRoi J. King, thirty-nine, an unemployed short-order cook from Los Angeles, had died instantly when someone broke his nose and the blow sent a sliver of bone sliding up into his brain.

Sandy folded back the newspaper and looked at Ananda, her dark hair tangled on the pillow beneath her, her face wide and innocent in sleep. He reached over and turned off the lamp just as the phone rang.

He started for it, but Ananda was right there, and she got it first. "What?" she said into the receiver blearily. The answer seemed to wake her up. She pulled herself to a sitting position, rubbed the sleep out of her eyes, and nodded as she listened. "All right. Yes. He's awake already. We'll be right up. Yes. Right away." She hung up and turned to Sandy. "Get dressed. That was Gort. Edan wants to see us."

"How is he?"

"Don't ask," Ananda snapped en route to the bathroom.

In less than ten minutes, they were up on Morse's floor. Gort admitted them to the suite and ushered them to the bedroom. The curtains were tightly closed, the room dark. Morse was propped up against his pillows, covered by blankets, an indistinct figure in the dimness. "Come on," he said impatiently. He sounded as though speech was an effort. Ananda reached for the light switch, but Gort stopped her and shook his head. They seated themselves in the shadows, shadows that grew even blacker when Gort shut the door to the connecting room.

"The morning news," Morse said weakly. "You hear?"

"We've been asleep," Ananda said.

"It was on . . ." he coughed, raised a pale bandaged hand to his mouth ". . . the news," he repeated. "Albuquerque. They're banning the concert.

They're afraid. Already...already there's forty, fifty thousand on hand. Camping. Waiting. More pouring in every day. They banned us."

"So?" Ananda said sharply. "You've seen this coming all along, right? In the visions? They can't stop us now. There are too many of us. We'll have Sandy announce that the Nazgûl are going to play anyway, play for the people, for free, and fuck the fascist authorities. Let's see them try and evict a hundred thousand people, two hundred thousand, three hundred thousand. We'll fight back this time. We'll burn their fucking city to the ground and dance in the ashes."

"No," Edan Morse said hoarsely. "Sandy, I want...want a press conference. Tell them."

"Tell them what?" Sandy asked.

"We're canceling," Morse said. "Canceling West Mesa."

"No!" Ananda said. Her voice was soft steel. "What's wrong with you, Edan? It's going down just the way you said it would. The way it was shown to you, right? What is this shit? We can't sell out when we're so fucking close!"

"What's *wrong* with me?" Morse said in a high, hysterical voice. He laughed, but the laughter turned into a fit of coughing that doubled him over. When he recovered, he said, "It's out of control, 'Nanda. It's not right. Not right! It was supposed to...it was supposed to stop."

"What?" Ananda demanded.

"Blood," Morse muttered.

"You're sick, Edan. Sick and scared, right?"

Morse laughed again, shrilly. "Gort," he said. "The light."

"You sure?" the big man asked.

"The light," Morse repeated.

Gort turned on the light.

Edan Morse was drenched in a sweat of his own blood. It seemed to be oozing from every pore, crawling down his flesh, soaking through bandages, bedclothes, blankets. Twin rivulets ran from his nostrils. The sheets beneath him bore the stains of his bleeding, the pillows behind him were smeared and reddish, and dried brown blood was crusted in his beard. It cracked when he opened his mouth. The whites of his eyes had gone crimson, and his pupils looked small and frightened. Even his gums were bleeding; his smile was raw and red and wet.

Ananda gasped. Sandy felt sick. "Jesus H. Christ," he muttered. He started to rise. "You got to get to a hospital," he said. But Gort caught him by a shoulder, pushed him back into the chair.

"No time," Morse said with surprising firmness. "And it wouldn't help.

There's no...no reason for this. Unnatural. Doctors couldn't do shit." He lifted his left hand wearily. "My blood," he said. "Part of the price. But not so much. Didn't think it would be so much."

"I'm sorry for you, Edan," Ananda said in a hard, flat voice. "But it doesn't make any difference. Stay behind. I hope you pull through. But if you don't it will still be worth it. The revolution is more important than your life, or mine."

Edan Morse closed his red, pained eyes briefly, and then forced them open again. His hand dropped back to the blanket. "You don't...don't understand. Not just me. The promises...shit...father of lies. It's not *right!*"

Ananda stood up, defiant. "What the fuck are you *saying*, man?"

Morse forced his left hand up again, reached over with his right and held it up. "The price was blood!" he said with all the force he could muster. "I paid it, bled myself, yeah. Quick cuts, deep, painful. Only they *closed,* 'Nanda! They healed. And afterward, scar tissue...stronger than uncut flesh, you know, stronger, *harder.* It was supposed to be like...like *that.* A short, clean struggle, and then we heal. Better. Stronger. Harder." He released his hand, grinned a hideous bloody grin, thin lines of red between his white teeth. "Not like this. Don't you understand, you bloody bitch? The bleeding won't stop! *The fucking bleeding will never stop!*" He screamed the last words at her.

Ananda was unmoved. "You were always too squeamish, Edan. You wanted to use the power of the music—but you wanted to control it. Well, you can't, sucker. It makes its own demands. You can't give only a little, you've got to give everything." She frowned, glanced at Gort and then at Sandy, hesitated a moment, then shook her head and plunged ahead. "You can't make the fucking omelette without breaking a few goddamned eggs, right? Only you'd rather sit around and wait for the eggs to break themselves mystically. The music can't do it all by itself—it needs us to make it come true. You want to pretend it's all sweetness and light. Well, it's not. It's *ugly* out there, and you can't fucking fight it without getting *ugly* yourself. You really think a few damned drops of blood from your *hand* was enough to pay the price? Do you?" She laughed scornfully.

"My...I haven't done..." Morse winced, looked away.

"That's it. Pretend you don't understand. Pretend you don't see. You've done it all along. You were willing to pay the price for the visions, but I was the only one willing to pay the price for the revolution. I was the one to do what the music demanded."

Sandy rose from his chair and faced Ananda, feeling very cold inside, as if something deep within him had just died. "It was you," he said with iron certainty. He had suspected it, he realized, had suspected it for...how long? Too long. But he had loved her, and she had been all that was left him, and so he had denied it, even to himself. "It was you all along, wasn't it?"

Ananda thrust out a hip, planted a hand on it, assumed a mocking exaggerated, provocative pose, ran her tongue across her lower lip. "Lil' ol' *me*? Why, I's just a hot-pants hippie chick. You think *I* could do something *violent*?"

"Jesus H. Christ," Sandy said.

"You know your problem, Blair? You think with your cock. Just like Jamie Lynch. Getting to *meet* that fucker was the problem. Once I did, it was all real simple. He was so hot to get me out to his place that he almost came in his pants." She glanced over at Morse. "Blood sacrifice, Edan. Someone had to do it."

Morse said nothing.

"And the Gopher Hole?" Sandy asked.

"Slozewski had to have his mind changed, had to become the Ash Man. Locking the doors...the blood made it easier. So many deaths, it made all the rest go down smooth and simple."

Her voice was ice cold. "You don't care," Sandy said accusingly.

"Of course I care. That's why I'm doing this!"

"It doesn't matter," Edan Morse said wearily. "Not now. Don't you see? If we don't stop, it won't...it won't be like we want. Too much blood. It will just go on. On and on. No...no resurrection, that's the lie. Armageddon forever."

"You're just scared to die, Edan," Ananda said.

"Maybe," Morse said. "But I'm right."

"We'll see about that, right?"

"No. We won't. I'm stopping it. I told you. Stopping it."

Ananda smiled. "How are you going to do that, Edan? Look at you. You going to call up all the soldiers one by one and give them the news? *I'm* your mouthpiece, you stupid motherfucker. I give your orders. What the hell makes you think they'd listen to you anyway? They listen to me. Mirrors, Reynard, Gull, Beca, we been through the wars together. They're mine. And I say go ahead."

Edan Morse pushed himself up higher. It was an enormous effort. "They listen to Gort, too," he said. "Gort, give the word. Sandy, set up that press conference. Cancel West Mesa. Cancel it. You hear?"

Sandy nodded.

Ananda sighed. "You suckers give me no choice," she said. "There's too much at stake here for me to let you screw it up. The Armaggeddon Rag is beginning to play, and none of you can stop it now. Sorry." Her hand moved quickly. Snuggled against her palm was a strange small silvery gun. "I guess no one here gets out alive."

"That only shoots darts," Morse said confidently. "Gort, take it away from—"

Ananda's finger jerked twice. The gun made a tiny spitting sound. Morse shrieked and his hand went to his face, covering his eyes. His body jerked wildly, spasming, feet kicking on the bed, and a terrible stench filled the room as his bowels let go.

Sandy scarcely had time to think. No sooner had she fired than she'd dropped the gun and whirled to face Gort. The big man was strong and fast. Ananda was faster and better trained. They met at the foot of the bed. Gort got a hand on her briefly. Then she spun and broke his precarious hold, and his wrist. Slammed back the big square chin with an open palm, dropped him with a devastating kick to the kidneys. He grunted as he fell, tried to roll away from her, but he was too slow. She came down on his back, hard, wrapped her hands around his head, jerked back. Sandy heard the neck break. Gort went limp, and blood trickled from his open mouth. She let his head sink back to the carpet.

Sandy had taken two uncertain steps forward.

She was rising, quickly, ready for him.

He scooped up the dart gun she had dropped, stepped back as fast as he could.

They were alone in a room full of corpses. He trained the gun on her with both hands.

"That only shoots darts," she said, smiling crookedly. "Drugged, yeah. But they won't stop me in time. They couldn't have stopped Gort, either."

"You killed Morse with it."

"Sure. I put a dart in his eye. You that good a shot, lover?"

She swept her dark hair out of her eyes. Her face was flushed with excitement, exertion. She looked beautiful; beautiful and deadly.

"Jesus," Sandy muttered. "I *loved* you!"

For a moment, a sad look flickered across her face. "I was getting sort of fond of you myself," she said. "Not at first. At first it was all fake. When Edan told me you'd be a part of all this, and that we had to have you, I read your books quickly, got ready. You put all your wet dreams in your books, you know. So I became just what you wanted. Worked great, right?" She grinned. "Later on, though...you are a nice guy, Sandy. I've got nothing against you. In a better world, maybe I could have loved you. As it is, love is impossible. It's a tool of oppression. A soldier can't love anyone while the war's on. Love makes you weak. Look at you. You still feel something for me. If I come for you, you won't be able to pull that trigger."

"But you could, correct? You could kill me easy."

She smiled ruefully. "Edan and I went all the way back to the Days of Rage." She gestured to the bed. "We're all expendable. Him, you, me."

Keep her talking, Sandy thought wildly to himself. Keep her talking and you're safe. "Wasn't he committed enough for you?"

Ananda shrugged. "When it came to rhetoric, to passing out money, to making big plans, sure. But deep down, he was just another damn candy-ass liberal. Like you. God save me from the idealists with no stomach for the battlefield."

"I'd think his goddamned war record would be enough even for you," Sandy said.

Ananda laughed. "Sandy, you're so innocent I could kiss you. His *war* record! Hell. You ever wonder why they couldn't pin any of that old stuff on him?" She shook her head. "Edan liked to pretend he was a people's executioner, to take credit for all kinds of stuff. I didn't mind. It worked out real well for me."

"Oh, Jesus," Sandy blurted. "You. It was *all* you—Sylvester, Maxwell Edison, Victor Von Doom. Morse just let the rumors—"

"He did have his gifts. The visions made him very useful. He saw the power in *Music to Wake the Dead* and he saw how we could use it. He saw it all coming. Sometimes it was hard to make sense of what he saw, and sometimes the visions were contradictory, and sometimes they were just wrong...but not often. He paid the price and he saw all of it, hazily. You, too."

"Me, too," Sandy repeated.

"Right."

"So you set out to recruit me."

"Wasn't too hard, either."

Sandy ignored that. "Why?" he demanded.

"Maybe we needed you to do our public relations."

"Media flacks come cheap for someone with Morse's money. There's more to it than that."

She grinned and taunted him with a slow lascivious glide of tongue across lip. "Maybe he saw what a stud you'd be."

"Cut the fucking games. Give me the truth!" He made what he hoped was a menacing gesture with the gun.

"Listen to the music," she said.

"The Nagzûl? You mean I'm in there, too?"

She nodded. "The visions were never completely clear. But Edan felt you'd be a key player somehow. He was right. You stirred up a lot of memories, got things moving. And Edan saw you at the end. You'd come down one way or the other, he said. No telling which, or how it would affect things. So I flirted you up and you warmed quick enough. Remember when we got to Malibu, and I gave Edan a weather report on our trip? If the weather had been less promising, we would have offed you then and there. Instead we drugged you. Gave you a taste of what was coming down. That always hits them hard. And the next morning I told you that we'd made it. I knew from your books that you'd feel that as a bond between us, and that it would weaken your other bonds. And it worked, right?"

Sandy wanted to rave at her, curse her, blast her with words, but for once none of them would come. "I ought to shoot you right now."

"You ought to, but you won't. I know you. Can't shoot a bod you've fucked as often as mine, can you?" She took a step toward him, slowly, confidently.

"Stop right there," he said.

Ananda smiled. "You don't believe in violence. Shoot me, kill me, and you're just the same as I am, right?" She took a second step, a third.

"Stop," Sandy said. His hands shook.

"I don't think so," she replied. A fourth step, a fifth, and her hand came up quickly and took the gun from his grasp. She sighed. "I told you so."

Sandy's stare was cold and angry and bitter. "So now you kill me, too. Well, go on. Get it over with."

Ananda cocked her head to one side. "Death wish? Sandy, if I wanted to kill you, you'd be dead by now. I don't stand around chatting up the enemy. Maybe it'd be safer to off you, but I can't take the chance."

A wave of relief washed over him. He felt dizzy. "Chance?" he repeated weakly.

"It's all so murky, your part in this. But one thing Edan was clear on. You're there at the end, for good or bad. I don't dare eliminate you. Charlie is the joker in the deck, and we do need a full deck, right?" Her finger jerked; the gun spat once, twice. Sandy felt a brief small pain in his shoulder, another, higher, biting into his neck. Numbness spread outward from where the needles had penetrated. "Goodnight, sweet prince," she said lightly. Then she leaned forward and gave him a quick, soft kiss as the world ran with kaleidoscope colors and his legs turned to silly putty beneath him.

TWENTY-SIX

**But my dreams they aren't as empty/
As my conscience seems to be**

Night. The cobbled street is slick and wet. He walks, endlessly, restlessly, without a destination. The street is thick with flowing gray mist. There is no traffic, no noise. Even his boots do not ring on the cobblestones as they should. To either side he glimpses the flashing light of neon signs calling to him, but the mists cover them so he cannot read the lettering. He does not know how long he has been walking this long, straight, dark street, but he is tired. Still, he walks on. The damp chills him, right through to his bones, and he turns up the collar of his coat, but it does not help.

Someone is walking beside him, with footsteps as silent as his. He looks over. Through the mist, he perceives the figure dimly. It is a young woman. She wears a short skirt and a halter top. Long tanned legs flash as she matches his stride. The chill does not seem to bother her. She is very attractive, he thinks, though he cannot see her clearly. Her long, straight hair falls down to the small of her back. A flower is tucked behind her ear, a rose, its vivid redness shocking in this damp gray world. They walk together for a while, and finally he asks her where they are going.

"To San Francisco," she tells him. Her voice is joy and music and innocence. "Why don't you have a flower in your hair?" He recognizes the voice now. It is Maggie's voice, Maggie the way she sounded a long time ago. "We're going back to the things we learned so well in our youth," she tells him, "to the days when we were young enough to know the truth." It's

Sharon's voice, sleepy after lovemaking, full of affection and the playfulness of newborn love. "Come on the rising wind," she urges, "we're goin' up around the bend." It is Donna speaking to him, big-eyed and serious; it's Alicia's soft shyness, it's Becky's dry, self-deprecating wit, it's Barbara who he had the crush on in junior high but never dared to date. It's Ananda who walks beside him, young and smiling and vital, and up ahead of them is the Summer of Love, where the skies are a deep cerulean blue and the sun is always shining and the dope is good and the girls wear flowers in their long blond hair.

"Ah, my friend, you're older but no wiser," another voice says. "For in your heart the dreams are still the same." Froggy is walking on the other side of him now, grinning, wearing a bright-red dinner jacket, a vest, a bow tie. His face is painted green, and his teeth are yellow. "Sander m'boy, that ain't the green, green grass of home waiting up ahead of you, and not only is your date the *ugliest* broad I ever laid eyes on, or laid anything else on for that matter, but in her eyes I see nothing. Nothing at all."

He does not understand. The woman is beautiful, was beautiful, has always been beautiful. He looks over at her again. But now the red that pierces through the fog is not a rose but a raw, open wound, still pulsing with fresh blood. It is a tall dark youth who walks beside him, his temple laid open by a nightstick. It is Bobby Kennedy, empty-eyed and broken. It is a slim black girl killed in a riot. It is Martin Luther King, his dream shattered. It is a shambling hulk of a man in a uniform, his face half blown away by a mortar, intestines spilling out of a gaping red hole in his belly. He holds them in with his hands and walks on blindly, toward the fog-shrouded distance. Others, dimly seen, are following behind him. A platoon of them, a company, an army.

"Who are they?" he asks Froggy. "Where are they going?"

Froggy waltzes in circles, holding a phantom partner in his arms, grinning. "Oh, can't you hear the drumming? To the battleground they're coming. Why, they're playing their song, they are, they are." He snaps his fingers. "What's the title of that album again? Slipped my mind, it did, it did."

"*Music to Wake the Dead*," whispers Sandy.

Froggy winks at him broadly, jerks a thumb at the stumbling dead. "It's gotta be rock 'n' roll music if you wanna march with them."

Edan Morse walks among the dead now. Even in death, he still bleeds. His bare feet leave dark red footprints on the cobblestones as he walks. He is coughing, dragging himself onward in a halting, pained, jerky shuffle, coughing. He sees Sandy. "Stop, stop, stop all the dancing," he cries out, pleading, "give me time to breathe." He clutches for help, his hand covered by a fine mist of blood, but Sandy is suddenly afraid and he lurches away, runs from the parade.

The side street closes in, growing narrow and crooked. Sandy is alone now, lost, frightened. Huge, tortured, familiar faces leer at him from shadows and come rushing out of the rain. He cries out, runs, stumbles and falls. When he pushes himself up again, his hands are raw and scraped.

A doorway looms in front of him. It is brightly lit, a haven in the choking dark, spilling the most wonderful radiance, a shining translucence that draws him closer. Bambi sits in the doorway in the lotus position, a dozen wide-eyed children at her feet. She is huge with child, and smiling with a deep inner peace, and she speaks in a soft, contented voice of what lies beyond that door. He has to hear what she is saying, hear the words of wisdom, learn the answers. He pushes through the children, into the light. Bambi looks up at him, smiles, opens her mouth. "Oo ee oo ah ah," she says, "ting tang walla walla bing bang. Oo ee oo ah ah, ting tang walla walla bing bang."

"No!" he shouts, shying away. Around him, the children turn savage. They pull at his ankles, pelt him with chocolate cupcakes, with incense sticks, with crosses, with tiny cups of grape Kool-Aid. Wild and afraid, he kicks at them, breaks free, runs back into the dark, away from the false light.

The shadows grow deeper all around him. The street becomes a mere footpath now, pressing in, turning and twisting. He moves through a misty labyrinth. The brick walls are wet, slimy, and covered with graffiti, mocking slogans in strange tongues. He cannot read the words. From darkened doors to nowhere, brightly painted whores call out to him. They wear mini-dresses in Day-Glo colors over huge breasts and meaty thighs, but the darkness makes the colors repellent, and their faces are skeletal, eyes hungry and worn under all that green eyeshadow.

Ahead, another light is flickering. He runs to it, gasping, and emerges in a great square full of people. Tall black buildings tower on all sides, blotting out the sky. Huge electric billboards flash insistently. The crowd is chanting, bowing, kneeling in worship to the signs. They are singing advertising jingles, offering money. Fights break out as the billboards compete for attention, turning sections of the crowd against one another. The atmosphere crackles. Slogans and cartoons loom impossibly large and threaten to fall on him. Neon tubes sizzle everywhere, blinking, stabbing, beckoning. He feels a hand on his shoulder and turns. Lark smiles at him and begins to speak, but no sound comes from his mouth. Sandy backs away. Again the dark closes around him.

For hours he stumbles through blind alleys and wicked streets that loop back upon themselves, until finally he emerges on the main thoroughfare again, the long, straight avenue with its tall iron street lamps haloed in the fog. But the street is empty now and he has lost all sense of direction and does not know where to go. He wanders to the middle of the street and stands there, baffled, helpless, looking first in one direction and then in the other, afraid to move, the blank gray walls of fog growing solid all around him. Around and around and around he turns, in dizzy circles.

Then the fog parts a little and the Nazgûl are there. They are carrying their instruments, playing them as they walk, and others are walking behind them, an army of shadows, an army of memories, an army of good intent. Sandy walks with them for a while. "Where are you going?" he asks Gopher John, Maggio, Faxon. None of them will answer. Faxon bleeds from old wounds, and only the songs will salve his hurt. Maggio's body is a ghastly thing of skin and bones, running with open sores. Gopher John beats on a big bass drum as he strides, and his eyes are far away. But Hobbins walks in front, sure-footed, laughing, and he draws Sandy aside. His red eyes are burning, pinpoints of fire in the fog, and his mouth twists in grim amusement. "C'mon now," he says, "we're marching to the sea," and then he whirls and leaps out on ahead. The Nazgûl follow, and behind them the long, long column winds, but Sandy is no longer sure. He moves to the side, huddles in a door. The door has been bricked shut and he finds no refuge there; eventually the column passes, and he is alone again.

He sinks to the ground and sits there, his back against the cold wet bricks, his face blank. He sits for days, but the fog does not melt away, nor does the sun come up. Sometimes he thinks he hears familiar music, dimly and far off, from the direction the Nazgûl had taken. Yet sometimes it is not music at all, but only the sound of battle. He is tempted to go that way. He feels abandoned and lonely.

His head is cradled in his hands, so he does not see Maggie emerge from the fog, does not see where she has come from. But suddenly she is there. She holds his hand, and he looks up at her. "Where have all my lovers gone?" she asks in a plaintive voice. He knows what the answer should be, but he cannot say it. She smiles at him, a brave crooked smile, but her eyes are tired and sad. She pulls him to his feet, back out into the street, back out into the fog. But then she hesitates, and Sandy knows that she is as lost as he is. He hears the music once more. It gives him a direction, the only direction left in this terrible gray world. He takes her hand, pulls her, and they set out down the street. The music grows louder as they walk. Maggie is smiling now, and they hurry, although once, when he is near to running, she holds him back and complains that he moves too fast. He slows, and they move on, tireless. Her hand feels good in his, and her face is familiar, accepting, content.

Then, in the center of the road, they come upon the motorcycle. It is a big motorized trike, painted red, white, and blue, and Slum is seated upon it, bare feet up on the handlebars, flowers threaded through his massive beard, a gentle smile on his face. He sees which way they are walking and shakes his head. The motortrike is pointed in the other direction.

"You don't understand," Sandy says patiently. "There's nothing for us there. This way. Come this way." He points.

The porkpie hat on Slum's head moves of its own accord, lifts, and a tiny black kitten peers out from underneath. Slum takes it down, pets it, sighs. "I'm sorry," he says, "that's a war down there. I don't believe in killing."

"But we're fighting for . . . for things that matter," Sandy says.

"That's what Butcher says," Slum observes.

"You're a coward," Maggie says accusingly. Or is it Maggie? Her voice sounds strange, and her hand has gone cold. It is ridged with callus along the edge of her palm. "Coward," she repeats.

"That's what Butcher says," Slum observes again.

"War is just if the cause is just," Ananda says with passion. "Sometimes killing is necessary."

"That's what Butcher says," Slum observes.

"If you're not part of the solution, you're part of the problem," Ananda argues. "If you're not one of us, you're one of the enemy. We got battle lines being drawn."

"Nobody's right if everyone's wrong," Slum says.

Butcher Byrne steps from the fog, holding a shotgun. He is dressed in khaki, with a face like death. "Beware," he says. He trains the gun on his son. Ananda draws a gun of her own and faces him. "Beware," she says. Or is it Butcher again? Their voices sound just the same.

"One, two, three, what are they fighting for?" Slum asks, shrugging.

"Slum, I'm lost," Sandy says. "Where do I go?"

"Follow the river," Slum suggests. "Follow the children. Follow the neon in young lovers' eyes."

"How?" he says. "I can't . . . can't leave it all. Froggy, Maggie, Lark, Bambi, me. You. You especially. I have to go back with her, have to help it change. You don't know the things that he's done to you."

Slum reaches into his Slum suit and brings out a photograph. He hands it out to Sandy and says, "Time, see what's become of me." It is a snapshot of a different Jefferson Davis Byrne, a clean-shaven gaunt man whose eyes are wary and wasted, dressed all in white, mouth open in surprise or pain.

Sandy nods. "You see?" he says. "You know, then. Why I have to go with her? Why we have to go back?"

"Nope," Slum says.

"The picture. The way you've hurt. All of us."

"Ah, but I was so much older then, I'm younger than that now." Slum taps the photograph again. It is changed. The man in the picture is heavy almost to the point of fat, with a big spade-shaped beard streaked with gray. He is wearing a denim shirt and a red bandanna; his cheeks are full and ruddy, and his smile is very broad. It is Slum; an older, healthier, happier Slum. Sandy looks up at him. "It's never too late," Slum explains. "I got life, right?"

Sandy is confused. He takes a step back, looks around. The fog still moves silently around Ananda and Butcher, who face each other with drawn guns, faces hard, locked in an eternal tableau.

"I don't know," Sandy says. "I'm so confused."

"The best lack all conviction," Slum tells him, "while the worst are full of passionate intensity." He pets his kitten, tucks him back into his hat, replaces the hat on his head. Maggie is on the motortrike behind him, her arms wrapped around his waist. She is smiling too, and Sandy does not know how he could have overlooked her. Slum grabs the handles, kicks down, and the motortrike roars to noisy life.

"Where are you going?" Sandy asks, desperate. He does not want to be alone in the fog. He does not want to be left with Ananda and Butcher. He is afraid of them.

Slum points. "There is a road, no simple highway, between the dawn and the dark of night."

"Take me with you."

Slum shakes his head. "Sorry. If I knew your way, I'd take you home, but where I'm going, no one may follow."

"Slum, I have to stop it. It's all coming down. Confrontation, war, armageddon. They don't understand. It will destroy all of them, the Nazgûl, Larry Richmond, Francie . . . they're going to use her in some kind of sacrifice, Slum, and the gates of hell are going to open and all the dead are going to come back."

"Then stop it, Sandy. Change it." He revs the trike.

"Wait," Sandy calls out. "I can't do it alone."

Maggie grins at him crookedly from beneath her broken nose. "Sure you can, love," she says. She jerks a thumb upward. "Superman and Green

Lantern ain't got nothing on you." Slum presses the accelerator, and they roar off, ripping through the billowing fog, rending it into fine white ribbons. Sandy stands and watches as they vanish in the distance. The tunnel they drive through the mist does not close. He begins to follow it, moving faster and faster. At last he begins to run, and finally, finally, he sees a sun, a great white sun shining down at the end of the road. He rushes toward it, and the sun grows and grows until it fills his universe and drives away the shreds of dream.

He came to lying on a narrow rollaway bed in a cluttered motel room. The curtains were open, and sunlight was streaming through the window onto his face. Sandy threw a hand across his eyes and struggled to sit up. His head swam. He was groggy and disoriented. He looked around, not recognizing the room. Where was he? How had he come here? For a moment, his only memory was a vague terrifying recollection of wandering endless fog-shrouded streets and holding strange surreal conversations. And then the dream began to unravel, and the other memories came rushing back. He remembered Denver and the room in the Hilton, Edan Morse and Gort lying dead, and Ananda's three soft kisses.

"Jesus," he blurted. He got up with a real effort, reeled, almost fell again. He was very unsteady. His head was pounding.

The room was empty, the twin beds unmade. A newspaper had been thrown on one. He picked up a section, stared at the letters for a long moment, unable to make any sense out of the headlines. Then he realized it was the sports section, and suddenly it all clicked into place. The paper was the *Albuquerque Journal*, dated September 20. He threw it down on the bed, glanced out the window again. It looked to be late afternoon from the position of the sun.

Sandy was sick and hurting. Strange pains seemed to be stabbing at his body at random. He had a bad case of the chills, and there were needle marks all up and down his right arm. But he forced himself to move to the bathroom, to undress and shower and stand under the cold, icy spray until the water had washed away the dregs of his long drugged sleep. When he dried himself, he felt better, a lot better.

His car keys were on top of the television set. In the closet he found fresh clothes...and something else. A rifle. Black and oiled, with a sling strap and a big telescopic sight. Sandy knew nothing about guns, had never fired a gun in his life. But he picked up the rifle and held it, ran his hands over it, drawn to it. He had to stop them, he thought. He remembered the way the Nazgûl had been stopped once before, in 1971.

Daydream was parked right outside. She was filthy, streaked with road dust, her nose and windshield covered with dead bugs. It made him incredibly, irrationally angry. He opened the rear hatch, tossed in the rifle, emptied a duffle bag of dirty laundry on top of it. He climbed in and started her up. His digital watch said it was 4:49. He would have to hurry.

TWENTY-SEVEN

This is the end/
My only friend the end

He had expected to fight the afternoon rush, but the streets of Albuquerque were oddly empty as Sandy sped west toward the lowering sun. The sky was pale eggshell blue, a shade somehow magical and very fragile; he knew it could not last for long. The people he glimpsed on the sidewalks seemed too quiet, almost hushed; of the other cars he spotted infrequently, at least half had their headlights burning. He wondered what that meant. It was as if an eerie stillness hung over the city, reminding him of the stillness of dawn on that morning, so long ago, when Peter Faxon had taken him up to the mesa to ride in the Flying Eye.

Someone told me long ago, there's a calm before the storm, he thought. And he feared that he'd see rain, and plenty of it, before the night was through.

On the edge of town, he hit the roadblock.

Daydream hugged a long dusty curve, and there they were; two state police cars blocking the road, and on the shoulder a big brown canvas-covered truck and jeep. The jeep had a machine gun mounted in the back, Sandy saw, and armed National Guardsmen were crouched on both sides of the road. He heard a shrill whistle and saw a cop waving him over. He braked and swung Daydream off to the side of the road. Popping his seat belt, he opened the door and started to climb out, but someone grabbed him and spun him around hard, shoving him down against the hood of the car. "Assume the position!" a harsh voice barked.

Sandy spread his hands and legs and held very still while they patted him down. He got a thwack across the ass with a rifle butt when it was over. "All right, move it! Where the hell do you think you're going?"

He turned to confront a short dark Guardsman with NCO's stripes and hostile black eyes. Sandy was pretty angry himself. "What the hell is the meaning of this?" he demanded.

The Guardsman looked him over, taking in the beard, the longish hair still wet from the shower, the jeans. "Don't mouth off to me," he said. "I asked you where you thought you were going. I'm waiting for an answer."

"Up to West Mesa. To the concert."

The Guardsman was studying the Mazda. He looked at Sandy again. "You got papers on that car?"

"Yeah, sure."

He held out his hand. "Let's see 'em." Another Guardsman had moved around to the hatch. "And open her up."

"What for?" Sandy said. He thought of the rifle in back, under those dirty clothes, and for a moment he was close to panic. "You got no authority for a search."

The NCO smiled. "You going to argue with me?" He waved, and two more men came over, rifles at the ready.

This was getting scary, Sandy thought. He backed up a step. "Wait a sec!" he said, holding up his hands. "Let me get my wallet." Reaching back slowly, he pulled it out of his jeans, flipped it open, rifled through it quickly, hoping like hell the cards were still there. He found one, pulled it loose, proffered it to the Guardsman. "See. I'm a reporter. National Metro News." He pulled out his driver's license, too. "See, look, that's me before I had the beard."

The Guardsman glanced at the card, squinted at the license, and studied Sandy's face. Reluctantly, he nodded. It was a nod Sandy remembered from the old days, a nod he'd tasted more than once before, when his press card won him a grudging change of status from one authority or another.

He pushed it. "I want to talk to whoever's in command here."

The NCO looked unhappy, but he turned to the Guardsman by his side. "Chavez, get the captain. We got a reporter here wants to see him."

Captain Mondragon was a swarthy, heavyset man about Sandy's age. He studied Sandy's ID briefly and shrugged apologetically. "I'm sorry if my men gave you a hard time," he said. "We're not used to this, you have to understand. And they're young. Boys, really. This is all very exciting to them, and some of them do get carried away."

"What's happening here?" Sandy asked.

"You don't know?" the captain said. He seemed puzzled.

"I got put on this story this morning, flew out from New York. I hadn't been paying much attention to the wires. Give me a little background."

Mondragon was sympathetic. "Didn't give it much attention myself, until they called us up. Well, not much to tell. After all them hippies ignored the order to break up, the police figured they couldn't handle it, and we were called up. We closed off the roads, but it hasn't made much difference. They've been coming through fields, over the hills, through the mountains. I hear one bunch even flew in with a balloon. We don't have enough men to cordon off the whole area. Right now, we're just waiting for reinforcements. There's talk of sending us in to disperse the crowd. I guess it'll come to that if there's trouble."

"Yeah? How do you feel about that?"

"Some of my men are eager for the chance. There have been some scuffles already. The cops tried to go in and make some arrests and got the hell beaten out of them. Personally, I'd just as soon let 'em play their damned music."

"How many are up there?"

Mondragon shrugged. "Our official estimate is a hundred thousand."

Sandy whistled. That was almost twice as many as had come to West Mesa in 1971. "I'm supposed to cover this," he said. "I have to get by."

"I know how it is when you got a job to do," Mondragon said. He plucked at his uniform unhappily. "Well, go on then. You'll have to take the car around the shoulder, but if you take it slow you shouldn't get stuck. I warn you, get out quick if there's trouble. I heard there's talk of sending in tanks, calling up the Regular Army. Things could get nasty real fast, and no one will know that you're just a reporter. They say they got some guns in there, too."

"They say," Sandy said grimly. He thanked the captain, got back into Daydream, and edged it off the shoulder, over a bumpy, rutted, hard-packed field, until he was past the roadblock. Back on the road, he took off.

He saw other Guardsmen, patrols sweeping through the surrounding countryside, and once he spotted a man crouched behind a juniper, reporting into a walkie-talkie. He passed an old school bus parked by the side of the road. Then other vehicles; Volkswagens and Cadillacs, pick-ups and panel trucks, vans and campers, more and more until both sides of the highway were lined solidly with them.

By then he could hear music, the faint but unmistakable sound of "Johnny B. Goode." It was not the Nazgûl. In 1971, the Nazgûl had come on at dusk, after a succession of lesser bands had played all day; Ananda had no doubt made the same arrangements this time. The road turned to dirt, and Sandy drove more slowly. Couples walked arm-in-arm and moved out of his way, waving cheerfully as he passed, while children careened past on bikes made unsteady by the rocks. The surrounding fields were spotted with tents and sleeping bags and fires and small knots of dancers, although the sound was still weak this far off. Sandy had to swerve around one couple making love in the middle of the road; a minute later he passed through a running swarm of laughing, bare-chested men playing some game with a basketball.

Finally he could take the car no farther. At the intersection of two dirt roads, a huge semi was parked at an angle, cutting off all access. On top of it stood a woman in a jumpsuit and red armband, directing traffic. She waved him toward the field on the right, a solid mass of parked cars on top of a prairie dog village. As he climbed out, he saw one prairie dog pushing a beer bottle out of its hole. It spied him and vanished. Sandy felt sorry for it. Other vehicles arrived from God knows where, boxing him in. He waited until he was unobserved, opened the hatch, and fit the rifle into the duffle bag he used to carry his dirty laundry. He carried it as he proceeded on foot.

With every step, the crowds grew thicker and the music louder. He passed the first sound tower, a hastily erected metal skeleton looming over the landscape, a ring of amps atop it, booming out the music. The stage itself was not even in sight; the tower must be rigged for radio transmittal, Sandy realized. There had been no towers at West Mesa in 1971, just the huge amplifiers up on the stage, but what worked for a crowd of sixty thousand would not suffice for this larger assembly.

How much larger he realized only slowly, as he slogged onward. He made a rough guess that the big sound towers were two miles apart, and he passed three more of them on the road. By then the sun was low against the western sky, and the clouds that were forming there were an ominous purple-black color, like great bruised fruits about to burst with blood. Against that sky, the towers stood in stark black silhouette. They reminded Sandy of the nightmares he had had of Martian war-machines when he read *War of the Worlds* as a kid; like the deadly Martian striders, each sound tower had three great metal legs, but instead of heat rays they were armed with sound, sound that thundered through the pregnant air of dusk and shook the earth, sound that filled the world and burned the soul. The music was a living, pounding, deafening thing near the towers, but it was there that the people clustered most thickly. They lay on blankets and on towels, fully clothed or naked or half-dressed, alone or in pairs. They sat on rocks and passed joints or bottles around. They clapped their hands and sang along with the music. They danced, and danced, and danced. A few brave souls even climbed the towers and stretched out on the hot metal, enveloped in the music. The crowds ringed the towers, each tower circled more densely than the last, until there was no empty space at all between towers, until the world was a solid sea of people, on the road and off it, bright clothes and music and human flesh everywhere. And then Sandy knew that the "official estimate" that Captain Mondragon had given him, like all the official police estimates of rock gatherings and demonstrations in the old days, was ridiculously, deliberately, infuriatingly low. One hundred thousand, Mondragon had said. Sandy was still enough of a journalist to gauge the size of a crowd. West Mesa held at least three times that number, and maybe considerably more. *By the time we got to Woodstock, we were half a million strong.* He shivered as from a sudden chill when he recalled that Albuquerque itself had fewer bodies than had gathered here on its fringe.

He passed a line of porta-sans, with hundreds waiting patiently for the use of each facility. The band was playing "Proud Mary" hard and hot. To the west, the sun was fading fast. The clouds filled the horizon, a wall of sullen purple. He passed a hot-air balloon, tethered to the ground below, its envelope a bright yellow smiley face. Three women in the gondola waved to friends below, while a man studied the distance through a telescope. The band played "Summer in the City," but the heat was beginning to dissipate now with the setting of the sun, and in a few hours the high desert would actually be cold. He passed a white hot-dog truck, shut tightly, a big sign on its side that read SOLD OUT. Spray-painted, disapproving comments overlay the lettering. PROFITEER! had been written in red and CARNIVORES! even larger in green. A different band played "Riders on the Storm." Faces grew indistinct in the twilight. His feet hurt.

Far ahead, across a surging plain of humanity, Sandy saw the stage, awash in shifting colored light. Nearby stood a slim black man with a Fu Manchu mustache and binoculars around his neck. Sandy borrowed the binoculars and took a closer look. He studied the instruments, the musicians, the crowd that eddied and danced around the stage, the security force pushing off those who tried to climb up. The platform stood ten feet off the ground; behind it loomed a metal gridwork thirty feet tall, supporting banks of amps and lighting tracks. Two huge hardwood beams braced the whole structure, crossing in a great X behind the performers.

Sandy tried to return the binoculars, but the man who had lent them to him had vanished. He kept them and moved on. The last two sound towers stood about two thousand feet from the stage, one on each side, angled outward. He made his way toward the closest, the one to the right of the crowd.

It was slow going. Darkness was settling fast now and the ground underfoot was uneven and rocky. People were everywhere, pushing him first this way, then that. He had to fight through them, clutching tight to the duffle bag, sometimes carrying it before him, chest high, like a baby. Once a woman pressed up against him, a slender, pretty redhead with vacant eyes. Her blouse was tied around her waist, and her small breasts touched his chest. "Want to ball?" she asked. Wordless, he moved away from her. Later he collided with a hairy man in denim colors ornamented with swastikas and peace signs, and the man glowered and said, "Who the fuck you pushing, man? You want to get cut? I'll cut you, asshole." Then he was gone too, swept away by the crosscurrents of swaying flesh.

When Sandy was a hundred yards from the tower, the stage lights went off, and the world grew silent.

You could feel the silence spread through the crowd. The music stopped and the dancing died and conversations ceased, out and out in ever-widening ripples. "Yes," he heard a woman near him whisper in a low, hoarse voice. "Yes," the way she might urge a lover who was riding her to climax. "Yes, yes, yes."

He glimpsed motion on the darkened stage. The sound system made a sibilant hiss and spoke.

"THIS IS THE HOUR," it said.

"THE *HOUR!*" the audience screamed back, half a million voices rending the silence. Miles away, Captain Mondragon and his men must have heard the sound, like some vast tidal wave breaking against the mountains. Sandy lifted the binoculars just as the smoky red light came on, all blood and fire, and there was Gopher John Slozewski scowling on his throne among those black-and-crimson drums.

"THIS IS THE DAY," the amps roared.

"THE *DAY!*" answered the crowd, and a second light came up, a sickly green light, alive with decay, and there stood Rick Maggio sneering, fingers poised over the strings of his guitar.

"THIS IS THE YEAR."

"THE *YEAR!*" they shrieked, and a deep violet spot came up and outlined Peter Faxon and his Rickenbacker, making him a dim, bruised, expressionless shadow. He was wearing a familiar jacket, a white leather jacket with long trailing fringe, and in the violet light the old bloodstains looked almost black.

"OF..."

"THE NAZGUUUUUUUUUUL!!!" the multitudes screamed and all the lights came up at once, sweeping back and forth across the stage, shifting, dancing, flashing on and off in a wild hypnotic strobelike rhythm, a rhythm that caught every small motion and froze it and magnified it and etched it clear to see. And Patrick Henry Hobbins came walking out on stage in a black denim suit with an American flag sewn on the crotch, the Eye of Mordor where the stars should have been, and he put on his Gibson and laughed the largest laugh in the world, said, "Yeah! All right, you fuckers, get set. We're gonna rock you till your ears bleed!" and they screamed even more, frenzied in their welcome, and Hobbins pounded on his guitar and the music surged out of the amplifiers, fiercer and more terribly alive than any sound in the world, and Hobbins' voice rang out across the miles.

Hey baby, what's that in the skyyyyy?!

Fireworks arched overhead, spreading sheets of phantom flame, while the Nazgûl sang "Napalm Love" and the audience clapped and cheered below. Sandy lowered the binoculars. He could feel the impact of the music. It was coursing through his bloodstream, touching him, shaking him. He wanted to join in, to let go of his rifle and slap his hands together and melt into the mass around him, to let it all happen. But he couldn't, he couldn't. He bit his lip and pushed on, toward the tower.

It was the same set as Denver. Red Rocks had been the dry run; West Mesa was for real. He could feel the excitement in the crowd around him, could feel the change begin, all those thousands and hundreds of thousands flowing into one another, becoming as one, one vast beast with half a million pairs of eyes and a single voice, a single heart, beating faster now, beating faster and harder and stronger. He glanced up, and the stars looked back at him with a billion yellow eyes. He could not see them twinkling. They were hard and icy and oh-so-steady, looking down.

With every step the sound pulsed louder, the crowd went wilder. Sandy found that he was fighting the music almost as if it were a living thing, a tenacious dark creature that wrestled against him every inch of the way. Song after song, he shoved his way through, forcing people aside, moving into the teeth of the music. The sound grew louder as he neared the tower, louder and still louder. It roared at him, it hissed and snarled, it buffeted him like some ancient preternatural wind sweeping out of nowhere, out of unimaginable blackness. It took him endless effort to make a yard of progress. He pressed on, through "Elf Rock" and "Cold Black Water" and "Crazy Cara," struggling against the foot-stomping beat of "Jackhammer Blues," against the bodies that swayed to "Poison Henry" and boogied to "Schuylkill River." He heard the screams when Maggio took off his shirt and tossed it out into the crowd, saw the colored smoke billowing off the stage when the Nazgûl plunged full-force into "Makin' War." As they did, a small gap opened in the wall of bodies in front of Sandy. He saw it and plunged through, up against the base of the sound tower. Movement in the crowd threatened to tear him away from it; he grabbed hold of the great metal leg and held on for dear life. "*Makin' war, makin' war, makin' war, war, WAR!*" the crowd was singing, over and over again as Maggio and Hobbins jammed.

"*Get the fuck off there!*" he heard a familiar voice shout, close at hand.

A few feet away, a girl had climbed up on the scaffolding. The shout was directed at her, from above. "*Get the fuck off the tower!*" the voice said, and a burly man leaned over from the girder on which he balanced, swung a nunchaku hard against the girl's fingers. She screeched, let go, and fell down onto the others below.

On the stage, red and yellow and white lights flashed in blinding explosive sequence. The reflections shone off the silver-mirror sunglasses on the man above. "*Makin' war, makin' war, makin' war, war, WAR!*" Gopher John lit into a long drum solo. Everyone was screaming, whistling, writhing. Sandy, silent, stared up at Mirrors. There was no help for it.

He waited until Mirrors had glanced away, then pulled himself up onto the tower, and began to climb. The thing had been put together with bare sharp metal. It dug into his palms painfully when he pulled. Under his arm, the duffle bag was awkward and heavy, and it kept slipping. Again and again he had to stop, adjust it, start over. He was scarcely ten feet up, on the same level as the guard, when Mirrors turned and saw him.

Sandy tried to flinch away, to conceal himself in the shadow of the tower's leg, but it was no good; he had been seen. Mirrors came toward him, walking along a girder as sure-footed as a cat, his nunchaku in hand. No retreat, Sandy thought. He braced himself against the leg, prepared to use the rifle as a club.

Then Mirrors stopped. "You," he said. He nodded. "Didn't recognize you. Go on up." He smiled and turned his back.

For an instant Sandy stood in disbelief, his body stiff with tension. Then he grabbed the rifle awkwardly again and resumed his climb.

He was not in good shape. He had to stop three or four times to catch his breath. The duffle bag with the rifle was impossible, and twice he almost dropped it. Finally he stopped, stripped off his sweater, and used it to tie the duffle bag to his back in a crude sling. That was better, but even so, he was only sixty feet up when the Nazgûl took their break, to cacophonous applause, whistling, shouting. The steady, rhythmic clapping from hundreds of thousands of hands was so loud that it sent tremors through the sound tower, and there was an awful moment when Sandy was certain that the resonance was about to bring down the entire structure. But then the Nazgûl came back out, in answer to the summons. Sandy hung on the side of the tower and watched. Hobbins took a swig from a flask, and Maggio took a pill, and then the sound started again as they opened the second and final set with "Blood on the Sheets." He was only twenty feet from the top then, and the shrill whistle from the amps so close at hand was an ear-shattering knife of sound that hurt his teeth and almost pried him loose from his precarious perch. He hung on, wincing, swaying, his teeth gritting together. Then, almost desperate, he scrambled up the final twenty feet, and pulled himself onto the platform where the amplifiers were mounted. They *shook* with the volume of the music. The sound level was deafening. Sandy pulled Kleenex out of his pockets, wet them in his mouth, stuffed them in his ears. That helped, a little, but there was no escaping the music. It was all around him. He rolled over on his back, gasping from the climb. His hands were raw and bloody. For long moments, he just wanted to lie there.

They did a long, driven version of "Blood on the Sheets," and they did "Ash Man" too, and still Sandy could not find the strength to move. Then he heard Rick Maggio's slashing, rumbling, pissed-off voice screaming out from the huge amps, right through the makeshift earplugs he had rigged. "The fuckers tried to keep us from playing here tonight," Maggio was saying. "What do you say to that?"

"FUCK 'EM!" the crowd screamed back.

"They said this gathering was il-*legal,* wouldja believe it?" Maggio snarled. "They said to stay home. They said to break it up."

"FUCK 'EM!" shouted a half million hoarse voices.

Maggio laughed. "Damn right! They're out there now, you know. The fuckers still want to stop us. They got tanks and they got guns and they got fucking *napalm,* but they ain't gonna stop us, not this time, I guaran-fucking-*tee* it! *Are* they?"

"*HELL NO!*"

"But maybe they're gonna try. And if they do, I don't give a damn. Know why? 'Cause I'm *mad!*"

"How mad are you?"

A stab of sound from the Fender Telecaster, amplified thousands of times; a single, jolting, searing, blazing, screeching chord that shuddered through the night. "Why," said Maggio, "I'm positively *ragin'*!" The Nazgûl exploded into sound, the beat came hammering down and Maggio sang his fury.

> Ain't gonna take it easy
> Won't go along no more
> Tired of gettin' stepped on
> When I'm down here on the floor

Sandy rolled over, crawled to the edge of the platform, unzipped the duffle bag and drew out the rifle. He kicked the duffle bag off the platform and watched it fall into the crowd that raged and seethed below. Sandy braced the rifle, sighted down on Maggio. He was closer now, and the telescopic sight had greater magnification than the binoculars. He could see everything clearly. Maggio was sweating profusely. The sores on his ravaged face had been covered with makeup, but the sweat had made the pancake run and now they looked open and ugly and painful. Rivulets of moisture ran down Maggio's chest under the lights. Sandy could count the ribs. Maggio was putting everything he had left into his song, pouring vitriol over all the injustice of the world, sneering down at his guitar as he bled it dry. The song roared from the sound system like a demon wind, but it was only one man's hurt and pain, all the bitterness and insecurity and fear that lived inside of Rick Maggio, coming back with a vengeance.

"How I'm ragin'," sang Maggio.

"RAGIN'!" they answered, taking his pain.

The music was hot enough to raise blisters.

Maggio was square in the crosshairs. Sandy slid his finger around the trigger. He could end it now. Maggio was the worst of them, he thought. A weak man, a bitter man, a man who didn't know how to love, only to hurt. He wouldn't be missed. Take Maggio instead of Hobbins, he thought, and the world will be better off.

"RAGIN'!" they screamed.

In the scope, Maggio's perspiration looked almost like tears. Sandy took his finger off the trigger. Not Maggio. No. Maggio, vile as he might be, was an innocent. He couldn't kill him, no matter what the price. The Nazgûl were pawns in this, all of them but one. All of them but Patrick Henry Hobbins. It would be different with Hobbins, Sandy thought. That would not be murder. After all, Hobbins was already dead.

As Maggio sang, Francie appeared on stage, dancing around, hands clapping above her head, eyes closed. The sight of her, moving to the music in front of that vast X, gave Sandy a cold feeling.

When the song ended and the applause finally wound down, Hobbins moved up front again. The lights narrowed in, shining on his face alone, on that pale white mask and those blazing red eyes. "Are your ears bleeding yet?" he asked with a grin.

"FUCK NOOOOOO!" they roared back.

"Well, well," Hobbins said. "Guess we got to play *louder*, then!" The opening bars of "Survivor" surged up around him.

> *Well, he came back from the war zone all intact*
> *And they told him just how lucky he had been*

It was the slowest song on the album; Hobbins stood stationary as he sang. Sandy sighted down on him. The crosshairs framed the pale forehead, covered with wisps of white hair. Now? he thought. He hesitated, then lowered the rifle. Not now. It wasn't . . . wasn't right, somehow. It had to be later, during a different song.

He looked up. The stars still shone overhead, but the clouds were moving in quickly now, eating them up one by one. Still, there would be no thunderstorm tonight, no wild lightning strikes scoring the blackness. These were a different sort of cloud, darker, quiet, sliding across the night sky like ink. With them came a coldness, and a stillness, and a silence that threatened to engulf even the music of the Nazgûl.

Sandy found himself listening to that music now, really listening to it for a little while, putting aside all thought of the thing he must do in a minute or two or ten. The song was as sad as heartbreak, and as inevitable. The music had a power to it. Whatever else they might be, the Nazgûl were still a hell of a rock band. They touched him now as they had first touched him many years ago, when he was a teenager listening to their first album on his first record player. His parents never understood. They could never hear the joy in rock, the life in it, the beauty. "Noise," his father called it. His mother, who went to too many PTA meetings and church services, was worse. "The devil's music," she would snap. He had to hide his Doors albums from her.

Sandy thought of Jamie Lynch, screaming his anguish in the night, tied to his desk, bleeding his life away on a concert poster. He thought of the teenagers burning in the Gopher Hole, pounding at locked doors until the metal grew red hot and the smoke rose around them. He thought of Balrog, gutted in an alley, and of the blood in Edan's eyes, and the sound Gort's neck had made when it snapped. Maybe she had been right, he thought.

But the music poured from the great amps behind him, a song that was liquid and haunting and made him want to weep and storm and make things better, and Sandy knew that it wasn't so, had never been so. He took up the binoculars again and looked through them, not at the stage now, but at the crowd. He did not know what he was looking for. He found only faces. A fat man with a stoned smile. A gorgeous young woman riding on the shoulders of her boyfriend, her eyes closed. Another woman, plain and fat, dancing now, dancing all by herself but not alone, because she was part of it all, part of the crowd and part of the music and part of the night. A biker, maybe the same one who had threatened to cut him earlier, bobbing awkwardly to the beat, the tension gone from his face. Good and bad, old and young, male and female, happy and sad. Faces. People.

It was a good concert, he thought numbly as he lowered the glasses. West Mesa had been a terrific concert back in 1971, he recalled; everyone had agreed about that; it had been fantastic until that shot had been fired from the darkness, until Hobbins had died in blood and silence, his song incomplete. And now it had to happen again, and he had to pull the trigger. Didn't he? *Didn't he?*

The thought made him sick.

Out there, below him, they were applauding again, in the hundreds and the thousands, they were gathered round their fires and their towers, they were holding hands and hugging one another and dancing together and singing and whistling and clapping, while he lay up here alone. The song had ended, Sandy realized dimly. And now the music began once more, but the bottom was harder and heavier, and the guitar licks taunting, wicked.

Turning and turning in the widening gyre

From a half million throats came a whispered promise that sighed across the darkness.

He's coming!

Hobbins leaned into the lyrics while the guitars sang.

The falcon cannot hear the falconer

And Sandy studied him through the rifle's scope. It seemed as though Hobbins was staring straight back at him, as if those dark red eyes looked deep into his own, as if Hobbins sang only for him.

> *The best lack all conviction, while the worst*
> *Oh, they're full of passion, and intensity*

Now, Sandy thought, as an ocean of people sang, *He's coming!* louder and still louder with each repetition. But he did not pull the trigger. *The best lack all conviction.* Why did he hesitate? It wouldn't be murder. Patrick Henry Hobbins had died in 1971, after all. This was only some demonic doppelgänger. That was a dead man singing down there.

> *Oh, yes, I know, I know*
> *That twenty centuries of stony sleep*
> *Were vexed to nightmare by a rockin' cradle*
> *Oh, a rocknrollin' cradle!*

But what about Larry Richmond? Maybe that was Hobbins singing, but it was Richmond's body. Kill Hobbins, and Richmond died, too. And Hobbins...Sandy remembered him from the old days. Arrogant, brash, full of himself and his own success and his talent, maybe a little fucked up on drugs, maybe just starting to crack...but a monster? No. Just a rock singer, a good rock singer, hardly more than a kid. Faxon had known him best of all, and Faxon had loved him.

"*HE'S COMING!*" they screamed.

"*HE'S COMING!!*"

"*HE'S COMING!!!*"

And the lights went down, all but one, and Hobbins stood there, looking out at all of them, out at the stars, and he smiled at them and he said, "*I'm here.*"

"Yes," Sandy whispered. And he knew it was true. But who was here, who, *who*? The Antichrist? The devil? Some monster? Or only the Hobbit?

The Nazgûl went into "Prelude to Madness." Stretched out on the tower, the cold metal underneath him, the amplifiers pounding at his back, Sandy listened and watched them. One more song, only one more. Then it would be "The Armageddon Rag," but Edan Morse had said it, the resurrection was a lie, it would be armageddon forever and the blood would never stop flowing. He had to stop it. Didn't he?

Charlie is the joker in the deck

And he was Charlie. "Sorry, Charlie," Hobbins said to him at Red Rocks, and Ananda had admitted it later, and that was why she hadn't killed him. Morse had seen it coming all along, had seen him there at the end, had seen him up here between the earth and stars, with this rifle in his hand. Sandy felt a coldness along his spine. If Morse knew it, Ananda knew it too, didn't she? Knew where he'd be. Knew why.

The car keys on top of the television.

Unguarded.

Waking at just the right time.

Mirrors smiling, turning his back.

Queens beat aces every time, yeah!

Do queens beat jokers, too? he wondered. He wasn't sure; he wasn't sure of anything. The Nazgûl were singing, and half a million people sang along.

Wolfman looked into the mirror
and Lon Chaney looked back out

Sandy stared up at the black, churning, overcast sky. A cold wind shivered through him. The rifle felt heavy and oily in his hand, alien. Wavering discords and strange echoes vibrated through the air around him. He studied the stage again, saw Francie dancing, saw the huge X behind her. Unless he shot, they would nail her up, bleed her, strip her, rip her eyes out while the crowd danced to the Rag, the endless Rag, while the demons gathered outside and no one listened to his warning. Unless he stopped it. Unless he shot.

Or ... or maybe ... *if* he shot?

West Mesa, 1971. A bullet from nowhere, Hobbins dead, sixty thousand people in a blind panic. Eight dead, hundreds injured. And now? Another shot, another bloody body, the music shattered for good and all, but the crowd was so much bigger tonight, and they would know the enemy had done it, the enemy who had tried to stop them all along, the enemy out there in their tanks and jeeps and uniforms, the enemy that ringed them, penned them in like animals. For a moment he could see it clearly, as real as the ghosts who had warred in the streets of Chicago that night. They would tear down the towers in their rage and grief, they would pull one another to pieces, and Ananda and her red-armbanded cadres would nail up Francie and make the blood sacrifice and seize control, and Hobbins would rise again from the dead and the band would play on, play on and on forever, play "The Armageddon Rag" to the darkness and the cold while the corpse armies gathered and spread out across the night.

The music had stopped. "Prelude to Madness" had run its course. And now, very slowly, it began.

> This is the land all causes lead to,
> This is the land where the mushrooms grow.

He could see them on the horizon again, could hear the long gasp from below as the crowd saw them, too; phantom towers of red and purple and burning indigo, crowned with blinding fire, blossoming slowly, engulfing the world with fury and hate.

> To the battleground I'm coming,
> Oh, don't you hear the drumming?
> They're playing the armageddon rag, oh!
> Playin' the armageddon rag!

What if he was wrong, though? What if he did nothing and he was wrong? Hobbins danced through the gunsights. Hobbins was moving, strutting, singing with his body as well as his voice. Sandy shifted the rifle and found him, lost him, found him, lost him. Through the scope he glimpsed Faxon, standing behind Hobbins in the line of fire. He drew a bead on the Hobbit again, hesitated, finger on the trigger. He heard Bambi telling him to believe. In what? His instincts? Or his nightmares? "You know what to do," Maggie whispered. Froggy laughed rudely and made his loud wet noise. "And then you put spaghetti in their hair, you do, you do."

> This is the day we all arrive at,
> This is the day we choose.

The world swam dizzily. The night sky was striped, bands of overcast alternating with bands of stars in clear black ink. Below was an endless army. Below was a small and frightened crowd. The sound tower seemed insubstantial. He looked down through solid metal at the ground below. On his wrist, Spiro Agnew had both hands pointed straight up.

Sandy pushed the rifle aside and stood.

He had taken three steps toward the back of the tower when she stepped out from behind the amps and stared at him, her face baffled and angry. "What are you doing?" she demanded, screaming it at him above the music. "Get back there. Shoot!" Mirrors must have told her, Sandy thought. She was so lithe and quiet, he had never even heard her ascend the tower.

"That's what you want," he shouted back at her. "It's been me all along, right? The joker in the deck. The assassin."

"Shoot him!" she screamed. She was not beautiful now. Her hair streamed in a black icy wind, and her face was distorted with an almost animal rage.

"Go put the fucking spaghetti in your hair!" Sandy told her.

> Well you're a killer too
> All the dead look just like you
> When they're playin' the armageddon rag!
> YEAH! They're playin' that armageddon rag!

She lunged for him, caught him. "Do it!" she screamed. "Do it or I'll break your fucking neck for you, just like I broke Gort's. Do it. DO IT!"

Sandy relaxed. Somehow he was not afraid. He was not afraid anymore. "It's armageddon day, baby," he said to her, "and you and me chose different sides. Shoot him yourself."

The Nazgûl went sliding off into the bridge, the long instrumental, guitars keening, wailing, drums pounding, the bass thrumming way down deep, while the vast audience below shook and stomped and called its deafening approval. Ananda looked up in panic, and poised with her hand in the air. "It's too fucking *late*," she shrieked. "I'll do it myself." She was incredibly fast. In an instant she was off him, and in another she had the rifle.

"It won't work," Sandy called out to her.

Hobbins was moving around wildly, dancing to the song, laughing. A half million people laughed and danced with him. "Hold still," Ananda muttered. "Hold *still*, fuck it!"

He moved behind her. "It's not a choice for you. It won't mean a thing. It had to be me, the joker in the deck, shooting and killing everything I used to believe in. Give it up, 'Nanda. It won't work."

She ignored him. The rifle moved in small circles as she tracked Hobbins. "Ahhhh," she breathed at last. She squeezed the trigger. The whine of the shot was lost in the whine of the electric guitars.

Hobbins staggered back just as Sandy raised his binoculars. A ripple of shock went through the crowd. Faxon broke off playing. Maggio's guitar screeched with feedback, and died. Gopher John's drums sounded lonely and lost for a moment, until he too froze.

Silence like an indrawn breath.

Hobbins flipped white hair back from his eyes, and grinned. "Sorry, Charlie," he said. "Must be the drugs." They laughed, thousands of them. Hobbins' face was red, but it was a hot flush, not blood. He looked right at Sandy and Ananda, and drew a short, exuberant sound from his Gibson, a chord that bubbled and soared. Then he led the Nazgûl back into the song, and music filled the darkness.

Overhead the clouds were breaking up. Sandy saw stars twinkling in a clear sky.

"No," Ananda said, her voice thick with disbelief. She squeezed off another round, and was rewarded with the click of an exhausted magazine. Again and again she fired; the rifle clicked and clicked.

"You only get one shot," Sandy said. "You missed."

She discarded the rifle, leaped up, whirled on him. "It was a full magazine! I loaded it myself! And I couldn't have missed, I had him right in the crosshairs!"

"Then maybe you killed him," Sandy said sadly.

Ananda didn't understand; she was wild and confused. Down below, the Nazgûl played "The Resurrection Rag" as it had never been played before, and half a million people clapped along and smiled and swayed to the beat. Sandy felt weak and weary, yet somehow very good. It was as though he'd found something, something precious that he'd lost a long, long time ago.

> *This is the day we'd dreamed about,*
> *   This is the land where the flowers grow.*
> *And all my hopes I'm bringing,*
> *Oh, don't you hear the singing?*
> *And all my dreams I'm bringing,*
> *Well, can't you hear the singing?*
> *And all my pain I'm bringing,*
> *   and I'm joinin' in that singing!*
> *They're playing the resurrection rag, oh!*
> *Playin' that resurrection rag!*
> *YEAH! That everlovin' funky goddamned*
> *   RESURRECTION RAAAAAAG!*

The four Nazgûl sang the final line together in a single wild, joyous shout. Bass, guitars, and drums melted into one another and delivered a thunderous, tumultuous crescendo, a great throbbing burning sizzling slambang piledriver assgrabber finish that went louder and louder and *louder* and *LOUDER* and then cut off sharply. For the merest fraction of a second the silence was absolute. And then the noise began. Applause. Laughter. Whistles. Cheers. Shouts. Pandemonium.

Far away, over the miles, through the darkness, the sound came sweeping and surging and climbing.

The ovation went on for five minutes, ten, fifteen. Twice Faxon tried to lead the Nazgûl into an encore, but the applause did not diminish appreciably even when the music began, and both efforts were stillborn. Finally the Nazgûl just stood and let it overwhelm them.

Sandy clapped with the rest. The cuts on his palms reopened and bled again, but he hardly felt it. He clapped until his hands were sore and swollen. He clapped and clapped and clapped.

Ananda stood beside him, silent and lost.

Finally the tumult began to diminish, dying away little by little, dwindling, softening. And the quiet came again. Patrick Henry Hobbins, his song complete at last, moved to the edge of the stage and opened his arms to all of them. "I love you goddamned assholes," he said to them. "Are your ears bleeding yet?"

"*YES!*" they screamed back at him. "YES, YES, YES!"

Hobbins smiled a small, sad, wry smile. Somehow he seemed to glow with an inner light now, and there was something wraithlike about him as he stood there, something translucent and larger than life. For one long moment, it seemed as though he did not stand alone, it seemed as though others were crowding the stage on either side of him. There stood a slender young black in phantom finery, long bright scarves dripping from his neck and waist, an electric guitar slung against his ruffled shirt. There was a pudgy young woman in oversized glasses and a flowered dress, a purple feather boa curled around her neck, smiling a wide, vibrant, crooked smile. There moved a handsome, unsmiling man with a full beard, wearing lizard boots and tight leather clothing. And behind them were others, so many others, dozens of them, hundreds maybe, bright and dim, shades from a restless yesterday only now put to rest, and all of them were dead, and all of them would live forever in the music, in the sounds that would never ever die.

The wind blew gently, and they were gone. The Nazgûl stood alone upon an empty stage. And up in front stood Larry Richmond. He stared down at the vast, awed, silent crowd with a baffled fear on his face, and turned away in panic. By then Peter Faxon had unslung his bass and moved to help. The two men embraced. Through the binoculars, Sandy could see that both of them were crying.

TWENTY-EIGHT

Lately it occurs to me/
What a long, strange trip it's been

All things considered, it had been a terrific party. Sandy had stocked the hotel suite with nothing but the best, and everyone ate too much and drank too much except for Bambi, who wouldn't touch anything but tea and kept talking about how inorganic and unhealthy all the rest of it was. Sandy got her good. He slipped the bellman a ten, and fifteen minutes later the man returned, carrying a silver platter. He placed it right in front of Bambi and lifted the lid, and there was a stack of Hostess chocolate creme-filled cupcakes piled a foot high. Bambi stared at them in horror for a moment, then broke down helplessly, and afterward she got up and pushed one into Sandy's face before sitting down to consume six. "They'd go good with raw milk," she said.

Sandy was left with chocolate cupcake and creme all over his face, but that didn't matter too much, since Maggie had been drinking a lot of champagne, and champagne always made her sweetly, drunkenly amorous, so she sat on his knee and licked at him until it was all gone. Froggy watched the process and made rude comments. "And then you bite his ear right off, you do, you do," he suggested in an evil croak, but Maggie giggled and ignored him. Froggy was left to wander off and talk about aura balancing with Fern.

Bambi had brought both Fern and Ray from the commune. Froggy had brought Samantha, a statuesque brunette who proved a disappointment to

Sandy, since she looked more like Raquel Welch than Andy Devine. She had a good sense of humor, though, which you needed if you were going to live with Froggy Cohen. "I'll never forget the first time I let the poor guy get lucky," she told them all. "There we were on my bed, and he was on top of me with his old magic twanger pumping in and out, and suddenly he leans over, leers, goes into that voice, and says"—her own voice dropped into a commanding, froggish croak—"'*You're gonna come now, you will, you will.*'" Froggy actually blushed. "The hell of it was, I did," Samantha finished, and they roared with laughter.

In the end, though, neither she nor Bambi's friends had the requisite stamina, and one by one they drifted off to sleep, until only the four were left. Sandy ordered up some more champagne, and Bambi sat knitting while he and Froggy and Maggie put away bottle after bottle and sang up all the old TV theme songs. Sandy had a nice buzz on, Maggie was nuzzling his neck, and Froggy was singing endless obscene imaginary verses for *Have Gun, Will Travel* when the knock came on the door. It was almost one at that point. "Probably a noise complaint," Sandy said, but he went to answer it anyway.

Outside stood a trim, short man with wavy chestnut hair and a pencil-thin brown mustache. He was wearing designer jeans, a vest, an open-collared chambray work shirt, high boots, and carrying a guitar. Sandy stared at him, mouth agape.

"That looks real intelligent, Blair," Lark said with his old mocking smile. "Close your mouth before a bee flies in."

"I didn't think you were coming," Sandy said.

"Who?" Maggie asked from behind.

"You sent me an invitation," Lark said.

"Yeah, sure, but you weren't here...I mean you didn't rizvip, and the party started hours a—"

"Spit it out, Blair," Lark said. "Hell, the star always arrives last." He sauntered past Sandy into the room.

"*Lark!*" Maggie exclaimed. "Couldn't keep away, huh?"

Bambi got up from her knitting and rushed across the room to embrace him warmly.

Froggy looked askance and made his rude wet noise. "He's brought that guitar. He's going to sing. I know it, I do, I do." He rolled his eyes.

"This is a reunion, correct? I always used to play when we got together in the old days, so I thought it'd be fun if..."

"You used to *try* to play for us in the old days, Lark m'boy," Froggy said. "Which is an entirely different matter."

"What are you drinking, Steve?" Sandy asked him.

Lark gave him that old mocking smile. "Lark," he said.

Maggie whooped. "He done it again!"

"Can you get me into the Name-of-the-Month-Club?" Froggy asked. "I'll be a good member, I will, I will."

Bambi gave him a smile and a supportive hug. "Good."

Lark stretched out in a chair, his leg casually flung over one arm. "Got tired of that whole advertising scene, you know? Three-piece suits and three-martini lunches get boring after a while. It's an exciting life, but superficial. So I figured I'd take a break from life in the fast lane, come out and see how you clowns were getting along."

"Life in the fast lane," Sandy echoed.

"It'd burn you out in a week, Blair," Lark told him.

"No doubt," Sandy said.

"Sander is more suited to life in the rest stops," Froggy suggested.

"So," Sandy said, "when did you get fired, Lark?"

The Ellyn smile flickered, then faded entirely. "I didn't get fired," he said with a touch of petulance. "The account I was working on went to another agency, and I was let go. It happens all the goddamned time in advertising, and it's no reflection on—"

Maggie sat down in his lap. "Shut up," she said. She kissed him on the nose. "Bambi will hit you with a cupcake if you keep on."

"A *chocolate* cupcake," Bambi said dangerously. "With creme filling. Very inorganic."

"It'll throw your aura right out of kilt, it will, it will," said Froggy.

Lark Ellyn looked from one smiling face to the other and gave a disgusted shake of his head. "I can't believe I'm here with you losers," he said.

"We may be losers, but we're *your* losers," Froggy told him.

Sandy brought Lark a glass of champagne. He accepted it, sipped, gave Maggie a sip, and then looked up. "Blair, it kills me to say so, but I guess you've got congratulations coming. That book of yours is doing real well, I'm told."

"It's paying for your champagne," Sandy said. "Six weeks on the *Times* bestseller list."

"And counting!" Maggie said. Her grin was crooked and very drunken. "I bet it stays up there *forever!*"

"We could have a pool," Froggy said.

"I haven't had time to read it yet," Lark said, "but I will. I promise."

"You'll probably wait for the paperback, you will, you will," Froggy said accusingly.

"It's dedicated to you," Sandy said.

Lark Ellyn almost choked on his champagne. He came up gasping and spitting. On his lap, Maggie was roaring with laughter and kicking her legs in the air. "*What?*" Lark said finally. "You're bullshitting me. Come off it, Blair. We don't even *like* each other."

Sandy grinned. "I didn't say it was dedicated to you *alone*. I've got better taste than that. It's dedicated to all of you."

"A cheap trick, Sander m'boy," Froggy complained. "A mass dedication is just a sleazy way of driving up sales of the book, don't think I don't know it. If I don't get a solo dedication soon, I swear, I'm going to stop teaching you how to pick up girls."

"I want to see it," Lark said.

Sandy nodded. "I've got a copy in the bedroom." He went back and picked it up. It was a nice, thick, heavy hardbound book. On the dust jacket was a photo of the Nazgûl in concert, with the crosshairs of a rifle over Pat Hobbins' face. *The Year of the Nazgûl,* read the title, in bright letters. In smaller print, below, it said *An Insider's Account, by Sander Blair.*

He brought it back and handed it to Lark, open to the dedication page, which read:

> *To Maggie, Lark, Bambi, Froggy and Slum*
> *. . . I got by with a little help from my friends*

"But what does it mean?" Lark said, "Got by what?"

"Read the book," Sandy said. "It's all in there. I hope you understand it better than the reviewers. They don't even know whether it's fiction or journalism." He shrugged. "To tell the truth, there are times that I'm not sure myself." He went to the bar, poured himself some champagne, and took a small sip. "I appreciate the congratulations," he said, "but sometimes I wonder if I really deserve them. It was a book that . . . well . . . almost wrote itself."

"Modesty alert!" blared Froggy, cupping his hands over his mouth. "Modesty alert, modesty alert. Stop him before he gets humble."

Lark flipped through the pages, frowning. "That woman is going to go on trial soon, isn't she? What's her name?"

"Ananda Caine," Maggie said. She made a face. "Tacky bitch."

"That was only one of her aliases, as it turned out," Sandy said. "She had a lot of names. A lot of hurt, too. Her father was an old folk singer who killed himself after he was black-listed. Ananda herself had been gang-raped in Alabama in the early Sixties when her mother was doing civil

rights work down there. She was only thirteen. At times I can almost understand everything she did. At times I can't understand at all. I guess it'll all
come out in the trial. I wonder if they'll believe even half of it." He sighed,
drank some more champagne. "My publisher figures the trial will be page
one for months, and that it will send sales of my book through the roof. So
much for literature."

Lark was looking at the dedication again. "Thanks, I guess," he said. He
looked up once more and said, "Hey, what about Slum? Where's the old
Slummer?"

That wiped the smile off everyone's faces quickly enough. "I forgot,"
Sandy said, "you don't know about Slum." He told him, wearily. Lark
looked incredulous by the time he was finished. "That's why I did the book,
really," Sandy concluded.

"I don't get it, Blair," Lark said. "How's the book going to help Slum?"

"The story was wild enough so I knew it'd be a cinch to hit big. And I
was right in the middle of it." He smiled wanly. "My publisher tells me it's
outselling Butcher's latest by a nice comfortable margin now. And every
fucking cent is going into a fund to pay Slum's legal costs. I've already gotten some high-priced hotshit lawyers, and Froggy has gotten some of his
ACLU friends interested. And if I run out of money, Peter Faxon has offered to help. Faxon and I have gotten pretty close since West Mesa, and
believe me, Peter could buy and sell Butcher out of loose change. There's
no guarantees, but—" he raised his glass "—a toast, to Slum, who I hope
like hell will be here drinking with us next year!"

Lark raised his glass. Maggie climbed off his lap, moved unsteadily to
the bar, and poured for the rest of them. They all drank, even Bambi, who
did not believe in alcohol. It tasted damn good, sweet and cold and full of
promise.

Afterward Froggy told an elephant joke, and they went from there to
grape jokes to dead baby jokes, and finally everyone was drunk enough and
stoned enough so they were willing to let Lark sing. He sang "Lemon Tree"
and "Leavin' on a Jet Plane" and "If I Had a Hammer," and Froggy sat next
to him mumbling, "If you had a hammer you'd smash your thumb, you
would, you would," and the darkest part of the night came and went, and
they sat together and sang and joked and talked, and one by one they
passed out, even Froggy. "Badges," he was saying groggily, "I don't need no
stinking ba . . . badg . . ." and suddenly he was snoring, and Sandy was alone.

He sat bemused, sipping flat champagne and staring at his sleeping
friends. Perhaps he slept himself; he wasn't sure. But he was awake when
dawn came streaming through the window. The room was full of heavy

breathing and morning stillness, and it reminded Sandy of mornings at
Maggie's place in the old days, when the whole gang had spent the night.
Sometimes she'd wake them with the smell of frying bacon, and a blare of
music from the stereo.

He rose and went to the phone and called down for four orders of bacon
and eggs, and one bowl of crunchy Granola. As for the music, he'd had a
stereo brought up last night, for the party. He went over and glanced at the
albums.

But of course none of them would do. There was only one choice. He
had it in the bedroom, an advance promo copy given him by Faxon before
the general release. He had wanted to play it for them last night, but what
with one thing and another, he had never gotten around to it.

The photo on the album jacket had been taken in the Philadelphia city
dump. They stood there surrounded by abandoned refrigerators, old tires,
broken TV sets, and couches with the stuffings spilling out. There were six
of them now; the original three, Larry Richmond on rhythm guitar, a
damned good keyboard player, and their brand new lead vocalist, a whip-
thin young black kid whose voice was almost as exciting as Hobbins' voice
had been. *The Nazgûl*, the jacket read, *Back from the Junkyard!*

All new songs, rewritten and rearranged for the larger group. Sandy held
it in his hands, wondering how it would sound, how it would sell. There
were no guarantees. But there never were.

He carried the album back to the stereo, slit the plastic sleeve with his
thumbnail, and placed the record carefully on the turntable. They woke to
the song of "Thursday's Child," who has far to go.

ABOUT THE AUTHOR

George R. R. Martin is the #1 *New York Times* bestselling author of many novels, including those of the acclaimed series *A Song of Ice and Fire* — *A Game of Thrones, A Clash of Kings, A Storm of Swords, A Feast for Crows,* and *A Dance with Dragons* — as well as *Tuf Voyaging, Fevre Dream, Armageddon Rag, Dying of the Light, Windhaven* (with Lisa Tuttle) and *Dreamsongs Volumes I* and *II.* He is also the creator of *The Lands of Ice and Fire,* a collection of maps featuring original artwork from illustrator and cartographer Jonathan Roberts, and *The World of Ice & Fire* (with Elio M. García, Jr., and Linda Antonsson). As a writer-producer, he has worked on *The Twilight Zone, Beauty and the Beast,* and various feature films and pilots that were never made. He lives with the lovely Parris in Santa Fe, New Mexico.

georgerrmartin.com

Facebook.com/GRRMartinofficial

Twitter: @GRRMspeaking

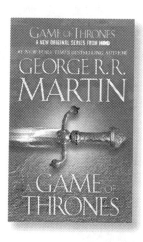
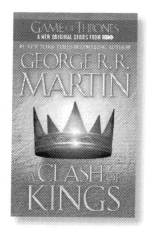
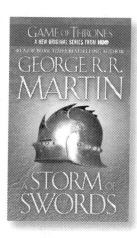
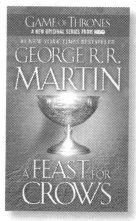
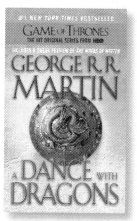

Westeros comes alive in these official *Game of Thrones* graphic novels!

A GAME OF THRONES:
THE GRAPHIC NOVEL: VOLUME 1

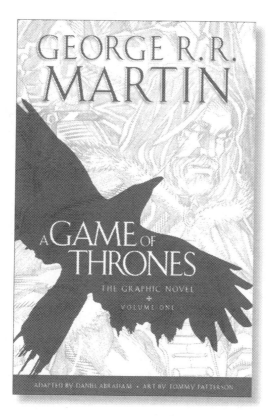

LOOK FOR
A GAME OF THRONES: THE GRAPHIC NOVEL: VOLUME 2
A GAME OF THRONES: THE GRAPHIC NOVEL: VOLUME 3
A GAME OF THRONES: THE GRAPHIC NOVEL: VOLUME 4

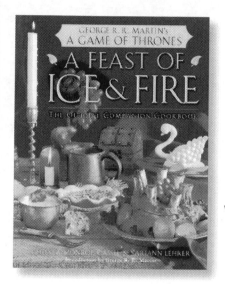

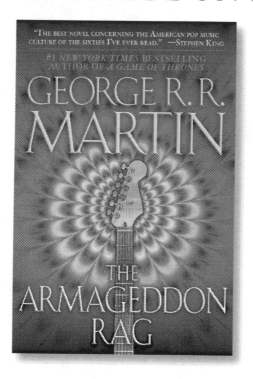

Printed in the United States
by Baker & Taylor Publisher Services